THE MOONS OF FATE DUOLOGY

A KINGDOM OF BLOOD & FATE

K.R. McRAE

For more information:

www.katimcrae.com

To all the girls dreaming of adventure but are held back by chronic illness...
This one's for you.

CONTENT WARNING

T his book is intended for audiences aged 18 and older.

This is a fated mates romantasy novel featuring a love triangle with why choose (MFM) scenes. Some of the content in this book may be triggering for some readers.

If you would like to learn more about the content warnings for this book, please visit the author's website:

www.katimcrae.com/content-warnings

CHAPTER 1

BRIAR

*C*hronic Fatigue Syndrome. It sounds like a manufactured disease for weak-willed women, like hysteria.

And yet, CFS is the reason I'm standing on my grandparents' doorstep in the middle of nowhere, a.k.a. Silver Ridge, Utah.

The fresh air will do you good, my mother said. But she and I both knew my parents were just frustrated with me, watching me throw my college scholarships, my prestigious internship—my entire future, really—down the drain.

I couldn't keep up anymore. I skipped class to sleep, made stupid mistakes on my homework assignments, and even dissociated during exams. But the day I got lost on the same university campus I'd called home for three years, I had a breakdown in the quad in front of a hundred people. Talk about humiliating.

That's the moment I realized I couldn't do it anymore.

When I informed my parents of my decision to drop out of college, my father said I was "lazy" and that I needed to "get my act together."

This fatigue is all in your head, he'd said. *We're all tired, but that's life; that's being an adult.*

So here I am, on a remote ranch over a hundred miles from the nearest city, on a parental-prescribed "spiritual journey of self-discovery and mental healing." Whatever the hell that means.

Before I reach the top of the porch steps, the screen door slams open, and my grand-mother rushes outside.

"Bri!" She crushes me to her chest in her warm, comforting embrace. "We've missed you so much, my dear."

"I've missed you too, Grandma." I cling to her, resting my cheek on her delicate shoulder, and try not to burst into tears.

When was the last time someone held me like this, in a way where it felt safe to fall apart?

Don't cry, Bri, don't cry...

"How are you feeling?" She steps back, holding my shoulders as she examines me. "You've lost weight since I saw you last."

I let out a weak laugh. It's been six years since I saw her in person, although we've kept in touch with weekly video calls, which made her feel not so far away.

As a child, I used to spend every summer here at the ranch. But as I got older, the summers quickly filled up with extracurricular activities and internship opportunities, and our family vacations to the ranch became shorter and less frequent. Eventually, my parents stopped bringing me altogether.

"Come, let's sit down while your grandpa brings in the luggage." Grandma grabs my hand and leads me to a set of white wicker furniture on the porch. "I just squeezed some fresh lemonade."

I take a seat on one of the chairs as she scurries inside. From here, I have a panoramic view of the Casey Ranch. The tall grass stretches out in a vast expanse around the farmhouse in all directions, and in the distance is a long, rocky mesa, towering over the ranch like an omnipresent sentinel. Tall, green trees dot the scenery beneath the setting sun, growing thicker near the base of the ridge.

It's the first moment of quiet I've had all day, far removed from the busy intercom of the airport, the scraping of suitcases on the floor as people hurry to their gates, or the country music crooning from the speakers of Grandpa's old Chevy truck on the two-hour drive from the airport. Most of which I slept through.

But right now it's just me and nature. An unfamiliar sense of peace washes over me, and for the first time in months, I take a full, deep breath, letting the oxygen slowly expand my lungs. When I breathe out, I sigh.

The tree closest to the patio still has a tire swing hanging from one of the branches, which creaks in the breeze. I would waste entire summers on that swing as a child, playing with the son of the ranch caretakers, Caz Nezara.

Grandma steps out of the kitchen with a tray, yanking me back to the present. She takes the seat beside me and pours us each a glass of lemonade from the glass pitcher etched with flowers.

I notice her wrinkled hands as I accept a glass from. Her thick, dark hair is more silver in person than I remember from our phone calls. It's pulled back in a long braid with loose strands falling around her dark eyes. They're serene, yet alert.

"Ah, fresh lemonade!" my grandfather exclaims, dragging my suitcases up the steps. "Pour me a glass, would you, Maeve?"

"Of course." She gives him a smile as he carries my luggage past us into the house. "He'll take your bags up to your room. Do you need any help unpacking?"

"No, I'll be okay, but thank you."

She sighs and tilts her head, examining me closely. "Oh, my dear, you look so tired."

But hearing those words from my grandmother, it feels like she really, truly *sees* me in a way my parents never did.

I swallow down the lump in my throat. "How are things here on the ranch?"

"Oh, you know, 'same old, same old.'" She waves her hand dismissively. "Nothing you need to worry about. Why don't you catch me up on you?"

I shrug. "There's nothing to tell. I'm not really doing anything these days."

"Oh, Briar." She clucks her tongue. "You're giving yourself a chance to heal. Ain't nothin' wrong with that."

That's the problem, though. I'm not sure I'll ever heal from this. How can I, when not even the doctors know what's wrong with me?

Although, in order to help me, they'd need to recognize that there's something wrong with me first.

I take a sip of lemonade. It's not quite as sweet as I remember it, and I can hardly smell the lemon fragrance as the rim of the glass comes close to my nose. But nothing tastes or smells the same anymore.

Grandma and I fall into a comfortable silence as we sip our lemonade and look out over the ranch. Grandpa steps out onto the porch and takes a seat on the loveseat beside my grandmother.

"Here's your lemonade, Henry." My grandmother passes another glass to him. "How was the drive?"

"Pretty quiet," he grunts, giving me a sly wink. At least he isn't upset that I ignored him for the past two hours while I slept in the truck.

He has much fairer skin than my grandmother, who is a descendant of the local Silver Ridge tribe. His blond hair has given way to gray wisps on his balding head, which he keeps covered with a cowboy hat, and he wears a pair of leather boots and his signature plaid button-up shirt tucked into his belted denim jeans.

Grandpa's sharp, blue eyes crinkle at the corners as he settles back in his chair and surveys the ranch. His parents bought this land almost a century ago and named it Casey Ranch, raising cattle and making a decent living here in Silver Ridge. Grandma and Grandpa raised my father here, but he left for California as soon as he could save up for a car. The ranch life wasn't meant for him.

Which is why my dad believes sending me here is a punishment, not a vacation.

I squint my eyes in the direction of the setting sun above the mesa and shield my eyes with my hand. "Wait, who's that?"

A cloud of dust plumes at the base of the ridge, kicked up by another old Chevy nearly identical to my grandfather's.

"Must be one of the Nezaras." My grandmother frowns. "But it's a bit late in the day for them to be out."

We watch silently as the dust plume grows closer, the truck speeding at full steam toward the farmhouse. The truck comes to a stop in front of the porch, and the roaring engine dies. A man in a cowboy hat climbs out of the driver's seat, his brim pulled low over his bowed head. His white T-shirt is pulled taut with his broad chest and strong biceps, though the hem hangs loose over a pair of jeans and hiking boots.

I don't remember any of the Nezaras looking this ripped.

His sun-kissed copper skin glistens with sweat, and when he removes his hat, he swipes his arm across the thick, raven hair clinging to his forehead. And I'd do anything to feel those thick, full lips on my body...

When his deep, brown eyes catch mine, my breath sticks in my throat like molasses.

"Bri?" The cowboy's voice is low and deep, sending a shiver down my body.

I tilt my head, studying him. "Do I know you?"

His shoulders drop. "You don't remember me? Caz?"

"Caz? No way." I clap a hand over my mouth and laugh. "I don't believe it."

The Caspian "Caz" Nezara who I spent my childhood summers with was a lanky, awkward boy—not a cowboy who looks like he belongs on a GQ cover.

He scales the porch steps two at a time with his long, muscular legs, and I stand up, arm outstretched to greet him with a hug. When we embrace, his thick arms envelop me, crushing me against the hard planes of his chest. I catch the faintest whiff of leather when my nose grazes his shoulder, but my sense of smell is weak, and to my disappointment, the delicious aroma is fleeting.

He steps away from me with a wide grin. "I had no idea you were coming out this summer."

"Yeah, it was sort of a last-minute decision." I gesture toward the tray on the wicker table. "Are you thirsty? Grandma made lemonade."

"Actually, I can't." Caz's expression turns serious. His gaze lingers on me for a moment longer before turning to my grandfather. "Mr. Casey, there's been a cattle mutilation. I came straight away after I found her."

"What?" My grandfather leaps to his feet with surprising agility. "Shit, let's go take a look."

My grandmother stands, wiping her hands on her apron. "We haven't had one of those in years."

Cattle mutilations happened from time to time during my summers on the ranch. The adults used to hide it from the kids, but we would hear them whisper about the gruesome details. I looked them up on the internet once, and the prevailing theory was that aliens caused them, which began a lifelong curiosity for anything supernatural. Aliens, ghosts, demons, you name it. I live for a good local legend or ghost story.

"Can I see it?" I ask.

My grandmother shakes her head. "Absolutely not! It's horrific."

"I know what they look like. I promise I won't be shocked."

My grandfather strides down the porch steps. "Fine, you can come.. But let's get a move on before the sun sets."

I follow them down to Caz's truck. He opens the passenger door for me and lowers the seat to give me space to crawl into the back. His warm, broad palm engulfs my petite hand as he helps me onto the running board, and I stoop low to avoid hitting my head on the roof.

As I climb inside, I'm hyperaware that my ass is in his face.

Once Grandma, Grandpa, and me are settled in, Caz jogs around to take his place in the driver's seat. He turns the key in the ignition, and the truck roars to life. We take off in the direction of the dead cow, the farmhouse getting smaller in the rearview mirror as we leave it behind us.

"Were they in an enclosure?" I ask.

"No, they were out grazing near the northwestern corner of the ranch." Caz narrows his gaze on the dirt path ahead. "I noticed a hole in the fence on my way home, so I stopped to fix it. They were all clustering together real close, and they were agitated about something. When I went to investigate, that's when I found the fallen cow."

"A hole in the fence?" Grandpa repeats. "Did it look man-made?"

"It could have been. Hard to tell if it was human or animal."

I lean forward, resting my elbows on their headrests. "How would you know either way?"

"A split rail fence with chain link runs along the entire boundary of the property," Caz explains. "It's high enough that it would be difficult for a coyote to jump over and harm the cattle. The only natural cause would be rust, but in one section, the rails were just gone."

"Did you find the missing rails?" Grandpa asks.

He shakes his head. "No. We'll need to order some more material to repair the fence. It's not big enough for the cattle to get out, but I'll do a temporary patch first thing in the morning, just to be safe."

When we reach our destination, twilight is beginning to settle over the ranch. Caz pulls out a flashlight from a toolbox in the bed of the truck before leading us on a short walk away from the dirt road.

A dark mass lies motionless in the tall grass. As we approach it, my chest squeezes at the sight of the dead cow, its black hair glinting softly under our flashlights.

My grandfather paces around the length of the carcass, brows furrowed. "There aren't any flies." When he examines the cow's head, he utters a string of curse words under his breath.

My grandmother's shoulders are so tense they nearly touch her ears. "What's wrong?"

"Her eyes are gouged out," Caz answers. "And her udder, too."

When I glance at him, Caz is already staring at me, his expression grave. His gaze is intense, almost like he suspects *me* for doing this, and I glance away, folding my arms. I just got here an hour ago, so I don't know why he'd think that..

"An animal couldn't have done this," my grandfather says, folding his arms. "There's no visible damage on the cow. No scratches, no bites, nothing. How do you strip a cow of her eyes and udder so cleanly without surgical instruments?"

"Is there a gunshot wound?" Grandma asks.

He shakes his head. "No."

"There's something else, Mr. Casey," Caz adds. "I think the animal was drained of its blood. We'll need to call the vet out to confirm, but there's no sign of blood in her eye sockets or belly."

My grandfather sighs. "Did you see any footprints or animal tracks nearby?"

"None."

"I'll call the vet out to test the carcass for poison. What a waste," Grandpa mutters, shaking his head. "We're already struggling as it is. We can't be losing cattle like this."

I hadn't realized that the ranch had fallen on hard times, but I'll wait until later to press them about it.

"Grimwalkers," my grandmother says on a breath. All of us turn to look at her.

"What are grimwalkers?" I ask.

"That's nonsense, Maeve," my grandfather chides. "That's just an old tribal superstition. Don't pay it any mind, Bri. No, I think this is Findley's doing. He's been out to get me for years."

"Findley is another cattle rancher in the area," my grandmother supplies for me before rounding on my grandfather. "Henry, you have no proof."

"Well, he's not going to just show his hand, is he?" He folds his arms, staring at the cow carcass in deep contemplation. "I'm getting too old for this shit. There's a housing developer who's shown some interest in the area. Maybe we should sell—"

"No!" Caz steps forward, hand outstretched, eyes wide with panic. "Please don't sell the ranch."

"I know this ranch means a lot to you, Caz. But if we can't turn a profit, we can't afford to keep the ranch going, much less pay you for your work."

"I-I don't mind." Caz lowers his eyes to the ground. "Look, this place means too much to let it go to a developer."

My grandfather claps him on the back. "It's just some preliminary interest in the area. They haven't approached me with an offer or anything."

Grandma interrupts the tense silence by clearing her throat. "Let's head back. It's getting dark out here, and I'm sure Bri is hungry after a long day of travel. Caz, care to join us for dinner?"

"I'd love to, but I better go check on my family and make sure everyone is okay. I'll ask if they've seen any suspicious activity around the ranch."

I assume he's referring to his siblings, but at the mention of *family*, I instinctively glance at his hand, searching for a wedding ring. His fingers are bare, but it's possible he takes it off while he's working.

Caz and I are the same age. Even though we're a little young, one of my college friends got engaged to her boyfriend last month, so it's not unheard of.

The thought that someone else already claimed him makes my chest squeeze. But look at him—if I was his girlfriend, I'd be quick to lock him down, too.

My eyes travel up his broad, muscular body until I reach his face, and I shudder when I find him staring right back at me. His dark eyes are sultry and soulful, studying me with interest.

Or, at least, I'd like to believe they are.

When we return to the farmhouse, Caz hops out and jogs around to help my grandmother out of the backseat of the truck. I follow, hunching over to avoid hitting my head on the ceiling and keeping my eyes on the floor to avoid tripping.

Out of nowhere, vertigo slams into me, causing my head to spin. A wave of nausea washes over me, and I lose my footing.

Caz catches me in his strong arms before I hit the ground. I blink a few times, trying to bring the world back into focus, but it's still spinning.

When I look up at Caz, our noses are mere inches away from one another. My breath hitches at our proximity, my heartbeat quickening when I realize my arm is wrapped around his neck.

"Bri, are you okay?" Concern is etched across his features.

"What happened?" Grandma's voice is brimming with panic.

"Y-Yeah, just had a little dizzy spell," I say weakly.

Caz sets off for the porch, cradling me in his arms. "I'll carry her inside."

"Please, I can walk," I protest. Even though I've lost about twenty pounds since I got sick, I still feel self-conscious about him carrying me.

"Don't worry; I've got you." When his voice husks in my ear, a flood of warmth hits between my legs.

My grandmother beats us to the door and holds it open. Caz turns to sidestep into the house, and I'm reminded of a groom carrying his bride over the threshold into their new home.

He sets me down on the sofa in the living room, and my grandmother fluffs the couch pillows behind my head.

I haven't been in this living room in six years, but it's exactly how I remember it. Yellow wallpaper with burgundy flowers, the plaid, worn-in sofa, and an old 90s television set in an oak TV cabinet. A photo of me from my high school graduation sits in a gold frame on one of the bookshelves stretching across the wall.

"Thank you, Caz," she says. "Thank goodness you were here."

"Happy to help, ma'am." His eyes are trained on me as he speaks. "Are you okay now, Bri?"

"Yes, much better, thank you."

Both my grandparents and Caz are staring at me with worry on their faces, and I hate being fussed over.

"I'm fine." I wave them off. "Thank you, Caz. I'm sorry to keep you from your... family."

He gives me a small smile. "It's no problem. I'm just glad you're feeling better."

Caz gives me one last look before turning to leave, and my cheeks grow warm under his watchful gaze.

CHAPTER 2

The clock on the nightstand reads 4:07 a.m. It's pitch black in my room, but when I try to will my mind to go back to sleep, it's no use.

Wandering downstairs through the dark house, I'm not sure what to do with myself. I don't want to turn on the TV and wake my grandparents, but I'm not hungry enough to fix breakfast either. One of the activities my doctor recommended was meditation and light yoga, so I wander onto the porch to practice.

As I step outside into the dark, the chilly morning breeze kisses my cheeks. Goose bumps rise on my arms beneath the long sleeves of my sleep shirt, making me miss the warm summer weather of L.A. I could be on the beach right now with my friends, but instead I'm in the Utah wilderness, far from civilization.

I take a seat on the top step and cross my legs, closing my eyes.

Deep breath in, deep breath out. Deep breath in—focusing on the breath entering through my nose—deep breath out. I imagine my energy flowing downward with each exhale, grounding my body to the wooden floorboards of the porch.

The tests show there's nothing wrong with you, the cardiologist said. *I don't want you to spiral trying to find answers that aren't there...*

No, Bri. Focus.

My parents' disappointed faces when I told them I was dropping out of school flashes across my mind.

Deep breath in, deep breath out.

The failure and self-loathing I felt when I called to cancel my summer internship. That marked the moment I gave up on myself.

I clutch at my chest to calm my racing heartbeat. I'm not trying hard enough to focus. I'm not trying hard enough to get better.

If I'd not eaten that candy bar at the airport or drank that soda, maybe I'd feel better.

If I cut out all carbs and sugar, or exercised every day, I would be fixed.

Or maybe my parents were right. What if I'm keeping myself sick on purpose to avoid my responsibilities? I was finishing up my junior year of college and feeling the pressure to get the best internship, make the right connections, and figure my life out. What if my brain made up this illness because growing up was too fucking scary?

It's the days where I feel better when I question myself the most.

"Bri, are you okay?"

Startled, my eyes shoot wide open with a gasp. Caz stands at the bottom of the steps, illuminated only by a single porch light behind me.

My chest is heaving up and down, a cold sweat clinging to my forehead.

"Bri?" he repeats, taking a cautious step toward me.

I take a ragged breath. "Sorry. Yeah, I'm okay."

He climbs the steps and takes a seat beside me, and my heartbeat can't decide if it wants to relax or speed up when he's near.

Caz rests his elbows on his knees. "You shouldn't be out here alone at night."

I give him a weak smile. "I doubt I'll get lost on the porch."

"It's not that." He sighs, keeping his gaze fixed on me. "Weird things happen on this ranch, especially at night."

I raise an eyebrow at him. "Then why are *you* out all alone at night?"

"I'm a ranch hand." He gives me a pointed look. "It's my job to be an early riser. Besides, I can take care of myself out here."

"What makes you think I can't take care of myself?" Nevermind the fact that I couldn't even get out of the truck last night without Caz's help.

"Maybe it's because you have such skinny arms." He grins, reaching for my bicep to give it a ticklish squeeze.

I giggle and push him off, but I enjoy the warmth of his hands through the fabric of my sleeve. "The last time I saw you, I could fit one of my hands around your entire arm."

He sits up straighter. "I've grown up quite a bit since you last saw me."

"You certainly have." I rest my chin in my hands as we sit side-by-side beneath the starry night sky.

"I'm, uh—" Caz stutters, clearing his throat. "I'm surprised you're back after so long. You stopped coming to visit during the summer. Your grandparents said you were busy with school and stuff."

"Yeah, I was." I look down at my feet. "But not this summer."

"Oh yeah? How long are you planning on staying this year?"

I pluck a stray hair off my slippers. "I don't know. I might just stay here forever."

Caz cocks his head. "Really? Growing tired of Los Angeles?"

"Something like that."

Silence settles between us. I feel him studying me, but I can't bring myself to meet his gaze. This is the first moment Caz and I have been alone this summer, and my negative death spiral of thoughts is spoiling it. I hate that I can't shake them off.

But my mind isn't in the present. It's on the future that I envisioned for myself, the one I can't accept I'll never have.

Caz slides closer, and our knees almost touch before he hesitates. "Something's going on with you. You can talk to me, you know. I'm a good listener."

Where do I even begin? He waits patiently for me, with nothing but the night breeze rustling the grass to fill the silence.

"Well," I begin, "I got sick last winter, and I never really recovered. I was going to college and had a summer internship lined up with this prestigious Hollywood event planner." My voice catches. "But I had to give it all up." I try to take a deep breath, but it's shallow and unsteady as I blink back hot tears.

"You know, I always admired you." He looks upward to the night sky, his expression nostalgic. "I remember as kids you used to talk about what you wanted to be when you grew up. Every summer it was something different—an astronaut, a ballerina, the president. We used to play make-believe and act out those plans, and I was always your sidekick, supporting your dream."

Caz turns his deep brown eyes onto me, which sparkle beneath the soft glow of the porch light. "I never once doubted that you could do anything you set your mind to, Bri. You were always so ambitious, which is why I know this has to be hard for you, giving up on your dreams like that. And I know you wouldn't give them up unless you absolutely had to. I guess what I'm trying to say is I'm sorry you're going through this."

Without thinking, I lean my head to rest against his shoulder, closing my eyes to soak in the warmth of his body. I take deep breaths, trying to resist the urge to cry, and he gives me all the time I need to compose myself.

"Thank you for saying that," I whisper.

Caz wraps his arm around my shoulder. "You'll figure out something else. Just because the future looks different than you imagined, it doesn't mean you can't find happiness another way." He gives me a little shake. "And if anyone can do it, you can."

Caz has been on my mind all day. I don't know when he got so good at pep talks, but I haven't felt this hopeful in months. Somehow, when Caz says it's going to be okay, I believe him.

The Nezaras are coming over for dinner tonight, and I want to look nice for Caz. He's grown up into a hot cowboy, but I'm... sickly looking. The bags under my eyes are so dark they look like bruises. My blonde hair lost its luster after I got ill, and the blue eyes looking back at me in my reflection are dull and lifeless. Hell, even my skin looks tired. I've always been pale—I take after my grandfather's Irish side—but it looks like I haven't seen daylight in years.

It's going to take a lot of makeup to look halfway healthy.

I'm finishing the final touches on my lipstick when I hear voices floating up the stairs. Fatigue seeps into my bones at the thought of facing all the spirited Nezara siblings. Of having to explain—again—why I'm here and wondering if they'll believe how sick I am. I'll be lucky if I don't fall asleep facedown in my mashed potatoes.

My limbs feel like they're made of lead as I make my way downstairs. As I get closer, a cacophony of excited voices grows louder.

It's only two or three hours, and then I can crawl in bed like a hibernating bear. I can do that, right?

I finish my internal pep talk and step into the kitchen.

"BRIAR!"

Before I can identify the source of the squealing, a small pair of arms wraps around me, practically knocking me off my feet.

"Talia, leave her alone."

I turn toward the deep, familiar voice, and when I meet Caz's gaze, a small thrill weaves its way around my body.

He gives me an apologetic smile and shrugs. "Sorry about her."

"Briar, I've missed you!" Talia exclaims, staring up at me with big, brown eyes. She looks so much like her older brother, with dark raven hair flying wildly behind her and soft, honeyed cheeks stretched into a beaming grin.

I take a step back and take her in. "Wow! You've grown a lot since I saw you last."

She was the youngest Nezara sibling the last time I stayed at the ranch. Back then, there were only four of them: Caz, the eldest, followed by Sebastian, Seraphine, and Talia.

But now, I count seven Nezara children in the kitchen. A young boy, who couldn't be any older than five, giggles and runs after twin toddler boys around the table.

Caz leans down to whisper in my ear. "That's Luke, chasing after Jonah and Micah."

His breath on my neck sends a delicious shiver down my spine, and I would give anything for it to be just the two of us right now. Caz's presence is calming.

This chaotic scene is pure sensory overload.

"Sybil, you remember Briar, don't you?" Grandma says, ushering me further into the kitchen. She leads me to a familiar elderly woman sitting at the table—Mrs. Nezara, Caz's grandmother.

She offers a warm smile. "Yes, of course I remember Briar. Come, sit by me." She pats the empty seat beside her.

The longer I stand, the weaker I feel, and my knees are about to give out at any moment. I accept her invitation to sit, and I'm delighted when Caz takes the chair on my other side.

"Maeve tells me you've been feeling under the weather?" Mrs. Nezara's wrinkled face peers out between strands of silvery hair, studying me with a look of concern.

It's difficult to focus on the conversation with the children screaming in the kitchen. Pots and pans clang against the stove as my grandmother finishes the cooking. Grandpa chats with Seb about cattle, and Seraphine and Talia argue about the best way to make flower crowns.

Every clink of silverware, every scrape of the chair on the tile, jars me. My mind starts to slip into that familiar, dreaded fog, and the stronger it gets, the harder it is to wade out of it.

I'm untethered from my own body, floating away and disconnecting from the present. Here, but not really here. A casual bystander to the events around me rather than being a part of it.

My eyes land on Caz, and I blink at him as he stares back.

"Are you feeling okay?" he asks under his breath.

I nod, my head heavy on my neck. "Mm-hmm."

Mrs. Nezara's long, silver braid hangs delicately over her thin shoulder as her aged hands remain clasped on the table. Her brown eyes are sunken into her face with age, but they're sharp and compassionate. "Luke, please stop running around the table and take a seat with your brothers. We are guests of Mr. and Mrs. Casey. Show respect."

The boys come to a sharp halt, chiming, "Yes, Grandma," in unison. Young Luke helps his brothers take seats at the table without complaint.

"Dinner's ready!" My grandmother starts bringing various dishes of food to the table.

Mrs. Nezara turns her attention to the girls. "Seraphine, Talia, help Mrs. Casey, please." Her voice is warm, yet firm, and they obey immediately.

There's no question that Sybil Nezara is the matriarch of the family, and the children have a deep reverence for her.

Once the food is on the table, Mrs. Nezara offers to recite the evening prayer. Caz wraps his broad palm around mine when we all join hands, forming a circle around the table. Mrs. Nezara's hand feels small and fragile compared to Caz's, but both are warm.

"To the Silver Shell Woman, thank you for your blessing of abundant food and the warm company of family and friends."

The Silver Shell Woman is the Silver Ridge tribe's deity. From what Grandma's told me, she's something akin to a moon goddess.

Mrs. Nezara continues. "We mourn the loss of my son, Robert, and his wife, Laurel. May their seven children grow into fine young adults who honor their legacy. And may She bless Briar as she begins her journey of recovery. Amen."

"Amen," echo our voices around the table.

Caz squeezes my hand, even as the others let go of each other to begin their meal. Glancing at him, my heart breaks—I knew his parents very well.

I remember when Grandma called to tell me Mr. and Mrs. Nezara died in some sort of accident on the ridge. The details were vague, but it happened about three years ago.

None of the Nezaras have cell phones, so the only comfort I could offer Caz was to ask Grandma to convey my condolences.

I look around the table. Seven children left without parents at far too young an age. Even though I'm not close to my parents, I can't imagine losing them. I'm not emotionally equipped to bear the loss of either of them, let alone both.

Caz gives my hand one more comforting squeeze before releasing it and digging into his meal.

Talia waves her hand to grab my attention. "Briar, do you have any boyfriends in Los Angeles? Maybe a TV star?"

Caz stiffens and throws Talia a menacing glare.

I laugh. "No, I don't have a boyfriend."

"Or a girlfriend?"

"Talia!" Caz hisses. "Mind your own business."

"But I haven't seen Briar in forever," she whines. "I want to know everything about her life. Gosh, it must be so glamorous living in California."

"Maybe we can go to Provo one of these days and go shopping together?" I suggest. "We'll catch up, just you and me."

Her face falls. "But I can't leave the ranch."

"Talia, eat your dinner," Caz snaps, giving her a stern expression.

She remains quiet for the rest of the evening, a dark cloud hovering over her mood.

As the meal carries on, I only half-heartedly listen to the others chatting around me. My eyelids are growing heavy, and after dessert is served, I close them for a moment, pressing the heels of my hand against my eyes to relieve the pressure building in my head.

Caz's voice cuts through the fog in my mind. "We have an early start tomorrow. Let's get back to the homestead."

When my eyelids flutter open, most of the Nezaras are already at the door. My eyes land on Caz, who is the last one to file out, and he throws me one last look over his shoulder.

"Thank you," I mouth silently.

He gives me a wink, the way he always used to do when we shared a secret.

That night, I drift in and out of sleep despite the exhaustion gripping my body.

The clock on my bedside table reads 2:47 a.m. I close my eyes once again, and as I hover on the cusp of sleep, an otherworldly howl cuts through the silence.

Startled, I sit up quickly, peering out between the curtains above my bed. However, the sight awaiting me makes cold dread seep into my veins.

In the distance, an eerie crimson glow lights up the top of the mesa. A beam of red light shoots upward from the middle of the ridge into the dark sky like a searchlight, but stationary. Transfixed, I try to wrap my head around what could cause this strange phenomenon, though the sinking feeling in the pit of my stomach tells me this is outside the realm of human understanding.

Whatever it is, I hope it's not a threat.

When my grandmother enters the kitchen to prepare breakfast, I'm already waiting for her at the kitchen table.

She gasps and clutches her chest. "Goodness, you startled me! What are you doing up so early?"

"Grandma, did you see those lights?"

"What lights?"

I gesture at the window. "There was this weird, red glow on top of the ridge. It happened before sunrise."

"Sounds like the northern lights." My grandfather walks into the kitchen and takes a seat at the table. "We see them here from time to time."

"We're in Utah," I point out. "We can't see the northern lights from here."

He shrugs. "It's not completely unheard of, especially with solar flares."

I fold my arms. "Then why were they red, not blue?"

Grandpa leans back in his chair. "They're usually more red and pink this far south."

I huff. "Okay, fine, but these lights weren't in the sky; they were coming from somewhere on the mesa, and one was shooting up like a searchlight."

My grandmother comes over to give us both a cup of hot coffee before turning back to the stove. Grandpa opens up his newspaper and starts reading.

I stare between the two of them, waiting for one of them to give me a response. But they act like there's nothing peculiar about the rocks on their ranch glowing as red as the devil.

"Grandma," I press, "you mentioned grimwalkers the other day. I tried looking them up on my phone this morning and read that they're evil beings that can turn into wolves or something—"

"Again, Bri, that's just an old superstition." My grandfather shakes his head. "Do you really believe in shapeshifters? It's nonsense."

"Grandpa, how can you see this crazy, unexplainable stuff happen on the ranch and not believe it's paranormal? Cattle mutilations, strange lights coming from the ground, otherworldly wolf howls—"

"It's simple," he says. "You probably heard a coyote, and we already talked about that dead cow. There's a rival rancher, Findley, who's out to compete for my business, and he's just trying to scare us off."

I clench my fist on the table. "But Grandpa, how can a person drain cattle of their blood like that?"

My grandfather chuckles. "Lots of people 'round these parts think it's aliens. Maybe that's the cause of all this spooky stuff."

My grandmother turns away from the stove and leans against the counter, wiping her hands on a kitchen towel. "I don't know, Henry. Remember that strange wolf we saw last year?"

I straighten in my chair. "Wait, what wolf?"

"Maeve..."

Grandma folds her arms. "It was the size of a cow, and it was leaving the cattle enclosure. It got up on its hind legs and walked off, just like a person, and when we followed its footprints, the trail disappeared. It frightened me—it still does. And the only place I've heard of such a thing is the legend of the grimwalkers."

"Grandma, what exactly does the legend say about these grimwalkers?" I ask.

I've never heard of wolves the size of cattle before, and to think that they can walk like people... the image is unsettling.

She takes a deep breath before speaking in hushed tones, glancing around the kitchen as if afraid someone will eavesdrop. "In old Silver Ridge tribal folklore, there are creatures called grimwalkers. To speak of them invites evil, so the elders rarely share the stories. But essentially, grimwalkers are evil beings with an insatiable thirst for blood and flesh, and they disguise themselves as animals to do harm. They're bad omens, and they say death follows them wherever they go."

"So, they could disguise themselves as giant wolves?" I ask.

My grandfather rolls his eyes. "Come on, Maeve, stop scaring her. I'll go up to Findley's ranch today and give him a piece of my mind. This has gone too far."

Grandma and I exchange a skeptical look, but we let the conversation end there and eat our breakfast. The rest of the morning passes by quietly after Grandpa heads out, and my grandmother works around the house doing her daily chores.

I spend the morning out on the porch, scrolling through my phone as I research everything from cattle mutilations, grimwalkers, UFOs, and everything in between. By the time lunch rolls around, my head is spinning with more questions than answers, and I have no idea what to believe anymore.

When a plume of dust rises in the distance, I squint into the sun and hold my hand to shield my eyes. Caz is driving toward the farmhouse, and my stomach does a little flip.

He pulls up and climbs out of the driver's seat, my gaze drawn to the muscles tugging at his white T-shirt. He's handsome in a rugged way, and I struggle to suppress a few cowboy fantasies as he takes off his hat.

He approaches. "Hey, Bri, how are you feeling today?"

"Not too bad, actually."

"In that case, I have an extra sandwich." He runs his fingers through his thick, dark hair. "Do you want to take a drive around the ranch with me?"

"I'd love to!" *God, Bri, don't sound too eager.* "Uh, let me just tell Grandma I'm going out."

I pop into the kitchen, hands flush against my hot cheeks. It gives me a chance to compose myself.

Grandma is nowhere in sight, so I scribble a quick note on the pad of paper beside the phone. On my way out, I take one last look in the decorative mirror hanging by the window.

My sunken eyes are rimmed with dark circles beneath them. I'm wearing leggings and Nike running shoes, along with an oversized sweatshirt, and my dull hair is pulled into a messy bun, which I didn't even brush out today. I hurriedly take out my scrunchie and run my fingers through the tangled strands.

I guess it's a slight improvement.

Caz waits patiently at the bottom of the porch steps for me to return. When he sees me, he perks up and leads me to the passenger side of his truck, and like a true gentleman, he opens the door for me to climb in.

As much as I miss Los Angeles, I can't help but compare Caz's chivalry and manners to the guys I used to date back home. Caz makes them look like complete douchebags.

He gets in on the driver's side. "Turkey or ham?"

"Turkey, please."

He passes me a sandwich in a plastic baggie. When he turns the keys in the ignition, the truck roars to life before we speed away across the ranch.

"Caz, I have a question for you."

He glances at me before turning his eyes back on the road ahead. "Okay, shoot."

"Do you believe in aliens?"

"What?" He tries—and fails—to stifle a chuckle. "Aliens? Like from outer space?"

"Yeah, do you think they exist?" I take a bite of my sandwich. It's a simple stack of meat, Sara Lee bread, and mayo, but it hits the spot.

"I mean, it's hard to believe we're alone in the entire universe," he says. "But I'm not sure I believe that little green men come to visit us in silver spaceships."

I nod. "Okay, that's fair. What about grimwalkers?"

He bristles but doesn't say a word.

"You're part of the Silver Ridge tribe, right?" I press. "Have you heard of them?"

"Yeah, I've heard of them." His voice holds a dark edge.

A few moments of silence pass, but he doesn't elaborate.

"Do you believe in them?" I prod.

Caz's grip tightens on the steering wheel. "Technically, you're a descendant of the Silver Ridge tribe, too. So you should know we don't talk about them."

His tone puts me in my place. Grandma explained to me earlier that mentioning them invites evil. I may not believe it, but she does, and so does Caz.

I'm being a complete ass.

"You're right; I shouldn't have brought them up. I'm sorry." I turn my head away from him and stare out the window.

Caz lets out a long breath. "It's okay. Look, I'll say this: I believe there are things in this world that humans can't explain. Fair enough?"

I turn just enough to steal a glance at him out of the corner of my eye. "Can I tell you what I saw last night?"

His brows furrow. "Is everything okay?"

I launch into everything that happened during the night, including the eerie wolf howl, the lights on the ridge, and the conversation I had with my grandparents afterward. Caz allows me to speak without interruption, giving an attentive nod every so often.

"Do you think we could drive up there?" I ask. "To check it out?"

Caz sighs. "I'll take you up there, but on one condition: promise me you won't go up there by yourself, especially at night. It's dark and treacherous up there; you could slip and fall."

"Got it. Only go up there during the day."

He huffs. "Only if you're with someone who can protect you."

"So, does that make you my Secret Service bodyguard?" I reach across the seat and ruffle his hair.

He laughs and pretends to tip his hat, which is sitting on the dashboard. "It would be my honor, Madame President."

A warm glow flames in my chest. I used to insist I would be the first female president of the United States, and he would pretend to be my Secret Service detail. He'd shoot at make-believe bad guys as we ran wildly through the tall grass, and he would tackle me to the ground and shield me with his body from the path of imaginary bullets.

I clench my thighs together at the idea of him on top of me now, pressed beneath his strong, muscular torso, between his legs…

"We're here." Caz brings the truck to an abrupt halt.

When he jumps out and shuts the door, it gives me a moment to cool off. My skin is scorching at the illicit fantasy of Caz, naked…

Geez, Bri, get a grip.

Caz opens the door and offers his palm to help me down. After I slide out of the cab onto my feet, he lets go of my hand, and I already miss our contact.

Time to focus on the task at hand—our alien investigation.

"See anything unusual?" I ask.

He glances around. "No, nothing out of the ordinary."

I take a few steps forward, soaking in the panoramic view. It's more forested up here on the mesa, which offers a breathtaking perspective of the ranch below. I can see the farmhouse from here, but it looks so tiny in the middle of the vast landscape.

"I can't believe I've never been up here," I say. "It's beautiful."

When Caz doesn't respond, I glance over at him. However, when I find him staring at me with a soft gaze, I nearly melt into a puddle in the grass.

I don't know what comes over me, but I'm drawn to him by something I can't explain. It's like my feet move on their own as I take a few slow steps toward him. His eyes grow wider as I move closer, until I'm pressed against his broad chest.

The longer I stare into his eyes, the more the magnitude of this moment grows.

This doesn't feel like a casual flirtation. Whatever this feeling is, I've never experienced it with anyone else. It feels like more, like our lives, intertwined so inextricably throughout the years, have led up to this moment. Although we come from two different worlds, fate made our childhoods collide, knowing we would be standing here one day all grown up.

All I know is I'm desperate to kiss him, to feel his lips on mine for the very first time. And judging by the way he's looking at me, I'm certain he feels the same.

That is, until he clears his throat and steps away from me. "We should head back." His curt voice cuts through the silence.

The thread between us snaps, and my heart plunges into my stomach. He may as well have dumped a bucket of ice water over me.

How did I misread his signals? I used to be so good at reading guys, which is why I never had trouble with boyfriends. *I'm* the one who does the leading on, then the breaking up. Not the other way around.

His rejection is brutal. My cheeks grow hot, but before he can see, I turn away from his intense gaze and head back to the truck.

Caz's boots crunch in the dirt behind me. "Bri, I'm sorry—"

"It's fine." My voice comes out in a strained, high-pitched squeak.

How am I supposed to look Caz in the eye again? I've completely ruined my relationship with the only person my age within a one-hundred mile radius.

I'm already in the truck before Caz has a chance to open my door for me, so he walks around to the driver's side and gets in. Neither of us knows what to say, and the ride back to the farmhouse is more than uncomfortable.

I'm desperate to get away from him, to escape this confined space we're both trapped in. I roll down the window for air.

As soon as we pull up to the farmhouse, I unbuckle my seatbelt and open my door before we roll to a complete stop.

"See you later," I say, slamming the car door behind me.

"Bri, wait—"

I don't stick around to hear the rest.

CHAPTER 3

I t's been almost a week, and I haven't seen Caz since our awkward encounter on the ridge. It was so humiliating I even called my mom to beg her to let me come home.

Are you ready to go back to school?

No, I replied.

Then I think it's best you stay with Grandma Maeve and Grandpa Henry for the time being.

Between the fatigue and brain fog, I've barely been able to move from my mattress, trapped in a body that may as well be made of solid lead. The days feel long, and I'm a prisoner of my own thoughts, which mostly consist of Caz.

Grandma took pity on me and brought me trays of food, though I hate her seeing me like this. So... weak.

That's probably why Caz isn't interested. If we started a relationship, and things got serious, my illness would condemn him to a caregiver role. If I was in his shoes, I wouldn't want to date me either.

Today is the first day I'm able to leave my room, though I spend the afternoon on the sofa downstairs watching trashy reality television. Grandma joins me for an episode of *Real Housewives of Beverly Hills*, and since I'm desperate for human interaction, I point out some of the places I used to go to with my friends. She nods and listens, though the scandalized expression reveals what she really thinks about the outrageous behavior of the housewives.

When dinner approaches, she gets up to start preparing a meatloaf in the kitchen, leaving me to distract myself with TV. It's the first real distraction from Caz I've been able to get.

Until I hear two pairs of boots walk into the kitchen, along with two male voices.

"Spooked, you say?" my grandfather asks.

"Yeah, the cattle have been running to one corner of the ranch, and they've been staying tight-knit all afternoon."

Oh, God, it's Caz. The absolute last person I want to see when my hair is unbrushed and knotted into a messy bun. I haven't showered in three days.

I throw the blanket off me and tiptoe toward the staircase, praying that he doesn't venture into the living room.

"Have there been any coyote sightings?" Grandpa asks.

"None, sir. Did you have a chance to talk with Findley?"

My grandfather lets out a heavy sigh. "Yeah, but he's sticking to his story that he's not involved."

"And do you believe him?"

"I'm not sure." A chair scrapes against the kitchen floor. "When I brought up Bri, he insisted he'd never intentionally scare the family. But I don't know."

"Speaking of Bri," Caz says, "where is she?"

No. No, no, no.

A spoon clacks against a pot before Grandma responds. "She's in the living room."

"Fuck," I mutter. I'm halfway up the stairs, making my way as quietly as possible so as not to make the old floorboards creak.

Caz's boots tap against the kitchen floor, then onto the carpet of the living room.

Shit, shit, shit.

I'm nearly up the stairs when Caz calls up behind me. "Hey, Bri?"

My heart sinks. I'd prefer not to rehash his cruel rejection from last week. Can't we pretend I never tried to kiss him and avoid each other for the rest of our lives? That seems easier.

I turn around slowly to face him. "Uh, hey."

He runs his hand through his dark hair as he fiddles with the brim of his cowboy hat with the other. It's tense being in the same room as him, and I brace for the additional rejection about to come.

"I wanted to ask if you'd like to go on a picnic tomorrow afternoon?"

I blink. "A picnic?" My brain fog must be bad because it sounds like he's asking me on a date, and that's impossible.

"Yeah, in our old spot where we used to go." He gives me a lopsided smile. "Do you remember?"

My hand loosens its grip on the banister. "Of course, I remember."

Caz beams. "Great. So, I'll pick you up at five?"

Before I can formulate a response in my head, I nod.

He beams up at me before walking back into the kitchen. I have no idea how long I'm staring after him, even after I hear the screen door shut.

What the hell?

I should have given him a taste of his own medicine and played hard to get. But instead, I just nodded like a desperate, blonde idiot. Pathetic.

When I make my way back down the stairs, I plop down on the sofa, staring blankly at the television. It isn't long before Grandma wanders into the living room and takes a seat beside me. She doesn't say anything at first; she just gives me a knowing smile.

"I'm going on a date with Caz," I blurt out.

"I heard." Her smile falters. "I'm glad to see you getting out. I just..."

I furrow my eyebrows. "What is it, Grandma?"

"I just want you to be careful, is all."

"I thought you loved the Nezaras?" I ask.

She places her hand on my knee. "Of course I do. The Nezaras are like family to your grandpa and me. It's just, they've always held us at arm's length."

I settle back against the sofa cushions. "How so?"

"Well, they have family secrets, which isn't any of our business," she says. "I know it's just one date, but I don't want you to be disappointed when he keeps you at a distance."

I think back to my almost-kiss with Caz last week. At the time, I was so sure we were on the same page, only for him to pull away without any explanation. I thought I'd misread his interest in me, but perhaps my grandmother is right.

"Just have fun tomorrow." My grandmother pats my hand. "You're young. Now is the time to have lots of fun with lots of different young men."

My jaw drops open as I laugh. "Grandma!"

She gives me a wink before rising to her feet, and she returns to the kitchen to finish dinner.

Grandma makes a good point. I'm only twenty-one, so it's not like Caz is the guy I'm going to settle down with.

But if this relationship runs its course, will we still be friends in the aftermath?

I want to be close to him. To know him on a more intimate level. When we were children, I thought I knew everything about him, but maybe my grandmother is right. Maybe I don't know anything about Caz after all.

Although, perhaps that's why I'm so drawn to him—he's mysterious, and I relish the challenge of unlocking his secrets.

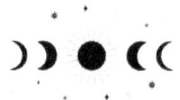

I spend the morning taking my time getting ready, but it's difficult to ignore the building anticipation. After sliding into a floral print sundress, I make my way downstairs and wait for Caz to pick me up.

My grandmother glances up from the kitchen sink. "Ah, Bri, you look lovely." She rummages in a cupboard for a moment before pulling out a bottle of wine, which she hands to me. "I thought this might be a wonderful addition to the picnic Caz planned."

I accept the bottle with a wide grin. "Thank you, Grandma."

A heavy knock comes down on the screen door.

"I'll get it," she whispers. "A lady never answers the door for her gentleman caller." She shoots me a quick wink over her shoulder before opening the door. "Ah, Caz, come on in. Bri's ready for you."

As Caz steps into the kitchen, he removes his hat from his bowed head. Once over the threshold, he looks up at me, hat held against his chest, and pauses. "Wow, Bri, you look..." His voice trails off.

"Lovely," Grandma supplies.

"Yeah." He runs his thumb over the brim of his hat with a small smile. "Lovely."

My cheeks burn hot.

"Ready to go?" I try to keep my eyes on his, but it's hard not to admire the neatly pressed button-up shirt and dark jeans he wore for the occasion.

He nods. "Yep, follow me. I'll have her home before dark, Mrs. Casey."

"You two have fun." She gives me a pat on the shoulder before I head out the door.

After the door closes behind us, I turn to Caz on the porch and pass him the bottle of wine. "This is for you."

He holds it out to read the label. "Thanks. I've never had wine before."

I follow him down the stairs toward the truck. "I hope it goes well with the food. What are we having?"

"It's a surprise." He winks at me before opening the passenger side door.

Once I'm settled into my seat, he closes the door and makes his way around to the other side. A picnic basket sits between us on the long seat with a red checkered blanket on top.

I've gone on plenty of picnics with him over the years. So why am I so nervous?

I wipe my clammy palms on my skirt.

Caz drives us out toward a grove of trees on one end of the ranch, which surrounds a small fishing pond.

"Remember how we used to have to hike all the way out here from the farmhouse?" I reminisce.

"I sure do." He smiles, his eyes focused on the road ahead. "I used to be stuck carrying the picnic basket."

"Ha! You volunteered, even though your lanky little arms could barely lift it."

He laughs and pulls the truck to a stop near the pond. I grab the blanket and wine while Caz takes the picnic basket, and we set off toward a spot near the water.

He sets up the blanket and pulls out an artisanal charcuterie platter from the basket. The spread includes baguette bread, a variety of gourmet cheeses, and assorted cold meats, complete with nuts, grapes, and strawberries.

When he's finished, I take a seat beside him on the blanket. "I'm impressed."

"Well, I know you L.A. girls have high expectations." He glances at me with a shy smile. "Especially one as classy as yourself."

A flutter beats in my chest.

I've never had a guy put this much effort into a date. It was always a meetup for cocktails or coffee followed by a night on the town, with the expectation that we'd usually end up at either his place or mine.

But this time, there's no pressure. He simply enjoys the pleasure of my company, and for whatever reason, that makes me *more* nervous.

"Here you go." He passes me a small porcelain dish with an intricate floral pattern.

I trace my finger along the edge of the plate. "This is really pretty."

"It's my grandma's china set," he explains, pouring the wine into crystal goblets and passing one to me. He holds his up in the air. "To starting over." He clinks his glass gently against mine, and his eyes never leave my gaze as we both take a sip.

We spend the meal chatting easily with one another, catching up on our lives and reminiscing about the past. The hours fly by, but neither of us notices. The two of us fall into our familiar pattern, and in some ways, it feels like no time has passed at all. I'm comfortable around Caz, and with him, it's safe to let my guard down, to tell him the things I can't tell my friends and family.

Caz turns to lie on his side, his elbow propping up his head. "I want to clear things up about the other day." He picks at a loose thread on the blanket. "Out here on the ranch, we don't get to have much of a social life. I don't exactly have a lot of experience with women. Well, any experience at all, really." Caz lets out a nervous laugh. "So, I guess I'm trying to say that as much as I wanted to kiss you, I panicked. I hope you don't hate me."

"No, not at all." I would have thought a handsome, rugged cowboy like him would have lots of girls falling at his feet. I mean, look at him—he's any girl's wet cowboy fantasy.

He smiles coyly up at me. "Just to make things clear, I do want to kiss you."

"Good. Glad we cleared that up." My lips stretch into a confident smirk, which masks the butterflies in my stomach.

"Me too," he says in a husky voice. "You know, city girls like you can be very intimidating to country boys like me."

I let out a breathless laugh. "You? Afraid of me?"

"I don't want to screw this up," he admits, looking away again. "I-I've liked you for a long time."

My laugh dies. "You have?"

He nods. "I'm really glad you came to the ranch this summer."

"Me too." I lie beside him until our faces are level. Gazing into his eyes, I hope he takes it for what it is: an invitation.

Our faces draw closer, so close I feel his warm breath on my lips. My lashes flutter as my eyes fall closed.

A deep howl echoes in the distance.

We both freeze. My body tenses as a chill runs down my spine, but I'm too frightened to move.

Caz wraps his arm around my waist, pulling me close against his warm chest. He looks around us, his gaze narrowing. Twilight is descending over the ranch, and the low moon is already visible in the sky. It's almost a perfect, round circle, but not quite.

He clutches me even tighter. "We have to go."

With feline agility, Caz rises to his feet and scoops me into his arms. He's able to reach the truck in just a few long strides, where he opens the door to set me inside on the seat.

"I'm going to clean up the picnic so it doesn't attract animals," he says in a hushed voice. "Lock the doors as soon as I walk away and only open them when I get back."

My heart rattles against my ribcage. "Caz, what's going on?"

"I'll be right back, I promise." He shuts the door and returns to our picnic spot.

I do as he says and lock the doors, and I only unlock them when he returns with the basket, which he shoves onto the seat.

"Let's get out of here." He turns the keys in the ignition, and we speed away.

As we drive, I take a look in the rearview mirror and see the same eerie red lights from the other night appear on top of the mesa.

"There they are!" I shout, pointing at the mirror. "The lights!"

Caz looks up and sees what I'm seeing, then steps harder on the gas pedal.

I gulp. "Caz, what's going on around here?"

His brow furrows as the truck barrels forward. "Bad things happen at night on the ranch."

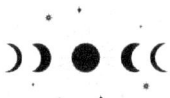

When we reach the farmhouse, the lights on the mesa have already disappeared. However, as we climb out of the truck, Caz's eyes keep flickering toward the top of the ridge.

He holds me close as we walk up the porch steps, his large hand on my waist pulling me against him. "Tell your grandma I'm sorry I kept you out late." He comes to a stop right outside the door.

I turn to face him, wondering if there is any way to salvage our date. "I don't mind. I usually find the nighttime to be quite romantic."

His expression darkens. "Unfortunately, there's nothing romantic about this ranch at night. I'm sorry things didn't go as planned. I wanted everything to be perfect for you, Bri."

I want to ask him about these "bad things" that happen at night, but when I open my mouth, the conversation with my grandmother replays in my head.

If I bring it up, it might only increase the distance between us, and that's the opposite of what I want.

I wrap my fingers with his. "I had a good time, even if it ended in an unexpected adventure."

The slightest hint of amusement reaches his eyes as he looks down at me. "You really are fearless, aren't you?"

I laugh. "I wasn't very fearless back there, but I knew you'd protect me."

"Of course." He squeezes my hand. "I'll always protect you."

There goes my heart again, fluttering against my chest.

I've missed my chance to kiss him twice already; I'm not about to lose out again. I lean forward ever so slightly, tilting my chin up to invite him closer. The seriousness on his face melts into a soft gaze.

As he leans in, I close my eyes, waiting for his lips to touch mine. His breath fans my face, laced with red wine, and my body is vibrating as I wait for us to finally take things to the next level.

The door beside us creaks open, and I gasp, practically jumping out of my skin.

"Oh!" My grandmother stands in the doorway, glancing between us. "I'm so sorry—I was just getting worried because it was dark out."

She shuts the door, leaving Caz and me in an awkward silence. The heat of the moment has passed.

Thanks, Grandma. Just my freaking luck.

"I should get going." Caz runs his hands through his hair and puts his cowboy hat back on. "Good night, Bri." With a wink, he turns to walk down the porch steps.

"Will I see you tomorrow?" I call after him.

He opens the door of his truck and pauses, his hand resting on the handle. With a grin, he calls back, "I hope so. We have unfinished business."

I rake my bottom lip between my teeth, biting back a girlish giggle as I press my back to the screen door. "Yes, we do."

CHAPTER 4

The next morning, I wake up late and make my way downstairs where Grandma sits in the living room, reading a book.

"Bri! Good, you're up. Are you hungry?"

"Not really." I rub my temples. "Do we have any ginger ale and crackers? That's all I'm really up for eating."

"Sure." Her eyes twinkle in a way that throws me off as she holds back a smile. "Just head into the kitchen. I'll be right there."

"Um, okay." *Weird.*

When I step into the kitchen, I'm greeted by a large vase filled with yellow, orange, and purple wildflowers, along with some baby's breath. They look like they've been picked by hand from around the ranch.

A small, plain note card sits on the table beside the vase. I pick it up and open it to a note scribbled in masculine handwriting.

These flowers made me think of that time when you wanted to be a florist, even if that dream only lasted for a day. Looking forward to date #2. Are you busy tonight? —Caz

A wide smile breaks across my face. I lean forward to sniff the flowers, only to remember I've lost my sense of smell.

"They're beautiful, aren't they?" Grandma enters the kitchen and crosses over to the table to touch one of the petals with her fingertips.

"They are."

Her dark eyes sparkle in the sunlight from the window. "Your grandfather and I are expected at the neighbor's for dinner tonight. Just a small gathering of ranchers in the area. So, we won't be back until after dark." Without another word, she exits the kitchen and heads back into the living room.

Did my grandmother just give me permission to have Caz over... unsupervised?

Well, I'll be damned.

It's her way of apologizing for last night's interruption. Granted, they aren't going to be gone all night, but at least this gives Caz and me a little time to ourselves.

The porch door swings open with a rattle, making me jump. I turn to find Caz standing in the doorway, heaving breathlessly. His brother, Seb, follows closely behind him, his eyes narrowed in concern.

"Are you guys okay?" I ask.

"Where's your grandpa?" Caz stamps into the living room in just a few quick strides.

"I think he's upstairs." I follow behind him and Seb, and my grandmother looks up from the sofa with wide eyes.

"Mr. Casey, are you up there?" Caz calls from the bottom of the stairs.

Footsteps come down heavily before Grandpa appears at the top of the stairs, buttoning his shirt.

"Is everything alright?" he asks.

Caz shares a look with Seb before answering. "We've had another cattle mutilation."

"You've got to be shitting me." Grandpa shakes his head and utters a string of curses.

"And that's not all, sir." Seb winces, bracing himself to deliver more bad news. "It's sitting in the middle of a crop circle."

My grandfather stops midway down the stairs, staring at the two of them with his jaw hanging open.

"My God," Grandma whispers, clutching her chest.

My grandfather bangs his fist on the banister, making all four of us jump. "That's it, I've had it! I'm gonna give Sheriff Callahan a piece of my mind. This is harassment, I tell you! Findley's gonna be sorry—"

"I'm not sure Findley did this, Mr. Casey." Caz lowers his eyes to the floor. "I drove by the same spot last night after dark and didn't see a thing. I have no idea how a person could make a crop circle and mutilate a cow in such a short time without being detected."

"Wait, a crop circle?" I ask. "Like, a pattern aliens make in cornfields?"

"Crop circles are a hoax." Grandpa continues down the stairs to join us in the living room. Agitated, he begins to pace. "We don't even grow corn."

"It's in the grass," Caz says. "And if it's a hoax, it's a really good one. The blades of grass are woven like a basket, not stomped on with feet or machinery."

Grandma gasps. "Woven grass?"

Seb nods. "Yes, ma'am. And the calf wasn't mutilated like the other, older cows. This one's insides were completely picked clean. The bones are completely bare, and there's no sign of blood on the ground nearby."

My grandfather practically spits with fury. "I'm going to bring Findley down and have the sheriff launch a full investigation—"

Grandma reaches up to put a hand on his arm, bringing him to a stop. "Henry, before you go hurtling accusations, think about this. You don't have any proof."

He folds his arms and shakes his head, and when he lets out a heavy sigh, his age is evident on his face. "At this rate, half the herd will be picked off by Labor Day. We're barely hanging on as it is. I'm getting too old for this shit, Maeve. Maybe it's time to sell the ranch."

"Please, don't do that, Mr. Casey," Caz begs.

"I'm sorry, son, but we can't keep on like this," Grandpa answers. "Cattle ranching just isn't as profitable as it used to be."

"Please, don't sell the ranch," Caz begs, and there's desperation in his eyes I've never seen before. "This ranch is our home. We can't live anywhere else. We'll monitor the fence line day and night if we have to, just... please don't give up."

My grandfather studies him for a moment before breathing out a long sigh. "I'll talk to the sheriff at tonight's meeting. Maybe some of the other ranchers have dealt with similar incidents and have some leads."

"Thank you, sir." Caz lets out a low breath.

My grandfather sits down to pull his boots on. "Maeve, get your purse. I want to head out now."

"Grandpa, do you want a snack for the road?" I ask. "It's almost lunchtime."

"Sure, Bri, that's very thoughtful of you." He gives me a half smile. There's worry on his weathered face, and I want to do everything I can to ease his stress, even if it's as simple as a snack.

"Caz, Seb, would you guys like anything?" I offer, turning to them.

Seb grins. "I'll never say no to food."

"I'll help." Caz follows me into the kitchen.

The atmosphere in the house is tense, and he's just as eager for a respite as I am.

"Lunch meat sandwiches?" I ask.

"Sure." He steps to the kitchen sink to wash his hands. "What can I do to help? Put me to work."

I task him with spreading mayonnaise on bread while I clean some grapes.

"I want to see it," I say quietly.

Caz glances up with an arched brow. "The crop circle? Absolutely not."

"I can handle it. I saw the last cattle mutilation."

"Bri, this one is different. It's really gruesome. I don't want you anywhere near it."

I set the grapes down and turn to face him head-on. "Then take me to the top of the ridge. So we can get a good look at it from above."

He sighs. "Alright, fine. I'm going up there anyway to scout it out."

"Maybe the pattern will offer clues as to who's behind this."

"Yeah, maybe." Caz's voice doesn't hold much hope.

I study him for a long moment as he absently puts the sandwiches together. His face is drawn with dark circles under his eyes. He looks like he didn't get any sleep last night.

He's worried about the fate of the ranch. We all are. Strange events are happening, and whoever or whatever is behind them is a mystery—an invisible enemy.

"We're heading out now," Grandpa says as he steps into the kitchen, followed by Grandma.

I hand them little baggies of sandwiches and grapes for the road. "I love you." I give them each a swift hug, hoping it offers a little bit of comfort.

Grandma pats my hand. "Thank you, dear. I love you too."

I watch from the window as they make their way down to the truck, and soon they're off down the road.

I turn to Caz. "They're gone. Let's head up to the mesa."

Caz, Seb, and I pile into the truck. We make our way up the steep dirt road in a weighted silence, each of us apprehensive about what we'll find at our destination.

When we reach the top, Caz parks and we climb out. Caz is the first to the edge, and he lets out a gasp. The corded muscles in his shoulders grow tense beneath his white T-shirt.

"What is it?" I ask.

He says nothing, continuing to stare downwards. Every step I take toward the edge feels heavier, like my body is warning me to turn back.

As soon as I reach the edge, I'm grateful I haven't eaten lunch yet. I'd throw up the entire contents of my stomach if I had.

I'm unable to make out the details of the cattle mutilation, but my eyes aren't focused on that. They're drawn to what's around it, a pattern made in the tall grass stretching across the open field. It's so large it would be visible from an airplane flying overhead.

A pattern depicting a pentagram encased in the outline of a circle.

My grandparents need to know what we've found.

I hold my phone up in the air. "Damn it. I don't have any service up here."

"Come on," Caz says. "Let's head back. Seb, I'll take you back to the homestead. I'm going to stay with Bri until her grandparents get home."

Caz and Seb turn their backs and start heading for the truck, their boots crunching along the gravelly dirt. But something compels me to take one last look at the crop circle below, like it's calling out to me and me alone.

Except I don't know what it's trying to tell me.

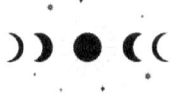

After dropping off Seb at the modest Nezara homestead, we return to the farmhouse and sit on the sofa. Caz's thigh grazes against mine, which sends a thrill weaving through my body.

Leave it to me to get turned on in the middle of a crisis.

We call my grandparents on speakerphone to tell them what we saw, and my grandfather starts cussing in the background.

"What does it mean?" my grandmother asks.

I scroll through a myriad of search results on my phone. "It could mean anything—protection, the devil, the five wounds of Christ, a sign of life and connections... the list goes on."

"We'll make sure the sheriff is aware," she says. "We'll be back after the meeting. Stay safe, you two. Thanks for staying with Bri."

"Of course," Caz replies. "She's safe with me."

"Drive safe. I love you." I hang up, then set the phone down on the coffee table.

A comfortable silence settles over Caz and me. I lean back against his hard chest, seeking his warmth and strength, and he wraps his arm around me.

"You okay?" he whispers.

"Yeah. You?"

"I'm fine."

I crane my neck to look at him. "Why are you so freaked out about my grandpa selling the ranch? You seemed upset earlier."

He lets out a hollow laugh. "I don't want to lose my job."

"There are so many ranches in the area. I'm sure you would get hired somewhere else."

He shakes his head. "This ranch is all I've ever known. It's where my siblings and I grew up, where my parents and my grandparents grew up, and generations before them. I can't just leave. This is our land. This is where I belong."

If I'm going to pursue a relationship with Caz, will our future together be tied to this ranch? I never imagined a life cut off from the outside world, although it's not like I have much of a future at the moment, anyway. I gave all that up when I left Los Angeles.

There isn't much I can do about that, but what I can do is help solve this mystery entangling the ranch.

"Let's start from the beginning," I say. "The day I got here, there was a cattle mutilation. Grandma mentioned there hadn't been one in years, but now we have two in two weeks. You said the cattle were acting spooked, plus we have a crop circle and strange lights on our hands."

Caz nods. "All true."

"I remember cattle mutilations happening from time to time when I'd visit the ranch, though the adults tried to keep it from us. Do you remember when all this first started?"

His brow furrows. "Yeah, as far back as I can remember, but it's never been this often before. These things used to happen so rarely."

"Why do you think that is?"

Caz shakes his head. "I'm not sure. Nothing has changed except—" His gaze flickers down at me, but his voice cuts off.

"Except what?" I ask.

His body tenses. "It's nothing. Nevermind."

I sit up straight, turning my body to face him squarely on the sofa. "The activity has picked up since the moment I arrived, hasn't it?"

He doesn't meet my gaze. "I'm sure it's just a coincidence."

When I looked at the crop circle, it felt like a message intended for me. Are all of these strange events signaling something? What was that pull that I felt standing on top of the mesa?

"Caz, does something want to hurt me?" My voice catches at the end as my lip trembles.

"Bri, I will never let anyone hurt you." He pulls me forward against his chest, and I burrow my face into his shirt, desperate for the safety I feel when I'm with him. "That's a promise."

The scent of leather and earth clings to his shirt. God, he smells good.

I lean back, staring into his eyes, and reflected back to me is the sincerity of his promise: he'll always save me.

I'm done waiting to show him how I feel.

I bring my hands up his chest, feeling every hard line of muscle beneath his cotton T-shirt. As I snake my arms around his neck, I lean forward, capturing his lips with my own.

Finally. *Fucking finally.*

His mouth tastes delicious—salty with a hint of sweet cinnamon.

When I take his lower lip between mine, a soft moan rumbles in his throat. His broad palms grasp my waist, pulling me even closer. One of his hands slides up my back to my neck, and he tilts my head to the side to trail kisses down my jawline to my neck.

I let out a soft, audible exhale at the sensation of his lips near my ear. His teeth nibble on my earlobe, driving me absolutely wild.

For a guy with zero experience with women, he kisses like an expert.

Our kiss quickly turns heated, and he kisses me like he needs my breath to keep breathing. It's hungry and desperate, and a blaze of need erupts in my core.

I need to feel his body settled over mine, need to forget the terror and uncertainty of today's events and lose myself in him.

I shift my position, straddling his lap on the couch, and grind against him. My lower belly clenches as I seek that delicious friction through our clothes—

Suddenly, he pulls back, breathing hard. "We should slow down."

His words are a bucket of ice water, extinguishing the flame of need with a smoking hiss.

I gaze into his eyes, catching my breath. He's a great kisser, but I'm guessing he's still a virgin.

"Sorry." I shift off his lap, taking a seat on the opposite end of the couch. "I guess I got a little carried away."

"No, it's fine. Really," he rasps. "I liked it. I *really* liked it."

I glance down at his lap, where the thick bulge in his jeans shows me just how much he liked it.

"I'm sure you have tons of experience with this kind of thing." Caz pauses, his eyes growing wide. "Wait, that came out wrong. I just meant that I imagine you had all kinds of guys who wanted to date you in school. I mean, look at you." He waves his hand at me up and down.

I have no idea why this rugged, masculine cowboy has melted into a puddle of vulnerability with me, but it somehow makes me even more attracted to him.

He leans forward and tucks a stray hair behind my ear. Holding my gaze, the depth of his affection is evident in those deep brown eyes, and it almost frightens me how much passion I find there. No one has ever looked at me that way before.

How long has he been pining for me, and how come I've never noticed it before?

I tear my eyes away from his intense gaze. "Are you hungry?"

He grins. "I'm always hungry."

I wish that was a euphemism.

"Let's have an early dinner, then." I rise to my feet, but when I do, a wave of dizziness hits me, making me stumble backward. I reach for the sofa arm, but I'm met with strong, muscular arms that steady me.

"Bri, are you okay?"

"Yeah." I try to bring the world around me back to a standstill. "Just stood up too fast."

"Sit down." Caz gently pushes me down onto the couch. "I'll get you some water."

After a few moments, he reappears from the kitchen with two glasses in his hand, one of which he passes to me. He sets his water on the coffee table and stands over me, his brows knitted together.

"Thank you." I take a small sip. "I'm sorry about that."

"Why are you sorry?"

I let out a bitter laugh. "You work so hard on this ranch every day, and I can't even make you dinner."

He kneels on the floor in front of me until our faces are level. "It's not a competition, Bri."

"Isn't it, though?" Frustrated tears prick my vision. "I can't keep up anymore, and it makes me feel so fucking lazy."

"You are a lot of things, Briar Casey, and lazy isn't one of them." Caz clucks his tongue, staring at the glass of water in my hands. He tilts his head and points at it. "Look at this cup. It's almost filled to the top with water." He reaches behind him and picks the other water glass off the coffee table, then downs most of its contents, leaving only a little at the bottom. "But this cup doesn't have much water. It's not the cup's fault, is it?"

I quirk an eyebrow at him. "No, it's just a cup."

He grins and takes my water glass from me, holding it up. "Let's say this cup is mine. I have a lot more energy in my cup to draw from than the other one, right? I can do a lot more with this cup."

"So, I'm just an empty, useless water glass?"

"No." He sets the two cups down and reaches for my hand. "I'm saying you have a lot less energy than I do, but that's not your fault. So, don't ever call yourself useless because it's not true. And if I have to keep telling you that until you believe it, I will."

I stare at him for a long moment. Truth be told, I never thought about it that way, but when he puts it like that, it makes sense.

Somehow, Caz is able to say all the right things that I need to hear.

He rises to his feet. "Now, you're going to sit here and drink your water, and I'm going to make us something to eat."

It's almost midnight, and I'm watching TV on low volume in my grandparents' living room. I'm curled up in a blanket on the sofa, unable to sleep. I keep thinking about my kiss with Caz and grinning like an idiot.

I can't stop thinking about him. My body has this magnetic attraction to his, almost as if it's painful to be apart. I don't know why I'm falling so hard, so fast, for him, but I've never felt this way about another guy before.

It's making me restless. I stand up and walk toward the window, but my body aches, protesting with every step. A full moon is out tonight, but that's not why the entire ranch is bathed in light.

The top of the mesa is lit up once again in that eerie, scarlet glow, reaching up to touch the velvet night sky. Tonight, it's brighter than before, as though it's trying to capture my attention.

Like it's beckoning me to come investigate. To unravel its mystery.

I'm mesmerized by it. Drawn to it the same way I'm drawn to Caz, as strange as that sounds.

Without hesitation, I grab my grandfather's truck keys off the hook by the door. Ignoring the pain in my joints, I barrel toward the truck and climb inside. When the truck roars to life, I slam on the gas pedal and make a beeline across the ranch toward the mesa.

Promise me you won't go up there by yourself, especially at night. It's dark and treacherous up there...

"Sorry, Caz," I mutter under my breath. But something in my gut tells me to follow the lights. I'll just head up, check things out, and head back to the farmhouse before anyone is awake.

The truck shakes and rattles on the steep path up to the ridge, slowing my progress. I keep checking the top to make sure the lights are still there, and I pray they don't disappear before I have the chance to investigate.

Finally, the truck levels out when I reach the top, and I pull over and turn off the truck, killing the ignition and headlights.

Peering through the window offers a view of the forested mesa, and the trees are lit in the same eerie glow. But the trees part to form a clearing, as if giving a wide berth to the source of light.

Like a warning.

In the clearing is a rectangular shape of red light, like a doorway. It's too bright to see through it to the other side, but small, white orbs of light are bursting forth.

What are these mysterious specters? Ghosts? Aliens? Angels? My mind races as I sit in the dark truck, a voyeur to this otherworldly, unexplainable event.

The orbs of light bounce around like dust motes, circling and dancing around one another in the air before their descent to the ground. The moment they touch the grass, they begin to take form, slowly growing and morphing into the shape of a human. Pressing my nose to the window, I count five beings with long, white hair and pale, translucent skin.

One of them turns, giving me a clear view of his eyes. Eyes the color of blood, glowing brightly in the dark night.

As he narrows his eyes, my blood runs ice cold. He's staring right at me across the clearing, his gaze menacing, and the others around him whip around to face me as well.

Oh, shit.

I'm frozen with fear, too terrified to move lest they see motion in the dark truck. But despite being at least fifty yards away, those crimson eyes look like they're staring straight into my soul, leaving me shivering and breathless.

They have pointed ears peeking through their long, white hair. Their black outfits look like they stepped straight from the Dark Ages, like demonic Vikings who have come to pillage our world from another dimension. Are these the creatures behind the cattle mutilations and crop circles?

Suddenly, the five of them dart forward, running like bullets across the grass—heading straight toward me.

I leap backwards, trying to scramble into the backseat of the truck. All I want to do is put as much space between me and whatever those things are, but my back slams against the seat.

This is how I'm going to die.

Will they find my body mutilated like the cows? Drained of blood, with the muscles picked clean from my bones?

My last thought is of Caz, and his face enters my mind, smiling at me.

Caz, of all the people in my life, is the one I see in my final moments. And my soul tells me what it's known deep down for a long time, even if I didn't. A bond that doesn't make logical sense, but a bond that's there nonetheless.

If only I could tell him that I—

A loud roar rips through the quiet night, the sheer force of it shaking the truck around me.

A hairy beast the size of a buffalo sprints across the clearing, but despite its size, it moves at the speed of a cheetah. It knocks the strange beings in its path like bowling pins to the ground, taking one of the demon creatures in its maw and shaking it like a rag doll.

The beast clamps down and rips the demon into two.

The torso and legs fall to the ground in a bloody pile at the beast's feet, and the demon's red eyes lose their glow, devoid of life.

I can't even muster a scream when the beast turns its eyes onto me. It's staring through the window into my eyes, and it speaks to something in my soul that keeps me transfixed on its gaze.

Its eyes are two luminous, golden orbs in the dark night. The beast's silhouette is visible beneath the full moon, revealing the largest wolf I have ever seen. When he steps closer, his giant paw lands on the ground with a loud thud.

Grandma said she saw a wolf last year the size of a cow, one that could get up on its hind legs and walk off without a trace.

This is the same creature. A *grimwalker*. An evil being disguised as a wolf to cause harm.

But as this wolf takes another slow, cautious step closer, I don't feel any malicious intent from it. Its fur is a soft shade of dark brown, illuminated by the light of the portal behind it. I'm unable to look away from his gaze, which feels familiar...

The remaining demons rise from the grass, attracting the wolf's attention. It whips its head around and emits a low, guttural growl.

Another deep howl echoes across the clearing. Two other grimwalkers appear in wolf form, slightly smaller in size than the first.

A battle breaks out between the three wolves and four demons. Their paws swat at their agile enemies as they bare their sharp teeth. Spittle flies from their mouths as they attack, their thunderous growls ripping through the quiet night and shaking the truck.

They're protecting me.

Why I believe this so fiercely, I don't know, but deep in my bones, I believe they're protecting me... and the ranch. The grimwalkers aren't the cause of all the bad things happening lately, but rather trying to *stop* them from happening.

I press my fingertips to the cool window, captivated by the battle outside. But the demons are worthy opponents, and the two sides seem evenly matched.

"Wait a second." I resist the urge to curse at myself, reaching over the console into the front seat. When I open the glove compartment, I dig around inside, looking for the handgun my grandfather keeps in there. At least I hope he still keeps it there. I've only ever seen it once six years ago on my last trip to the ranch.

I don't know how a gun will protect me against demon creatures from another realm, but my body is moving on autopilot at this point. There's nowhere to run with the sharp drop over the edge of the mesa mere feet away, so my options for survival are limited.

All three wolves are locked into a heated battle with a demon, leaving the fourth to turn its sights on me. It darts forward like a bullet train, its glowing red eyes fixed on me.

I scream.

The gun is nowhere to be found. I throw myself onto the floorboards, covering my head with my arms as I curl up into a fetal position.

This is it. This is how I die, and if the cattle are any indication, it'll be a gruesome end to my short life.

A loud rip tears through the night like a lightning strike. The truck lurches from the impact of something heavy against the side, like a body, and I peer up to see the demon hit the window—without its head.

Blood smears across the windowpane as the body falls to the ground with a soft thud.

There's a ringing in my ears, drowning out any other sound of the battle taking place outside. Shaking, I pull myself onto my knees, just enough to peer out the window.

The largest of the three wolves stands only feet away, blood dripping from its maw as its golden eyes find mine.

Why does he seem so familiar?

A movement behind him catches my eye, and I rip my gaze away from his. The last two demons are stalking toward my protector, leaving the other two wolves lying in the grass, breathing hard and completely spent of their energy. This wolf managed to win his fight, as evidenced by the body lying behind him, but the other two weren't as lucky.

But the wolf isn't turning around to face the final two attackers. I have to warn him. To save him, just like he saved me.

Without a second thought, I leap from the truck, thrusting open the door with all my might. "LOOK OUT BEHIND YOU!" I scream at the top of my lungs, pointing at the impending threat behind him.

With a snarl, the wolf turns around, only to be knocked down by the two demons. One of the attackers raises its hand, revealing long claws growing out of its fingertips. While one demon holds the wolf down, the other strikes him across the head, causing him to become still.

"No!" A sob is wrenched from my throat, tears pricking my vision. I take a few steps forward without any regard for the imminent danger ahead. A desire to save him overwhelms me, propelling me toward the familiar beast whose soul called out to mine.

As the demons continue their assault, the wolf's form begins to shrink and morph into a human being. The rich, brown fur gives way to honey-toned skin as the naked form of a man is left in its wake.

No way.

No fucking way.

The man lying motionless in the grasp of the two demons is Caz.

Caz Nezara is a grimwalker.

This can't be real. There's no way this is real.

Maybe I'm asleep in my bed at my grandparents' farmhouse, and I'm having a bad dream. A nightmare I can't wake up from.

It takes a moment for the shock to wear off. The two demons are pulling Caz closer to the glowing portal behind them, dragging his heavy, muscular form across the clearing by the arms.

They're taking him back to whatever hell they came from.

My feet turn to lead, and I struggle to take a step forward. I have to get to Caz before he disappears.

What I need is to find that gun. That's my only chance to save us both.

In a split-second decision, I hurl myself back toward the truck, flinging open the driver's side door. I climb in, lying across the front seats to reach for the glove compartment, and I shove everything out of the glove compartment onto the floor.

There!

My fingers wrap around the handle of the gun, the metal cold against my skin. It's jarring. It's been years since Grandpa taught me how to handle a gun, and it's heavier than I remember.

This is a weapon designed to kill—and it's my only chance to save Caz.

I spring into action and push myself out of the truck. It takes a few steps, but my body gives way to momentum as I sprint forward as fast as I've ever run in my life toward Caz, unwilling to let him get away.

But I can't start shooting until I'm close enough to know I won't hit him.

The demons are at the portal now, dragging Caz's motionless body through the scarlet glow. The neon outline of the mysterious doorway starts to shrink when they step through, pulling Caz's torso into the light.

I'm so close. The portal starts shrinking into a circle. I can't let it disappear if Caz is on the other side.

In order to make it, I leap forward, diving headfirst into the abyss.

Darkness consumes me, save for the glowing red eyes of the demons right below me as I enter into free fall.

This is my last chance.

Aim. Take a deep breath. Grandpa's lessons swim through my brain.

Aim. Take a deep breath.

Aiming between each pair of eyes, I take a breath, then fire two shots before I black out.

E verything hurts.

I'm engulfed in darkness. The hard surface I lie on feels like it's tilting. Spinning. Every inch of my body aches like it was hit by a freight train.

Slowly, I blink my eyes open, but everything around me is blurry. After giving myself a moment to adjust, the starry, velvet night comes into view above me. The full moon hangs high in the sky, but it's glowing a deep shade of blood red, with red clouds floating around it.

That's... weird.

The last thing I remember is jumping into a supernatural portal after a bunch of demons who kidnapped Caz.

Caz! Where is he?

I sit up quickly, the abrupt movement making me dizzy, and I drop my hands to the ground to steady myself. The texture beneath my fingertips is stony, and when I glance down, I find cobblestone pavers beneath me.

Around me is a dark, empty square with a circular fountain in the middle. Quaint, medieval buildings enclose the square, like I've fallen into a remote village in Europe trapped in the Dark Ages.

Where the hell am I?

When I glance over my shoulder, I gasp at the sight of a limp, naked form nearby. "Caz?"

I crawl over and roll him onto his back, and as I do, he lets out a groan. Three deep gashes mar his neck, and blood is smeared across his skin. With a chill, I realize it's where the demons clawed at him during their battle.

"Caz, you're hurt."

He winces but doesn't open his eyes. "Where are the blood wraiths?"

"The *what*? Do you mean those demons who attacked us?"

He grimaces and nods.

I search the square for any sign of them. It doesn't take long to spot the two on the opposite end of the square, each with large holes blown through their heads. They're lying motionless on the cobblestone, surrounded by a large pool of blood, and their red eyes are devoid of any life.

"They're dead." I turn my focus back on Caz. "Oh, my God. I did it. I actually did it!"

His deep brown eyes flutter open, and he stills when his gaze locks onto mine. "You were always a good shot."

I brush my fingers across his forehead. "That's when I was practicing on empty cans. These were different."

"That's the understatement of the century." When he tries to sit up, I help him, careful to avoid his wound.

He looks around at the square, his brows knitting together as he studies our unfamiliar surroundings. His head turns up toward the sky, and when his eyes land on the moon, his body stiffens beneath my touch.

"No." He shakes his head. "No, no, no, this can't be right..."

"Caz, what's going on? Where are we?"

"We're not supposed to be here." He attempts to scramble to his feet, but he winces with pain and gasps. I manage to get to my own feet and pull him up with me.

"Where are we?" I ask.

"In the Crimson Vale." A dark look crosses his face. "Come on—we have to hide."

He grabs my hand and leads me across the square, following the perimeter to stay in the shadows of the buildings.

"What about those two?" I whisper, nodding my head toward the two dead blood wraiths.

"There's nothing we can do."

He pulls me behind him through the shadows, leading me down a dark, narrow street. We dart behind wooden crates and empty market stalls as Caz keeps a watchful eye out.

When we come across a barn door, he rolls it open as quietly as possible and leads me inside. Horses huff in agitation at our arrival. I stand still as Caz closes the door behind us and shuffles around in the dark, and after a few moments, a small gas lamp lights up.

He holds the lamp near his waist, blocking my view of his private areas as he approaches. Heat rises to my cheeks, and I glance at the straw-covered ground.

A horse beside me lets out an angry snort. Grandma and Grandpa taught me how to ride horses during my summers at the ranch, so I approach it to calm its nerves. I reach out to give it a gentle pat on its snout, but when I come face-to-face with a pair of glowing, red eyes surrounded by hair as dark as night, I gasp.

I fall backwards onto the ground. "Holy shit!"

"Shhh!" Caz rushes forward to help me back to my feet.

Large, black wings unfurl in distress, releasing a couple of long feathers into the air.

"Is that a fucking *pegasus?*" I hiss.

Caz gives the beast a weary look. "Yeah, I think so."

"What is this place?" I round on Caz. "And what the hell are you?"

"Let's start with why you were on the ridge." He narrows his gaze at me. "Bri, you promised not to go up there by yourself."

I fold my arms. "You would have been hurt if I hadn't been there."

"If I hadn't been so worried about your safety, I could have handled those blood wraiths all by myself."

"Oh, please. It's lucky I was there to kill those—oh, shit." I stop, my eyes widening in fear.

Caz stiffens. "What? What's wrong?"

"Grandpa's gun... I didn't see it when we woke up. It could be anywhere."

"Damn." He runs a hand through his hair. "Well, we can't go looking for it. Until we can figure out a way back home, we have to stay hidden."

"Where are we?"

Caz lets out a long breath. "You better sit down." He crosses over to a cupboard and rummages through the shelves. "I have a lot to fill you in on. Here."

He tosses me a saddle blanket, then turns his back toward me again to continue searching through the supplies. Despite the terrifying and confusing situation we've found ourselves in, I can't help but admire the lines of muscle on his strong shoulders and back, and my eyes trace the curvature of his spine down toward his firm ass.

Damn, that's a great ass.

Much to my dismay, he finds a pair of equestrian pants and a loose-fitting cotton shirt and shrugs them on. He looks like a medieval poet in that outfit, and under different circumstances, I would find it funny.

Caz leads me into one of the empty stalls at the end of the row. Thankfully, it's cleared of excrement, and Caz begins to rake some straw into a pile in the corner. He takes the saddle blanket from me and lays it out on the makeshift bed.

He takes a seat and pats the spot beside him. "Sit."

I do as he says. A shiver runs down my spine at the cool temperature in the barn, so I pull my knees against my chest to keep warm.

"Where do I even begin?" he mutters, running his hand along his jaw with a heavy sigh.

I snort. "Let's start with the fact that you're a grimwalker."

"Well, we're not so much grimwalkers anymore as we are werewolves."

I do a double-take. "Werewolves? Like howl-at-the-full-moon werewolves? And who is *we?*"

"My siblings and I, we're all werewolves." The corner of his lips curl. "My grandmother too. And we can shift into werewolves of our own free will, not just on the full moon."

"Sounds like a grimwalker to me." I push a pebble around on the floor with my shoe. "So, the two other wolves who fought with you in that battle...?"

"That was Seb and Seraphine." His face falls. "I hope they're okay. Those blood wraiths were pretty strong compared to what we normally see."

"What the *actual* fuck, Caz?" I can't wrap my head around all this.

The Nezaras are werewolves. I wouldn't believe it if I hadn't witnessed Caz transform with my own two eyes. Actually, I'm still not sure I believe it.

"Let me start from the beginning," Caz says. "My family is directly descended from the Silver Ridge tribe, but we haven't been recognized as members for centuries. Long ago, the tribe cast my ancestors from the tribe as punishment for being grimwalkers."

"So you *are* grimwalkers."

Caz lets out a hollow laugh. "Not anymore. Grandma says the medicine woman ripped the evil part of our ancestors' souls from their bodies and cast them into the Crimson Vale. What was left was the good half of their soul, but they cast the Curse of the Werewolf on their bodies as punishment for the havoc the grimwalkers caused. They also cursed them to guard the portal to the Crimson Vale, chaining them to the land around the portal to ensure they fulfilled their duty to protect."

My face scrunches together. "I don't get it."

He clucks his tongue. "I'll just tell you the story the way Grandma tells it."

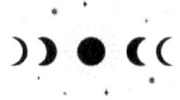

Azumi and Elior sat cross-legged outside the chief's wickiup hut, where a plume of smoke rose overhead. The tribe's elders were inside, discussing the fate of the two brothers.

Azumi glanced through the trees, where some of the members of their tribe were huddled in a group. They kept their distance from the brothers, but they whispered behind their hands and threw suspicious glances their way.

"Our fate has already been decided, Brother," Elior said bitterly. "Even if they allow us to stay, why would we want to?"

"No other tribe will accept us once they find out what we are," Azumi argued. "It will be difficult to survive on our own in the vast expanse, not to mention how difficult it will be to meet our mates and start a family."

"The Silver Shell Woman will ensure our mates find their way to us," Elior replied. "It is the way of the lunar goddess. Do not fear."

The cloth that covered the entrance to the hut was moved aside, and the elders emerged from the hut. Azumi and Elior sat up straighter and waited for the chief to speak.

"Azumi and Elior, sons of Nezara, you have witnesses who claim you wear stolen forms to steal flesh and blood. Do you deny it?"

The brothers glanced at one another before Azumi, the eldest, spoke on their behalf. "No, we do not deny it."

"This is most troubling," the chief replied.

The other elders recoiled in fear and disgust.

"There are witnesses who claim you drank the blood of wild horses in the form of wolves," the chief continued. "Is this true?"

Azumi bowed his head in respect. "We cannot help what we are, but we do not pose a danger to the tribe."

"Grimwalkers are an abomination against nature," the chief said. "Your very existence poses a danger to us. We cannot allow you to stay."

Elior rose to his feet. "Then we will go in peace."

"We cannot allow that, either," the chief said. "The medicine woman will advise us.

Makara, how do you suggest we handle this?"

An elderly woman, with eyes covered in a milky haze, stepped forward. She could not see with her eyes, but she was a highly respected seer and healer, and her word was considered final.

"The grimwalker is too evil to exist in this world," Makara said. "There is a way to cast it to the Spirit Realm, but it will come at a price."

The chief nodded. "Whatever it is, we shall pay it."

"We will need to settle new lands and leave them behind." Makara hobbled forward. "By casting away their evil nature to the Sprit Realm, it will create a connection between the two worlds, and this land will no longer be safe for our children." Makara raised her withered hands toward the sky. "I ask the Silver Shell Woman to cast the evil within these two souls from this world. Whatever is left of these young men will be tied to this land forever."

Thunder clapped in the distance as dark storm clouds rolled in.

Suddenly, Elior clutched his chest and doubled over. "What is happening?"

Azumi had the same reaction, and as he grasped at his heart, his eyes were wide with fear.

"No more will you drink the blood of the Silver Shell Woman's creatures!" Makara shouted as her body trembled, channeling a mystical power. "Begone from this earth!"

A flash of crimson light blinded the brothers, and they held their hands up to shield their eyes. Azumi gasped when a cloud of black mist escaped from his chest. His eyes followed it toward the red light, which was a portal to an unknown realm. The mist disappeared inside of it, followed by a similar cloud of dark mist from his brother.

"You are hereby bound to this land to protect the goddess's creation," Makara declared. "This portal will reappear on the night of the full moon, and it is up to you to protect it from the evil beings that lie in wait on the other side. But I will not leave you defenseless. I cast the Curse of the Werewolf upon you, and upon your children, and upon your children's children, for now and evermore, to give you the strength to fight the evil of the Spirit Realm."

"How do we prove ourselves worthy, Medicine Woman?" Azumi begged. "How do we break this curse so we can venture out to find our mates?"

"The goddess will reward you for your protection, but not for the evil cast to the other side," Makara said, lowering her hands. "Otherwise, your fates are tied to one another. If one half of your soul dies, so does the other. And until the dark becomes light once again, you will remain cursed."

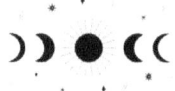

When Caz finishes his story, a weighted silence falls between us. The gears in my mind are spinning, trying to remember every detail and each of the dozens of questions swirling around in my head.

"And that curse," I say slowly, "that curse was passed down through the generations? To you and your siblings?"

He nods. "Yeah. I can't physically leave the ranch. And in order to protect the area, my family and I can turn into werewolves to prevent the blood wraiths from entering our world."

"Are the blood wraiths the ones who were causing all the cattle mutilations and crop circles?" I ask.

"For the most part, yeah. There are all kinds of creatures who reside in the Crimson Vale. The portal only appears on the full moon, so we're prepared to fight. We can go for a year or two without seeing anything cross through, but for some reason, this summer has been particularly active. The portal appears when it shouldn't, and more blood wraiths cross over."

A shudder rolls down my spine. "Ever since I stepped foot on the ranch."

Caz glances down at a piece of loose straw on the floor. "Maybe it's just a coincidence." But his voice isn't convincing.

I hug my knees tighter against my chest. Every bad thing that's happened this summer—the cattle mutilations, the crop circles, the lights from the portal—it's all because of me.

I clear my throat. "Have you been here before?"

He shakes his head. "No, never. None of the Nezaras have been through the portal as far as I know."

Hot tears spring to my eyes, so I squeeze them closed. "Which means we don't know how we'll get back." Caz's body heat radiates off him, and I scoot closer to keep warm. "Is that how your parents died? Protecting the ranch from evil creatures?"

A moment of silence passes between us as Caz takes a shaky breath. "Yeah."

I lean my head on his shoulder. "I'm so sorry."

The gravity of our situation hits me, like *really* hits me. Caz and I are stuck in a realm full of evil blood wraiths and creatures who want to hurt us, and we have no way of knowing how to get out. When we woke up, the portal had already disappeared.

A lump forms in my throat that I try to swallow down. I have to be strong right now—not just for me, but for Caz—if we're going to figure out a way home.

My tears spill onto his sleeve.

"Bri, hey, don't cry." He touches my chin, lifting my teary gaze to meet his. "We'll hide out here and see if the portal reopens tomorrow night, okay? Nature has a way of balancing the scales. At least, that's what Grandma always says."

He reclines back on the straw mattress, pulling me down with him. When we're both lying flat, he wraps his arms around me and holds me close against his chest. "I promised I'd do everything to protect you," he whispers into my hair. "We'll find a way back home."

With a loud sniff, I nod my head against his chest. His steady heartbeat drums in my ear, and I focus on it to calm myself.

"I can't believe you dove in through the portal after me." Caz's chuckle rumbles against my ear. "Guns blazing and all."

I tilt my chin up to meet his gaze, our faces close. "I'd do anything for you."

When I watched him being dragged away by the blood wraiths, I realized something. At the time, I was terrified I would never get a chance to tell him how I felt.

That I love him.

Maybe it's too soon to feel this way, but deep down, I think I've loved him for as long as I've known him. It took me almost losing him to realize it.

I reach up to stroke his face and trace the rough stubble along his strong jawline. He closes his eyes to lean into my touch, urging me closer.

Adrenaline from our fight with the blood wraiths still races through my veins, heating the blood beneath my skin.

And maybe it's the adrenaline that makes me act irrationally, but I need Caz. To feel his protective embrace, his strong warrior's body on mine.

I climb on top of him, my breasts pressed to his chest, and descend my lips onto his.

His body responds to mine, like a lit match dropped on gasoline. Our kiss deepens as all of our unspoken emotions begin to pour out—desperation, fear, passion—and my hips begin to roll against the hardening bulge in his tight, equestrian pants. My hands roam over his shirt until I find the opening of his neckline to explore his bare, muscular chest.

The heady need in my mind is muddling my thoughts, and for a moment, I forget about his neck injury. My hands grasp at his neck, and he sucks in a sharp breath and recoils.

"Oh, shit, I'm sorry!" I sit up and ball my hands in front of my mouth.

"It's okay." He brings his hands around to my ass and squeezes. "Please, don't stop."

I let out a breathy moan as he kneads my backside, and I grind against his lap, desperate for his touch, for friction. For pleasure.

"I want you." I gaze down at him through my eyelashes.

Caz is a virgin, and I'm giving him one last chance to back out if he isn't ready. So, I wait for his response, breathing hard from the desire and adrenaline raging through my bloodstream.

But the way he's looking at me with that hooded gaze, cock erect in his pants, makes the desire explode between my legs.

"I want you too, Bri." The rest of his sentence remains unspoken, but we both feel the weight of it. *In case we don't make it out of here alive.*

Neither of us will die with regrets.

Caz rolls us both over, pushing me onto the straw mattress so that he's straddled on top of me.

When my back hits the blanket, an involuntary moan escapes my throat as a flood of arousal pools in my underwear.

He yanks his shirt off over his head, tossing it to the side before diving down to meet my mouth. Our lips crash together, tongues moving in a frantic dance. My hands glide up his bare torso of their own accord, and I find his skin burning hot to the touch, fueled by wild desire.

He sits up again, bringing me with him by supporting my back. I hastily tug my sweatshirt off before he begins to fiddle with my bra, but after struggling with the clasp, he gives up and rips it off over my head.

He leans down to take one of my nipples into his mouth, his tongue swirling around it with surprising skill. It sends wave after wave of pleasure down my body, and as I throw my head back, a part of me wonders if I might just orgasm right now.

I gasp. "Oh, God..."

To my frustration, he stops, forcing a small, pitiful whine from my throat. He lays me back down on the blanket as he gazes upon me—not my body, but *me*—with a soft look. It takes me aback.

No one has ever looked at me this way, especially during sex. Rather than a look of pure lust, his expression is filled with devotion and a hundred promises that send my heart on the verge of bursting. He leans forward, crouching over me, to place a long, sweet kiss on my lips.

His mouth begins to trail downward, leaving a path of hot kisses that grow more intense the further he descends. When he reaches the waistband of my leggings, his fingers come up to fiddle with the elastic and tug downward. He takes his time peeling them off, leaving kisses along my inner thigh in his wake. It's an excruciatingly slow process as he teases me, exposing my womanhood to the cold, ambient air around us.

"I've dreamed about this moment for so long," he says, his voice husky.

Once my leggings are bunched up at my ankles, he pulls my sneakers off one by one, staring down at me with a gentle smile before sliding everything off my body.

I'm completely exposed to him, and just seeing his face admire my body with a mixture of awe and desire ignites my passion within me.

I can't wait any longer. My fingers move toward my entrance, placing featherlight touches on my skin as I spread my legs for him, showing him where I want him.

He unbuttons his pants, watching me touch myself as he slides them off, eager to witness every single moment. Refusing to blink, Caz continues to watch as his erection springs forth, and my eyes widen at his thick length standing at full attention.

He catches my reaction. A flicker of fear crosses his face as he looks down at the mouth of my arousal. "I don't want to hurt you."

"You won't," I encourage him with a soft purr, sticking a finger into myself to show him the way.

His hand grips the base, holding it steady as he presses it against my finger. Once he is in position, I slide my finger out and guide him inside as I let out a deep moan. He's big and thick, stretching me as he fills me to the brim.

Once he is fully seated within me, he begins to pull back out slowly, savoring the sensation he's experiencing for the very first time. I love that no other woman has given this pleasure to him, that I get to introduce him to a whole new world of sexual delights.

Just before he withdraws to the tip, he slides back into me, taking his time to find his rhythm. But little by little, his control unravels, and as he increases his tempo, my body is thrown backwards with each thrust of his strong hips. We begin to rock in tandem, our speed growing faster and more aggressive. He lets out a low, beastly grunt with each thrust inside of me, and I have to bite down on my wrist to stifle my cries of pleasure.

I have to keep quiet, even though I want nothing more than to scream his name.

I've never been brought to climax this quickly before. Wave after wave of ecstasy hits me as I fall to pieces beneath him, and each hard thrust extends my orgasm, making my eyes roll back in my head as my body convulses between his thighs.

"Oh, Bri," he groans, throwing his head back. His body shakes as he empties his seed inside of me. His thrusts become less powerful as the last of his energy is spent on his finish, and when he falls to the blanket beside me, his cock slides out, leaving me empty yet satisfied. His hot release coats my insides, dripping out onto the blanket beneath me.

With heavy breaths, we both stare up at the ceiling. I relish the cold temperature on my skin, which is burning with heat.

"Hey, Bri?" he whispers.

"Hmm?"

"I'm sorry for... you know. Not pulling out."

I let out an exhausted laugh. "It's alright. I have an IUD."

"Oh, okay. That's good." He lets out an audible swallow. "I don't want to pass on this curse to my children."

Well, shit just got real. A weighted silence falls between us.

If he got me pregnant, I would have his werewolf babies. Because that wouldn't be weird *at all*.

But he doesn't want kids. Having kids means passing on his curse to another generation of Nezaras. And even if I don't want them now, I don't know how I feel about not having children one day.

Because Caz is everything to me, and a future with him means giving up a lot. Children. The ability to leave the ranch with him.

Coming down off my high, the allure of sleep grips my exhausted body. I'm about to succumb to it when Caz pulls me closer and folds the excess blanket over my body. His body is emitting so much warmth I don't need the blanket, but I enjoy him doting over me nonetheless.

My last thought before falling asleep is the two of us sitting on the porch of the farmhouse, with Caz cradling a small infant in his arms.

CHAPTER 6

"**B**ri, get up." Caz's whisper is urgent.

I blink against the sunlight streaming in from the rafters as the pegasuses stomp with agitation in the stalls beside us. Caz crouches low behind our stall door. He's pulled his clothes back on already, his brow is furrowed in intense concentration.

"Caz, what's wrong?"

He holds his finger to his mouth to quiet me and whispers, "Put your clothes on, but don't make a sound."

I nod and pluck my clothes from the straw before dressing.

As I tie my sneakers back on, rhythmic, heavy footsteps reach my ears. It sounds like an army marching toward us, though I have no idea how many soldiers there are.

"Stay here, out of sight," Caz whispers, standing up.

"Where are you going?" Panic rises in my chest as I reach out to grasp his hand. "Don't leave me!"

"I'm just going to keep an eye on the door," he says in a low voice. Caz stoops to give me a quick kiss before stepping away. "Hide."

I do as he says, sitting low to hide my entire profile behind the stall door.

A few minutes pass by as the footsteps march closer. Voices in the street float inside the barn.

"...do you recognize this weapon?" A threatening voice asks. "Answer me!"

"N-No, sir!" replies a different, meek voice.

Cold dread seeps through my veins. Did they find the gun? Is that what they're showing around to the villagers, asking for clues to the whereabouts of its owners?

If so, they are *very* close to finding out.

The barn door creaks, and I clap my hands over my mouth to stifle a gasp.

Chaos erupts. Shouting echoes outside as heavy footsteps thunder into the barn. But there's a more chilling sound, like bones cracking and flesh tearing, which makes my blood turn to ice. A familiar, low growl shakes the entire barn, and straw falls from the ceiling.

Caz's wolf form is so massive that I can see the tips of his pointed, fur-covered ears from where I'm crouched.

The pegasuses around me stomp in their stalls, bucking and neighing at the threat.

"Take down the werewolf!" a voice commands.

Caz lets out a ferocious snarl. Spotting a small opening between the wood slats of the stall door, I shift to get a better view of the fight.

In the light of the sun streaming in through the open barn doors, this is the first clear view I get of Caz in his wolf form. His sheer size takes up most of the barn, and there's barely enough room for the army to enter. The chain mail of the first row of soldiers rustles as a barrage of axes hurtle toward Caz's wolf, which he manages to bat away with his massive paw. A few of the ax heads slice into his arm, and he lets out a snarl as he shakes them off.

"Second line of defense!"

The first row of soldiers retreats to give way to a line of archers, who raise their bows and take aim.

Fear grips me as I hide away like a coward, unable to help Caz. All I can do is watch on as he fights for our lives, but I'm not sure how he'll survive this.

Hot tears well in my eyes. This is it.

A loud series of thwaks rips through the barn as strings release their arrows, which fly straight toward Caz's massive form. He's an easy target since he's trapped inside with no escape, and he cries out in pain as they strike.

My hands fly to my mouth to cover my screams as tears stream down my cheeks. With a low whine, the wolf shrinks into itself, replaced by Caz's naked form lying on the ground. The arrows fall out as he transforms back into his human body, but he's bleeding profusely as a puddle of blood pools around him.

No, no, this can't be happening.

Why isn't he moving?

"Please, don't hurt him anymore!" I cry out, leaping to my feet and yanking open the stall door. I reach Caz before the soldiers can, and I fling myself over his limp body.

One of the soldiers points at Caz. "Captain, his face…"

They all stop walking toward us, leaving me sobbing over Caz's unconscious form as their hushed whispers echo around us.

"It can't be—"

"It must be an imposter…"

"It's the alpha king!"

"Gather them both and tend to his wounds. We're taking them to the castle immediately."

One of the soldiers peels me off of Caz, but I struggle against his tight grasp.

"Get off of me!" I scream. I land a good kick to his shin, making him stumble back.

He grabs his leg, his face twisting with rage. "You bitch!"

I turn back toward Caz, but I'm met with a strong slap across the face. My body falls to the floor from the force of the officer's hand, sending my vision into a blur as the barn swims around me. My cheek stings from his blow.

His dark figure towers over me. "You will come with us quietly." He steps around and grabs my wrists, forcing them behind my back to tie a rope to bind me. Pulling me behind him, he drags me toward the exit of the barn.

The other soldiers surround Caz's limp, naked form to lift him up and carry him out behind us.

When we step outside, I blink against the blinding sunlight. It takes a moment for my eyes to adjust, but when they do, I'm met by villagers peering out from their windows and doors of the buildings lining the street, and others staring at us from their market stalls of food and wares.

They look normal at first glance, but when I catch a villager's eye, I realize their skin has a green hue to it. Another person has pointed ears and red irises, reminding me somewhat of the blood wraiths who attacked us last night. A beggar nearby leans against the wall, peering her face up at me from beneath her cloak—the spitting image of an old witch with a long, pointed nose, warts and all.

And yet, they all look at *me* with fear and apprehension.

The sunlight possesses a red tint, which casts a strange glow on the street. I look up to see red clouds in the sky, and like the moon, the sun is tinged blood red.

The soldiers carry Caz past us and load him up into a wagon, which is pulled by two black-haired, red-eyed pegasuses like the ones we just spent the night with. One of the soldiers climbs into the wagon with him, pulling out bandages and a bottle from his rucksack. He pours out a clear liquid onto the cloth and cleans the wounds. Caz groans in pain and stirs, but his eyes remain tightly shut.

He's still alive.

I let out an audible sigh of relief, and the tears begin anew.

When the wagon creaks and rolls forward, the officer shoves me toward it to follow. I stumble, but I'm able to steady myself before plummeting forward. I fall into step with the wagon, and the clip-clop of hooves on the cobblestone pavers creates a steady rhythm. The onlookers are silent as they watch us, their eyes wide with fear and confusion.

But they aren't focused on me—they're staring at Caz. At least someone had the decency to cover his lower half with a blanket.

We make our way back to the village square where we landed late last night. My eyes fall on the fountain, and in the light of day I realize that the water falling down the stone tiers looks strange. Too dark to be water.

As we march closer, I jolt when I realize it's not water in the fountain. It's blood.

This confirms it: we really are in hell. Or some version of hell, I suppose.

We cross through the square onto a wooden bridge, which leads to a main road stretching up a steep hill. A dark castle looms at the top of the hill, surrounded by stone turrets reaching high into the sky. It's utterly massive and imposing, watching over the village like a sentinel.

And it's our destination.

As we begin to climb the steep hill, a sharp pain shoots through my legs, radiating from my lower back. It isn't long before my breathing becomes ragged, gasping for air as my heart hammers in my ribcage.

Even though the village is small and we haven't walked far, fatigue grips my body, like I'm dragging a heavy ball and chain behind me. Each step feels unsteady beneath me as vertigo sets in, making the ground feel so far away.

But asking for a break isn't an option. Every time I slow down, the officer behind me pushes me forward and barks, "Pick up the pace!"

Sweat beads on my forehead, and all I can do is pray my legs don't give out. If they do, I'm not sure they'll let me survive.

As we near the top of the hill, we cross a wooden drawbridge. I peer over the edge just enough to see a long, long drop to the moat of water below, and I gulp. That's not just a moat. It's a craggy ravine of dark stone.

If I fall, I'd be dead before I hit the water.

After crossing the drawbridge, we pass beneath a stone archway into an expansive castle courtyard. People dressed like medieval nobles meander leisurely along the covered walkways framing the four exterior walls, where thick, green ivy creeps up the stone. However, as soon as the spectators spot Caz's face in the wagon, they stop and begin whispering to each other behind their hands.

One of the soldiers referred to Caz as the *alpha king* earlier. I don't know what that means, but how would they know what he looks like if he's never been through the portal before? Have they seen his human form on the other side?

My head is spinning with questions, but there is no time to dwell on them. Not that I could if I wanted to because the brain fog ratchets up the longer we continue to march. My mind disassociates from my body to manage the pain. So, when the wagon finally comes to a stop in the courtyard, I send a silent prayer of gratitude upward for the break.

The soldiers lift Caz out, keeping the blanket draped over him. Two soldiers take his arms, while two more lift him by the legs, and they carry him in like a sack of potatoes as I follow behind, my wrists still tied with rope.

We make our way to the interior of the castle, which is furnished with the most luxurious decor. Black marble floors and intricate, woven rugs mark our path through the castle. Crystal chandeliers hang above us, illuminated by candlelight casting intriguing shadows on the stone walls. Opulent paintings in gilded frames hang on either side of us, and rich wooden credenzas line the passageways with expensive vases and tabletop sculptures.

I'm limping as fast as I can, fighting the fiery pain in my legs, but when we reach an archway with open doors, the officer pushes me forward with an impatient grunt. I stumble into the room and lose my balance, falling to the floor. With my hands tied behind my back, I'm able to catch myself on my knees, but it sends a sharp pain up through my body, making me cry out.

And the cry echoes against a cavernous ceiling.

My vision waters at the pain, so I blink a few times to bring the room back into focus. The massive, circular room around us towers into a domed ceiling with a painted mural on the roof depicting a vicious battle scene with wolves. A silver chair—or throne—upholstered in black velvet sits atop a raised platform, its high back stretching taller than me. Above it hangs a long, black flag from the ceiling, with a red dire wolf symbol sewn in the middle with a pentagram around its head.

Exactly like the crop circle.

A masculine figure emerges from the shadows behind the throne, and all the soldiers bow before him. His dark form steps into the light, revealing an all-black, Victorian-style suit that shows off his broad, muscular chest. On top of his dark, thick hair is a black crown adorned with onyx stones.

But when my eyes drop to his face, I gasp.

This can't be.

"Bow before His Majesty, King Caspian of House Nezara, King of Alphas and Ruler of the Crimson Vale!"

King Caspian... of House Nezara? As in Caz's full name, Caspian Nezara?

I glance beside me at Caz, where the soldiers have set him down face-up on the floor. I scan his face, and it is definitely, undoubtedly, Caz.

And yet, the king himself looks *exactly* like Caz, but... different.

I stare between Caz and the king, unable to comprehend the mirror images reflected back at me in their faces.

The room is plunged in complete silence as the figure steps down from the platform, his prowling footsteps silent and feline as walks slowly toward us.

My knees threaten to give way beneath my weight. He walks directly toward me, and my body erupts into shivers as he grows closer. It's unnerving how he looks exactly like Caz; however, when he stops before me, I realize his eyes are a deep shade of burgundy rather than the familiar brown of Caz's irises.

I've never seen a shade quite like it.

As I stare up at his towering figure, he reaches out a finger to caress my jawline, his dark gaze boring into mine. He breathes out a subtle sigh as his fingers make contact with my skin, lingering there for a moment.

I feel inexplicably drawn to him and his dark, mysterious aura.

Who is he? He's Caz, but he's *not* Caz, and I don't know what to make of that.

"Are you hurt?" he asks me in a low voice. Like his appearance, he sounds like Caz, but different. Darker.

I shudder and shake my head no, unable to form a worded response.

"Don't lie to me." He tilts my head to the side. "I can see the handprint on your face." Glancing up, he narrows his eyes at the officer standing behind me. "Did you lay a hand on her, Captain?"

Tension charges the air as the soldiers around me visibly stiffen.

"S-She was resisting arrest, Your Majesty," the officer stammers.

The king barely spares a glance at one of his guards before settling his gaze on my face again. "Kill him."

The way he issues this command so casually, without an ounce of emotion, is unnerving. It's as though he's entirely unaffected by the weight of those words, like he issues that particular command the same way he asks for a cup of tea or the weather report.

An armored knight steps forward from the entrance to the throne room, heeding the order given by his king. I turn my head just in time to see the knight raise his ax high above his head, bringing it down on the neck of his victim. Blood spatters everywhere, including my face as warm flecks hit my cheeks. My eyelids scrunch together just in time to prevent it from going into my eyes.

A distinct thump of a head rolling on the stone makes bile rise in my throat.

The king wipes his thumb across my face, sending a violent shudder rolling down my spine. When he releases me, I open my eyes to find him licking the blood off his finger as he gazes down at me, a shadow of a smile playing across his lips.

Dragging his focus away from me, he steps toward Caz's limp figure, walking in a slow circle around him. "I never thought I'd meet my light one. What an auspicious day this is."

Caz's eyes remain shut, his chest heaving with labored breaths. I'm not even sure he's aware of his surroundings right now. My eyes roam over his exposed chest and arms, which are covered in fresh scratches and bruises.

The king completes his inspection and steps back. "Bring in the witch to heal his wounds. I wish to speak to him."

Almost immediately, an older woman appears in the entryway, head bowed, and she approaches Caz's body. She bends down beside him and waves her hands above his chest, and glowing light forms on the palms of her hands.

The visible wounds disappear in an instant, and Caz's skin returns to a perfectly smooth surface. All evidence from his battle is erased from existence like it never happened.

Caz's brown eyes slowly open, and after he sits up, the witch takes her exit without a single word.

"Welcome to the Crimson Vale, Light One." The king folds his hands behind his back. "You are the first to cross over since the dark ones were cast into this world by our ancestors."

Caz adjusts the blanket around his waist before glancing up at the king. "You must be the evil half of my soul, then."

"Evil is such a strong word." The king's lip stretches into a smirk. "But yes, I am the half of your soul that is cursed to remain in this realm. And yet, we've done pretty well for ourselves here, as you can see." He gestures around the throne room.

Caz glances around, but when his eyes land on me, they widen. He reaches out his hand to take mine, giving it a comforting squeeze.

The king's gaze snags on our joined hands. He pauses, his smirk dissipating. "It took time, but House Nezara has built an empire here. We brought peace to the Crimson Vale by uniting all creatures suffering at the hands of the warring werewolf packs. Now, they all answer to me."

"There are werewolves here?" Caz furrows his eyebrows. "Does that mean you're under the Curse of the Werewolf too?"

The king shakes his head. "No. While I am the king of all the werewolf clans, I myself am not actually a werewolf."

"Then what are you?" I ask.

The king turns his gaze onto me, the smirk returning to his face. "A far superior being."

"We're here by mistake," Caz explains, forcing the king's attention back onto him. "We were in a battle with some powerful blood wraiths who crossed over to our world when we fell through the portal."

The king's expression turns severe. "You allowed your fated mate to be near the fight? How could you be so reckless, exposing her to such danger?"

Caz grits his teeth. "She wasn't supposed to be there."

"Hold on." I hold my hand up. "What do you mean by 'fated mate'?"

How do we break this curse so we can venture out to find our mates?

Wait... the story of the brothers that Caz told me last night. He mentioned something about "mates."

The king raises his eyebrows in surprise. "You haven't told her?"

"She had no idea about the supernatural world before last night," Caz explains. "She wouldn't have understood."

I shake my head. "Understood what?"

Caz chews on his lip, debating. "Each werewolf has someone out there who destiny has chosen for them. A werewolf knows this from the moment they set eyes on them for the first time. It's an undeniable attraction."

"You mean, like love?" I ask.

He nods. "Yes, but it's so much deeper than love."

I point at myself. "And... I'm your fated mate?"

Caz's lips twitch like he's holding back a grin. "Yeah, and I've known it ever since I met you for the first time as kids. It's hard to explain, but it's this feeling you get, deep in your bones, that we were meant to be together."

It's why I fell for Caz so quickly. Why I'm drawn to him—and why his initial rejection stung so badly.

I take a breath. "If that's true, why did you push me away the first time I tried to kiss you?"

The king scoffs and shakes his head. "Imbecile."

Caz's throat bobs. "Because I know what a life with me means for you. I can't leave the ranch. I don't want kids. You would be giving up so much to be with me, and I love you too much to let that happen. At the end of the day, it's your choice to either accept me or reject me, but—"

"Stop rambling," the king interrupts, rolling his eyes. "She'll reject you if you keep acting like a weak little puppy instead of the alpha that you are."

An awkward silence befalls the room. I'm still reeling from the information that Caz just revealed: that we're destined to be together. How could he know that when he saw me for the first time? We couldn't have been older than five.

I've liked you for a long time...

But Caz brings my focus back to our more pressing task. "How do we get back through the portal? We don't want to stir up any trouble here. We'll return to our world and leave you in peace, the way our ancestors intended."

The king quirks an eyebrow. "You won't be able to go back until the next full moon."

Caz recoils. "Why? The portal has opened before without the full moon."

He scoffs. "Impossible."

"It's true," I add. "I've seen it. Ever since I stepped foot on the ranch—"

Caz shakes his head at me to not say anything more, but it's too late. The king—King

Caspian—turns to look at me, a serious expression on his sharp features. Even though he's staring at me, his burgundy eyes are far away, lost in thought.

He hums low in his chest. "Fascinating. Almost as if..." His voice trails off.

"As if what?" I demand.

"As if the curse wanted to make sure you found your way here." His voice, although quiet and introspective, reverberates around the room.

I remember being drawn to the lights from the portal the way I was drawn to Caz. It felt like the portal was calling out to me to explore it, like it wanted me to solve the mystery of it.

When I swallow, the king's eyes dip to my neck, his gaze a heated caress on my skin.

"So, unless another portal magically opens for Bri," Caz says, "we have to wait here until the next full moon?" Caz glances at me. "I guess we'll have to find somewhere in the village to stay."

"Nonsense," the king says. "If my light one dies, I die. I can't risk you being attacked outside of the castle, so you will remain here, as my guests."

Caz looks weary. "Thank you."

The king waves over a couple of his guards. "Take him to the dungeons."

"Wait, what?" Caz looks behind him in panic, scrambling away from the approaching guards.

I shout over the ensuing chaos, "But you just said we could stay here as your guests!"

The soldiers grab Caz's arms on either side. The blanket slips down to the floor as they yank him to his feet, baring his nakedness in a betrayal of Caz's dignity.

"Like I said, I can't risk you being attacked," the king says matter-of-factly. "I can't control what happens to you in your world, but while you're here, I can't have any of my enemies finding out about you. The only way I can ensure my survival is to keep you under guard at all times." He turns toward his throne and walks back toward the dais, waving his hand to dismiss him. "Take him away."

"Caz, no!" I scramble to my feet to chase after him, but with my arms bound, I lose my balance and stumble.

The king appears at my side with dizzying speed, catching me in his arms before I fall to the floor. One moment, he's walking toward his throne, and in an instant, he's beside me. Am I losing my mind?

"You will not be subjected to the dungeons." His cold breath tickles my skin against my ear, sending a shiver down my body. "I have other plans for you."

For a split second, it's easy to forget I'm not in Caz's arms. But gazing into his calculating, red eyes, I'm reminded that this is *not* Caz. This is his dark one, and I need to be careful.

I try to move from his grasp, but I'm no match for his strength. "What the fuck do you want with me?"

He lets out a low chuckle. "What a foul mouth you have, my lady."

"I'm not your lady. Let me go."

"Leave us." His deep command is addressed to everyone else in the room, but his gaze continues to bore into mine.

I'm transfixed as the guards' chain mail rustles. Soon, the door closes with a heavy thud, plunging us into a ringing silence.

He leans his face close to me, his nose almost grazing mine.

"Fated mates are when two souls are tied together by destiny," he whispers. "My light one's soul is drawn to yours in an undeniable bond, stronger than anything in both your world or mine. As the other half of his soul, you are also my fated mate."

My lips part as I suck in a sharp breath.

"However," he continues, "the ancient curse dictates that the dark ones will never meet their mates, who are firmly planted on the other side of the portal in your world. This is a unique opportunity I cannot pass up."

He shifts me until I'm on my feet, but his arms pull me closer against his chest. I'm unnerved by being in his arms because he looks exactly like Caz—but a more unfamiliar and dangerous version of Caz.

I'm afraid of him.

"I have a proposition." He smirks, and his eyes glint with mischief. "You will remain here at the castle until the next full moon. If you don't fall in love with me by then, I will let you return to your realm."

An incredulous laugh bubbles up from my chest. "Fall in love with you? Are you serious?"

But he is undeterred. "However, if you do fall for me, you will remain here as my queen, and I will make all your dreams come true." He brushes his nose against mine, sending shivers of electricity through my body. "And rest assured, my lady, I will do everything in my power to make this go my way."

It's not like I can refuse to stay here. He has Caz. All I can do is wait it out until the next full moon and, in the meantime, figure out a way to break Caz out of the dungeons.

And if *Caspian* thinks I'm falling in love with him, he's insane. There's no danger of that happening.

"Fine," I snap. "You have a deal, but only if I have your word that you'll let Caz and I both go, alive and unharmed, if I don't fall in love with you."

His eyes bore into mine as he grips my waist, keeping me close. "Upon my honor, you have my word."

Whatever his honor and his word are worth.

"And you need to let Caz out of the dungeons."

His gaze narrows. "Trust me, it is the safest place for him. I don't need my enemies to find out about my weaknesses, and too many people have seen him already." He unties the ropes around my wrists.

When my arms fall at my sides, the room starts to blur. My knees buckle under the crushing weight of everything that's transpired in the past twenty-four hours. I haven't endured this much physical stress since before my illness, and the emotional stress isn't helping either.

The king catches me as I melt in his arms. "Are you alright?"

"I need to sit down."

He scoops me into his arms. In a split second, we're standing on the dais, where he sets me down on the seat.

How the hell did he do that?

He kneels down in front of me until our faces are level. "My light one called you Bri. Is that your name?"

"Yeah. Short for Briar." I rub my temple. "Can I have a glass of water?"

King Caspian lifts his hand and snaps his fingers. Within seconds, the door opens as a butler hurries in, carrying a tray with a water goblet. He hands it to the king, who brings it to my lips.

"Drink." He tilts the goblet so the water trickles into my mouth. A few drips run out the corner of my lip, and his thumb reaches up to wipe them away.

I push him off. "I can hold my own cup."

His only response is a low chuckle, which annoys me even more. I take another slow, careful sip of water and breathe in deeply through my nose to keep the nausea at bay. After a few breaths, the room finally stops spinning.

"Feeling better?" he asks.

I nod and set the goblet down on the small table beside the throne.

He remains kneeling. He is so close to me my legs are spread apart on either side of his torso, making me instantly recoil. My back hits the tufted upholstery of the chair. "You're not Caz."

He stands up, his expression steeled into an unreadable mask. The king grips both armrests and towers over me to cage me in. "And yet, I am. We are two halves of the same whole."

The reality of my situation hits me like a boxer jab to the nose. Caz and I are trapped here for an entire month. Him in the dungeons, and me alone in the Crimson Vale without him.

I'm truly, absolutely terrified.

"I want to see him," I say, holding back a fresh wave of tears. "Let me see Caz."

King Caspian straightens, allowing me space to breathe. He takes a step back, eying me closely with a scowl on his face. "No."

"Fuck you!"

He clucks his tongue. "Insolent girl. I should throw you down in the dungeons just to teach you a lesson."

"Fine, then do it. I dare you." I meet his frightening gaze, challenging him.

If I can get down to the dungeons, at least I'll be with Caz. But I'm also terrified to find out how King Caspian, the dark one, would punish me down there.

However, I can't let him win, so I continue to hold his gaze with my chin held high, even if it's just a ruse to disguise the terror inside.

"You'd like that, wouldn't you?" he says, breaking the silence between us. "But I won't allow it. You're mine."

I huff. "I don't belong to you. You literally just met me."

Suddenly, sharp nails dig into my cheeks. King Caspian stands in front of me, angling my face up to meet his cold gaze.

He grits his teeth. "You are my fated mate as much as my light one's. You may only care for him now, but you will come to feel for me in the same way very soon. And at the end of your thirty nights here in my kingdom, you'll feel even more deeply for me than you do for him because I can give you things he can't."

His hand releases my face, but only to pull me to my feet. Placing his hands on my waist, he holds me still.

And then he grinds his hips against mine, pressing his unmistakable erection against me through our clothes. I gasp.

He skims his lips over my ear. "I'm going to treat you like the queen you are, and you will want for nothing except for my cock to be buried deep inside of you, night after night." The king growls. "You'll be on your knees before me, begging to stay when the next full moon arrives."

My cheeks grow hot as his growing hardness presses against me. I close my eyes, remembering the things he did to me last night in the barn, the way his strong, muscular body covered mine as he took me, making me experience the best orgasm I've ever had. An uncomfortable feeling grows between my thighs as desire sets in, begging to be sated.

I open my eyes, but when I find his deep, ruby-red irises staring back, I remember myself.

This is *not* the man I shared my body with last night.

I push him away, taking him by surprise, and he stumbles back. But his shock is quickly replaced with rage as he clenches his hands into tight fists.

He grinds his teeth. "I'll have Elowen escort you to your room. Perhaps some time to settle in will help you see things more clearly."

The throne room doors swing open, and a woman dressed in a frilly maid's uniform enters. She approaches the platform and dips into a deep curtsy.

"Elowen will be your personal attendant," King Caspian explains. "Her sole purpose is to ensure that your every whim and desire is met. Consider this my first gift of many to you, Lady Briar."

With that, King Caspian turns his back on me and exits the throne room, leaving me breathless and clutching the armrest to steady myself.

CHAPTER 7

After Caspian leaves the throne room, Elowen clears her throat. "If you would follow me, Lady Briar, I will show you to your chambers." Her gaze is lowered to the floor in submission.

She vaguely resembles the wraith-like creatures that emerged from the portal to attack the ranch. Her skin is almost translucent, with pointed ears like an elf's. However, her hair is black as night, and her eyes are a brilliant shade of violet.

"Does he make you wear that?" I gesture at her uniform, which resembles a sexy French maid's outfit.

"It is the uniform of the castle waitstaff." Her voice doesn't give away any emotion.

"The men too?"

Her cheeks turn pink, but her voice remains steady. "No, they have a men's uniform."

"I see." I step down from the platform and follow her out of the room, my gaze snagging on the beheaded officer being dragged from the room by a pair of guards.

She leads me through a maze of corridors of the castle and up multiple flights of stairs. Great, more walking. My body feels like it's giving up, and the brain fog grows stronger and stronger the longer we climb.

We stop in front of a massive set of oak doors on the top floor of the castle. Elowen opens them up to reveal a luxurious living room, and when we enter, I notice an en suite bedroom through a set of double doors to my left.

I'm astonished by how bright and airy the room feels. I was expecting all-black, Gothic-style décor to match the king's personality. But I'm pleasantly surprised by the color palette of the room with shades of blush pink, gold, and white—a suite fit for a princess. A crystal chandelier shimmers brightly overhead, casting rainbow flecks of light on the paneled ivory walls. The plush living room furniture faces a white marble fireplace, which already has a cozy fire burning inside.

"You guys have electricity in the Crimson Vale?" I ask, pointing to the chandelier.

Elowen blinks. "Electricity, my lady?"

"Yeah, uh..." Okay, maybe not electricity. I tap my chin. "How are the lights powered?"

"Oh, by elven magic, my lady."

Well, that's going to take some getting used to.

I take a peek into the bedroom, where I find the largest bed I've ever seen in my life. What's bigger than a California King? This bed, apparently. The headboard stretches high toward the vaulted ceiling, and soft, sheer curtains flow down on all four sides from the four-poster frame. A fluffy, floral duvet lays across the mattress, complete with numerous pillows that take up half the bed.

"Shall I draw up a bath for you, Lady Briar?" Elowen asks.

I glance down at my sweatshirt and leggings, which I've been wearing since yesterday and probably smell like a barn. Flecks of blood from that beheaded guard stain the fabric. "Sure. Thanks."

When I wander into the bathroom behind Elowen, I gasp. It's nearly as large as the bedroom and tiled in white marble. White walls with gold paneling surround the room, and at the center is a tub—the size of a small swimming pool—depressed into the floor. Water begins to flow out from the gold plumbing fixtures, and Elowen makes a move to add a bubble bath to the water.

"Wait!" I hold my hand up. "Do you have anything unscented?"

She pauses for a moment before nodding. "Of course, Lady Briar, I will remember that as your preference."

I can't stand the smell of soap these days. No matter what scent it is, it smells wrong, like stale cigarette smoke and industrial-strength chemicals.

It takes a bit of time for the tub to fill, so I take a seat on a tufted stool at the vanity while I wait.

"Shall I help you disrobe?" Elowen offers.

I wrap my arms around myself. "No, I can manage. Thank you."

Once the bath is full, Elowen turns off the water, curtsies, and exits the bathroom. As soon as the door shuts behind her, I yank off my sweatshirt and leggings and toss them on the floor. I'm eager to enjoy this luxurious bath and rinse off the horrible day.

As I sink my entire body into the steaming water, I wonder if King Caspian thought I smelled like a barn. It would be better if my scent put him off.

Although, I think my attitude did a pretty good job of that. He seemed angry when he left.

Sitting in the bubbles and steam, my body begins to relax. I close my eyes, trying to allow the hot water to soothe my sore muscles and joints. However, when my eyelids shut, the image of Caz with deep, burgundy eyes comes to mind, and he's staring at me with insatiable desire.

"Lady Briar?"

A delicate hand gives me a gentle shake. My eyes flutter open and I see Elowen standing over me.

"Lady Briar, it's time for me to get you dressed for dinner."

"Dinner?"

"Yes, you are expected for dinner with His Majesty, the king. You've been asleep all day since your bath this morning."

That's right. I put on a robe and slid into this soft, dreamy bed. Best sleep I've had in a long time.

I slowly blink my eyes at her, but I can't seem to bring the room into focus. Despite sleeping all day, a hazy fog grips my brain, and when I try moving my limbs, they feel heavy like lead. My hands and feet are completely numb, and my right leg and lower back are in pain.

The fatigue rears its ugly head yet again. Although, given everything that's happened in the past twenty-four hours, it's no wonder I feel like this. I overexerted myself.

"Lady Briar?" Elowen looks me over. "Are you ready to get out of bed?"

"I'm not hungry." Even my voice sounds weak. "Tell King Caspian I'm not feeling well."

"Yes, Lady Briar." She gives me a small curtsy before exiting the room.

There's a window in my peripheral vision. I'm curious if it's dark already, but I can't seem to muster the energy to even turn my head, and the eye strain causes a wave of dizziness to wash over me. Closing my eyes, I try to remember to breathe in and out through my nose, allowing the oxygen to reach into my lower lungs.

All I can do is wait for the dizzy spell to pass.

With my eyes closed, my other senses are heightened—except for my sense of smell. Cool silk sheets cradle my body, and the room is quiet in a pleasant way, without the sound of electronics buzzing or mechanical equipment whirring. The only sound is the comforting crackling of the fireplace coming in from the living room.

That, and the sound of quick footsteps approaching.

The door to my room flies open with a loud bang, startling me.

"Are you sick?" a familiar voice demands.

I tilt my head up to find King Caspian towering in the doorway of the bedroom. My head feels heavy and falls back against the pillows as I let out a sigh. "Wow, you got here fast."

Unnervingly fast.

This is really the last thing I wanted to deal with right now, and I especially didn't want him to see me so... weak.

Rather than leave me alone, he enters the bedroom and takes a seat beside me on the bed. Elowen hovers in the doorway, wringing her hands.

King Caspian stares down at me with surprising gentleness. "If you are sick, I will call the castle's mage to heal you."

It takes me a moment to adjust to the sight of Caz's face with different eyes peering back. "I don't think that will help."

"Why not?" he asks. "I assure you, my mage is quite skilled in healing illnesses."

"This isn't a little cold." My voice is biting. "It's a chronic illness, and I don't even think it's made its way down here yet."

He cocks his head. "What do you mean?"

I let out a heavy sigh. The sooner I can explain this to him, the sooner I can get back to sleep. However, when I try to sit up, I struggle to get my arms to hold my weight.

King Caspian moves closer to help me sit up against my pillows. The moment his hand makes contact with my back, it sends a shiver down my spine that isn't entirely unpleasant.

I settle back against the thick layer of pillows. "Back on Earth, there's a pandemic going on. I don't think the virus could have made its way to the Crimson Vale already, especially if no one here has made contact with humans."

"A pandemic?" His brows knit together. "I'm afraid I'm unfamiliar with the term."

Geez, this is going to be harder to explain than I thought.

"A pandemic is a widespread illness. Like a plague." I pause, and when he nods in understanding, I continue. "This particular illness is one the world had never seen before. I caught it, but I never seemed to recover from it. There's no known cure, at least not yet, because it is so new. I mean, there is a vaccine—"

He holds his hand up to stop me. "What is a vaccine? I will have the mage bring it immediately."

Seriously? It's like I'm explaining current events to a recluse who's been living under a rock for decades.

I take a deep breath to quell my growing frustration. "Have you heard of, oh, what's the word?" Why can't my brain function the way it used to? "Oh, right. *Inoculation.* Have you heard of inoculation?"

He nods. "Yes, I'm familiar with the term."

"A vaccine is a form of inoculation against disease," I explain. "But I wasn't able to get it before I got sick, because it wasn't my turn yet."

"Your turn?" Anger flashes across his eyes, and I swear they glow brighter than his usual shade of burgundy. "Who's life could possibly outweigh yours?"

"Well, the elderly, the immunocompromised, essential workers..." I tick off each group with my fingers.

"Unacceptable." He huffs. "And you are certain there is no cure?"

"They're trying to figure it out." I rub my aching temples. This is utterly exhausting, explaining this to him. "But, not yet. People either recover or they don't, it seems."

King Caspian taps his chin, lost in thought. "I will insist all the mages look into this immediately."

"You really don't have to go to all the trouble."

"Of course I do." His expression softens a bit as he examines me. "I want you to be well, Bri."

Hearing him call me by my name—not Lady Briar—is jarring. It makes him feel more familiar to me, and I don't need that messing with my head.

"Look, you don't want me." I glance down at my hands folded in my lap. "You're looking for a queen, but I can't be that for you. I'm a burden. I'm pretty useless most days."

He grabs my chin, turning my face to force my gaze to meet his. And the furious expression he's wearing makes me gulp.

"Do not ever speak about yourself that way again," he says in a low, dangerous voice. "I will not hear this ridiculous talk about you being a burden. Do you understand me?"

There's no room for argument, so I just nod.

"Good." He lets go and gets up from the bed. "Elowen, please bring up a bowl of soup for Lady Briar."

Elowen curtsies and scrambles off.

King Caspian follows but pauses in the doorway. "Oh, and Bri?"

There he goes with my nickname again, like we've known each other for years.

I swallow. "Yeah?"

He glances over his shoulder, regarding me with a mischievous look, "If I ever hear you speak of yourself disparagingly again, I will take you over my knee and spank you."

"Is that a promise or a threat?"

The words spill out of my mouth before I even have a chance to stop them, and if I had the energy to move my arm, I would clap a hand over my mouth.

His expression shifts. For a moment, he seems taken aback by my boldness, but it is quickly replaced by a lustful hunger, drinking me in with his deep, ruby gaze.

"Consider it both."

And with that, he disappears from the room.

After sleeping the rest of the night, and half the following day, I still wake up feeling unrefreshed. That's more common than not these days, but at least I'm able to get out of bed.

My thoughts drift to Caz. How is he doing down in the dungeons? Is he being treated right? Is he eating enough?

I'm sure my grandparents and his whole family are worried sick about our disappearance. Surely, the Nezaras wouldn't tell my grandparents that we were sucked into another dimension full of blood wraiths and werewolves. Would they say that we ran away together as young lovers? I hope so; I hate the idea of my grandparents worrying about whether I'm alive or dead.

Elowen comes in to let me know she's drawn another bath for me, and I take my time soaking in the unscented bubbles. She insists on drying and styling my hair for me once I'm done, and to be honest, I'm grateful for the help. These days, it feels like an extra chore I'd rather not waste energy on, and tonight, I know I'm going to need all my strength to stay on my toes during dinner with King Caspian.

I'm sitting in a comfortable chair in a fluffy white bathrobe while Elowen wraps my hair into a towel to dry. She begins putting on my makeup for me, and I'm amazed at how skilled she is.

I glance at her in the mirror. "How did you come to work at the castle?"

"My family has served House Nezara for generations." She brushes powder across my face. "I was raised by my parents to do the same."

"Have you ever wanted to do anything besides being a servant?"

Her brows knit together. "I'm not sure what you mean, Lady Briar."

"I mean, wouldn't you rather have a different career?" I clarify.

She shrugs. "Not really. It's safer here at the castle than anywhere else."

"Is the Crimson Vale a dangerous place?"

She nods. "Generally speaking, yes. The werewolf packs are constantly at war, and oftentimes the villagers in their territory will get caught in the battles. Witches usually keep to themselves, but they make money by offering their services for hire, and most use their dark magic for revenge on others. The lower blood wraiths don't usually cause too much trouble, but it's the stronger ones you definitely want to watch out for."

I glance at her ears. "And what type of being are you?"

"I'm an elf."

This place is so weird. "Do you have any cool powers as an elf?"

She grins. "We can manipulate nature to a certain extent. For me, I have an affinity for plants, but other elves can work with other elements, either as weapons or to improve the lives of others."

She glances at a vase on the counter, which has a simple bouquet of flowers in it. When she passes her hand over it, the flowers sprout additional petals, growing bigger and more vibrant in color. New flowers sprout from the stalks, giving the bouquet a fuller, brighter look.

"Wow, that's incredible." I reach out to run my finger along the velvety flower petals.

"Hey, can I ask you something, Elowen?"

"Of course, Lady Briar."

"What type of... being is King Caspian?" I ask. "He said he's not a werewolf, even though he's the alpha king. If he's not a werewolf, what is he?"

"Close your eyes, please." She begins to apply eyeshadow onto my eyelids. "I'm not supposed to say, but I have a feeling you'll find out at dinner tonight."

Now *that* has certainly piqued my interest.

"Am I expected to have dinner with him every night?" I ask.

Elowen nods. "Yes, and I hope you'll find the abundant spread to your liking."

I wince. King Caspian probably eats way better than his servants, and here I am complaining about it.

"Hey, Elowen, can you just call me Bri? You don't have to address me so formally."

She bites her lip. "But King Caspian insists we call you Lady Briar."

I hum. "Okay, what if you call me Bri when it's just the two of us in here, alone? You can call me Lady Briar when there's other people around. Deal?"

"Deal." She nods, a warm smile spreading across her face.

Did I just make a new friend in the Crimson Vale, of all places? I have a feeling I'll need all the friends I can get to make it to the next full moon.

When she's done with my hair and makeup, she leads me to the bedroom, where she's laid out a dress for me to wear. "Dinner is a formal affair here at the castle. King Caspian has requested the kingdom's top dressmaker to come fit you for some custom designs, but in the meantime, I hope you'll find this to your liking."

She holds up a sultry black gown to me, and I swear my jaw drops to the floor. The dress is an A-line shape with a small train behind it, and the material is dark satin beneath black tulle. The bust has a deep V-neck, with dark lace and crystal sewn along the hem, with sheer, lace sleeves stretching down to the wrists.

It's stunning, and I can't wait to put it on. It's got Goth princess vibes that pair well with King Caspian's aesthetic.

Not that I care about matching his aesthetic. I'm trying to get out of here, not play dress-up doll with Caz's evil twin.

The guilt hits me all over again. I'm up here being wined and dined while Caz is trapped in the dungeons. I need to convince King Caspian to let me see him, though the last time I asked, it pissed him off.

I'll just need to approach it in a different way. Catch more flies with honey than with vinegar, or however the saying goes.

When it's time for dinner, I steel my resolve and follow Elowen downstairs. She leads me into a cavernous dining room, where a long mahogany table stretches the length of the room beneath a crystal chandelier. Which is powered by *eleven magic*.

I'll never get used to that.

Three sets of French doors open up onto a terrace beneath the starry night sky, allowing fresh air inside. A fireplace roars on the other side of the table, illuminating the room in a romantic, mysterious glow.

King Caspian stands from his seat when I enter the room, wearing an all-black fitted suit similar to the one he wore yesterday, but this time, he left the crown upstairs. "Ah, my lady, you are a vision. I have just one more thing to add."

He approaches and holds out a square velvet box, opening the lid to reveal a necklace of black crystal, which shimmers under the light of the chandelier. It's woven into an intricate, filigree design.

"If I may?" He steps behind me, brushing his fingers across my neck as he moves my hair to the side, sending a shiver of electricity down my body.

"It's going to take a lot more than jewelry to win me over." But I stand still as he clasps the necklace around my neck.

He leans in to whisper in my ear. "Perhaps a little wine will help soften your affections toward me."

I try not to show any reaction, but my body tingles from the sensation of his lips so close to my neck.

Clearing my throat, I step away from him.

There are only two seats at the table, placed on the far ends of the long table. I stride toward the available one, where a butler pulls out my chair for me. An outrageous amount of food is displayed on the table from elaborate fruit displays to a seafood tower almost as tall as me. "Is anyone else joining us?"

"No, I have you all to myself tonight." He takes his own seat at the opposite end of the long table.

Honestly, I'm thankful for the distance the table provides.

"This is a ridiculous amount of food for two people." I raise my voice to call at him from across the table. "It seems like such a waste."

"Don't worry, the leftovers are distributed to the staff." He waves his hand at the food. "Now, unless you have any further objections, please eat."

After giving him a very obvious eye roll, I examine the different trays of food. The sheer number of choices is overwhelming, but I opt for some roast chicken, a helping of carrots, and a slice of warm, baked bread.

A butler appears beside me, holding a rounded, silver decanter with intricate flourish designs etched into the outside. I admire it for a moment before realizing he's pouring red wine from the spout.

I hold my hand out to stop him. "Actually, do you have ice water instead?"

"Of course, my lady." He nods, turning back to retrieve the water.

The king eyes me closely. "No wine for you?"

"No, I don't really drink much these days," I reply. "When you feel hungover all the time, it's not very appealing."

Besides, I need to keep my wits about me when in the presence of the king.

He lets out a snort of amusement but doesn't say anything more on the subject. The butler fetches my water, and then he returns to the king's side to pour a glass of red wine.

I notice that the decanter he uses for King Caspian's wine is different from the one offered to me. It's made of glass, not silver, and the liquid is a much darker shade of red than the wine I was given.

As King Caspian swirls the glass, the viscous liquid sticks to the sides of the glass in a way I've never seen before.

"That doesn't look like wine."

He glances at me over the rim and smirks. "Very observant."

I gulp. "That's not... blood, is it?"

"It is." He briefly raises his glass toward me before taking a long sip, keeping his gaze locked on mine.

It takes a few moments to put the pieces together. "Wait, are you a *vampire?*"

A wicked grin appears on King Caspian's face as he lets out a low, deep chuckle. It sounds so different from Caz's laugh—darker and more dangerous.

"How are you a vampire if Caz is a werewolf?" I ask.

"Because I am not subjected to the Curse of the Werewolf. Our ancestors were grimwalkers, which meant they could turn into any animal at will, but they also had an insatiable bloodlust." He swirls the contents of his glass once again, watching the blood roll down the sides and leaving snaky, red trails in its wake. "When the Silver Ridge tribe cast our ancestors out, they separated our souls into two: our light one and our dark one. The bloodlust in us was seen as evil, and thus cast to the Crimson Vale with the dark ones."

I take a moment to wrap my head around that. "So, the light ones are werewolves, and the dark ones are vampires?"

"Indeed." He takes another sip from his glass.

"So, you're a vampire, but you're also the werewolf king?" I say slowly, trying to wrap my head around it.

"Yes, all of the alphas of the werewolf packs answer to me as their one true alpha." He gives me a patient nod.

"Except for Caz, who is the alpha of the Nazara Pack."

"Caz is me, and I am Caz." He sighs as he sets his glass down. "As I've explained, we are two halves of the same person."

"Speaking of Caz," I say, "what's it going to take for you to let me see him?"

He runs a fingertip along the rim of his wineglass, making it chime. "I'd be willing to let you see him. That is, in exchange for something in return."

I jump at the chance to see Caz. "Yes, anything."

In seconds, he appears by my side, leaning over my chair and crowding my space. "Anything?"

Superhuman speed. That's how he's able to move so fast.

I gulp.

His eyes possess a dark glint as he licks his lips. "How about a visit with my light one in exchange for a night in my bed?"

CHAPTER 8

This asshole.

I should have seen that coming. Of course, King Caspian would exploit my feelings for his selfish desires. He may look like Caz, but he is nothing like him. Instead, he's a manipulative son-of-a-bitch.

But when he looks so much like Caz, it's easy to forget he's the dark one.

I raise my hand and bring it toward his face to slap him, but he grabs my wrist before I can deliver the blow.

"Fuck you!"

"I thought you would do anything to see him?" He caresses a cold finger along the vein of my wrist and turns his face to skim his lips over the lace. "Hmm, I bet your blood tastes so sweet—"

I yank my arm out of his grasp, then throw my napkin on my plate. "I'm done."

He frowns. "But you've hardly touched your food."

"I've lost my appetite." Without a single glance back, I stand up and hurry out of the dining room.

He could catch up to me if he wanted to—I've seen firsthand how fast he is—but he lets me go.

Remembering the path back to my room proves difficult, but after a few wrong turns, I finally find it and slam the door behind me, breathless from the climb.

As I storm into the bedroom, I yank my dress and necklace off, tossing them to the floor. The last thing I want right now is to be dolled up for King Caspian's pleasure, and I'm eager to put on a pair of pajamas and forget this night ever happened.

But when I open the closet, all I can find are short, lacy negligees made of satin, which barely cover my ass. They each come with a matching, full-length dressing gown, but the fluffy white robe I've been sleeping in is gone.

Is King Caspian responsible for this? Fucking pervert.

I pick out a black nightgown and yank it over my head, then crawl into bed and pull the covers up to my neck.

I miss Caz. I miss his kind words and gentle touch, and I wish he was here beside me to help me face these monsters in the Crimson Vale.

Yes, I would do anything to see him. But sleeping with the enemy? That's going too far, and if Caz were here, he'd tell me not to do it.

But Caz isn't here. He's locked away in the dungeons, enduring God-knows-what. I need to see him and make sure he's okay, no matter the cost.

If I truly love Caz, wouldn't I do anything for him? Do I have any other choice?

No, I don't think I do.

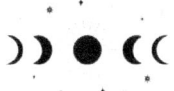

I slip on my black, satin robe over my negligee and make my way to King Caspian's room. How I'm able to find it so easily, I'm not sure, but something called me here. Led me to this door.

When I raise my fist to knock, I hesitate. My heart is racing; my stomach is in knots.

Before I can make up my mind whether to knock or leave, the door opens. On the threshold stands King Caspian, wearing nothing but a pair of loose-fitting cotton pants. His bare chest is exposed, revealing his bronze, muscular physique. He's built exactly like Caz with his broad chest and shoulders, but his ruby-red eyes examine me with a look of triumph.

He folds his arms and leans against the doorframe. "Did you change your mind?"

I avoid his gaze. It's not difficult to do when his ripped abs are staring me in the face. "I'm here for Caz. Remember our deal?"

He nods. "A night with me in exchange for a visit with my light one." He opens the door further and gestures for me to enter. "I remember. Although, I wonder if you'll even want to visit him after tonight."

I scoff.

When I walk past him, I have to turn my shoulders to avoid brushing against his bare chest. "Let's just get this over with."

He shuts the door behind me, and my eyes wander around the king's private quarters. It's much more grand and impressive than my room, and the wood furniture is made from the darkest mahogany. The bed is made up with red silk sheets with black curtains drawn back along the four-poster canopy. I am sure there is a living room and a bathroom attached, but all the doors are closed, trapping me inside.

A fire is roaring in the fireplace opposite the bed, framed in black marble and gold. A Victorian-style seating area sits in front of the fire, where two sets of whisky glasses wait for us atop a coffee table.

He knew I would come and prepared accordingly.

I gulp. "I think I'll take that drink now." I'm going to need a bit of liquid courage to get through this night.

King Caspian materializes in front of me with two full glasses of whisky. I glance at the table, and sure enough, the empty glasses are gone.

Goddamn, he's fast.

His fingertips brush against mine as he passes me a glass, and I withdraw my hand.

"Is that a vampire trick? Being so fast?" I sling half the glass back.

"It is one of my many talents, yes. But rest assured, I'll take my time with you." He smirks. "The night is long, and I have plenty of time."

"Oh, goody." I roll my eyes.

"Cheers to your beauty and intelligence, Bri." He clinks his glass against mine before taking a sip.

I chug the remaining contents of mine in one gulp, eliciting a low chuckle from him.

He takes the empty glass and sets it on a nearby table. "Anxious to get started? I feel the same way."

"Where do you want me?" I glance at the bed.

He follows my gaze and smirks. "I figured we could start with a little foreplay, but if you'd prefer to go straight to the main event, I'm happy to oblige."

Nerves grip my body, and I start to tremble. Goose bumps erupt across my arms as I glance at the floor.

It feels wrong to be here because I'm cheating on Caz. And yet, I'm doing this *for* Caz. God, I'm so confused.

King Caspian steps in front of me, taking my head into his hands. He tilts my gaze up to meet his, and his smirk is replaced with a softer expression. "You have nothing to be afraid of, Bri. I would never hurt you."

As I gaze into his burgundy eyes, my anxiety dissipates—except the anxiety between my thighs. Clenching them together, I try to fight the excitement and lust that seem to be building in my body.

I shouldn't feel this way, but I can't help it. He looks like Caz, and just as handsome. If I pretend I'm sleeping with Caz and not his evil doppelgänger, I might actually enjoy this.

I step up onto my tiptoes and plant a soft kiss on his cool lips. They feel so familiar, and yet, his reaction is unexpected.

He meets my mouth with expert skill, sucking on my lower lip as his fingers snake through my hair. It's like he can't get enough, devouring my mouth with insatiable hunger.

I think I might drown in his kiss.

God, he tastes divine. His salt mixed with a hint of cinnamon creates a heady mixture on my tongue.

He groans against my mouth, sending vibrations down my body. When his hardness presses against my lower belly, I gasp against his mouth. He takes the opportunity to slip his tongue inside, dominating my mouth while he explores.

He's an excellent kisser. The best, if I'm being honest.

How many women has he been with to kiss like this? Something tells me he's not a virgin like Caz was.

An unexpected pang of jealousy jabs my heart.

I break away from his kiss, both of us panting hard as we stare each other down with hooded gazes. Challenging one another, daring the other to make the first move.

My fingers grab at the waistband of his pants, hovering mere inches above his thickening erection. With a fistful of fabric in my hand, I step backwards toward the bed, leading him there with a tug.

A smile pulls at his lips as he follows, willing and eager. "Mmm, I like a woman who takes charge."

I push him down onto the bed as hard as I can. He lets out a low laugh when his back hits the sheets, propping himself up on his elbows.

When I untie my robe, it slips off my shoulders onto the floor. I'm left in nothing but my lace negligee, and when I climb onto the mattress to straddle his waist, he glances between my legs. The skirt is riding up... and I don't have any underwear on.

Breathing hard, I gaze down at him, supporting my weight with my hands on his broad chest.

I want him. Even if it's wrong. I just can't remember *why* it's wrong...

I want him. And my body is powerless to stop it, like it's moving of its own accord.

My body feels strange. Foreign. Like it's being controlled by someone other than me.

I pause and shut my eyes, trying to get this feeling to pass. This isn't like when I dissociate. It's something different. Something darker.

When I open my eyes, I'm disoriented. I'm standing in front of King Caspian's chambers once again in the dimly lit corridor.

But I was just inside, on his bed. I could feel him beneath me as I straddled him...

So how did I wind up out here?

As I glance around, I notice my vision is clearer. Before, while in his bedroom, everything was rimmed in a haze.

"Couldn't get enough of me at dinner?" asks a familiar voice.

Glancing up, I find King Caspian standing in the doorway with that villainous smirk on his face. He's shirtless, wearing the same loose-fitting pants that I just saw him in.

I bring a hand to my head. "What's going on?" I point at his door. "I was just inside your room, and then... how did I wind up out here?"

He says nothing, just standing in the doorway, examining me with a smug expression.

"Was that all a dream?" I ask. "Did... did you fuck with my brain?"

"Beautiful *and* intelligent, as always, Bri," he says. "I'm actually surprised you woke yourself up. It takes a lot of mental strength to awaken from one of my dream spells."

I take a step back. "How did you do that?"

He rests his arm against the doorway above his head, towering over me. "A vampire doesn't just drink blood, my lady. We have other abilities as well."

"Like your super speed?"

He nods.

It was all just a dream. A dream that had me sleepwalk all the way across the castle to his room. A trap he laid out to manipulate me.

I clutch my robe tighter against my chest. "What if I hadn't woken up from your dream spell?" My voice quivers. "Would you have just taken advantage of me while I slept the entire time?"

He stiffens. "Of course not. I prefer my partner to be awake and willing."

SMACK!

I land my palm across his face with such force it shocks even me, and this time, I make contact. His head knocks to the side, and he raises a palm to rub the red handprint I left on his cheek.

"Your Majesty!" a guard shouts from down the hall. He and a fellow guard start running toward us. "Seize her!"

I gasp as they each grab one of my arms, and they start dragging me away from the king, who looks stunned.

"You're going to the dungeons," a guard says.

The dungeons? Will I be able to see Caz down there? Did I just figure out a way to see him? It's not the ideal situation, but at least we'll be together.

I resist struggling against my captors and go limp in their arms.

"No." King Caspian holds his hand up to stop them. "Release her."

"Of course, Your Majesty," they reply in unison. They release me from their grip and bow to their king.

"No!" My frustration manifests in hot tears, which threaten to spill down my cheeks. "Take me down there."

King Caspian digs his fingers into my cheeks, forcing my face upward. His cool breath fans my face, and my own catches in my throat under the intensity of his gaze.

And his eyes are glowing bright red with fury.

"You haven't upheld your end of the bargain yet, Bri," he whispers in a dark voice. "You don't get to see my light one so easily."

I tremble. "But I slapped you. Shouldn't I be thrown in the dungeons as punishment?"

"A slap like that is just foreplay." He regards me with heated anger blazing in his red gaze. "Besides, I have other punishments in mind for you, but not the dungeons."

Everything about this situation makes me furious. I have no control over what happens to me; I'm powerless against everything. Powerless against King Caspian and powerless to see Caz. I can't even go home.

There's nothing I can do to change my situation, unless I succumb to King Caspian's advances. And then where does that leave me? I get to see Caz, but only if I betray him and cheat on him with another man.

They're the same man, says a small voice in the back of my mind.

A tear slips from the corner of my eye.

His face falls. "It wasn't my intention to frighten you. I assure you, I would never force you to sleep with me under a dream spell. I merely... planted the seed in your mind."

When he runs his thumb along my cheek to catch my tears, I knock his hand away. I stumble backwards a few steps, the tears obstructing my vision. Anger and frustration have bubbled to the surface and burst forth like a volcanic eruption.

"I fucking hate you," I yell at him. "I hate you, and I hate this place. I just want to go home!"

Whatever home means now. The ranch? Los Angeles?

Before he has a chance to react, I turn and run off down the corridor in the direction of my room.

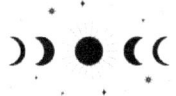

The next morning, Elowen comes in to wake me up, opening the curtains to bring light into the bedroom.

"Good morning, Lady Briar—I mean, Bri." She gives me a curtsy beside the bed. "I've had breakfast brought up, and it's waiting in the sitting room when you're ready."

"Thanks, Elowen." My joints are stiff, my mind foggy, and my stomach growls at the mention of food. Having eaten so little last night, I could use some sustenance.

I wrap my robe around me and wander out of the bedroom, my joints causing me to walk stiffly. But as soon as I enter the sitting room, I freeze at the sight awaiting me.

The room is covered in various flower arrangements of all colors and shapes and sizes. Bouquets on the coffee table, on the floor, on the writing desk in the corner. There has to be over a hundred different flower arrangements in here.

"Isn't it just beautiful?" Elowen claps her hands together. "They're from the king. Here, smell these ones."

She shoves a bouquet of red roses into my face, and I take a deep inhale. But despite a room brimming with flowers, I'm unable to smell them, no matter how hard I try.

I take a seat on the sofa. "King Caspian did all of this?"

There is barely enough room for my breakfast tray on the coffee table. I pluck a stray rose petal off my bowl of berries before I dig in.

Elowen beams. "He certainly did. I've never seen him do anything like this for a woman before. He must really like you."

My stomach roils. "Exactly how many women has he had?" I stir some honey into my hot tea.

"Ah, well..." Elowen shifts from foot to foot. "King Caspian is known as the most eligible bachelor in all the kingdom, but he's never shown an interest in settling down or providing an heir to the throne."

I tap my spoon on the rim of my cup before setting it down. "Does he bring women to his room?"

She wrings her hands together. "I, uh, I'm not sure if it's my place to say—"

I glance up. "Your secret's safe with me, Elowen. We're friends now, remember?"

"Well, okay..." She takes a seat on the opposite end of the sofa, then leans in and lowers her voice. "King Caspian has a reputation around the castle as a bit of a playboy. He's been known to hire women of ill repute to visit his bedchambers."

If King Caspian is supposed to encompass everything evil about Caz, his philandering is in direct contrast to Caz's...virtue, which I stole.

I'm not interested in King Caspian, so why does my heart clench when I think of the other women he's had?

I touch one of the flower petals on a nearby bouquet. Is he trying to make up for last night? The things I shouted at him were cruel, but he manipulated me. He deserved to be put in his place.

After finishing my breakfast, I pick out a book from the bookcase and retreat into my bedroom—away from the flowers. I spend the day reading in bed, trying to escape my current situation. All I can do is hide away from King Caspian until I figure out what I feel.

Who sends flowers to a girl who screams she hates him?

Should I apologize?

The dressmaker comes by after lunch, but I refuse to see him and ask Elowen to send him away. I don't want to accept any gifts from King Caspian at the moment, and I'm even tempted to throw all the flowers out the window. I probably would if only there weren't so many of them. Chucking a hundred flower vases out the window sounds utterly exhausting.

When the sun begins to set outside, Elowen enters the bedroom. "It's time to get ready for dinner."

"I'll take dinner in my room tonight." I flip the page of my book.

Elowen checks behind her, as if the king himself is standing right behind her. "I don't think the king will be happy to hear that."

I shrug. "Tell him I refuse to leave my room. I don't want to see him right now."

Elowen curtsies and exits the room.

Within five minutes of her departure, King Caspian bursts into my bedroom—without knocking. He stands in the doorway, his hands on the doorframe as if blocking me from escaping. "I see you received the flowers I sent you."

I don't look up from my book. "Yes."

He grits his teeth. "Then why aren't you joining me for dinner? Are you not feeling well again?"

"No, I feel fine today."

He clenches and unclenches his fist. "I apologized for my behavior last night. I sent you flowers this morning. So answer my question: Why are you not joining me for dinner?"

I close my book with a sharp snap. "Your apologies and your flowers do not mean you're entitled to my time."

His nostrils flare as he inhales a sharp breath. "We made a deal, Bri."

It takes every ounce of willpower not to slam my book on the floor. "Yes, but nowhere in that deal does it stipulate I have to have dinner with you."

He begins pacing the bedroom. "This is not how it was supposed to be. You are my *mate*. We're supposed to be inherently attracted to each other. Even if you're unable to feel the mate bond as we do, you should at the very least not be repulsed by me. How can you love my light one but hate *me*?"

My words caused this pain, and seeing how deeply they affect him makes me feel like an ass. Yeah, his actions last night were disgusting, but so were my words.

"Come here. Sit down." I sigh and pat the bed beside me.

He takes a seat on the mattress, looking at me with a pained expression in his gaze that's hard to meet.

Only because he looks so much like Caz.

"Caz has always treated me with respect," I begin, trying to find the words to explain it not only to him but to myself. "Caz and I have known each other since we were kids. We were friends first, and only recently did we become something more. Everything is consensual between us, and it's at a pace we're both comfortable with. That's what relationships are about: give and take."

He scoffs. "But I've given you everything you could possibly want. I've given you flowers, food, clothing, a servant, and one of the best rooms in the castle. So why won't you give me anything in return?"

It's like explaining the concept of sharing toys with a spoiled child. "It's not about gifts. It's about trust and respect, and when you coerced me to your room last night, you weren't showing me any of that. It made me distrust you."

My words seem to be sinking in, and he nods as his brows knit together in thought. Silence falls between us as he considers my words, and I pick at a loose thread in the duvet. I wrap it around the tip of my finger until the color drains from my skin, loosen it, and do it again.

"Then consider this gesture an olive branch." He looks at me with an unreadable expression on his face. "I will let you see my light one. No strings attached."

I'm stunned. "Wait, really? Just like that?"

"Just like that." He nods, but he's put up a wall that gives away no emotion. "We can go now, if you want."

My guard is up, but I decide to let this play out. "Okay, sure. Let me get changed first." I point to the door. "Out."

After tugging on a loose-fitting dress with renaissance sleeves, I rejoin King Caspian and follow him through the corridors of the castle, watching the back of his head as though I might find any sign of deception. But with each step we take, I dare to hope it's a step closer to Caz.

We approach a narrow passageway off of the first-floor courtyard, guarded by two soldiers and an iron gate. One of the guards unlocks the gate and opens it wide, allowing us to pass.

It closes behind us with an ominous thud, and a rush of cool air blows up the narrow, stone corridor. A low ceiling hangs directly above our heads, and there's only enough space for us to walk one at a time.

I follow King Caspian in silence as we descend further underground. The corridor, which is illuminated with lit torches, twists and turns a number of times, with many forks in the path. But he never once hesitates, so I continue to follow while remaining alert and try to memorize the path.

By the time we reach a large chamber at the end, I'm gasping to get air into my lungs. It's a domed, circular room made of stone with high ceilings. I glance around the chamber and see a number of wide cells surrounding us as we stride into the center of the cold, dim space.

King Caspian nods his head at one of the cells on the opposite end of the chamber. "There."

A familiar, warm voice calls out from the shadows. "Bri? Is that you?"

"Caz?" I take a step forward.

Caz's form steps out from the shadows, reaching his hand through the bars.

"CAZ!" I make a mad dash toward him. When I reach his cell, I start to sob and sink to the floor, and Caz sits down with me. I've finally found him, but the iron bars of his cell make him feel so far away. Still, he grabs my hand, and he reaches through the bars to stroke my cheek with the other.

His eyes are the familiar shade of brown I've known for years, and as I sit here in this cold, damp dungeon, I realize how badly I've missed him.

"Bri, shhh, it's okay. You're okay." He gives me a gentle smile.

"I s-should be comforting y-you." I hiccup between sobs. "You're in jail."

"It's actually not too bad in here." He tips his chin at the space behind him. "This is the best cell in the entire dungeon, and I get three delicious meals a day."

I wipe my eyes and peer through the bars. A four-poster bed sits against the stone wall, and it's covered in thick blankets and pillows. In the corner is a small dining table with a high-back upholstered chair. Flames glow in the fireplace, which has a small loveseat facing it. An array of books sits on the mantle.

"Is that a chamber pot?" I ask, eying a large basin by his bed.

"Yeah, I'm living like it's 1699 in here." He laughs. "It's a little boring, but I've been reading to pass the time."

I sniff. "Aren't you cold?"

He shakes his head. "The fire never goes out."

"So... they're not mistreating you in here?"

He squeezes my hand. "No. I only get whipped if I talk back to the guards."

I gasp. "What?"

"Shh, Bri, I'm kidding." He strokes my cheek with his thumb. "They don't beat me or whip me or anything like that. They really just leave me alone except to bring meals."

A sob wrenches from my throat. "God, don't even joke about that."

Caz presses his forehead against the bars. "Come here."

I lean my face forward to give him a long, yearning kiss, our cheeks pressed against the iron rails that separate us.

Reluctantly, he breaks our kiss and leans back. "What about you? How are you doing?" He looks me up and down as though looking for evidence of abuse.

"I'm... fine."

He glances at King Caspian standing behind us and narrows his gaze. "Are you sure? You seem upset."

The last thing I want is for Caz to worry about me. "No, really. I'm fine. My room is huge, and there's plenty of food."

"Good. I'm glad. We just have to wait until the next full moon, and then we can go home."

I nod. Caz doesn't know about my deal with King Caspian, but it's irrelevant. I'm not falling in love with the dark one, so he'll have to let us go once the portal reopens.

We sit here for a long moment, taking in the appearance of the other. I'm unwilling to let him go, so I grip his hand for dear life.

I don't want our conversation to end. I just want to hear his voice.

"Is it really true?" I ask. "About us being fated mates?"

A slow, gorgeous smile spreads across his face. "Yeah."

I lean into his touch, closing my eyes at the contact. "What's it like to be so sure about someone?"

"I don't know. The mate bond is a powerful attraction that's hard to explain." He hums in thought. "From the moment I met you, I just knew deep in my bones you were it for me. When I'm with you, my world feels whole and complete, and everything shines a bit brighter. Pushing you away this summer crushed me, Bri, but I would hate myself even more for holding you back from your dreams."

His selfless confession makes my breath catch. How could anyone feel so strongly about anyone, let alone *me?*

And yet, he loves me so deeply he's willing to let me go if that's what it takes for me to be happy. He's so selfless and good. I don't deserve him.

But I love him. I fell hard and fast, and I can't imagine letting him go. If that means I have to stay on the ranch to be with him, then I can accept that. He doesn't want to pass on the Curse of the Werewolf to his offspring, then we won't have kids. We can adopt.

We'll make it work. I want to make it work because I love him with every fiber of my being. Caz is a good man, and I would be insane to let him go to chase a degree and a career I'm too sick to have.

Perhaps fate had a hand in that.

If we weren't dragged—quite literally—into the Crimson Vale, would we have admitted our love to each other so soon? Would he have told me we were destined to be together?

But perhaps we were supposed to come here, to find ourselves in circumstances that made us desperate to ensure that nothing is left unsaid between us. Is that the power of the mate bond?

It feels like every road has led me to Caz somehow. So how does King Caspian play into all that?

Speaking of the alpha king, he clears his throat behind me. "It's time to go."

I lean my forehead against the bars. "I love you, Caz."

"Hey, stay strong, okay?" Caz strokes my cheek with his thumb. "We'll be out of here in less than a month."

I lean in for one last kiss, savoring every last second I have with him before it's ripped away.

Caz stands up first before helping me to my feet, offering his hands through the iron bars. I feel unsteady, but I follow King Caspian out of the dungeon, turning to wave at Caz before he disappears into shadow once again.

I eat my dinner in silence.

King Caspian sets his fork down. "You saw for yourself he's being treated well here."

I glance up from my meal. "Why lock him up at all, then?"

"I couldn't possibly let my rival be free to vie for your affections." He smirks, but the humor doesn't reach his eyes. "I told you; I have enemies. If he dies, I die."

"Why did you let me see him?" I ask.

He takes a sip from his goblet before answering. "Because relationships are about give and take, Bri."

I scoff and shake my head. "Let me guess: you *give* me time with Caz before *taking* my body?"

He sets his glass down. "I told you I would let you see him, no strings attached. I'm not the complete monster you think I am." He gets up from his chair, wiping the corner of his mouth with a napkin before tossing it onto the table. "Good night, Lady Briar."

Apparently, it's his turn to storm out on our conversation. Within seconds, he's gone.

CHAPTER 9

The next morning, I awaken after a restless night.

I'm comforted that Caz is okay and being taken care of in the dungeons. King Caspian is to thank for that, I suppose, although he's the one who put him down there in the first place.

So why do I feel so shitty about how we left things last night?

After hearing Caz describe how he feels about me as his fated mate, I realized that King Caspian might feel the same way. Does he feel that bond as deeply as Caz does?

Even though I'll choose Caz when the full moon returns, I suppose I could be nicer to King Caspian in the meantime. He's making an effort, and I've fought him every step of the way. If I can move past the dream spell incident, I think it will make my time here in the Crimson Vale much easier.

Elowen sets out what *she* says is a simple dress, but it's a purple velvet gown with long sleeves and a floor-length skirt. However, when I put it on, I'm surprised by the comfortable fit.

It's perfect for exploring the castle, and I don't want to spend another day locked in my room.

I head out on my own and start with my floor, which appears to be empty guest rooms. They're nice, but not quite as luxurious as mine or the king's.

The second floor is where I find a massive library, and I'm tempted to spend the rest of my day just exploring this room. It looks like the stock photos I've seen of the Admont Abbey Library of Austria but with darker bookcases. The painted fresco on the domed ceiling is mesmerizing, and I could stand here staring at it until my neck grows sore.

This one doesn't depict wolves at war. If I had to guess, it's about elven magic, with pointy-eared beings manipulating different elements, all illustrated in stunning pastels.

Footsteps echo behind me, but before I can hide, a familiar voice calls out to me.

"Bri?"

I turn around to find King Caspian emerging from one of the doors on the opposite end of the vast library. But with his vampiric speed, he disappears and materializes in front of me within seconds.

"Oh. Hi."

Yep, this isn't awkward at all.

"You've found the library, I see." He offers a tight smile. "I'm not surprised. You seem quite fond of reading, especially when I'm in the room."

Heat rises to my cheeks. "Look, I know I've been, uh…"

"Stubborn?"

I sigh. "Yeah, you could say that. You didn't ask us to fall through that portal, I guess. You've been generous to let us stay here instead of throwing us to the wolves—"

"Quite literally."

"—so thank you." I glance at the intricate weave of the rug under my feet. "And thank you for letting me see Caz last night."

"You are always welcome in my home. I'd never send you away."

I chance a glance at him. "Even when I slap you and scream at you?"

The corners of his lips tug. "It takes a lot more than that to break me."

His ruby gaze holds mine, and for some reason, I can't seem to look away.

He clears his throat. "Are you exploring the castle? I would be happy to give you a personal tour."

I wave my hands. "Oh, you don't have to. I'm sure you have better things to do, like running a kingdom and all."

He chuckles. "Then you'd be surprised by how much time I have on my hands. I have people for the day-to-day administrative responsibilities, but you won't find anyone more knowledgeable about this castle than me."

He's extending an olive branch, so I decide to accept it. "Well, if you have the time, I'd appreciate it."

"It would be my pleasure." He clasps his hands behind his back in a regal posture. "This is a great place to begin since the library is in the east wing. The books in this library have been accumulated by the royal family for centuries, and it is now home to over 75,000 individual texts. The murals painted on the ceilings were commissioned by the royal family…"

The sheer amount of knowledge King Caspian has about the castle is astonishing. I may as well be on a private tour with a museum docent as he leads me through his study, the council chamber, the portrait gallery, the music room, and a number of different sitting rooms. With each room, he spouts off historical facts and tidbits of information, even about specific paintings or objects.

He also takes me through the ballroom, which reminds me of the dance scene out of *Beauty and the Beast*. The floors are made entirely of marble, and windows overlooking a terrace stretch all the way up to the ceiling, which must be at least thirty feet above us. A massive crystal chandelier hangs above our heads.

King Caspian stops in the middle of the space. "We have a ball every Saturday night,"

"Every Saturday?" My eyes grow wide as I examine the room. "How many people could you fit in here for a formal dinner in rounds of eight to ten? Do you use this room on any other night besides Saturdays? Do you rent it out?"

King Caspian laughs, and I think it's the first genuine laugh I've heard from him.

"Why? Are you planning our wedding already?"

I throw him an exasperated look. "Back on Earth, I was going to school to become an event planner."

"Ah, excellent. That is an important skill for a queen to have."

I swear his ruby eyes glint with a hint of pride.

"Well, don't get too excited." I avert my gaze to the floor. "I dropped out of school and gave up my internship."

A deep crease forms between his brows. "Why?"

"I got sick."

This is the worst possible moment for tears to start welling in my eyes, but the wave of emotion that washes over me comes out of nowhere. I don't want him to see me like this, so I stride past him toward the terrace doors, eager for fresh air.

"Here, allow me." He zips past me with his supernatural speed and opens one of the large glass doors.

I swallow the lump in my throat. "Shouldn't you avoid the sunlight?"

He quirks an eyebrow at me. "Why would I do that?"

"Doesn't sunlight kill vampires?"

"Not that I'm aware." He chuckles and shakes his head. "Where did you get such an idea?"

Once again, my cheeks burn hot. "It's a legend back home. Vampires are immortal, but they can be killed instantly by sunlight or a wooden stake through the heart. Oh, and they can turn into bats."

"I imagine a stake through the heart would kill most creatures." He gives me an amused look. "But turning into a bat? I've never heard that one before."

"Well, I'm glad we cleared that up." And now I feel like an idiot.

I follow him out onto the balcony, and we look out over the castle grounds. Below the terrace is an outdoor area surrounded by stone columns, but the weeds and vines are overgrown, and the trees appear dead.

"So, King Caspian, is this considered quality landscaping in the Crimson Vale?" I swear I can see sludge in the defunct fountain. Gross.

"I suppose things have been let go since... well, it doesn't matter."

I steal a sideways glance at him. His eyes glaze over as he retreats into himself, and his brows furrow in a way that makes him look wistful.

He seems so far away. To bring him back, I place my hand over his, which is resting on the balcony.

"King Caspian?"

He looks down at our hands, then up at me. "You don't have to address me so formally. Just call me Caspian."

I nod. "Okay, *Caspian*."

He surveys the garden. "Perhaps you would be interested in redecorating this to your liking?"

"Me?" I examine a dead bush with withered flowers below. "I don't think it's my place to redecorate your home."

He scoffs. "Nonsense. I trust that you have good taste. Besides, it will give you something to do during the day when I'm unable to entertain you."

I pause, considering his offer. "Let's say I accept your offer. Do you have a budget for me?"

"We can discuss it with the treasury next week."

My mind is working in a million different directions as I imagine the garden parties the castle could host. I could hang paper lanterns from the stone archways, and if I could light the fountain with elven magic, it would be ethereal. What types of flowers could I get in the Crimson Vale to bring some color to the garden? Elowen might know.

"I love watching your mind work." Caspian shifts closer, gazing down at me with a soft expression. His ruby-red irises captivate me, holding me frozen in place.

I suck in a sharp breath at our proximity. My hand is still on top of Caspian's. He shifts it to lace his fingers with mine, and I don't draw away.

This is the first day we've managed not to argue, and I have to admit, it's... nice. A part of me doesn't want the moment to end, but I'm not sure if I want this to go further.

But before I can voice my hesitation, Caspian leans forward and places his lips on mine.

This is our first real kiss. The first time didn't actually happen except in a dream, but even then, he tasted like Caz—salt with a hint of sweet cinnamon. He still does.

I can't resist. I close my eyes, savoring his lips. They become more passionate and demanding as he deepens our kiss, and his hands move to my waist to pull me closer to him.

It steals my breath away. An involuntary moan escapes my mouth, which spurs him on. As he presses into me, his growing erection brushes against my stomach, and the effect is like a bucket of ice water being dumped over my head.

I place my hands on his hard chest and push him away. Between ragged breaths, I whisper, "I'm sorry, I can't."

I spin around and rush into the ballroom without looking back. And I don't stop until I reach my room, locking the door behind me to ensure I remain alone.

To have time to think.

I cross into the bedroom and throw myself on the bed, burrowing my face into the pillows. It takes me a minute to catch my breath, but I'm not sure if it's from running or from that kiss.

I roll over onto my back to stare up at the ceiling. My fingertips brush against my mouth, and my tongue grazes my lips, still able to taste him. Caz's taste, Caspian' taste—they're the same.

Closing my eyes, I continue to savor the sensation, but my heart is filled with an aching guilt. I love Caz, but I can't deny that I really, *really* liked kissing Caspian.

They look and taste the same. Caspian even insists they're the same person, two halves of the same soul.

If that's true, why does it feel like I betrayed Caz?

As much as I try not to, I can't help but compare the experience of kissing both of them. With Caz, his kisses are sweet and full of tenderness. But Caspian's lips are full of lust, passion... *experience*. What Caz lacks in experience, Caspian certainly seems to make up for.

I have a strong suspicion that Caspian knows how to please a woman and that he could take me to places I've never been before. Even the images he implanted into my mind the other night were hot as hell.

They really are complete opposites. The light and the darkness. Like the sun and the moon.

I request to eat my dinner in my room that night. Perhaps an evening away from Caspian will help me see this situation with a clearer perspective.

I expect Caspian to come barging in, demanding to know why I'm refusing to join him for dinner.

But he doesn't come.

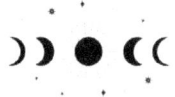

The next morning, Elowen brings me a handwritten note.

Dinner will be on the terrace tonight. I expect your attendance. —Caspian

I guess we're back to making demands.

You like that he's taking charge, says a nasty little voice in my head. *You're always the one initiating things with men, but you don't have to do that with Caspian. He knows what he wants, and he wants you.*

But what about Caz? He's locked up in a dungeon while I'm out gallivanting with his evil twin.

I have to eat, and I can't avoid Caspian until the next full moon. It's just dinner, so no use trying to resist or justify it. It will give me a chance to clear the air and set some boundaries with him.

No more kissing. Period. I don't trust myself to stop things if it happens again.

For dinner, Elowen helps me pick out a black cocktail dress with a lacy A-line skirt that comes down to my calves. It's an off-the-shoulder dress with a sweetheart neckline, which I finish off with the woven crystal necklace Caspian gifted me at our first dinner. We finish it off with a pair of black gloves and a small fascinator hat with ravens feathers, and I look like I'm ready for a gothic tea party.

I make my way downstairs, but with each step I take, the more butterflies seem to flutter around in my stomach.

When I step out onto the terrace, I find Caspian leaning against the balcony, staring out over the garden. My heel taps against the ground, which pulls his attention onto me.

The moment he lays eyes on me, he licks his lips. He doesn't even try to hide his reaction as he examines me from head to toe.

He approaches to give me a kiss on the cheek. "You are a goddess." His face lingers close to mine for a moment, but he steps back, clearing his throat, and leads me to the table with his hand on the small of my back.

When he removes his hand to pull out my chair, it leaves little electric sparks dancing on my skin long after we take our seats.

It's just the two of us at a small café table covered in a white tablecloth. A four-pronged candlestick lights the table for us, along with the soft glow of the chandelier through the windows.

With a start, I realize the table is set up in the exact spot where we kissed.

I ignore the flutter of my heart. "So, why are we dining *al fresco* tonight?"

"I figured you would be... inspired." He places his chin in his hands as he rests his elbows on the table.

"Inspired?"

"Yes, for the garden renovation."

"Oh, right, that." I glance out at the garden to avoid his heated gaze. "Yes, good idea. When are you wanting it done by?"

A servant steps out onto the patio and approaches the table. Without a word, he sets down our salad course in front of us.

Caspian waits to speak until the servant disappears. "I wanted to speak to you about that. How would you feel about planning a garden party for next Saturday night?" He reaches for a silver goblet at his place setting and takes a sip.

I check mine to find it full of ice water. "Me? Plan a garden party?"

He looks at me over the rim of his glass. "If it's too much to ask, we can postpone it to a later date or cancel it entirely."

I shake my head. "No, I can do it."

"Are you sure? I don't want to put any undue stress on you in your condition—"

"I'll be fine." I roll my eyes, but there's no real irritation behind it. It's kind of sweet for him to worry.

Caspian nods. "Then it's settled. I'll make sure you have resources at your disposal to delegate to. But if it becomes too much, please let me know."

Actually, this project couldn't have come at a better time. It will keep me busy, which means less time to slip up and kiss Caspian.

I glance out over the gardens. "It will be the best garden party this castle has ever seen."

It's not much now, but I see so much potential beneath the gnarled vines.

"I have no doubt in your abilities."

I blink and glance back at him. "How do you have so much faith in me? You haven't even seen my work."

"Because you are the most stubborn woman I have ever met." He lets out a low chuckle. "If anyone can set their mind to something and deliver, it's you."

My cheeks are flaming hot, and I glance down at my salad to avoid his intense stare.

"However," he says, "before we focus on next week's ball, we have one tomorrow night to get through."

"Tomorrow?" I glance up. "Tomorrow is Saturday?"

After spending a few days here, I already lost track of the time. It's been almost a week here in the Crimson Vale, which means I only have about three weeks left before the next full moon.

I thought I had more time here.

Caspian reaches across the table to take my hands in his. "Bri, would you do me the honor of accompanying me to the ball tomorrow night?"

I glance down at our joined hands. His skin is so cold to the touch that it sends chills up my arms and down my spine.

"But I don't have anything to wear," I say.

"Well, if you hadn't turned my dressmaker away the other day, we might be more prepared." He gives me a pointed look, but a faint smile crosses his lips. "But do not fear. I will have Aurelius come first thing tomorrow morning to get you fitted into one of his dresses. All the ladies of the kingdom are clamoring to wear his designs."

"Thank you."

"Anything for you." His expression softens. "I look forward to having the first dance with you."

I straighten up in my chair. "Dancing? What kind of dancing?"

Somehow, I doubt they'll be blasting hip-hop and electronica in the ballroom tomorrow night.

Caspian must notice my apprehension. "You need not worry. I am an excellent dance partner, if I do say so myself. You'll be just fine in my arms."

My crossed legs tighten in response to his remark. The idea of dancing the night away in Caspian's arms sends a thrill down my spine, and the heat grows between my thighs.

I need to calm down and think of something else. Anything else.

This dinner was supposed to be about setting boundaries between Caspian and me, but instead, I'm going to the Crimson Vale equivalent of prom with him.

The rest of dinner passes by with me fighting this uncomfortable desire in my seat, while Caspian talks about who will be at the ball tomorrow night. I nod periodically to show I'm listening, although I'm barely taking in a word.

After dessert is finished, he sets his napkin down on the table. "Shall I escort you back to your room?"

I inhale a shaky breath. "Sure. Thank you."

We walk upstairs side-by-side in comfortable silence. At least, he seems comfortable. I'm trying—and failing—to maintain my composure.

Why did I let him walk me back? This is a bad idea waiting to happen.

I can already see how this will play out. He's going to walk me to my door and kiss me, and I'm going to cave and invite him in because I can't keep it in my pants.

I've been turned on all night, and I wouldn't mind if he helped to satisfy this aching lust in my lower belly.

The Bri I used to be would have slept with my dinner date without a second thought. But now, I have Caz to consider.

But if Caspian and Caz are the same person, is it really cheating?

We reach the door to my guest chambers, and I turn to face Caspian, wondering what he's going to say next. Is he going to ask to come in?

His nostrils flare as his gaze dips down my body. "I should wish you good night."

But he doesn't move, almost like he's waiting for me to invite him in.

"Yeah," I whisper, breathless from the stairs. "That's probably a good idea."

With a curt nod of his head, he steps back. "Good night, Bri."

He doesn't even kiss me goodnight before disappearing around the corner. The night is over and the temptation has passed.

But I'm confused. We had a great time tonight, or so I thought. Why wouldn't he kiss me?

Granted, the last time it happened, I pushed him off and ran away, so there's that. And the time before that, I slapped him, even if the kiss only happened under the dream spell.

He's being respectful of my boundaries, which is exactly what I wanted in the first place, so I should be thrilled.

With a heavy sigh, I turn the door handle to retreat into my room for the night.

Alone.

CHAPTER 10

I wake up to a whirlwind of activity the next morning. Elowen brings my breakfast tray to me in bed, but a man comes flying in behind her with an entourage of assistants.

"I am Aurelius!" he declares as he steps inside. He wears a flamboyant suit threaded with a blinding array of colors, and he flashes a confident smile from the foot of my bed.

When he grins, I nearly yelp at the sight of his teeth, each of which is filed into sharp points. Judging by that and the pointed ears, I'd guess he was a blood wraith if it weren't for his kaleidoscope irises that gleam in the light.

"Lady Briar, it is an honor to fit you for a dress for tonight's ball." He comes around the side of my bed and places a kiss on the back of my hand before giving an exaggerated bow. "But we have little time to work. Bring in the mannequins!"

His flurry of assistants dressed in black suits bring in seven mannequins, each with an extraordinary ballgown draped over the shoulders. They set them up around the bed in an arc for me to view.

"Please accept my deepest apologies, but I'm afraid we don't have time to do a custom dress, Lady Briar." Aurelius frowns and clutches his heart. "However, I hope one of these is to your liking. My ladies will take your measurements and leave you with fabric samples before the day is over. Moving forward, I will design you the most beautiful dresses, my lady; I assure you."

It's way too early for this chaos. The beginnings of a headache start piercing my skull, and I rub my temples with my fingers, digging deep.

Aurelius gives me another bow. "Please, take your time to review the dresses as you eat, and we will tailor your selection for you."

Everyone in the room stares at me, waiting for me to do something. Feeling far too exposed in my little negligee, I pull the covers up over my chest. My stomach grumbles, so I reach over and pluck a cherry off my breakfast tray.

The seven ballgown options are overwhelming. Each is a different brilliant hue with plenty of sparkle and ostentatious embellishments. None of them are anything I'd ever wear.

I pause on a ruby-red ballgown on the far end. The material is a stiff satin, with the skirt flowing down into a wide A-line. A slit runs high up the left leg, and the bodice is well-fitted to the mannequin's torso. The neckline is a deep V-shape that hangs off the shoulders.

The color reminds me of a certain someone, and I point at it. "That one."

"Splendid choice!" Aurelius claps, encouraging the entire room to applaud.

Ugh, please stop.

"You will be the belle of the ball in this design," he gushes. "The envy of all the ladies, and the object of every man's fantasy..."

There's only one man's opinion who matters tonight.

Elowen steps forward and curtsies. "I will let His Majesty know of your color selection. He wanted to coordinate his suit to match."

A small blush creeps into my cheeks. Yeah, this really is like prom. Maybe he'll give me a corsage.

Every head in the room turns toward me when I let out a giggle at the ludicrous thought.

"Ah, she is rendered giddy by her dress!" Aurelius beams and gestures toward me. "I am truly honored to delight you, Lady Briar."

I attempt a smile at him, but it feels more like a grimace.

It takes all day to get ready. I try on the dress before Aurelius and his assistants whisk it away for alterations, and Elowen draws me a bath before we move on to my hair and makeup. She styles my blonde hair into a loose chignon and finds a deep burgundy lipstick to match my dramatic eyeshadow. Somehow, she's able to cover my pale, sickly skin and the dark circles under my eyes. Only elven magic could do that.

Elowen's cosmetic skills are unrivaled, and she pulls off an astonishing transformation.

"Before we put on your dress, King Caspian wanted me to give you a gift to wear tonight." She reaches over to a stack of velvet boxes on the countertop. The first consists of an elegant gold necklace and matching earring set, each set with large rubies.

I run my finger along the center stone of the necklace, which reminds me of Caspian's eyes.

"And one more finishing touch." Elowen opens a large, square box and takes out a gold tiara inset with black diamonds. It's dainty, but when she places it atop my head, it completes the entire look.

I look like a fucking princess, and I can't remember the last time I felt this glamorous... or beautiful. It's been a while. My confidence was just another victim of my illness, but this is a glimpse of the old me. Even if it's only for one night.

Once Elowen is satisfied with her handiwork, she brings me downstairs to the ballroom, but we wait in the wings of the second-floor balcony. The dull roar of the crowd lilts upward toward us.

I take a step back and clutch the wall. "I don't know about this."

Elowen's eyes grow wide with alarm. "What's wrong?"

"There are so many people here." I point at the doorway. "I haven't been in a crowd since..."

Since before the pandemic.

My heart starts to race, and I lift my hand to my chest to quell the palpitations. I close my eyes and breathe through my nose.

What sort of diseases could they be carrying here in the Crimson Vale? Certainly nothing we've ever seen in my world. I'm going in there unvaccinated and unprotected.

"I can't get sick again," I whisper. "What if—?"

A soldier taps his staff in the doorway. "His Majesty presents, Lady Briar Casey!"

My mouth falls open, and I look at Elowen.

She motions me forward and gives me a comforting smile. "Everything will be fine. Have fun."

I glance at the open doorway into the ballroom, willing my feet to step forward.

This moment was bound to come. It's not like I expected to stay cooped up in my house forever. I had to navigate the airports to get to Utah, but at least then I had a face mask. It's become a sort of security blanket since I got sick.

Tonight, I have nothing to hide behind.

Elowen taps my back to usher me forward. It's now or never.

When I step through the doorway, I find myself on a small landing overlooking the ballroom. Below me is a crowd of people, who all turn their faces upward to stare at me. The chatter falls silent, and only a few whispers can be heard as I begin to descend the staircase.

My knuckles turn white as I grip the banister for dear life.

But when I find King Caspian in the crowd, I take a steadying breath. His presence is reassuring, and the tension in my shoulders releases on the exhale.

He gazes up at me from the center of the crowd, his conversation completely forgotten as he runs his palm over his chiseled jawline, drinking me in. When I reach the bottom of the stairs, he makes his way over to offer his hand..

Although his skin is cool to the touch, it ignites an unexpected warmth in my belly.

He leans down to whisper in my ear. "Bri, you are the most beautiful woman I have ever laid eyes on." King Caspian takes a step back to examine me up and down. "Musicians, play the first dance!"

Oh, shit. Here we go. I'll be lucky if I don't fall on my face.

He leads me to the center of the room, and the crowd parts to create a path for us. When the music begins, an upbeat waltz, Caspian steps off and sways our bodies in time with the melody. With expert skill, he leads me around the dance floor while keeping his ruby gaze locked on mine.

The crowd melts away, and it feels like it's just the two of us. He's rimmed in candlelight, creating a golden halo around him, and his strong arms support me as he spins me around, pushing me out and pulling me back into his firm, broad chest.

The song comes to an end, and the crowd applauds us, bringing me back to reality.

He takes a bow before leaning in. "How are you feeling?"

My legs wobble beneath my weight as I curtsy to him. "I think I need to sit down."

Caspian nods and leads me over to a pair of thrones set up at the front of the room. After he gets me settled he snaps his fingers, and a servant approaches with a tray of water goblets. I grab one of the glasses and take a long pull, drinking deeply.

Caspian doesn't take a seat but rather hovers over me, keeping close watch.

"Caspian, are you going to introduce us to your mate?"

Hold on. I recognize that voice...

As Caspian turns around, a trio of familiar faces comes into view. My eyes go round.

Caspian clears his throat. "Lady Briar, may I present my siblings, Prince Sebastian, Princess Seraphine, and Princess Talia of House Nezara."

Although they're identical to their counterparts on Earth, their eyes have a burgundy color to them—just like Caspian. The only other difference is that they're dressed like royalty rather than ranch hands.

I catch myself staring, so I incline my head to them in respect. "Nice to meet you."

Sebastian regards me with a frosty expression. "She should bow before the Prince and Princesses of the Crimson Vale."

Seraphine folds her arms across her chest. "She looks rather comfortable up there on the throne."

Talia says nothing, but she gives me a cold stare I've never seen her wear back on Earth. It looks out of place on her young, sweet face.

These are *not* the same Nezara siblings I know and love. But I shouldn't be surprised that Caz isn't the only Nezara with a dark one here in the Crimson Vale.

I glance at Caspian. "The others, Luke, Jonah, and Micah...are they here as well?"

"The little princes are too young for these balls." Caspian turns his furious gaze onto his siblings. "And you should show more respect toward the mate of your king."

The three of them shrink back, averting their gazes to the floor as they bow their heads.

"Of course, Brother," Sebastian says. "Please excuse us."

The three of them turn and disappear into the throng of people, but not without Talia throwing one last nasty glare back at me.

Caspian sighs and turns his gaze back onto me. "I assume you're acquainted with their light ones?"

I look out into the crowd. "Yeah, I am. They seem much different here in the Crimson Vale."

Caspian rests his hand on the chairback above my head and leans down, shielding me from the rest of the party. His eyes study my face for any sign of distress or illness.

He's my protector, and I'm surprised how quickly I came to rely on him in such a short time.

A sharp click against the marble floor grabs our attention. Caspian stiffens.

"My grandson, there you are. You've been avoiding me all week."

Caspian plasters a smile on his face before turning toward our new guest. "Lady Briar, may I present the queen dowager, Sybil of House Nezara."

The face of Caz's grandmother stares back at me, but her demeanor is unrecognizable—it is neither comforting nor compassionate. Her sharp, burgundy eyes peer out from her wrinkled face, which has a thick layer of makeup that looks out of place on her copper skin. The silver hair atop her head is combed back into a tight bun adorned with a tiara, and her dress comes up into a high, frilly collar.

"So, this is the human who has stolen my grandson's heart." She steps onto the raised platform with the help of both her cane and Caspian. She takes a seat on the throne beside me, sizing me up and down over her upturned nose.

Caspian grits his teeth. "Yes, Grandmother." The tension between them is palpable, thickening the air.

"I take it she's the reason you haven't joined us for dinner a single night this week?" She throws Caspian a severe glance. "Remember, family is everything."

He throws his hands into his pockets, steeling his expression into cool indifference. "As the king, I choose how and who I spend my time with. My fated mate has crossed into the Crimson Vale, and as you know, this is an unprecedented opportunity."

She stomps her cane against the floor. "None of the Nezaras have met their true mate in all the centuries we have been here. You are playing with fire and tempting fate, Grandson."

Caspian's eyes flash with rage. "You are the queen dowager, but I am your king. You will speak to me with respect."

She rises to her feet. "Robert would never have spoken to me in such a way. May he rest in peace." Queen Dowager Sybil gives me one last condescending look before she retreats back into the crowd.

"Don't pay her any mind," Caspian says.

However, the encounter has left him agitated, as evidenced by the twisted expression on his face.

I have no idea what to say to comfort him. Not after his entire family snubbed me.

A throat clears below Caspian, and we glance down at a throng of people milling near the platform. The receiving line has begun.

Lucky me.

Caspian nods curtly at the subject at the front of the queue. "Malrick."

"Your Majesty." Malrick bows. "And who is this vision of beauty that sits upon the throne?" He turns his jaundiced eyes onto me, giving me a smile with his sharp, yellowed teeth, and his long, black hair hangs in greasy strands down his back.

"This is Lady Briar Casey, my mate." Caspian gestures at him. "And this is Malrick, the alpha of the Ravenrock Clan."

"A pleasure." Malrick smirks and bows to me. "Your Majesty, does this mean you will be announcing your engagement tonight? It's about time this kingdom had a queen upon its throne once again. We need an heir."

Caspian steps closer to me and places a possessive hand on my shoulder. "There is no rush. Unlike you, I'm in my prime."

"Ah, I see." Malrick winks. "Trying to keep your options open before tying yourself down and marking her—?"

Caspian cuts him off. "Enjoy the party, Malrick. You're holding up the line."

"Apologies, Your Majesty." He gives us a deep bow. "Lady Briar, I look forward to seeing you again."

The hairs on the back of my neck stand on end. He turns around and stalks away toward the food display.

I glance at Caspian. "What was that about?"

He sits down on his throne beside me and leans in. "The Ravenrock Clan would rather see their alpha on the throne than a Nezara. They've coveted the kingdom for years."

I stare at Malrick's back across the room. "Isn't that treason?"

"It is." Caspian scoffs. "But unfortunately, we need them. They are one of the most powerful werewolf clans in the Crimson Vale, and they're very useful when it comes to war. It's a tenuous relationship."

One of the servants approaches Caspian and whispers something in his ear. He nods and turns back to me. "I must attend some business with one of the other werewolf packs. Will you be alright on your own?"

I glance at the receiving line, which is getting longer by the minute. "I can handle this. Go ahead." I give him a small smile.

He caresses my cheek with his thumb before standing up, and the corners of his hard mouth tick upward at me before settling back into that schooled expression of indifference. When he disappears into the crowd, the receiving line disperses; it seems they're only interested in me if I'm on the king's arm.

Rather than stay put, I climb off the dais and explore the buffet of treats and snacks. When I reach the table, the first thing I see are petit fours, so I pick one up and pop it into my mouth while perusing the many options. It's even more opulent than the dinners I spend with Caspian, and the assortment of food would rival the best buffets in Las Vegas.

Caspian will probably be gone awhile, and I don't know anyone else here. The dark Nezaras hate me, and no one else dares to approach me without a formal introduction.

This party sucks. I glance at the exit and think about heading back to my room.

Or... I could go visit Caz. I know where the dungeons are, so I could go there without Caspian escorting me.

Do I have enough time to check on Caz before coming back? I don't want Caspian to notice my absence, but I could use a friendly face right now.

I grab a cloth napkin off the end of the row and load it up with treats, and with one final glance around the ballroom, I slip out the door unnoticed.

After a week here at the castle, I've grown familiar with the first floor layout and make my way toward the courtyard. However, my heart sinks when I spot two guards standing watch at the iron gate, and I retreat into the shadows along the wall.

Shit. I didn't think this through.

Should I return to the ball? Head back before anyone notices my absence?

An idea pops into my head. It's reckless, but it might just work.

Mustering up as much confidence as I can, I adjust my tiara and emerge from the shadows, walking directly toward the guards. I school my expression the same way Caspian does, and meeting both their gazes, I give them a curt nod of acknowledgement.

I straighten my back to appear taller. "I wish to enter the dungeons."

One of the guards bows. "My apologies, Lady Briar, but we are under strict orders to not let you inside."

"But I was just here the other night, accompanied by the king himself," I protest.

"My lady—"

"Are you disobeying a direct order from the future queen of the realm?" I raise an eyebrow at him. "I won't forget this."

The two guards glance at one another, shifting with unease.

"Very well, my lady." The first guard unlocks the gate and pulls it open, allowing me to pass.

I give them each a nod as I stride through, but I resist the urge to thank them. I doubt any of the dark Nezaras show gratitude toward their servants.

The gate closes behind me, and I bite back a grin. I can't believe I pulled that off.

I set off quickly down the narrow passageway, but when I come to the first fork, I pause. Which direction did Caspian take?

I take the left passage, trying to remember the way to Caz's dungeon. So far, everything looks familiar, but at the next fork, I realize I've made a mistake, and I have to backtrack to take the other route.

Soon, I come across a row of cells, but they are much smaller and brimming with all sorts of creatures who look like they've been down here for a long time. Their eyes are sunken in, and they're so thin I worry that they'll starve to death.

"Help us!"

"Show us mercy!"

One of them reaches a hand through the bars, grabbing onto my dress. He pulls me closer to him. "Just a taste of your blood, my lady?" His filthy hand skims my leg through the slit in my dress.

When I look up into his glowing, red eyes, I gasp. *Blood wraith.*

I push him off as hard as I can and run, heart pounding. Without stopping, I push forward until pain shoots down my legs, and even then, I keep going. I haven't run like this in a long time, and my body gives out beneath me as I trip onto the cold, wet floor. The napkin full of treats falls to the floor, and small cakes and hors d'oeuvres tumble out onto the cobblestone.

My crown clatters to the floor a few feet away with a metallic clink.

"Caz!" I cry out, desperately hoping he hears me. "Caz! Where are you?"

I'm met with silence, and I hang my head while pounding my fist against the floor.

This was a stupid idea. I'm lost in a cold, damp dungeon, and I am so turned around I'll never find a way out.

"Caz! Please... I need you."

"Bri...?"

The call is distant, echoing off the stone walls, but I recognize it immediately as Caz.

I turn in the direction of my voice. "Caz! Where are you?"

"Bri, follow the sound of my voice..."

I crawl over to the crown and grab it, then stumble to my feet and push forward, gripping the stone wall beside me for support. My legs are shaking from weakness, but I have to find Caz.

"Caz! I'm coming!"

"Keep following my voice, Bri..." It's stronger this time. I'm getting closer.

After a couple minutes, the circular chamber comes into view at the end of the corridor, and I sprint toward it despite the protest of my legs. When I reach the entrance, I seek out Caz's cell and rush forward, falling to my knees in front of him.

I release the tiara in my hand, and blood drips from my palm where I gripped it for dear life.

He crouches on the floor and reaches through the bars to take my hands, inspecting the injury. "Bri, what happened? What are you doing here?"

I squeeze his hands hard. "I took a wrong turn, and someone tried to grab me…"

"You're safe now." He gives me a gentle smile. "Wow, look at you. You're all dressed up."

I take a deep, shuttered breath. "There's a ball going on right now. I saw your siblings and your grandmother, but they were their dark ones. They hated me."

Caz's lips set into a hard line. "Don't take it personally. They're evil. It's in their nature."

I want to tell Caz everything I've seen before I have to go back, but I'm hyperaware of the limited time I have left. "There was this creepy werewolf guy. He wants the throne, and I get a bad feeling from him. I don't know, Caz. This place is dangerous. I just want us to go home."

"I know; me too." He rests his forehead against the bars. "Come here."

I take a breath and lean in, pressing my forehead to his and closing my eyes. "I miss you. I wish you were upstairs with me."

He cups my cheek. "Me too. I wish I could hold you right now."

"I'd love that."

I lean in to give him a longing kiss, but I'm frustrated that the bars are keeping me from his embrace. We've been separated since we spent our first night together, and all I want to do is reaffirm our love, to be with him without this wall between us.

Without Caz, I don't know how I'll make it until the next full moon. I'm terrified and alone in the Crimson Vale, and I need him by my side. I need his reassurance, his protection, his love. His body.

Words aren't enough. I need to *feel* his reassurance, and with the clock ticking, it only heightens my urgency.

I deepen our kiss, moaning against his mouth. His lips grow more insistent, our bodies desperate to be closer.

I reach my hand through the bars to touch him, resting it on his thigh. "I want you."

His brown eyes appraise me with a hooded gaze. "I want you too, Bri. Being down here without you is torture." He glances behind me. "But here? Right now?"

His husky voice sends all the blood in my body rushing to my core. "Yes. Right now.

Please, Caz. We don't have much time."

Is it the worst possible timing? Yes. Does my body care about that? No. All it knows is that I need Caz, and I don't know if or when I'll be able to sneak down here again.

He's trapped down here, and even though he's comfortable, he's isolated. He has no one except for me.

Caz gives me another kiss, hard and quick. "All I do is sit and think about you, about that night, and how much I want to do it again." He lets out a breathless laugh. "Now that I've had sex, it's all I can think about. If I had a choice, I'd live in bed with you and never come out."

I grin, running my hand up his thigh. "If we didn't need to take breaks to eat and sleep and make a living, I think most people would fuck twenty-four-seven."

My hand grazes his growing erection, and both of us suck in a sharp breath. The aching heat between my legs, the one smoldering for him since I took his virginity, is unbearable.

"We don't have much time," I whisper. "Stand up."

He follows my lead as I scramble quickly to my feet, both of us panting hard. Once we're upright, I push my body forward, my breasts pillowing against the bars.

I grab his hand and guide it through the high slit in my dress. His fingers find the hem of my lace underwear, and he moves them aside to slip a finger into my wet entrance.

My head rolls back at the sensation. "Oh, Caz, yes." I close my eyes at his touch.

I'm able to fit my arms through the bars to unbutton his pants, although it's hard to focus with the way Caz is touching me right now.

"You feel so good." He groans as I free his thick erection from his pants.

I grip his heavy length tightly and begin to stroke, keeping a slow, steady rhythm.

Our lips find their way back to each other through the bars. I whimper into his mouth as he explores my insides with his finger, and he slips a second one inside, making my lower belly full and tight.

The forbidden nature of our rendezvous hurdles me closer to orgasm—anyone could walk in on us as we claw at each other, more animal than human. The clock is ticking, and it adds a thrilling element to our encounter as we ravish each other without shame.

"I've missed you," Caz whispers, curling his fingers and making me shudder. "All I do in here is read and stroke myself, wishing it was your hand instead of mine."

"Then let me make your fantasies come true." I grip Caz in one hand while keeping a firm grip on the bars with the other to steady myself. I increase the tempo of my strokes on his hard length as my head swims with dizzy lust.

It feels good not to think right now. All of my loneliness, guilt, and fear melt away when I'm in Caz's arms, and the only thing that matters right now is him and our mutual release.

I want to make him feel good in this miserable place, to remind him that I'm real, that I'm here, and that I still love him.

Caz hits my sweet spot, and I cry out toward the domed ceiling. Ecstasy overwhelms me, making my body shudder against his. A tidal wave of pleasure crashes through me, a divine feeling I want to last forever.

His hot seed spurts forth, coating the floor between our feet. Ropes of cum spill onto my dress, but I'm too wrapped up in my own pleasure to care. I pump a few more languid strokes to ensure I fully empty him.

Caz opens his eyes, which are glazed over with the haze of his release. "Bri, I love you—"

"Lady Briar, if you were so desperate to come, you should have asked me."

A chilling voice echoes behind us, bringing my pleasure to a screeching halt. I whip around to find Caspian standing at the entrance to the chamber, and his expression cold but his gaze burning with a glowing red fury.

Caz and I hastily untangle from one another, like two teenagers caught in the act by a parent. I smooth my cum-stained dress as Caz turns away to button up his pants.

Caspian folds his arms and leans against the wall, his calm demeanor more frightening than the rage licking at the edges of his control. "I would never allow you to degrade yourself by getting on your knees for me in this filth." His gaze narrows at the dirt on my skirt.

"I didn't... Caspian, I'm so sorry," I whisper, unable to fully meet his eye.

But why am I sorry? Caz is my boyfriend, and Caspian is...

What is Caspian to me? We haven't defined anything between us, and he knows my heart belongs to Caz.

So why do I feel so terrible right now?

The king scoffs. "No, you're not. But you will be."

My stomach drops at his dark, foreboding tone, and my skin prickles with warning.

Caspian lifts his finger and curls it, beckoning me forward. I take a step back, but my back hits the bars, reminding me that I'm trapped, and Caspian is blocking the only exit.

I blink, and Caspian is standing in front of me. "Lady Briar, I will not ask you again.

Come. Here."

He grabs my arm and hauls me closer, skimming his nose over my ear. "I am on the brink of my control, Bri. You do not want to test me right now, especially when you're wearing another man's cum stains on a dress *I* gave you."

"I thought you were the same person?" I struggle, and fail, to yank out of his grip. "That's what you keep reminding me, anyway."

His jaw ticks. "Keep talking and I'll make your punishment even worse."

"Get your hands off of her!" Caz rattles the bars.

A sickening sound of breaking bones and tearing flesh rips through the air. I peer over my shoulder as Caz drops to the ground on all fours, his body twisting and contorting. He releases a pained cry that morphs into a deep growl as he shifts into a werewolf, a growl so loud it shakes the room.

He charges the bars, knocking over the furniture in his path. I squeeze my eyes shut and steel myself for him to burst through and charge us. But when I try to pull Caspian out of the way, he doesn't budge.

The wolf slams headfirst into the iron before stumbling backward with a whine.

"Those bars are enchanted to contain werewolves." Caspian says coolly. "Try not to slam so hard that you kill yourself. Or do I need to remind you that our mutual survival depends on both of us staying alive?"

I steal one last glance at Caz as his wolf form lies on the damp floor in a heap, heaving with ragged breaths.

The image burns itself into my memory before he disappears.

Before I know it, we're standing near the entrance of the dungeons, with me hoisted over Caspian's shoulder like a sack of flour. I don't know how much distance we covered in the blink of an eye, but it leaves me absolutely nauseous.

When he sets me down, I bend over and hurl up bile onto the floor, gripping the wall to stay upright.

He leans against the wall and waits for me to finish, but he doesn't make a move to help me. When I finish, I straighten up and wipe the back of my hand across the back of my mouth.

But the moment I meet his gaze, he turns his back on me, striding toward the iron gate that leads into the courtyard. I struggle to keep up with his brisk pace.

As we pass under the portcullis, he rounds on the two guards. "If you let her into these dungeons again, I will have your heads."

They cower in fear, pressing their backs against the wall. "Y-Yes, Your Majesty."

"Don't punish them!" I call after him. "It's all my fault."

"You do not speak." He lifts his finger and points it at me. "My patience is about to snap, and I cannot be responsible for what I do to you if that happens."

Caspian grabs my wrist, pulling me behind him into the castle. Rather than return to the party, he leads me up the stairs to my room.

Without a word, he pushes me inside. Before I can round on him, he shuts the door behind me, and the lock clicks.

I sink to the floor, my legs shaking from climbing up the stairs, and crawl to the door on my hands and knees. When I try the door handle, it doesn't budge.

With my fists clenched, I pound on the door with both hands. "Let me out! Caspian!"

But he doesn't return.

CHAPTER 11

The next morning, I awaken to the click of the door being unlocked. I sit up on my makeshift bed on the sofa in the living room, peering over at the door.

Has Caspian come to talk?

I glance down at my negligee and the robe tied around my waist. But when I reach up to touch my hair, the loose chignon it was styled in last night is a tangled mess of knots.

I imagine I look like a wreck. The tears I cried throughout the night have probably streaked my makeup and rimmed my eyes red. If Caspian sees me like this—

Instead, Elowen walks in with the breakfast tray. "Good morning, Bri."

"Morning." I slump back into the sofa cushions.

She sets up my tray of food on the coffee table, but she shifts one of the flower bouquets to the side to make room. A dead flower petal flutters onto the floor.

Elowen surveys the bouquets in the room that Caspian left for me last week. "Shall I refresh your flowers for you?"

I sigh. "No, it's okay."

"It doesn't require much magic—"

"It's fine," I interrupt. "They can be removed."

Elowen enlists the help of a few other castle servants to remove the vases of dead flowers. I remain on the sofa in my pajamas and robe, watching the people come and go from the room.

They can leave, but I can't. When Elowen leaves, she gives me an apologetic look before shutting the door and locking it behind her.

She doesn't return until lunch with my meal tray, but like breakfast, I don't touch it. "When should we start getting ready for dinner?"

Elowen busies herself by wiping some imaginary dust on the mantle. "King Caspian has canceled dinner tonight. I am to bring you dinner in your room."

I let my spoon fall against the side of the bowl. "Is he planning on keeping me locked in here until the next full moon?"

She gives me a pitying look. "I don't know."

I'm afraid to ask her how he seems today. If I'm locked up here, it's a surefire sign that he's still mad.

The rest of the afternoon passes by at a snail's pace. I try to occupy myself with reading, but it's difficult to concentrate on the words when my mind is swirling with all sorts of dark prospects.

Is he going to punish Caz for what happened? Has he changed his mind about letting us return to our world? Will I be kept prisoner here forever? These are the questions that I need to ask him, but I can't if he refuses to see me.

Elowen brings my dinner tray right on schedule. She doesn't stay long and leaves the tray behind, leaving me to pick at my meal in lonely silence.

I draw my own bath and soak in there to pass the evening, but even the luxurious tub doesn't lift my mood. After towel-drying my hair, I slip into one of the skimpy nightgowns in the closet and climb into bed. My neck is sore from sleeping on the sofa last night, and my body welcomes the soft mattress and fluffy bedding.

As much as I try not to think about my complicated feelings for both Caz and Caspian, I can't escape them. Since being locked up, I've had nothing but time to think, to lose myself in my thoughts.

And yet I'm no closer to sorting them out.

I love Caz. That part is obvious.

But I feel guilty for Caspian catching us together. That's the part I can't work out.

Caspian has feelings for me because I'm his fated mate, but I don't feel the same way... even though I liked it when he kissed me. Caspian intrigues me, and I can't deny our chemistry.

But Caspian only likes me because I'm his fated mate, not because he knows me. Not the way Caz knows me. Except, if I go by that logic, then Caz is only attracted to me because of the mate bond.

Without it, would Caz see me as anything more than a friend? I'll never know.

I groan and burrow my face in the pillows.

My eyes finally start to close when the lock clicks in the living room.

I sit up in bed. "Hello?"

The door opens, and Elowen enters the room. I deflate.

She wrings her hands together. "His Majesty requests your presence in his private bedchambers."

I glance at the clock. It's nearly midnight. "Now?"

She nods.

I slide out from the bed and slip my feet into a pair of slippers on the floor. Elowen picks up my robe off a chair in the corner and helps me put it on.

Peering into the mirror, I try to comb through my hair with my fingers, which is still flat from the bath. I have no makeup on to cover the bags under my eyes.

Is he ready to talk about what happened yesterday? Or is he about to deliver the sinister punishment he promised?

As we make our way through the dim corridors, different scenarios pass through my head. The closer we get to his chambers, the more my nerves take hold, making my stomach flip and my body shudder.

Elowen leaves me once we reach the door and disappears down the hall. I lift my hand to knock, resigning myself to whatever fate awaits me on the other side.

"Enter." His tone is commanding and dark, and my hands shake as I push the door open.

His room is just how I recall it from the night he cast the dream spell on me. A fire roars in the fireplace, casting eerie shadows that dance across the walls. He sits in front of the fireplace, sipping on a glass of whisky. A blush creeps up onto my cheeks when I realize he's not wearing anything. Not even a pair of underwear.

So, I was right. He *is* going to fuck me tonight.

That should disgust me. And yet, a thrill coils itself between my legs, squeezing my bundle of nerves and making my body tremble with need.

Caspian scoffs, but he refuses to look at me. He continues to sip on his whisky, staring into the fire with a pensive look on his face. "Do you know how worried I was when I returned to the ballroom, and you were nowhere to be found?" He stands up, setting his whisky glass on the coffee table with a sharp tap.

When he turns, I take a step back at the heated look in his crimson gaze.

Like an animal stalking its prey, he steps toward me, closing the distance between us. I don't dare to breathe or make a sound. I don't even steal a glance at his dick, even though I'm desperate to avert my eyes from his intense gaze.

"You broke my trust, Bri."

I gulp. "But I'm with Caz. You know that."

He stops only inches away, his tall frame towering over me and crowding my space. "Do you know how it feels to find your mate in the arms of another?"

I shake my head.

"Well, you're about to find out." He reaches out to grab my wrist with the speed of a snakebite.

When he hoists me over his shoulder, I gasp, but within seconds, he throws me onto the bed like a ragdoll.

Caspian materializes at the foot of the bed, facing me as he begins to whisper a strange chant in an unfamiliar language, bowing his head and closing his eyes.

"Are you..." I gulp. "Are you casting a curse on me?"

He ignores me, muttering eerie words that make my skin tingle.

At last, his eyes fly open. "You may enter now." He stares at me, but he addresses someone else in the next room.

A woman enters from a service entrance off to the left wearing nothing but a sheer lace corset and a string garter belt, which holds up a pair of black pantyhose. She saunters into the room as her long, blonde hair sways from side to side, her blue eyes holding no trace of emotion.

When she turns her back toward me, her ass is on full display with nothing but a string thong between her cheeks.

Caspian stands at the foot of the bed, watching me for a reaction.

"What the hell is this, Caspian?" I try to sit up on the bed, but to my horror, my arms and legs are unable to move. I'm lying face-up against his pillows, which prop me up enough to have a front-row seat to this surreal scene unfolding in front of me.

"Is this another dream spell?" My voice rises in panic. "Why can't I move?"

He growls. "This isn't a dream, Bri. I've put a body-binding spell on you."

"Why?" I struggle to move, but my efforts are in vain. "Let me go."

"Not until you understand." He reaches out and puts his hand on the woman's head, pushing her to her knees.

Her head is eye level with his manhood, giving me a full view of his bare chest. When her head begins to bob back and forth, my stomach churns, and bile rises in my throat.

I think I'm going to be sick. She's giving him a blowjob, and he's forcing me to watch.

Caspian wraps his fingers into the woman's hair, grunting in satisfaction as he forces her head even deeper onto his cock. Her gagging fills the silence of the room as he holds her still and fucks her mouth with quick, vicious thrusts.

"How does it feel, Bri?" he growls, his fiery gaze holding mine. "Watching this whore who looks just like you choke on my cock?"

I try to look away, but I can't move my head. Something is squeezing my heart with so much pressure it hurts. My frustration manifests in the form of tears, which well up in my eyes.

"HOW DOES IT FEEL?" he roars, holding her in place as he thrusts his hips forward with one final push. His eyes remain fixed on mine as his mouth falls open, and he lets out a low groan with his release.

The spell releases its grip on my body, but I'm too stunned to move.

He doesn't even spare a glance at the woman on her knees before him. "You're dismissed." His tone is cold. Unfeeling.

Without a word, she stands up and leaves through the door she came in through. But before she disappears, she uses her thumb to wipe off the excess cum leaking from the corner of her mouth.

Yep, I'm definitely going to be sick.

Caspian approaches the bed, leaning against the frame with his arms folded across his chest. But the icy expression on his face thaws slightly when he meets my tear-streaked gaze.

He turns his back on me. "Go back to your room." His voice is quiet. "I will see you tomorrow."

Clapping a hand over my mouth, I slide off the mattress until my feet touch the floor. My body is overcome with violent shudders as tears stream down my face.

This punishment wasn't physical, but I wish it was. That would hurt less than this.

No, this was personal. He wanted to hurt me the way I hurt him, and fuck did it hurt.

But I shouldn't be surprised. He's the dark one. For as good and kind as Caz is, Caspian is rage and cruelty wrapped into one person.

Two halves of the same soul. The light and the dark.

When I reach my room, I make a straight shot for the toilet and retch, bile burning my throat on the way up.

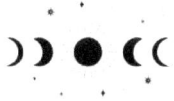

The next morning, when Elowen enters my bedroom, I'm already awake. She pauses beside the bed, staring down at me with her brows furrowed in concern. "Are you alright?"

I must look like shit.

With a groan, I pull myself into a sitting position. "Am I allowed out of my room now?"

She gives me a gentle smile. "Yes. In fact, His Majesty has requested your presence at today's treasury meeting with the Royal Council."

Fucking great.

Elowen does my hair and makeup before helping me into my dress for the meeting—a floor-length sheath dress in simple black with a turtle neck and billowy sleeves. I haven't prepared anything, and I have no clue what to expect or who will be there. I'm walking into this meeting blind, and I don't appreciate the short notice.

When I arrive, Caspian is sitting at the head of the table, joined by Prince Sebastian and another person I don't recognize. The unfamiliar man is elderly, with a pair of wiry glasses sitting on the end of his nose, and he wears a set of loose-fitting, brown robes.

Caspian waves me in. "Lady Briar, please, take a seat."

Okay, I guess we're going to pretend last night didn't happen. Fine by me, especially since he refuses to look me in the eye when addressing me.

I take the available seat beside the elderly man and glance around the empty table. "Is this everyone?"

Caspian nods. "For this particular treasury meeting, yes."

"If we were discussing matters of diplomacy," Prince Sebastian says, "we would have the full council here. But a simple garden renovation is too small a matter to bother the important heads of state."

I fold my arms. "So, they sent you instead?"

The corner of Caspian's mouth twitches, but just when I think he might actually smile, he steels his expression once again. "Brother, you are my royal advisor. I need you involved in all matters concerning the council."

Prince Sebastian pins me with a murderous glare. "And you just want to spend time

125

with your precious mate, even if it's wasted in a dull meeting."

"Lady Briar, may I present Lord Peter, the master of the Royal Treasury." Caspian gestures toward the elderly man.

Lord Peter nods politely at me, his eyes magnified behind the glasses like a bug. "A-A p-pleasure," he stutters.

It takes a moment to realize he's not stuttering in fear—it's age. This guy should have retired twenty years ago.

"Have you prepared the budget for the renovations for Lady Briar?" Caspian directs his gaze to Lord Peter beside me.

"Y-Yes, Your M-Majesty." He sifts slowly through a pile of papers in front of him with wrinkled, shaky hands.

Sebastian scoffs.

We all wait in a drawn out silence until he produces a document, which he passes to me. It's a simple handwritten budget, but I'm not sure how *850 pieces of gold* translates into a currency I'm familiar with.

"T-This is from a b-budget the late Queen Vaelora used early on in her r-reign to r-renovate the garden, may she rest in p-peace. The last time the g-garden was r-renovated was shortly after her m-marriage to His M-Majesty, K-King Robert, may he also rest in p-peace. I hope you f-find this useful."

Robert was Caz's father, who was killed in a werewolf battle back on Earth. But Caz's mother was named Laurel, not...

"Vaelora?" I ask. "I thought your mother's name was Laurel?"

At last, Caspian meets my gaze, his eyebrows furrowed together in confusion. "No. My mother's name was Vaelora."

"But Caz's mother was named Laurel, so shouldn't your mother be the same?"

"Ah." With a sideways glance at the door, Caspian's jaw clenches. "If Laurel was my father's fated mate, destiny would have kept them apart here in the Crimson Vale. That is the curse." Caspian rises to his feet, adjusting his suit. "Now, if you have everything you need, this meeting is dismissed."

Within seconds, he strides from the room, like he can't get away fast enough.

This hot and cold act from Caspian is giving me whiplash. He barely looked at me during that all-too-brief meeting this morning, and it bothers me more than it should.

I wish we could go back to our old dynamic, when he would tease me and I would rebuke his advances. But now that he's not pursuing me, my ego is bruised.

And tonight, I'm feeling rather petty.

According to Elowen, I'm expected to dine with the king—and I'll be wearing the sexiest dress I could find in my wardrobe. Two of us can play this game.

I bite my lip to suppress the conniving grin on my face.

Elowen helps me slip into a tight, burgundy bodycon leotard with a *deep* V-neck. A sheer black floor-length skirt attaches to my waist, accentuating my leg peeking out from the slit with a strappy black heel.

We pair it with the darkest shade of red lipstick Elowen can find, and the black crystal necklace Caspian gifted me.

If he won't meet my eye, fine, but at least I'll give him something else to stare at.

With one last look in the mirror, I wipe a bit of excess lipstick from the corner of my mouth and head downstairs.

College Bri was brimming with confidence. She knew her assets and exactly how to flaunt them to get attention from men. And tonight, I need to tap into that younger version of me to give Caspian a taste of his own medicine.

My heels click against the stone castle floor as I enter the dining room, announcing my arrival. Caspian glances up from his seat at the end of the table, and when his eyes land on me, they practically bulge out of his head.

Yep, the dress has the effect I was going for. I pretend to ignore him as I take my seat across the table from him. To drive the point home, I drag my fingertip along the steep neckline, all the way south until my hand disappears under the table.

"Leave us," Caspian barks at the servants.

They scatter quicker than a flock of pigeons.

The king clenches his jaw. "What in the nine hells are you wearing?"

I start to fill my plate, perusing the variety of foods presented on the table. "What do you mean?"

He clenches his fist beside his empty plate. "I cannot have you parading around the castle, showing off your body in an outfit that leaves very little to the imagination. It's not befitting of a future queen."

I look down at the outfit. "But this was in the wardrobe you provided."

His jaw ticks. "Not all those outfits are meant to be worn in public."

"Oh, if that's the case, I can take it off now." I slip one of the straps down my shoulder. "After all, if you can be naked in front of other people, so can I—"

Caspian's chair falls to the floor with a loud crash as he stands up, his hands coming down hard on the table. "Damn it, Bri! Why are you toying with me?"

I startle, recoiling against the back of my chair. "You mean the way you toyed with *me* last night?"

"Ah, I see." He folds his arms. "You're throwing a temper tantrum."

"A temper tantrum?" I scoff. "Please, this is nothing. If you want to hurt me, fine, but don't be surprised when I bite back."

A tense silence falls over the room, blanketing the air with a suffocating heaviness.

"What do you want?" he says through gritted teeth.

I grab my napkin off the table and smooth it over my lap. "A civil conversation, for starters." I arch an eyebrow at him. "Unless you want to keep up this dick-measuring contest to see which of us can be the biggest asshole? Because I'll give you a run for your money, Dark One."

He shakes his head and chuckles under his breath. "Such a waste."

I blink. "What is?"

"Not putting that filthy mouth of yours to better use."

My cheeks burn hot, and Caspian smirks in triumph. With a lazy wave of his hand, his chair lifts off the floor with magic, setting itself right again at the head of the table. He sits down and leans back, appraising me with heat in his gaze.

Well, at least we're past the not-talking-to-each-other bit.

I start to load my plate. "I wanted to ask you something this morning, but you left in such a rush I didn't get a chance. It's about the curse."

He lifts his glass decanter off the table and pours it into his glass. Blood. Ew.

I rip my gaze away from the contents of his glass and focus on not losing my appetite. "You mentioned your mother and Caz's mother are different people."

He sets his pitcher down. "I don't hear a question."

I resist the urge to roll my eyes. "You said your fates are tied. That if one half of your soul dies, so does the other. So, when Caz's dad, Robert, died, that means the dark Robert died, too."

He swirls his glass, but when he speaks, there's an edge of impatience to his tone. Probably from mentioning Caz's name. "Again, where is your question?"

I huff. "I'm getting to it. Not all of us have super speed, you know."

Unlike me, he doesn't resist the urge to roll his eyes.

"My question is: Did your father die the same way Caz's did? And how did your mother die if her fate isn't tied to anyone in my world?"

I steel myself for a snarky response, but to my surprise, Caspian sits back in his chair and considers my questions. He rests his elbow on the armrest and folds his fist under his chin as though deep in thought. His eyes glaze with a distant look.

He takes a deep breath. Judging by the dark expression on his face, he's coming up for air from a painful past he'd rather not revisit. When he finally breaks the silence, his voice is quiet and unsteady. "They were murdered by a rival werewolf pack." He continues to stare off at nothing. "Those traitors wanted to see Malrick on the throne. So, while my parents were traveling through the southern region, they were ambushed and killed."

"Oh, my God," I whisper. "I'm so sorry."

"They were coming for me next, but I sent our armies to find them and bring them to justice. To this day, Malrick insists he knew nothing of the plot, but I don't believe it. So for now, I'm keeping a close watch on him."

"How old were you?"

He sighs. "Seventeen. The Royal Council wasted no time planning my coronation, and I was instilled as the king of the realm the day following their deaths."

"I'm sorry." I bring a hand to my aching heart. "No one should lose their parents that young." I take a deep breath, knowing that Caz is a touchy subject. "That's the same age Caz was when his parents died, but they were killed by blood wraiths who came through the portal."

He continues to rest his chin in his hand, his eyes reflecting the flames crackling in the fireplace. "When our light one dies, that death is mirrored in our world, one way or another. As for the death of our mothers, it is simply an unfortunate coincidence."

Although he tries to hide it, there's a deep sadness he carries with him—the same sadness weighing Caz down. A sorrow that unites them, whether they realize it or not.

Maybe they're more similar than just their appearance.

"I'm so sorry, Caspian. I'm sorry for your loss." I push my plate away having lost my appetite.

He hums, staring into the fire. "You know, you're the first person to offer their condolences."

"What do you mean? It's been over three years, hasn't it?"

"Yes, well, I could never show my grief to the world, could I?" He drops his arm over the side of the chair, resting his head against the upholstered back of his tall chair. "Everyone believed me to be unaffected by their deaths."

I shake my head. "But it's normal to grieve for your parents, no matter who you are."

"Unless you are the king of the Crimson Vale." Caspian lets out a long, shaky exhale. "Growing up, I was never allowed to show weakness. I would receive a beating if I cried, so I learned how to mask my emotions at a young age."

"That's awful." That explains why he's so good at schooling his expression into cool indifference.

"But necessary," Caspian says. "In this world, you get eaten alive at the first sign of weakness. If anyone saw my grief, they would seize that opportunity to take the monarchy and put my surviving family at risk. It would mean the end of House Nezara—which means the end of the light Nezaras in your world, too."

I look down at my fingers laced in my lap. "You can show your grief to me. It's okay."

Caspian lets out a hollow laugh. "A grieving man is an unattractive one." His expression quickly sobers. "You don't need to see that side of me."

"But I want to see that side of you." When I rise to my feet, the chair scrapes the floor beneath me. "This is the most you've opened up to me since we met, and it's because you trust me enough to be vulnerable."

With caution, I approach Caspian on the opposite end of the long table, running my hand along the edge of the wood. He watches me, his guard going up little by little with each step I take.

I don't want him to throw the wall back up between us, so when I reach him, I bring my hand to his cheek. "Don't do that. Don't shut me out."

The tendons in his neck are strained as he tenses under my touch.

"Trust goes both ways, remember?" I say. "I opened up to you about my illness, and you were kind about it. What makes you think I won't do the same?"

His shoulders relax as he lowers his shields. But when they come down, I find a broken man sitting before me. All of my anger toward him, my guilt, my jealousy, dissipate as we stare at one another in silence.

Caspian closes his eyes and leans into my touch. "I never mourned their deaths. I just..." His throat bobs as he swallows, but there's an unmistakable waver to his voice that takes me by surprise.

"Hey, it's okay." I sit on the armrest of his chair and wrap my arms around his neck. "It's okay."

He burrows his face into my chest, inhaling my scent, while I stroke my fingers through his thick, dark hair.

"You can show your weakness to me," I murmur, bringing my lips to the top of his head.

He glances up, revealing a single tear stain on his cheek, which I wipe away with my fingertips.

"Bri..." he whispers longingly, his eyes searching mine. He pulls me down onto his lap and clutches me for dear life. "Bri," he repeats, sighing softly.

Caspian burrows his face into my neck, brushing his lips against my jawline.

I hesitate only for a second before I meet his mouth, planting my lips onto his with a delicate motion.

Our kiss starts slowly, exploring one another with caution. It's a side of Caspian I've never seen, and I peel back each remaining layer of his hardened facade little by little, until I find his rawest, truest self at the center.

And beneath the mask is a frightened young man carrying the weight of the world on his shoulders, with no one to shoulder his burden with.

His arms wrap around my waist, snaking his hand up my back to pull me closer against his hard chest. With a sharp inhale, his lips move with greater urgency against mine as if to devour me whole.

He doesn't just want me. He *needs* me. Desperately.

I let out a moan and roll my body against his, putting my entire self into this kiss. All I crave is more intimacy beyond what we're sharing now, to bring our bodies closer together, if that's even possible.

I want to melt into him.

He scoops me up in his arms and rises to his feet, kicking his chair backward behind him. Reaching behind me, he sweeps all the food and cutlery off the table, sending them to the floor with a thundering crash. He hoists me onto the edge of the wood, my legs falling open on either side of him.

I've never had a man take control like this. Desire explodes within me, sparking a throbbing need in my core. His burgundy eyes hold my gaze as he stares down at me, his face darkened with pure lust.

As I gaze back up at him, I forget everything: my loyalty to Caz, our argument, and the fact I don't belong in this world. I can't think of a single reason not to want him.

All I know right now is I'm ready for him to take me to places I've never been before.

He runs his hands along my thighs, inching upward toward my stomach. "Do you enjoy teasing me with this sheer dress of yours?"

Unable to form words, I nod while panting like a cat in heat.

Caspian runs his hands up my torso toward my breasts. "I can't have anyone seeing you in this." He grabs the front of my dress and tears it in half with a loud rip.

The shredded fabric falls open around me.

Did I mention I didn't wear any lingerie tonight?

The food is on the floor, but my naked body is sprawled out on the table like a buffet. And by the way he licks his lips and rakes his eyes over my body, he's ready to feast.

My nipples peak at the sensation of the cold air in the room, and my pussy clenches in nervous anticipation. The seconds pass by as he drinks me in, and the ache between my legs becomes unbearable.

I tighten my legs around his waist, pulling him closer against my entrance. "Are you going to fuck me, or what?"

When he bumps into me, I moan at the hard erection straining beneath his pants.

"Not only am I going to fuck you," he says, unbuckling his belt, "but I'm going to make you scream my name so loud the entire kingdom will know you're mine."

With a hard yank, Caspian lets his pants fall to the ground at his feet. His heavy erection springs forth to graze my inner thigh, and I gasp at the hard, velvety texture.

When he brings his fingers to my entrance, he begins to move in slow, tantalizing circles. He doesn't enter me, but rather uses his three middle fingers to stimulate my opening.

Caspian smirks. "You're so wet for me."

My head rolls back onto the table as I let out a low, animalistic groan. I've never heard such a noise escape my lips, but a primal need is consuming my body as he works against me. Caspian coils my need around his fingers, and I'm on the cusp of climax, panting hard and trembling with anticipation.

He brings me to the brink of orgasm... only to stop.

As he withdraws his hand, his knuckles brush against my entrance. A shudder rolls through my body.

"Caspian, please," I whimper.

"You can tease me all you want, but I can't tease you, is that it?" He leans over, caging me in with his arms on the table. "Don't play with fire if you don't want to get burned, Bri."

He presses me further against the table. I buck my hips to grind against his cock, and it twitches with arousal.

"Mmm, kitty has claws," Caspian hums.

He straightens up and rips off his tie, discarding it on the floor. He yanks his jacket off before ripping his shirt open, which sends buttons flying in all directions.

My eyes widen as he climbs up onto the table, his naked body sliding over mine. My legs wrap around his waist on instinct, drawing him closer, and he grabs my wrists and pins them above my head.

"What do you have to say for yourself, now?" he asks in a low voice, his cool breath fanning my face.

"I want it." My voice quivers.

"You want what?" He smirks, teasing my entrance with the tip of his manhood. "Use your words, Bri."

I moan. "I want your cock inside me."

With a rough thrust, he plunges his entire length into my throbbing sheath. We both let out a deep moan as he stills, our bodies adjusting to the other.

And, God, it feels so, so good. He fits me like our bodies were made to interlock together.

He slowly pulls out, but just before he withdraws the tip, he slams into me once more. He continues like this, slowly pulling out and plowing back in.

As he pumps inside me, I cry out, growing louder as he moves faster. My body slides back further on the table with the force of each subsequent thrust, and I'm on the brink once again, eyes rolling back in my head as his tempo increases with each entry. I want to clutch onto him, but his hands continue to restrain my wrists above me. I want to wriggle beneath him and release some of this tension, but his body is forcing me to hold still against this onslaught of pleasure, intensifying the experience.

And that's when I hit my climax, shattering beneath him as I shout at the top of my lungs. "Oh, God, yes!" My vision goes blurry, and I'm seeing stars as he plunges into me over and over. "Yes, Caspian, YES!"

The infinite wave of orgasm won't let up, and my cries devolve into incoherent, unrestrained screaming. I'm certain the entire castle can hear me, but I don't care because I'm swept up in pure euphoria.

Caspian slows his pace as he spills his seed inside of me with a long groan, using my pussy to pump himself empty.

His muscular body, glistening with sweat, collapses onto the table beside me, releasing my wrists in the process. My arms are boneless, and my legs tremble from clenching so tight around his waist.

We lie together, too breathless to speak as we come down from our high, slowly, gently, like feathers floating down to the ground.

This is wrong. I just betrayed Caz.

And yet, this feels so perfect, so... right.

CHAPTER 12

The next morning, I wake up in Caspian's bed, grinning from the mind-blowing sex we had last night.

To my disappointment, the spot next to me is empty, but a handwritten note sits on the pillow.

I had an early meeting with the Council, but please stay as long as you'd like. You look gorgeous lying naked in my bed. —Caspian

And just like that, my stupid grin returns.

I set the note down and stretch out, feeling the luxurious silk sheets slide against my bare skin. But then it hits me how complicated things are now.

I cheated on Caz. The whole they're-the-same-person argument won't hurt him any less when he finds out.

Caz puts me on a pedestal, worshiping me like a goddess. He puts his faith in me to show him what to do during sex, and the idea that I'm his one and only makes me want to show him everything I know.

But with Caspian, I want him to show me everything *he* knows. With him, sex is uncharted territory. He brings experience to the bedroom and thrills me with the way he dominates me..

When Caspian first made his proposition, I was absolutely certain I would choose Caz when the full moon rises again. But now that my heart is opening up to the alpha king, my resolve is wavering.

How am I supposed to choose between two halves of the same person? I am the fated mate of both Caz and Caspian, but the curse has always kept the dark ones from ever knowing them. And my heart breaks for Caspian, for growing up believing he'd never find true love because an ancient curse made it impossible.

But why me? Why am I the first fated mate to cross over into the Crimson Vale?

As if the Curse wanted to make sure you found your way here...

I bolt upright in the bed as my mind works on overdrive, racing with thoughts and questions about destiny and ancient curses.

Is the curse weakening after all these centuries? Am I supposed to break the curse by staying in the Crimson Vale?

Whatever the reason, the choice has been put in my hands. I'm destined to wind up with either Caz or Caspian, and my future hinges on the decision I have to make. When the full moon comes around, I need to be absolutely, one hundred percent sure I know what my heart wants. I love Caz, but what if I come to love Caspian just as much, if not more? Despite years of friendship, Caz and I had a whirlwind romance this summer, so why couldn't it be the same with me and Caspian? It's the mate bond at work.

Don't I owe it to myself—and to them—to find out?

I make a promise to myself, right here and now, to make the most of my time with the alpha king. Why fight the undeniable, *fated* attraction I feel toward Caspian, especially if I decide he's the one I want to spend the rest of my life with?

But the thought of never seeing Caz again devastates me. I'm not sure I could bear to lose him. And if I choose to leave, the decision to leave Caspian behind won't be as easy as I thought.

My heart starts thudding erratically in my chest. My pulse thrums in my ears, drowning out all other noise.

Heart palpitations. It steals my breath away, and I lean back against the pillows while clutching a hand to my chest.

A sudden onset of fatigue washes over my body, as though something is siphoning the energy right out of me.

Last night's sexual marathon—which continued into the wee hours of the morning—along with the hefty weight of my decision, has left me drained and headed straight into a crash. I need to rest, especially if I'm going to have this much cardio exercise between the sheets with Caspian in the coming weeks.

Taking up Caspian's invitation, I spend the rest of the morning in his bed, slipping in and out of consciousness. In that haze between sleeping and wakefulness, images of the garden renovation swirl in my mind, each more vibrant and elaborate than the last.

I awaken to the sound of the door creaking open. Elowen enters the room with a lunch tray, and I blush at the thought of her finding me like this—naked in the king's bed.

Tugging the sheets up to my chin, I whisper, "Good morning."

"Good morning, Bri." She sets the tray down on the bed, along with a fresh dress she brought for me. At least I won't have to do the walk of shame back to my room.

"Elowen, you've said you're good with plants, right?"

She blushes. "So I've been told."

"I need your help with something."

After I eat and change, Elowen accompanies me to the garden, where I call a meeting of the castle servants tasked with helping me. I run through my vision for the upcoming ball on Saturday, and although we don't have much time to complete all the work required, they appear enthusiastic about it. Perhaps they needed something to shake things up around here.

Elowen comes up with some creative suggestions. Her elven magic allows her to manipulate some of the dead shrubbery back to life, allowing us all to bounce ideas off of one another for the landscaping.

"I'd also like a light menu appropriate for a garden party," I mention to the castle's head chef. "Let's use garden herbs in the cocktails and incorporate fresh fruit into the desserts. Perhaps some more savory hand pies and canapes so people can mingle while they eat?"

He bows politely to me. "I will draft a menu for your final approval by tomorrow evening."

"Have the candlemaker send over a thousand candles," I direct one of the other servants. "I want floating candles in the fountain and the pond and pillar candles along the pathways."

I'm so wrapped up in the planning I don't hear another set of footsteps approach from behind.

"Excuse me, Lady Briar. Might I have a word in private?"

I glance up from my notes to find Caspian leaning against one of the stone pillars, which is covered in a thick layer of wild ivy. His expression is unreadable except for the wicked gleam in his eye.

"Of course, Your Majesty." I curtsy to him before turning back to the group. "Everyone, you have your tasks. There isn't much time, so let's get to work and make this happen."

I dismiss the servants before approaching Caspian. He motions for me to follow, then leads me down a stone breezeway lined by Roman columns. Once we're hidden behind a canopy of overgrown vines, he pushes me up against one of the pillars.

"I love watching you boss around my servants," he says in a low voice, burrowing his face into the side of my neck. His cool breath fans my skin, sending a pleasant tingle down the length of my body.

Grabbing his lapel, I pull him closer. "Is that so? What else do you like to watch?"

"Mmm, I have a few ideas." He nibbles on my earlobe, making me moan softly. "And they all involve you being naked."

God, the things he says make me want to climb him like a tree.

The two of us act like we've been in a relationship for months, not hours. But it's so easy with him. As easy as breathing.

But the unspoken tension underneath it all is the steady ticking of the clock, counting down to the moment I have to decide between staying here and returning to my world. It's not like we have the luxury of time to take things slow.

Caspian chuckles, his broad chest rumbling in a comforting, delightful way, but he pulls back just enough to meet my gaze. "I must say, Bri, it turns me on watching you work. You're a natural."

"If it turns you on so much, then why aren't you doing anything about it?"

He smirks, his ruby eyes glinting with mirth. "Don't worry. I have plans for you later, but first, I wanted to take you on a tour of the town."

I roll my eyes. "I think I saw enough when your guards captured me and brought me to the castle."

His hands splay over my hips, holding me close. "Which is why I'm making it up to you. You'll get to see the village from the royal carriage this time."

I sigh, fighting the growing discomfort between my thighs. He glances down and runs his tongue over his bottom lip. Almost as if he knows how wet I am.

How embarrassing would that be?

"Okay," I say. "It's a date."

"Excellent."

Caspian takes my hand and leads me into the castle, and we don't stop until we reach the courtyard. A black carriage pulled by two dark winged horses awaits us, and the familiar dire wolf sigil of House Nezara adorns the coach.

"I want to show you the kingdom you would rule over should you decide to remain here as my queen." His tone is serious, although the glimmer of hope in his expression is unmistakable.

Yep. Definitely *not* taking things slow.

After he helps me into the carriage, Caspian takes a seat beside me. The interior is private, with comfortable red upholstered seats and a black interior. Glass windows on the doors provide a view of the outside, but the red velvet curtains could be drawn for privacy if we needed it.

I might need it if I can't get this lust tampered down.

"I won't bore you with the details," Caspian says, "but for the longest time, the Crimson Vale was ruled by the werewolf clans. Each clan had control of a territory, but there were constant land disputes and power grabs, and the realm was a place of chaos." He glances out the window, eyes lost in thought, and smirks. "Of course, House Nezara saw an opportunity, and over the centuries my family seized control of the Crimson Vale, uniting all the werewolf packs, their territories, and their subjects under one monarchy."

"So that's why you're not only the ruler of the Crimson Vale, but also the alpha king?"

Caspian turns his ruby gaze onto me. "Intelligent as always, my lady."

As we ride through the quaint village square, I'm brought back to that night when Caz and I first arrived. It feels so long ago already, even though I only landed in the Crimson Vale ten nights ago.

Only twenty nights left until I have to make a decision. It's not enough time.

We roll past the barn where Caz and I first made love, and a pang of guilt spears my chest. Is he worried about what happened to me after Caspian caught us touching each other in the dungeons? For all he knows, Caspian strung me up and tortured me for sneaking behind his back.

But after he finds out about Caspian and I, Caz might want to string me up himself.

"Why the frown?" Caspian asks, placing a hand on my knee.

I glance up at him, plastering a smile on my face. "Nothing."

He leans forward to peer out the window. "This is the village that provides the primary goods and supplies for the castle. A witch's apothecary is just there, and they produce a number of medicines for the mages who care for the royal family and staff."

"Do the blood wraiths live here?" I ask.

"Some do. Most lower blood wraiths—the feral beasts—live in the forests. The more civilized ones live here in the village."

Staring at a little girl playing with a ball, I ask, "What other types of creatures live here?"

The little girl looks up at the carriage with startling black eyes, and I gasp. There's no white around her pupils, only endless black pits.

"Elves, witches, mages, werewolves, demons, goblins," he lists, using his fingers to count them. "Those are the intelligent lifeforms here, anyway. The blood wraiths are less civilized."

I straighten in my seat. "They left a message when they came through the portal. A crop circle in the shape of your house sigil."

He nods. "They're uncivilized, but very in tune with nature like the elves. No doubt they picked up on the ancient magic that binds the land in your world, telling them that my soul called out to you."

"I'd tell them thanks, but they tried to kill me," I mutter.

"Not that you left any of them alive to offer thanks." Caspian appraises me with a hint of... is that pride?

I glance out the window at the bustling market, where stalls line the street in front of the medieval buildings. "Are there any humans here?"

He shakes his head. "None. You are the first of your kind to pass through."

Some of the people have pointed ears or strange eye colors, and a few have a greenish skin tone. But do these small features really make them so different from me? From a distance, they could be mistaken for humans. They merely go about their daily lives, earning a living to make ends meet and care for their families.

Would it really be so bad, becoming queen? says that small voice in my head. *You could make a difference with your power; give your life meaning again...*

What do I have waiting for me back on Earth? Besides my grandparents, Caz is my only reason for going home. I can't stand my parents, and my life is so screwed up that I have nothing to return to.

But here, I could be someone important. Somebody more than the sick girl with no college education or future.

If Caz could stay behind, too, it would be perfect.

140

By the time we return to the castle, my eyelids are heavy. I lose my footing while getting out of the carriage as vertigo hits me on the way down. Caspian catches me, holding me steady while he gazes down at me in concern.

The same way Caz looked at me when I stumbled out of his truck.

His brows plunge. "I'm calling the mage."

"Really, it's not a big deal," I insist. "I just... pushed myself a little too hard today."

"I'm calling the mage, and that's final."

Caspian carries me all the way upstairs to my room in half the time it normally takes. He doesn't go at his full speed to avoid me getting sick again, but that still doesn't stop the nausea by the time we reach my door.

When he deposits me onto the bed, he orders Elowen to help me into my nightgown while he fetches the mage.

Once I'm in my negligee and robe, Elowen pulls the covers over my lap. Now that I'm settled in bed, I'm not sure if I'd be able to get up if I wanted to. Gravity weighs down on my limbs to keep me from moving, and the room is in a blurry haze as my vision blurs in and out of focus.

I don't want to see a mage or a doctor or anyone claiming they can help me. Back on Earth, every appointment left me with more questions, and I would usually sit in my car afterwards and cry. My faith in health care has been completely squashed by these so-called professionals who treat me like a hypochondriac.

Anxiety gnaws at my gut at the thought of another person telling me it's all in my head.

Your bloodwork came back normal. You're perfectly healthy.

You don't meet the criteria of any known disease.

I'm sorry, but we don't know enough about this virus to help you.

A knock at the door yanks me back to reality and away from the negative thought spiral. It opens, and Caspian fills the doorway with his broad shoulders.

One look at his face is all it takes to breathe easy again.

Caspian enters the room, followed by another man. "Bri, this is the mage, Lucius the Wise."

He gestures to an elderly man who looks quite a bit like Lord Peter, the master of the Treasury. However, his eyes seem more alert, and fortunately for me, his hands don't shake.

The mage bows. "Lady Briar, I hear you are dealing with a myriad of symptoms. Tell me what is going on."

I glance at Caspian, unsure how to explain my medical history in a way a non-human would understand. I'm not familiar with the medical terminology here in the Crimson Vale.

"Well, I had a nasty illness about six months ago," I begin, trying to frame this the right way. "But instead of recovering, new symptoms started popping up."

I sigh and let my head loll back against the pillows. My eyes close as I recall my list of symptoms, a script I've orated so many times it's muscle memory by now. "I have consistent brain fog and fatigue. I get confused easily and can't focus, and sometimes I have trouble remembering words. Oh, and don't forget the shortness of breath, vertigo and dizziness, and heart palpitations. My muscles and joints ache often, especially if I push myself too much, and sometimes I feel like my back can't even support my upper body. I can still read, but things just seem out of focus. And things either smell really foul, or I can't smell at all."

I open my eyes to find the mage eying me with a dubious look. The same look I've seen on every doctor's face.

"That's quite a list," he says. Based on my personal experience, he's either unsure of how to help me, or he believes I'm exaggerating.

I glance at Caspian. "See? He can't help me."

Caspian rounds on him. "Do something for her."

The mage shrinks away from the king. "I-I suppose I could give her a special tea blend to help ease her symptoms, but that's about all I think I can do."

A tea? A fucking *tea?* I'm in a realm full of magic, and all he can do for me is tea? Next thing I know, he'll be asking me, *Have you tried yoga?*

"That's it?" Caspian's hands clench and unclench, like he's itching to wring his neck. "You're the most powerful mage in the kingdom. Do better."

"My deepest apologies, Your Majesty." Lucius gives him a deep bow. "We don't have enough knowledge of humans to treat her."

Caspian lets out a growl as his eyes narrow in anger. "Isn't there some sort of magic or spell that will heal her?"

The mage winces at his tone. "Your Majesty, if that were so, I would be a very wealthy man."

"Give your tea blend to the kitchen," Caspian snaps. "Now, get out of my sight, you worthless toad."

The mage bows once more before scurrying from the room.

"This is why I didn't want to see the mage." My voice quivers as tears pool along my lashline. "It's always like that."

Caspian sits down on the bed beside me. "I only want to help you."

"I know—agh!" My heartbeat breaks into heavy flutters, so I clutch my chest and struggle for breath.

His eyes grow wide. "Bri? Bri, what's wrong?"

"It's fine," I say tightly. "This happens all the time." I take another breath, sucking for air. "It'll pass."

He shakes his head, his face twisted with helplessness. "I had no idea you were living with so much suffering."

"Really, I'm okay. I'm not dying or anything. And I've definitely come a long way from where I was. It's just... not enough." I sigh. "Don't look at me that way."

"Like what?"

"With pity." The last word comes out bitter. "Look, I'm tired. I'm going to get some sleep."

"Of course." He rises to his feet and straightens his suit, but his jaw is clenched. It's obvious he doesn't like being dismissed. "If you need anything, do not hesitate to call for me."

"Okay."

"Good night, Bri." He leans down to kiss my forehead.

I watch him go with regret. His intentions were noble, fueled only by concern for me, but I was short with him.

Because things with the mage went exactly how I expected them to go.

And just like that, I'm back to square one, no closer to a cure that will never come. But that's the thing—I'm starting to come to terms with it.

I just wish everyone else would, too.

CHAPTER 13

The next morning, I wake up when Elowen brings in my food tray into the bedroom, along with a mysterious package wrapped in black paper with a gold ribbon tied around it.

I accept the package from her and give it a little shake. "What is it?"

She shrugs. "I'm not sure. It's from His Majesty."

My curiosity wins out over my hunger, and I untie the ribbon as Elowen sets up my food tray beside me. Inside the gift box is a black filigree mask surrounded by white tissue paper. As I lift it from the box, my fingertips trace the intricate design of the mask.

It's stunning, but what is it for?

My eyes land on a gold envelope at the bottom of the package, and I slip a notecard out from under the flap.

Wear this tonight. We're going out for dinner. —Caspian

Going out? Like, on a dinner date?

What does dating in the Crimson Vale even look like? I doubt we're going to the local tavern to drink ale, if the mask is any indication.

After breakfast, I enlist Elowen's help to get ready, though I'm unsure how to dress. The most likely destination is a masquerade ball, but the castle hosts a ball every weekend. Why all the mystery for an activity we'll repeat on Saturday evening?

I decide to stick with a black outfit to match the mask and opt for a strapless, trumpet-style gown with silver sequins sewn in a damask pattern. Elowen styles my hair down in a vintage wave and completes the look with dark lipstick to match.

I just hope I'm not overdressed for whatever he has in store for tonight.

When I arrive downstairs, Caspian is waiting for me in the courtyard beside the carriage. His lips stretch into a grin when he sees me, and his eyes rake over my body without an ounce of shame.

"How is it possible that you grow more enchanting every night?" He closes the distance between us to place a lingering kiss on my cheek.

"Thank you." Heat creeps to my cheeks. "Are you going to tell me where we're going?"

He steps back to grab my hand and help me into the carriage. "If I told you, it wouldn't be a surprise."

We ride to the outside of the village where the forest grows thicker. About thirty minutes from the town, we come to a stop at a sprawling estate situated deep in the woods. A brick mansion sits behind wrought iron gates, which open for our carriage to roll through.

"We're here." Mischief glimmers in his eyes as Caspian puts on his mask.

I follow suit and tie the mask behind my head. "Is this a formal dinner?"

Caspian is the first to step out of the carriage, and he turns to offer his hand and help me down the narrow steps.

"Not exactly," he says in a low voice, and the corner of his mouth twitches with a smile.

He offers me his arm to hold on to as we ascend the steps toward the towering oak doors of the mansion. They open up onto a dark foyer lit with dozens of candles, and it reminds me of stepping into a Victorian-era estate.

A woman in a short dress smiles at us upon our arrival, and when I meet her gaze, I realize she has cat eyes and tufted ears on top of her head.

If I'm dressed wrong for whatever the hell this is, I'm going to kill Caspian.

"Welcome to the Manor of Salacious Appetites," she says. "To our left is the dining room, where refreshments will be served all night. To the right you will find a series of rooms, each with a different theme. Should you wish to participate in any of the activities, please let one of our guides know. We will be happy to teach you the techniques if needed."

Okay, now I'm confused.

"Thank you." Caspian nods to the woman and puts a hand on my lower back, leading me toward the right.

"What activities?" I whisper to him. "I'm guessing you didn't bring me to an arts and crafts show?"

"No, not crafts." He smirks. "Sex acts."

My stomach lurches, and I'm thankful I haven't eaten anything yet. "I'm sorry. *Sex acts?*"

Caspian lets out a low chuckle. "You don't have to participate in anything. I just want to watch your reactions and gauge what you like, Bri. I want to fulfill your wickedest, most salacious fantasies."

The way his voice grows rough makes my skin buzz.

"So, just to be clear," I ask, "you brought me to a sex club for a date?"

"I most certainly did." He licks his lips. "Are you ready for the first room?"

"Um, sure, I guess." As ready as I'll ever be.

Caspian laughs and grabs my hand, leading me through the first door.

As we step into a dark, spacious sitting room, my eyes are drawn to the floating orbs of light drifting near the ceiling. In the middle of the room, a woman hangs upside down from the ceiling in strips of red silk fabric, which are tied artfully across her body into a pretzel shape, her legs and wrists bound. Onlookers sit on antique sofas and tufted chaise lounges in a circle around her, their transfixed gazes turned upward.

I also see her lithe breasts peeking out between the ties, revealing hard, peaked nipples. From the looks of it, she's not wearing any clothing beneath the silk ties. It's so distracting I almost miss her pointed ears.

"W-What is this?" I whisper in Caspian's ear.

We stand in a corner by the bookcases, unnoticed by the others in the room.

"They're tying her up for sexual pleasure," he whispers back.

I roll my eyes. "I can see that. I mean, what is going on in general? What the hell is this place?"

He chuckles, low and dangerous. "The social elite come from all over the Crimson Vale to experience the Manor of Salacious Appetites. The membership fee is exorbitant, making this a very exclusive club. Each room has a different sex act, and if people like what they see, they are brought into a separate room to learn and experience the technique."

"So, this is like the IKEA of BDSM?"

"I'm not quite sure what the 'IKEA' is, but if you are implying a sort of retail shopping experience for kinky sex, then yes."

I turn back to watch the woman, who is accompanied by a man—who has a greenish complexion—standing on the floor beneath her. He has his hand on some loose silk ribbons, and he begins to twist and turn them. The woman above begins to contort into a different position as he pulls her strings like a puppeteer.

Caspian leans down to whisper in my ear, sending shudders down my spine. "What do you think? Do you like it?"

I breathe in through my nose. "It's... certainly mesmerizing." The woman flips onto her stomach in midair. It reminds me of a sexier version of acrobatics. "But I don't think this is something I would want to try just yet."

I'm definitely not that flexible. Besides, I'd get dizzy as soon as I got flipped over.

"Then let's move on." Caspian snakes his arm around my waist and leads me into the next room.

When we enter, it's pitch-black with the exception of a single red orb of light shining near the ceiling. It's illuminating a man dressed in leather from head to toe, his face completely covered except for his eyes. He's holding some type of flogging device, with multiple strands of leather attached to a long handle.

Below him is a woman on all fours. She's completely naked apart from a large red ball in her mouth attached to a leather strap around her head. A spiked dog collar adorns her neck, attached to a leash held in one hand by the leather man behind her. His other hand raises the flog high above his head, sending it down with a loud smack that cuts through the silent air.

She moans around the ball gag, and that's when I notice her sharp teeth biting into the rubber. They look like Aurelius's teeth, filed into sharp points.

I shudder when I see a red welt forming on the woman's bare behind.

BDSM was never my thing, but when I imagined what it entailed, it looked a lot like this.

"Not your cup of tea?" Caspian murmurs.

I can feel his eyes on me instead of the performance, carefully assessing my reactions and taking mental notes for later. No pressure.

Another loud smack reverberates around the room as the leather comes down on the woman's ass. I shudder.

"No, but... never mind."

He steps closer, crowding into my space and stealing all the oxygen with it. "Tell me, Bri. Tell me your fantasy."

I shift between my feet. "I... I wouldn't mind if you spanked me. Not with a whip or anything, but with your hand." Shaking my head, I bring my hands up to cover my burning face.

When I said it was easy with Caspian, this isn't the conversation I had in mind. This is the opposite of easy.

Caspian's cool fingers wrap around my wrists and pull my hands down. "Don't ever be ashamed to tell me what you want." He leans down to look me in the eye. "I want to give you everything you desire."

With a gulp, I nod, enraptured by the fervor in the dark rubies of his irises.

"Shall we continue?" he asks.

"Please." I'm eager to get out of this room.

As soon as we pass through the doorway, we find ourselves in a massive, marble-tiled bathroom. The brightness of this room is an assault on my eyes, and I bring my hand to shield my vision against the harsh white tile reflecting the chandelier light.

Multiple performances are taking place, each with a couple of onlookers huddling close to watch. In an oversized, clawed bathtub sits a naked couple taking a bubble bath, and the man massages the breasts of the woman lying against his chest, her mouth hanging open with uninhibited moaning. Another couple is having sex in the shower, the man pressing the woman's back up against the wall as he takes her, his grunts echoing against the tile.

To my surprise, the performers look almost human. You have to look really closely for the subtle signs that they aren't, though many I can't identify.

"What are they?" I ask.

"Werewolves," Caspian answers. "Except for him. He's a demon." He points to a naked man in the middle of the room.

A woman on her knees before him obscures his lower half from view. They seem to have the most onlookers, and out of curiosity, I step forward.

The crowd parts for Caspian and me, but when I look down, I realize she isn't giving the man a blowjob. Instead, the man is fisting not one but two cocks in his hands, holding them steady as a double stream of urine arcs onto her chest.

I sputter, both horrified by the act and enthralled with the two dicks. "I... I think I'm done here."

I grab Caspian's hand and march toward the door leading to the next room. His chuckles echo off the tile floors, and I throw him a withering look over my shoulder.

He laughs again, and I shush him as we step into the next room, which is dark. After the bright white light of the bathroom, I pause in the doorway as my eyes adjust to the dimness. Caspian, of course, has no problem with his vision, and he grabs my hand and guides me through the shadows, sticking to the perimeter of the room.

Once my eyes adjust, I realize we're in a bedroom, and in the center stands a four-poster mahogany bed. I count seven people in the performance, though none of them are actually on the bed.

And then I gasp.

The performers have hooks piercing their naked flesh, and each hook is at the end of a chain attached to the bed frame. They dance around the bed with wild, sensual movements as a drummer maintains a steady rhythm, much like a pulsing heartbeat. Blood drips from the incision sites, smearing across their bodies in a grotesque, yet captivating way. Sweat lingers in the air.

Caspian comes to an abrupt halt, and I bump into him from behind.

"Why are we stopping?" I whisper.

The air whooshes from my lungs as Caspian pushes me back against a dresser, which knocks against the wall behind it. He hoists me up so that I'm seated on top of the dresser, and my legs are splayed around his torso.

And when I look into his eyes, they're glowing—like *actually* glowing in the dark the way fire pierces the night.

He licks his lips as his eyes dip to my neck. "I like this room." His voice comes out like a beastly growl.

"Caspian, what are you doing?"

"The blood," he whispers. "Does it turn you on the way it does me?" He grinds his unmistakable erection against me, and if I weren't so terrified right now, I'd probably let him fuck my brains out right here in this dark corner of the bedroom.

But something's off with him. For someone so in control of himself down to his facial expressions, he's on the verge of losing it.

"Caspian, I don't think you're in your right mind now."

"But you look so delicious," he purrs. He leans down to scrape his growing fangs against my neck.

I try to push him back, but it's like pushing a concrete wall that won't budge. "Caspian, I want to leave."

"But why?" He licks my neck from my shoulder to my ear, and I quiver in response.

"Because you're not you," I say, trying to keep my voice firm. "I want to leave. And you promised to give me whatever I want, right?"

He leans back, his eyes round with surprise. When he blinks, the flaming glow leaves his eyes, and he stumbles back. "Bri, I apologize. The scent of blood..."

"It's okay," I whisper. "Let's get out of here. Hold your breath or something."

After hopping off the dresser, I grab his hand and lead him through the doorway into the next room. But I'm trembling.

Caspian never loses himself like that, and that's what scares me the most. I forget that he's a vampire, and if he succumbs to his bloodlust, I don't have a chance in hell of fighting him off.

He wouldn't kill me by accident, would he?

When the door closes behind us, he takes an audible breath. The air in here isn't laced with sweat and blood.

I eye a nearby sofa. "Let's sit down for a bit." My legs are weak and shaking, though I'm not sure if it's from fatigue or shock.

I pull Caspian over to the tufted loveseat. There are a few of them situated around a bed, although the lighting in this room is a bit better. It allows me a moment to take in the Victorian-style decor with green, floral wallpaper, rich wood paneling and furnishings, and an assortment of vintage perfume bottles on the vanity. It feels as though I've stepped into someone's private bedroom, and I'm simply a voyeur to the seemingly vanilla sex the couple on the bed are engaged in.

"Please, allow me to apologize for my behavior in the last room," Caspian whispers. His face is twisted with guilt. "I promise I would never hurt you, Bri—you must believe me."

"It's okay. I'm fine, see?" I gesture at myself.

He leans in, pressing his forehead to mine. "I assure you, when I taste your blood, you'll enjoy it."

His dark promise sends a violent shudder down my spine, and he lets out a low chuckle.

"You... want to drink my blood?" I lean away from him to check his eyes, and sure enough, they aren't glowing. He's completely in his right mind. "How does that even work?"

"Oh, Bri," a low chuckle rumbles in his chest. "That's a discussion for later." He rests his arm behind me along the back of the sofa and turns his gaze on the couple in the bed. "This is the final performance room. We can stay here as long as you like before heading into the dining room for refreshments."

This performance is very tame compared to the others, although it seems odd to end with missionary sex. However, we got all dressed up to come here to the Manor of Salacious Appetites, so we might as well enjoy one of the shows. This one is more my speed.

I turn my focus on the couple in bed, but upon closer inspection, there are actually three people in the bed. A naked woman rides one of her male partners, who is lying on his back beneath her, while the other man kisses her neck from behind. Like many of the other performers, the woman and the man lying beneath her—the one with his erection fully submerged inside her—look rather human, so I'm guessing they're either werewolves or witches, although the man behind her has a translucent quality to his skin and pointed ears.

These creatures of the Crimson Vale are a kinky bunch.

The woman gyrates her hips on the first man's cock as her head rolls back against the shoulder of the second. Her eyes are closed, lips parted, as she uses the men for her own pleasure.

This isn't too bad, especially after the more extreme performances earlier. In fact, I might even say this one intrigues me.

I'm transfixed as the translucent man pushes her forward until she is on all fours above the other guy. He begins to slowly enter her from behind, giving her anal while the man below her is inside her pussy.

I never imagined that was possible. Leaning forward, elbows on my knees, I keep my eyes glued to the performance.

The translucent man withdraws as the other drives his hips upward, taking turns filling her with their cocks. The woman is holding still, allowing the men to do all the work, although her head is arched upward as she lets out a low, guttural moan.

Working together without a word, the men increase their tempo, like musicians reaching an accelerando in a song. Alternating back and forth, in and out, until they're both plowing into her with such force I worry she'll break in two. But as their thrusts become more vigorous, her moaning grows louder until she reaches her peak, seizing with pleasure as she lets out an ecstatic cry. Both men slow their tempo, groaning in unison at their simultaneous release.

I lick my parched lips.

The three untangle from one another, and the room begins to clap politely. It plunges me back to the present, and I join in the applause.

I had plenty of sex when I was in college, but this night has opened my eyes to how much there is I still don't know. An entire world of experiences awaits me, and Caspian wants to give me whatever I want to sample.

"Shall we head into the dining room?"

Caspian's voice takes me by surprise, and I jump, my heart racing with erratic thumping. He studies me for a long moment, and my cheeks burn under his scrutiny.

I hate how he reads me so well.

Without a word, he stands up and offers his hand, pulling me to my feet. The other people in the room mill about, so he navigates us through the small crowd until we're back in the main foyer.

When we step into the dining room, my stomach rumbles at the savory scents wafting through the air. I approach the buffet table, but when I reach out for a canape, I gasp and yank my hand back.

The food is spread out on the naked body of a woman, lying on her stomach on the table as the platter.

"Help yourself." Caspian casually picks up a crab cake from the woman's lower back and pops it into his mouth.

After reaching for a small plate, I fill it with enough food and hope it's enough to avoid coming back for seconds. This night has shown me that I'm positively naive when it comes to sex.

I'm young, fumbling her way through sexual encounters while pretending like I'm an adult with experience. But I have absolutely no clue what I'm doing when I've only scratched the surface.

I'm eager for a place to sit down, but as I scan the room for a seat, I realize there's no furniture. Instead, a number of scantily clad men and women are contorted into different positions, and some of them have masked guests sitting on them like chairs.

"What the hell is this?" I mutter under my breath.

Caspian gives me a wicked grin. "Living furniture."

"I think I'll stand, then." Biting into a celery stick, I cast my eyes down toward the opulent carpet, looking anywhere but at them.

Yeah, I'm an innocent child compared to these people. And if Caspian is a member of the exclusive Manor of Salacious Appetites, he must be into BDSM.

How the hell can someone like me satisfy him?

A small crowd of onlookers are gathered around the fireplace. Slowly, I lift my gaze to peer through them, where a woman, also naked, lies on her stomach. But rather than lying on a table, she is being supported by two men on all fours, acting as the legs of a table.

Another man stands behind them, facing the crowd. From the fireplace, he pulls out a ladle and pours red wax onto her spine. She whimpers with pleasure as the man pours different colors of wax onto her back, her legs, and even her bare butt. By the end of the performance, a rainbow of colors completely covers her body, turning her into a work of art, and the small audience begins to clap.

I set my plate down on a credenza—one made of wood and not people—near the exit. "I think this was enough fun for one night."

Caspian offers me his arm, and I take it, weaving mine through his. He leads me outside to the front steps, and I cling to him for support while we wait for the carriage to pull around.

"You're quiet," Caspian murmurs.

I don't meet his gaze. "Is that what you're into? Because I'm not sure if..." My voice catches.

Caspian tilts my chin to look into my eyes. "I've tried many things at the Manor of Salacious Appetites. I grew up knowing I would never meet my fated mate, so I sought something to fill the void in my heart and ease the loneliness."

This is the second time Caspian has shown his vulnerability to me, and it catches me off guard.

"Nothing in my past has come close to the experience of being with you." He runs his thumb over my lip. "And since meeting you, I've wanted no one else. I'll never want anyone else."

Before I can say anything, the carriage rolls up, and Caspian helps me inside.

The ride back to the castle is quiet, and I watch the forest disappear through the window as we roll into the village.

The carriage rolls to a stop in the courtyard, but when the door opens, Caspian lets out a deep growl. "Shut the door. I need a minute alone with my mate."

The footman's eyes grow round, and he slams the door shut with a quick apology.

Caspian leans forward and takes his hands in mine, and his voice softens. "I'm doing everything in my power to make you fall in love with me. Which is why I want to fulfill your every whim and fantasy."

A lump forms in my throat. "You already have, Caspian. The sex between us is... intense. Explosive." I laugh. "At least, it is for me."

His smile falters. "Be honest, Bri."

I recoil. "Honest? I am being honest. You're the one who's familiar with all this kinky stuff."

He quirks an eyebrow at me. "Are you sure there wasn't anything in the Manor of Salacious Appetites you wanted to try?"

My cheeks are on fire. "I already told you I wouldn't mind a little spanking."

"What else?"

I think back through the performances one by one, but it was all too intense and aggressive for my taste, except perhaps... maybe...

"The threesome?" He gives me a pointed look.

"W-What?" I lean back in my seat, and my hands slip from his grasp.

"You enjoyed watching that threesome," he says. "I smelled your arousal. I watched your reaction to it; you were mesmerized. Did you like watching, or do you want to actually participate?"

Smelled my arousal? Surely I misheard him.

I shake my head. "I was more interested in the, you know, the mechanics of it."

"The *mechanics* of it?"

"Yeah." I fold my arms and stare out the window at the reddish hue of the crescent moon above. "I don't want to talk about this right now."

He stares at me for a long moment, and I feel his eyes boring into the side of my skull. After a moment, he sighs. "Suit yourself."

Caspian knocks on the door, and the footman opens it.

Without waiting for Caspian's help, I gather my skirt into my hand and climb out of the carriage as fast as I can.

"Bri, wait!" he calls after me.

"I need a little space," I say. "That was a lot, okay? See you at dinner tomorrow."

Without waiting for a response, I rush off to my room, and to my relief, Caspian doesn't follow.

The whole evening was just so... weird. I just had a crash course in some of the most mysterious facets of BDSM, and it was enough to make *Fifty Shades of Grey* look downright vanilla in comparison.

Of course, I know what a threesome is, but I'd never considered it for myself before. But when I watched one play out in front of me, it stirred up something in me. Curiosity, perhaps?

One woman, two men.

And I just happen to be one woman fated to two men.

Elowen allows me to sleep in, and I don't wake up until she arrives with lunch. Strange dreams from the Manor of Salacious Appetites kept me tossing and turning all night long, so the extra few hours of sleep were needed.

"How was your date with His Majesty?" Elowen asks, setting the lunch tray down on my bed.

I snort. "It was certainly... memorable."

"Do you have something special planned for dinner tonight?"

My stomach does an uncomfortable flip. "No, not really." After the Manor of Salacious Appetites, what sorts of things would Caspian attempt to do to me tonight?

The problem is that I gave Caspian all the control last night by admitting how inexperienced and frightened I was. I need to wrestle some of that control back from him and level the playing field. That's the only way this will work for me.

As I pop a slice of an apple into my mouth, I recall how my last meal was served on a naked woman's body, and an idea forms in my head.

"Actually, Elowen, I do have something in mind. Can you help me relay a small request to the kitchen for tonight's dinner menu?"

"Good evening, Bri." Caspian rises to his feet and crosses the dining room toward me. He takes my hand to graze his lips sensually along my knuckles.

"Good evening," I reply, unable to contain my grin. "I hope you don't mind, but I made a few special requests for tonight's dinner menu."

His eyebrows arch. "Oh, really? I'm intrigued."

The main course carries on as usual, but when our dishes are cleared, the dessert doesn't come. When Caspian notices, he straightens in his chair and shoots an annoyed glance at a servant in the corner.

"Looking for dessert?" I ask.

His guarded gaze settles on mine. "I am."

Caspian knows I'm up to something, and I'm positively giddy at the thought that I know something he doesn't. That I'm taking back a bit of control in this power dynamic.

And as the king, he can't stand not being in control.

I push my chair away from the table. "We'll be taking dessert upstairs in your room."

"Is that so?" With a slow grin, he rises to his feet and follows me out of the dining room. "What did you have in mind?"

"You'll see."

The tension is thick as the two of us head upstairs in silence. Caspian remains behind me, and I can feel his eyes on my back—well, mostly my ass—as we ascend the stairwell. I inject an extra sway in my hips with each step.

When we reach his door, I open it and let myself inside. Caspian follows, shutting it behind us with a firm thud and clicking the lock.

I turn and study his reaction as he scans the room with his burgundy eyes. When they land on a small cart beside the bed, his eyebrows raise, but the corners of his mouth curl upward.

"Bri, you continue to surprise me, each and every day." His voice is thick.

"Take off your clothes." I cross over to the cart and inspect the ingredients I requested. A bowl of whipped cream sits at the ready, accompanied by smaller bowls of chocolate sauce, raspberry sauce, and an assortment of small berries.

Caspian strips down, taking his time before tossing his clothes to the side. His heated gaze roves over my body the entire time. "Where do you want me?"

His gruff voice sends a shudder ricocheting through my body. "Lie back on the bed and get comfortable."

"As you wish, my lady." He crosses over to the mattress and sits, his thick cock rising to attention. Caspian lies back against the pillows with his arms folded behind his head. As I roll the tray closer, I feel his gaze on me.

"It hardly seems fair that I'm the only one in a state of undress here," he says.

"I agree."

I untie the large bow at my waist, which is holding my wrap dress together. Shrugging it over my shoulders, I let it fall to the floor at my feet, revealing a set of sheer, black lingerie.

"Fuck, Bri." He bites his lip as his eyes roam my body. His erection stands at full mast.

Standing beside the bed, I grab the whipped cream and a small spoon. I carefully place a white dollop onto a few choice places: the base of his neck, his chest, his belly button, and finally, the tip of his erection. At the last dollop, I hear him draw a sharp intake of breath.

"It's cold," he growls.

"Then let me warm you up." I crawl onto the bed, covering his lips with mine.

He responds to my kiss, drawing his head up to take possessive control of my mouth, but I don't let him. Slowly, I begin to descend, leaving a trail of kisses down his jawline. When I reach the base of his neck, I place my lips around the whipped cream, lapping it up as I move my mouth against his skin. He lets out a low moan.

I lift my head just enough to catch his eye and lick my lips. "Mmm, so sweet."

I continue working my way down toward his chest, taking one of his nipples into my mouth. Torturing him, I work my way to the other side with languid strokes of my tongue before sucking against the other one covered in whipped cream.

Caspian sighs beneath me, his hard chest rumbling against my ear.

I make my way down to his belly button, where I stick out my tongue to lap up the cream, and his back arches off the bed.

Grinning, I work my way down past his belly button, getting closer to my final destination. But at the last moment, I sit up on the mattress, and Caspian lets out a groan in frustration.

"Why are you stopping?" he asks through gritted teeth.

Without answering, I pick up a strawberry from the cart and take my time to inspect it. I shift my gaze to lock on his before lowering the strawberry to the tip of his manhood. Taking my time, I circle the strawberry around the head to get some whipped cream onto it.

This is just a preview of what I plan to do to him later.

Bringing it to my mouth, I stick out my tongue, swirling it around the berry and sucking off the cream before sinking my teeth in. The juices burst onto my tongue with bright flavors, and I let them roll down the corners of my mouth.

I set the leaves of the strawberry onto the cart, licking the berry juices off the corner of my mouth.

He groans, watching me with his lidded gaze.

That's right. I'm in control of the alpha king. I have what he wants, but I'll give it to him when I damn well please.

Hinging forward, I bring my face down toward his manhood and grasp it at the base with my hand. I take the tip of his erection between my lips, circling my tongue to clean off the remainder of the whipped cream from his body.

Caspian sucks in a breath. "Fucking hell..." He grabs the pillow behind his head, sinking his fingers into it to hold on.

Moving my head up and down his length, I take him so deep he hits the back of my throat. However, before I can fall into rhythm, he pulls me off and flips me over.

Caspian nips at my earlobe with his teeth. "My turn for dessert."

"Wait, no fair!" I struggle under his weight as he straddles me. "You can't hijack my idea."

"I just did." He makes quick work of the lingerie, ripping it down the middle into shreds with a loud rip. Within moments, I'm lying naked beneath him.

He leans over and grabs a small spoon, which he dips into the raspberry sauce. Slowly, he pours a bit on the base of my neck, continuing a trail of cold sauce down my chest and swirling a bit around one of my nipples.

After dripping the sauce over my belly button, he drops the spoon back on the cart and leans down, moving his mouth against my naked body. He trails his tongue in swirling patterns across my skin, lighting up every nerve ending as I writhe beneath him.

My hips buck off the bed as he laps the remaining sauce from my stomach.

Satisfied, he sits up, and his eyes hold a mischievous glint as he picks up the chocolate sauce. "It's so warm."

"Please," I beg, my body wriggling beneath him. A fire burns between my thighs, and I'm desperate for release.

He tilts the small bowl of chocolate sauce above my core, letting the warm sauce run over my slit. My back arches at the sensation of warmth between my legs, though I'm needy for something else to fill me up.

Caspian sits back further on the bed between my legs, wrapping his arms around the backs of my knees and spreading them apart. He lowers himself so that his face is between my thighs, his nose just inches from my sex.

As he stares up at me from between my legs, my heart pounds. How is a man this perfect mine? God, he's gorgeous.

Caspian flattens his tongue against me and licks upward toward my clitoris, and I moan. Although he works slowly at first, it isn't long before he becomes more aggressive. He pulls me closer against his face, and his mouth begins sucking at my folds.

I'm barreling toward my release faster than I want to, and when he hums against me, I shatter.

"Caspian!" Fireworks dance behind my eyelids as euphoria explodes. Adrenaline pumps through my veins as I seize with uncontrollable, jerky movements. I entwine my fingers into his thick, dark hair, holding him against me as I grind myself against his face and squeeze every last drop of pleasure.

Through my eyelashes, I peer down to see his bright, ruby gaze boring into mine from between my legs, his eyes glinting with triumph.

As much as I thought I was in control, Caspian has proven how delusional I truly am. He's the true puppet master of my body, and he knows exactly how to make me dance for him.

I never stood a chance.

CHAPTER 14

Caspian stirs beside me and wraps his muscular arms around my naked body beneath the silk sheets. "Mmm, good morning." He whispers into my hair before he plants a soft kiss.

"Good morning indeed." I yawn. "How am I still so exhausted?"

"Well, we didn't do much sleeping."

I laugh. "I suppose that's true. Maybe that's why I feel so foggy." As I glance around the room, nothing is quite in focus, like I'm observing the world through a hazy lens.

Caspian props himself up on his elbow to get a better look at me, his brows furrowing in concern. "Perhaps you overexerted yourself last night."

I grin at him. "I certainly don't regret it, though. Definitely worth it."

"Even so, you should spend the day recovering. I've been meaning to have dinner with my grandmother to appease her. Perhaps I'll do that tonight while you rest."

That's probably for the best. I don't need the queen dowager to hate me any more than she already does.

I give him a playful pout. "I'll miss you tonight."

He leans down to kiss the tip of my nose. "And I will miss your company tonight as well. However, you'll need to be well rested for tomorrow night's ball. Any hints as to what I can expect?"

"No hints. It's a surprise."

"Do I need to force it out of you?" He brushes his fingers along my inner thigh, dragging them up my leg and tickling me.

"Okay, fine!" I push him off. "All I will say is I've planned a couple of party games, just to give guests some different ways to socialize besides dancing."

"Ah, seems fun." His eyes twinkle with that mischievous look of his. "Is there anything you need from me to assist with the preparations?"

"Nope, I have everything handled. The only thing you need to worry about is showing up and having a good time, okay?"

"Then I shall leave you to it." Caspian draws me closer to him and plants one more kiss on my lips. "There's some work I must attend to, but feel free to stay here as long as you like."

I roll away from him and climb out of bed to begin gathering up my clothes from the night before, which are strewn about the floor in crumpled piles. "I think I'll head back to my room for the day. Enjoy your dinner with your grandma."

He grimaces. "Thanks." It's obvious he's not looking forward to it, and I don't blame him.

I give him one more kiss before sneaking back to my room, careful to avoid any of the servants who could see me in last night's attire.

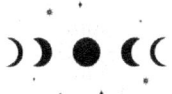

"Bri?" a familiar voice says, shaking me awake. "Bri?"

When I open my eyes, I find Caspian sitting on the bed beside me, but on closer inspection, I realize his eyes are a deep shade of brown, not red.

"Caz?" I swipe the back of my hand along my eyes.

He smiles down at me and strokes my hair. "Yeah. I've missed you."

I shoot up in bed and throw my arms around his neck. "How are you here?"

"My dark one let me out," he admits, although a strange expression crosses his face.

I lean back, but I don't release my arms from his neck. "Caspian let you out? Why would he agree to that?"

If Caspian is in competition with Caz for my affections, it makes no sense to let him out.

"Well, it comes with a price. I, uh..."

I look at him expectantly, waiting for him to finish, but he won't meet my gaze. "What is it?"

"Already starting the fun without me?" Caspian materializes on the threshold of the bedroom, leaning casually against the doorframe with his arms crossed.

His voice holds a sultry edge that sends a delicious shudder down my arms. I glance between the two of them. "Caspian, what's going on?"

"I'm fulfilling your fantasy, Bri." His arms drop to his sides as he stalks toward the bed with a dark expression on his face.

"My fantasy? What fantasy?"

"He's talking about the threesome, Bri," Caz answers, his voice quiet. "That's the condition of my release."

My jaw drops.

But when I assess Caz's tight expression, my chest twinges, and I take his hands in mine. "Hey, it's okay. You don't have to do anything you don't want to do."

"If this is what it takes to be with you, then I'll do it."

My hands grip his so hard my knuckles turn white. "What, of course that's not—"

"Show me what you like," Caz replies, his voice gruff as a hooded expression crosses his face.

A burning heat grows between my legs, but I don't trust myself to believe it.

Because I want this. I want this more than I've ever wanted anything in my life, and I had no idea until this moment.

When I said Caspian would take me to places I've never been before, never did I imagine... well, this.

Caz slides his hands up to my cheeks, holding my face still as he takes my mouth. But it isn't sweet or chaste.

This is heat. Pure, burning need.

Another set of hands presses into me from behind, roaming over my body and cupping my ass over my lingerie. Caspian leans forward, nibbling at my ear to make me moan against Caz's mouth.

"Is this what you want, Bri?" he purrs in my ear. "Both me and my light one at once?"

I wake up with a loud gasp, heart pounding, and shoot up straight in bed. Breathing hard, I search the room for any sign of Caz or Caspian, but I'm alone.

It was just a dream.

A fucking *hot* dream.

But of course, that isn't reality. After Caspian caught me with Caz, I doubt the two of them can stand to be in the same room as each other without fighting, much less to have a threesome. It's insane. Absolutely out of the question.

The sun is setting outside my window, which means I slept the entire day away. Caspian is probably getting ready for dinner with his grandmother right now.

But I'm so fucking turned on right now, and I wish Caspian were here to take care of it. I'm soaking wet.

I climb out of bed and draw myself a bath. As the water fills the tub, I stare absently at the water, unable to shake the lucid dream. It felt so real in the moment, but it was just something my mind had conjured up.

Unless...

Did Caspian cast a dream spell on me? He noticed my interest in the threesome performance at the Manor of Salacious Appetites, so it's entirely possible. Maybe he wanted to plant the idea in my head to gauge my interest. I have a strong suspicion that Caspian would be more open to the idea than Caz.

But as soon as they both began to kiss me in my dream, it felt... right. When I was wedged between them, it felt like the place I was always meant to be.

Technically speaking, I'm the fated mate of both Caz and Caspian. They are two halves of the same whole, separated by an ancient curse. Of course I'd want them both.

I just never imagined having them both *at the same time.*

And now that the seed has been planted, I'm not sure I'll ever get the image out of my mind—or the desire purged from my body.

The following morning, Elowen comes to wake me up with my breakfast tray.

"Rise and shine!" she trills. "I'm so excited for the party tonight. I can't wait for you to see the landscaping."

"Yes, we have a lot of work to do." I run through my mental checklist for the day. "After breakfast, let's head down to the garden. I'm sure you did a great job, Elowen."

She beams. "Thank you. Is there anything on your list I can help with?"

"If you don't mind being my personal assistant for the day, then I'll take whatever help I can get."

She nods. "Absolutely. Aurelius has sent over your dress, so we'll need to leave plenty of time before the party for a final fitting, along with your hair and makeup."

My notebook on the nightstand has the event sheet I finalized yesterday, so I grab it and pass her a copy to review. "After we inspect the garden and the floor diagram, we'll head to the kitchens to check on their progress. Can you help me ensure all the vendor shipments have arrived?"

She scans the handwritten page. "Of course. We haven't had a party like this for as long as I can remember. It feels like every weekend it's the same ball, with the same people, the same food, the same music, in the same room. All they do is dance and mingle, but between you and me, it's grown quite stale."

I grin. "Then let's shake things up."

We have a whirlwind of a day, darting around the castle to follow up on last-minute preparations. I make a few adjustments to the layout in the garden, praying for the lighting to turn out how I envisioned once the sun goes down.

I don't have time for lunch, but the kitchen allows Elowen and me to sample all the foods being served tonight, so that fuels me through the rest of the day.

When Elowen and I return to my room to get ready, Aurelius is already there waiting for me. He gives me a deep bow with a dramatic flourish of his hands. "Oh, Lady Briar, I have outdone myself with your dress for tonight. You will be the most enchanting flower in the garden, I assure you."

His assistants bring in a mannequin—and draped over it is the most stunning gown I have ever seen. It's a strapless ballgown in a pretty shade of pale pink, and the skirt is covered in a top layer of mint tulle hanging from the waist. Pink rosettes and sage leaves are sewn in a swirling pattern across the dress, trailing delicately in the back along the floor.

I approach the dress with outstretched hands and run my fingertips across the fabric petals. "It's gorgeous."

It's a welcome deviation from all the dark colors that seem so popular in the Crimson Vale. Elowen styles my hair into a chignon with loose tendrils of hair hanging free, but the final touch is a delicate rose gold tiara, which she fastens into my hair.

When I look in the mirror at the final result, it reflects back a strong and healthy queen who's ready to take on the Crimson Vale.

Maybe I can do this after all.

Maybe I could be the alpha queen. I could do it if I had both Caz and Caspian at my side.

With determined poise, I head down to the party, eager to soak it all in before the first guests arrive. As I step to the edge of the balcony overlooking the garden, thousands of candles illuminate the lush foliage in a soft, romantic glow.

It's not how I imagined—it's a thousand times better.

I did it. I actually pulled this off. The night is young, and there's still so much that could go wrong, but I take a moment to bask in the beauty of the garden.

"You've done well, Bri."

A deep, familiar voice envelops me with praise. I don't even have to turn around to know it's Caspian who steps up to wrap his arms around me from behind. He rests his chin on my shoulder while gazing out over the garden. "Seeing this is like getting a glimpse inside your spectacular imagination."

"I know this is probably a bit more feminine for your taste—"

"It's perfect," he whispers in my ear. "Just like you."

I'm far from perfect. I'm having obsessive thoughts about threesomes involving him and Caz, and it's getting to the point where there's no room left to think about anything else.

Caz pressed against my front, Caspian pressed against my back, and both of them touching me in ways that make me feverish with need...

With a quick glance around us, I make sure we're out of earshot of anyone else. There are guards stationed every twenty feet along the balcony and around the garden perimeter below, each in full uniform and holding a long staff with a mace on the end.

I bite my lip and keep my voice low. "Hey, can I ask you a question?"

Caspian releases his grip on my waist, turning me to face him. His brows are knitted together. "This sounds serious."

"Did you... cast another dream spell on me last night?"

He grimaces. "No. You made it very clear I shouldn't do that again."

"Oh, okay. Got it. Never mind."

So, if that threesome wasn't a dream spell, that means my mind conjured that all on its own.

If Caspian had initiated the thought, it would be easier to come to terms with it. I could blame him for making me feel this way.

The corner of his mouth tugs. "Are you having filthy dreams about me, Lady Briar?"

When I laugh, it comes out more like a nervous cackle. He cocks his head at me in concern.

Real smooth, Bri. *Real smooth.*

Caspian sighs and runs his hand along his neck. "Bri, I owe you a number of apologies."

I blink. "For what?"

Taking my hands in his, he stares at them for a long moment before meeting my gaze. "I am a king. I am not accustomed to making apologies. To apologize means to admit fault, and in my world, that is the equivalent of admitting weakness." He sighs. "But you *are* my weakness, and when it comes to you, I act irrationally. I've never been in love, and I'm still learning how to be worthy of it."

Caspian, the alpha king, is in love.

With *me.*

As soon as it registers, a strange, unexpected warmth spreads in my chest, starting from my heart and seeping into my veins.

My breath catches. "Caspian—"

"Please, let me finish. I never formally apologized for casting that dream spell on you, and I also owe you an apology for the way I retaliated after finding you with my light one. My behavior on both occasions was inexcusable. I will never hurt you ever again—you have my word."

Everything in my body is yearning to echo his sentiments, to tell him I love him and I'll never hurt him. It feels as natural as breathing.

But I stop myself.

I can't do that to him. I can't get his hopes up, because if I leave the Crimson Vale, it will hurt him so deep he may never recover. He may never open up his heart and be vulnerable with anyone again. How could he if the one person he's fated to be with leaves him behind?

How could I do that to him?

How could I do that to either Caz or Caspian?

Despite whatever dreams I have about being with both of them, it's never going to happen. Time for a reality check.

The day is coming when I'll have to choose between them, and it's approaching quickly.

A few guests enter through the archway of hedges at the other end of the garden, and I seize the distraction. "Looks like it's showtime."

Caspian offers me his arm, and we make our way over to greet the guests as they arrive. Many of them compliment the garden renovation, admiring the ambiance and thanking us for allowing them to be a part of the big reveal. I'm riding a high from all the praise.

Caspian leans over to whisper in my ear. "Enjoy this moment, Bri. You deserve it."

We exchange a long glance, his eyes twinkling with pride beneath the paper lanterns above. However, the moment is interrupted by a voice that sends a direct chill down my spine, and goose bumps rise on my arms.

"Well done, Your Majesty." Malrick approaches to clap Caspian on the back. "It's good to see the castle mixing things up every once in a while."

Caspian glares at his unwelcome familiarity. "Don't thank me. This is all to Lady Briar's credit. I just footed the bill."

Malrick throws his head back in laughter, revealing pointed, yellow teeth, and his greasy, long hair falls back from his shoulders.

"A woman's touch." He turns his scrutinizing gaze onto me and winks. "It was long overdue. Have a lovely evening, Lady Briar."

He bows before me and takes my fingers into his rough palm, planting a kiss on the back of my hand. His lips linger a few seconds longer than they should before he straightens up and joins the party.

When he turns away, I wipe my shuddering hand on my skirt.

Caspian's jaw clenches as he watches him walk away. "I should kill him and be done with it."

"No, you need him and his clan." I take his hand and squeeze it. "He's not worth your time."

"Or yours." He continues to glare daggers at Malrick's back.

We spend another fifteen minutes greeting the guests before joining the party ourselves. I glance around the crowd to ensure that everyone is eating and drinking, and it appears everyone is having a good time. Light laughter punctuates the chatter every now and again, and there's a relaxed atmosphere that wasn't present at the last ball.

Until I glance over at the queen dowager and the royal siblings standing on the opposite end of the garden, and by the way their ruby eyes narrow when they glance over, it's clear they're having a discussion about me.

I've managed to piss off four vampires just by existing. Great.

A butler passes by with a tray of canapes, and I snatch as many as I can fit in my napkin. I'm starving.

Caspian pulls me to the bar and catches the bartender's attention. When he turns back to me, he's holding a cocktail in each hand. "I know you don't often partake these days, but you should enjoy the menu you worked so hard to create."

I glance at the basil leaf floating delicately on top of the pink liquid in the glass and recognize the Basil Grapefruit Martini. When I accept the glass from him, Caspian clinks his against mine.

"Cheers to your moment of triumph." He takes a sip from his glass, and after a moment, his eyes widen. "Is that...?"

"Blood orange mixed with actual blood." As gross as that sounds, hopefully it will soften the vampiric royal family's attitude toward me.

He hums in appreciation. "It's exquisite."

A tap on my shoulder captures my attention, and I turn to find Elowen standing behind me in her maid uniform. "Lady Briar, according to the schedule, it's time for the first game."

I give her a nod. "Thanks. I'll make the announcement. Caspian, I'll see you soon."

Before I step away, he grabs my wrist, pulling me in for a swift kiss that leaves me breathless.

He smirks. "Now you may go."

How am I supposed to compose myself when he just claimed me with that kiss in front of everyone?

Clearing my throat, I step onto the small, raised platform where a group of musicians play for background music. Once they finish their song, I clink my fingernail against the glass to get the crowd's attention.

"Good evening, everyone! Thank you for coming to our little garden party." A few chuckles lilt up from the guests. "I want to take a moment to thank the wonderful and experienced castle staff who made everything possible tonight. And I couldn't possibly forget to thank His Majesty, King Caspian, for his generosity and hospitality."

I seek him out in the crowd, and when our eyes meet, I stop breathing.

The way he's looking up at me, brimming with such pride and tenderness, catches me off-guard. I open my mouth to continue, but the lump forming in my throat threatens to make my next words waver.

How am I supposed to leave him when the full moon arrives?

"Cheers to the King of Alphas!" someone calls out.

"Long live House Nezara!" another person shouts.

I welcome the interruption and raise my glass to Caspian to toast him. The guests follow suit, but Caspian ignores them all, his gaze snagging on my lips as I take a sip of my drink.

I take a deep breath, shoving my emotions into a little box deep down and locking them away. "We're going to kick off this party with something a little different." A few murmurs float up from the crowd. "It's a game of cat and mouse. I need all the ladies to gather on my right and all the gentlemen to the left."

It takes a few moments for the guests to organize themselves accordingly. Just like my sorority friends from college, these nobles are going to love this game, and it's a chance for me to steal a romantic moment alone with Caspian.

"All of the ladies will scatter and hide. Anywhere on the castle grounds is fair game, as long as you remain outside. We'll have a two-minute head start before the men come to find us. Gentlemen, you will have fifteen minutes to search for the object of your affection. However, if you don't find a companion when time runs out, you lose. Any questions?"

"What if I find a partner before the fifteen minutes is up?" a man calls out from the crowd.

"What you do with your fifteen minutes is up to you." I wink, and the guests begin to chuckle. "Ladies, our time starts now!"

With my drink still in hand, I gather my skirts in the other and descend the stairs. I steal one last glance at Caspian, who appraises me with a hungry expression, before I run off in the direction of the hedge maze Elowen designed.

As I get further away from the party, the atmosphere grows quieter around me. The only light in here comes from the dim glow of the red crescent moon, providing plenty of dark corners for romantic trysts. I pass a couple of giggling women who also retreated into the maze, but we set out in different directions. It isn't long before I'm alone.

I down the rest of my drink and set the glass on the ground. The basil leaf sits at the bottom of the glass as my first clue for Caspian.

A bit further along, I pluck one of the flowers off my dress and drop it in the middle of the path. The alcohol I just chugged makes me feel tipsy, and I giggle as I stagger deeper into the hedge maze. It doesn't take much to get me inebriated these days.

I continue until the sounds of the party completely fade to silence. Even though I'm certain I'm alone, I glance around to make sure the coast is clear before hiking my dress up over my knee. A frilly pink garter is wrapped around my thigh, which has a small rosette to match my dress. I slip it off and let it fall onto the ground before I scurry off to find my hiding place.

My legs are burning by the time I find a small stone bench at a dead end, so I take a seat and wait. Even though I'm gasping for air, a wide grin is plastered on my face as I imagine Caspian putting together the trail of clues I've left for him. Will he find me in time to steal a romantic moment before we have to get back to the party?

With his speed, he must not be far behind.

A movement in the shadows makes me perk up with excitement. However, when the figure steps into view, my heart sinks.

"Lady Briar." Malrick greets me and stalks closer, swirling my garter around his finger. "Fancy meeting you here."

He stole the last clue I left for Caspian.

A knot forms in my gut, along with the gnawing feeling that something isn't right. I'm surrounded on three sides by hedges, and Malrick is blocking my only escape.

"I noticed you didn't come here with a date," I say rather loudly. Caspian may have vampiric speed, but it's useless if he can't find me. If I make small talk, I can stall long enough for Caspian to hear me and come.

"No, I'm not really the type to commit to one woman." He grins, exposing his sharp, yellowed teeth. "Although, a lovely girl like you would make an excellent luna for the Ravenrock Clan. You are the most desired woman in the kingdom, after all."

I glance behind him. "What? Oh, I don't know about that."

"After your debut last weekend on King Caspian's arm, everyone is talking about the human girl who stole the heart of the alpha king." He steps forward and takes a seat beside me on the bench, but I scoot away toward the end, trying to keep as much distance between us as I can.

"Everyone in the kingdom wants a taste of you." Leaning closer, he whispers, "What's your secret? How were you able to tame the king of alphas? You must be quite... exceptional."

He slides closer to me, and I shift away until my ass is hanging over the edge of the bench.

I stare at the dark hedge maze ahead. If I run, I have no doubt he'd catch me. I'm in heels and a ballgown, and it's a miracle I haven't tripped yet tonight.

Besides, he's a werewolf, and if he shifts, I'm done for.

Malrick presses his thigh against mine, and disgust crawls up my spine.

"I-I should go find Caspian," I mumble.

"He won't be finding you. I have the final clue, remember?" He holds up the garter, stretching it between his two fingers. "I simply wanted to return it to you. Shall I put it back on?"

He kneels on the ground in front of me, blocking my exit once again.

When Malrick slips his hands under my skirt, all the air is sucked out of me. My body holds me prisoner, rendering me unable to move or run away as I shake with fear.

Goddamnit, Bri. Move. *Move.*

But move where? There's nowhere for me to run.

Malrick continues to move my skirt up until it's above my knee. He stops to graze the exposed skin of my thigh with his coarse hands, and my throat goes dry.

"So smooth," he whispers, glancing up at me with his beady, yellow eyes. "I wonder what other parts you keep smooth, Lady Briar?"

Why can't I move? Why can't I tell him to stop? If I scream, will he fly into a rage?

There's nothing I possibly do to overpower a werewolf and escape. *Nothing.* That's why my body is frozen in complete and utter terror. I'm not a queen; I'm a useless girl who's unable to protect herself.

My breathing grows ragged as he starts to push my knees apart—

A dangerous growl rips through the air, making the hedges tremble from the reverberation.

My head shoots up as a relieved sob looses from my throat. "Caspian!"

Caspian appears from the shadows of the hedges wearing an expression of pure rage. Within an instant, he appears beside us and grabs Malrick by the collar. He lifts him off the ground, into the air, and sends him flying backwards with an incredible show of strength.

Malrick tumbles through the hedge wall into the next section, leaving a gaping hole in the greenery as shredded leaves scatter in all directions.

I shove my dress back and hug myself, shaking violently.

Caspian leaps through the hedge wall to pounce on Malrick, where he pins him to the ground. His fists collide with his cheekbones in rapid succession, one after the other, turning Malrick's face into a bloodied, bruised mess.

When Caspian stops, Malrick lets out a croaked laugh, still wearing a smug expression. "You think you're so powerful, Alpha King? You aren't even an alpha... but I am."

My eyes widen in horror as Malrick's body begins to contort and shake. A sickening sound echoes through the air as his limbs twist into unnatural, painful positions, bones cracking and muscles tearing.

Caspian is shoved off of him as Malrick's figure grows larger and fur begins to sprout along his arms and legs. His suit rips into tatters before falling to the ground at his paws.

Malrick shifts into a black werewolf so massive he takes up the entire width of the hedge path. He lets out an angry snort as his bright yellow eyes focus on Caspian.

"Bri, get the guards." Caspian keeps his gaze trained on the wolf, but fury laces the edge of his voice.

I glance between him and the wolf. "I-I can't leave you!"

"I'll be fine. Go!"

I hike up my skirt and kick my shoes off. They'll just slow me down.

At full speed, I take off through the hedge maze, backtracking my way to the entrance. Even though Elowen and I designed this maze together, being inside of it is a completely different story. The terror has me taking wrong turns every which way, and as I wander the maze, twigs digging into my heels, I cry out. "Help! Somebody, help me!"

My shrieking echoes back at me through the empty, dark hedge maze. The silence terrifies me.

I come to a stop, gasping for air.

Every second I waste means another opportunity for Malrick to overtake Caspian.

I glance at the hedge to my left. It stretches maybe nine or ten feet above my head, and when I push my hand into the leaves, I find branches behind it wide enough to plant my feet on.

I scale the hedge wall, ripping my dress along the way. A sharp branch digs into my palm, making me cry out, and when I yank it out of the hedge, blood starts beading on my hand.

When my head peeks out over the top, I see the tip of a long mace weapon bobbing up and down along the far wall, which must be attached to a guard on patrol outside the perimeter.

"Help!" I scream. "The king is under attack! Come quickly!"

Someone shouts, and then another, and soon I see the tops of at least a dozen mace weapons making their way through the maze.

"Hurry!" I scream.

The next minute stretches endlessly before the guards arrive. At last, the guards appear around the corner, holding lanterns and all manner of weapons, not just maces.

"Where are they?" the captain asks.

Gripping the branches for dear life, I peer behind me to see if I can find any sign of Caspian or Malrick. It's so dark, and the crimson moon offers little light at this stage of its cycle.

A yelp cuts through the air in the distance, and I turn in its direction, squinting through the dark. It's subtle, but I can see a wolf's paw swipe through the air before disappearing behind the hedges.

"There!" I yell, pointing.

They take off in that direction, and one of the guards stays behind to help me down. We sprint to catch up to the others, and I pray we're not too late.

When we reach Caspian and Malrick, they're engaged in a full-on battle. The wolf snarls as he rushes at Caspian, but he is far too agile for Malrick to keep up. He easily dodges each attack.

Caspian comes to a stop beside the captain. I catch a glimpse of his mouth, which is covered in blood.

"I don't have any weapons to take him down," Caspian says. "I can only keep him occupied. Attack!" He spits blood on the ground before rushing back into the fray.

The guards follow. They cannot shoot their arrows or throw their axes without putting Caspian in danger, so they surround him and begin to slash at the wolf's feet.

"Give me your dagger!" Caspian calls out to a nearby soldier, who obliges by yanking it quickly from his pocket and tossing it to him. He catches it by the handle and seemingly disappears, only to reappear on top of one of the hedges.

The wolf snaps his canines at the soldiers surrounding him, spit flying as he whirls around in a circle.

"Malrick!" Caspian calls.

The wolf whips his snout to face Caspian. He lets out a vicious growl, baring his teeth before leaping.

"Caspian, look out!" I cry.

At the last second, Caspian lunges forward, his arm outstretched toward the beast's face. He plunges the dagger into his eye, and a high-pitched yelp reverberates around the maze.

The wolf's form slowly shrinks back into the unconscious form of Malrick. The dagger disengages itself from his eye as he transforms, falling to the ground with a clatter. Blood spews profusely from his socket and his arm where Caspian must have bit him earlier.

So much blood.

I think I'm going to be sick.

The guards rush forward to seize Malrick, and he stirs with a weak moan.

"Throw him into the worst cell in the dungeons," Caspian orders, leaning down to scoop up a bit of blood onto his finger. He pops it into his mouth, sucking on his fingertip. "Mmm, nothing tastes quite like the blood of your enemies, though I must say, yours is a bit sour for my palette."

"My eye!" Even in his human form, Malrick lets out a snarl that sounds more beast than man. "You will pay for this!"

As the guards drag Malrick off, Caspian materializes at my side. He grabs my shoulders and examines me up and down. "Bri, are you hurt?"

I shake my head, my wide eyes staring straight ahead of me, yet seeing nothing. Shock grips me, and I can't stop the violent trembles wracking my body. Each struggling breath I take feels like ice slicing the walls of my lungs.

"Bri, I'm here." Caspian wraps his arms around me. "You're safe now."

My feet lift off the ground when he picks me up. I curl closer into his broad chest as he carries me from the maze.

When we exit, a crowd of people waits for us in the garden.

"Lady Briar!" Elowen cries, rushing toward us. "Your Majesty, is she alright?"

"She will be. Tell the guests the party is over."

She curtsies. "Right away, Your Majesty."

The party has descended into complete chaos. People are milling around in agitation, trying to figure out why a dozen guards just pulled a naked, bloodied Malrick from the hedge maze and into the castle. A few guests whisper behind their hands as they stare at us, at least until Elowen ushers them away.

Caspian does not put me down. Instead, he heads for the castle, his strong arms holding me close as he carries me up to my room. He doesn't let go until we reach the bed, where he sets me down on the mattress with the utmost care.

"C-Can you lock the d-door?" My teeth chatter as the shock wears off.

He disappears for a moment before the lock clicks, and then he reappears beside me, sitting on the edge of the bed. "Did he..." He swallows. "How far did he go with you?"

I shake my head. "You got there just in time."

He grits his teeth. "What did he say to you before I got there?"

It's all a bit of a blur, except for the way he touched me, the way his yellow eyes burned as he looked at me. That's what I remember in vivid detail. "Something about how the whole kingdom wants a taste of me."

Caspian's eyes flash. "The idea of that disgusting dog's hands on you..." He closes his eyes and shakes his head. "I'll kill him. Alliance be damned."

"Don't worry about that right now." I wrap my hand around his arm and tug him close. "Will you stay with me tonight?"

"Of course, my love." *My love.*

Caspian slides into bed beside me and pulls the covers over us. He wraps his arm around my waist, whispering sweet, comforting words until I fall asleep.

CHAPTER 15

When I stir, Caspian sets his book on his lap and peers down at me. "Good afternoon, my love. I'm glad you're awake."

"Afternoon?" I rub my eyes, but the haziness in my vision doesn't go away. "What time is it?"

"It's after lunch. There's still some food on the tray if you're hungry."

"I'm starving."

Even though I slept all night and all morning, it feels as though I didn't get a single minute of sleep. Although thinking through yesterday's events, it's no wonder I feel like crap. Not only did I run all over the castle preparing for the garden party, but I also got tipsy, narrowly escaped a sexual assault, and scaled a hedge maze after witnessing a vampire and a werewolf battle it out. And to top it all off, I'm on my period, and my symptoms are always exacerbated during this time of the month.

Jeez, no wonder I feel like shit. Even if I weren't chronically fatigued, anyone would still feel exhausted after all that.

I'm still in my ballgown, dirty and ripped from climbing the hedges, and I'm eager to change into something more comfortable.

"I need to meet with the Royal Council," Caspian says. "But I've stationed multiple guards outside the door so you can feel safe."

"When will you be back?" My voice sounds needier than I intended.

He gives me a gentle smile. "As soon as I can get away. I've been putting this off all morning." Caspian reaches over for the lunch tray and sets it on my lap. "Eat."

I lift the lid to find soup and bread on the tray, and my stomach growls.

I hope he didn't hear that.

As Caspian gets dressed, his face is set into a hard expression. Every time he meets my gaze, he gives me a reassuring smile that doesn't quite meet his eyes.

Something is bothering him, and it has me worried.

After he leaves, I finish my food and take a bath, eager to wash off the memories of last night. I change into my leggings and sweatshirt and spend the rest of the afternoon in bed.

I attempt to read a book after a long nap, but my eyes hurt too much when I try. Without books and sex, the Crimson Vale is surprisingly dull.

When Caspian returns, he's followed by Elowen pushing a dining cart into the bedroom. He takes a seat beside me while Elowen sets up dinner for us on the bed.

"How are you feeling?" he asks.

I shrug. "Like crap."

"And yet, you look like a goddess."

I scoff and slap his arm, but there's no power behind it. "You don't have to lie."

"It's not a lie." He narrows his eyes at me. "I am many things, but I am not a liar. I find you to be the most alluring woman I have ever met."

Elowen sets a dinner tray on my lap, and I turn my focus onto it. I'm too tired and hungry to argue anyway.

Caspian settles against the headboard beside me and digs into his own meal. Elowen gives us both a curtsy before retreating from the bedroom and shutting the door behind her.

"I never ate in my bed before meeting you," he says. "Now I seem to find myself enjoying it far too much."

I swallow the bread in my mouth. "Can I ask you a question?"

"I love when you ask me questions."

I roll my eyes. "What was your meeting about today?"

Caspian pauses with his fork and knife in hand. "What meeting?"

I throw him a pointed look. "The meeting with the Royal Council."

"Oh, right. That meeting." He takes a bite of his roasted chicken and takes his time chewing.

"Yeah. *That* meeting. Why are you acting so weird about it?"

"I'm not acting 'weird.'"

I bump his arm with my shoulder. "Yes, you are. Now spill. What's going on?"

Caspian sighs and sets down his silverware. "I called the meeting to put an end to our weekly balls and execute Malrick." He refuses to meet my eye as his fist clenches and unclenches.

"Execute?" I repeat. "Don't get me wrong, the guy is scum, but that seems a bit extreme, don't you think?"

"It doesn't matter. The council said no."

I blink. "They can say no to you?"

Caspian lets out a hollow laugh. "Indeed they can. The Ravenrock Clan is one of the most powerful packs in the Crimson Vale, and the council worries that executing their alpha would trigger an all-out war. Which is fine by me, but they unanimously disagreed."

I glance down at my plate. "So, what now?"

"They agreed to keep him locked up until the next full moon. At that point, we'll decide how to move forward."

His statement says so little, and yet so much. Malrick's fate depends on whether or not I remain in the Crimson Vale, and the council is waiting to see if I'm worth all the fuss.

If I leave, I become a footnote in Caspian's long list of sexual conquests, and it doesn't make sense to unleash war over a fleeting relationship. But if I become his queen, it's a different conversation entirely.

Either way, I feel sick about it. "What did they say about canceling the balls moving forward?"

He leans his head against the headboard and closes his eyes. "They said no. If we cancel our events over this incident, House Nezara will look weak. That one werewolf frightened us into submission. And..." His jaw ticks. "I suggested we keep you under guard in your room during the balls for your protection, but..."

"But?"

"Your absence will only fuel speculation that Malrick had his way with the king's mate."

I'm speechless. I stare down at my dinner plate, but my hands grow numb and I set my silverware down.

These balls are for optics. They're about showing off the wealth and influence and strength of House Nezara. At the end of the day, Caspian is the king, but the king is one of the least powerful pieces on the chessboard.

And I'm just a pawn, easily sacrificed until I trade in for a queen.

"Who all sits on the council?" I ask. "Besides your brother and Lord Peter?"

Caspian rakes his bottom lip between his teeth. "There are a dozen seats on the council.

Most are influential merchants and alphas from our allied packs. And my grandmother."

The queen dowager, Sybil of House Nezara. Is *she* the most powerful piece on the chessboard?

"You have nothing to fear, Bri." Caspian reaches to take my hand in his, then pulls it up to lay a kiss against it. "I will have guards protecting you around the clock, wherever you go. They will not leave your side at the ball next week."

"Is the council okay with that?" My tone is biting. "It won't make you look scared and weak?"

His grip on my hand tightens. "If it does, I don't care. Not when it comes to your safety."

I let out a sharp breath. "I'm sorry. I didn't mean to be bitchy toward you. I'm just frustrated."

"Believe me, Bri, no one is more frustrated than I am."

I lean my head against his shoulder. "I wish I could attend without anyone knowing who I am."

"How?" Caspian asks. "Everyone knows who you are now. They all want a fucking taste of you..." He lets out a frustrated snarl, his anger rippling along the edges of his control.

I straighten up. "Wait, I have an idea."

He stares down at our hands joined together, then looks at me with wild eyes.

"You and I were anonymous at the Manor of Salacious Appetites once we put our masks on," I explain. "No one except the hostess knew who we were because of our masks."

He blinks. "What are you saying?"

"I'm saying we could do a masquerade ball next weekend. Rather than having all eyes on us, we could fade into the crowd."

"That... that could work." He taps his chin. "We could still have heightened security and keep some of them undercover. No one will notice. It will create the illusion that we weren't affected by Malrick at all." He looks at me with a hint of a smile. "It's a brilliant solution, Bri."

"The only issue is the council wants to make sure we're both seen at the ball." I fold my arms. "I think we would still need to reveal ourselves at the end of the night. Just to prove we were there."

He nods. "I agree. It would avoid rumors that we sent imposters in our place."

I release his hand and fold mine in my lap, picking at my nails. This is a good plan, but there's still a nagging feeling at the back of my mind that something could go wrong.

Knowing that the Royal Council is willing to sacrifice my safety to keep up appearances terrifies me. Besides Caspian, Elowen is the only other person here I can trust.

It's not enough. I need more people in my corner if I have any chance in hell of surviving the Crimson Vale.

"Caspian, one more thing," I say. "I... I want Caz to be there."

His eyes narrow. "Absolutely not."

"I'd feel safer knowing he'd be there if things went wrong. I... I really need someone else on my team to look out for me." My voice breaks at the end. Knowing there's a target on my back—from both Caspian's enemies and so-called allies—makes me feel like I'm on an island surrounded by a dangerous, tumultuous ocean.

It's a lonely and frightening place to be.

His hard gaze studies me. "Fine, I will agree to it, but he goes back into the dungeons at the end of the night. Understood?"

I nod. As much as I wanted more time with Caz, it's a sore spot for Caspian, and I'm not going to push my luck.

We resume our dinner in silence. I finish every last bite of my meal and examine the dinner cart by the door. "Is there any dessert?"

He glances at me. "I'm glad to see you have an appetite. You don't typically eat enough."

My cheeks burn red. "I just get really hungry this time of the month." I reach for my water glass and take a deep swig.

"Ah, I see." He nods. "Tell me, do you also get more aroused during your 'time of the month'?"

I sputter with water in my mouth and cough, swiping the back of my hand across my mouth. "Caspian!"

"What?" He shifts closer to me, pushing aside our dinner trays to the foot of the bed. "You forget, Bri, that blood turns me on. You have no idea how much your scent has been driving me crazy."

"Wait, you can *smell* it?"

You enjoyed watching that threesome, he'd said. *I smelled your arousal.*

I bury my face in my hands. "Ugh, that's so embarrassing."

"Not to me." He pulls my hands away from my face. "I want to taste it."

"What?" I recoil. "You've got to be kidding me." Unable to meet his eye, I climb out of bed and busy myself by cleaning up the dinner trays.

With my back turned to Caspian, I grip the edge of the cart and process what he's asking of me.

He wants to taste my period blood. *Gross.* I had a feeling he was into some kinky shit, but this one takes the cake.

Caspian gets up and follows me over to the cart. He spins me around and pushes my back against the wall. "Does it *feel* like I'm kidding you?" His husky voice is like velvet as he grabs my hand and brings it to the crotch of his pants. There, I find his unmistakable erection pushing against the fabric.

"Caspian, come on," I say, withdrawing my hand. "That's so... weird."

When I meet his gaze, I gasp. His eyes are glowing the same way they glowed in the Manor of Salacious Appetites when he smelled blood.

He's managed to rein it in since I started it yesterday, but it seems the last of his willpower is gone, and all that's left is a bloodthirsty vampire who wants to eat my menstruating pussy. A month ago, I never would have imagined this scenario to be in the realm of possibility. And yet, here we are.

I swallow. "But period blood isn't just blood. It's... other stuff."

"I am fully aware of the biological process, Bri. It's a different flavor profile than regular blood, but still delicious in its own way." He cages me against the wall and grazes his nose along my jawline. "I'd do anything for a taste."

I perk up a little. "Wait, anything?"

He licks his lips. "Anything."

Gazing into his eyes, I find nothing but feral desperation there. He's not entirely in control of himself right now, and it would be wrong to take advantage of that.

But if Caspian is feeling generous right now, I could use that to benefit someone else...

I shove the guilt down and take a deep breath.

"Do you wish to make a deal, Caspian?"

He gives me a savage grin, revealing his teeth. His canines are elongating into fangs. "I love making deals."

"I gathered that."

I remind myself that Caspian was the first to use sex as a bargaining chip. *A night with me in exchange for a visit with my light one.*

Sometimes, we have to use the tools available to us. And in this realm, sex seems to be my only asset. I'm already cheating on Caz, so I might as well use it to benefit him.

"I'll let you have a taste, but on one condition," I say.

"I'm listening," he purrs against my neck.

Fuck, that feels good.

Focus, Bri.

"After the masquerade ball, you don't put Caz back in the dungeons at the end of the night. You give him a night of freedom."

Caspian grows still. Unnaturally still.

I glance down, but his face is burrowed into my neck. "Caspian?"

A moment passes, then Caspian lets out a dark chuckle that has me both turned on and terrified at the same time.

He straightens, staring down at me with a wicked smirk. "You continue to surprise me, Bri. I didn't think you had it in you."

I gulp. "What are you talking about?"

He peers down at me through his narrowed gaze. "I see exactly what you're doing. Very clever, using my feelings to get what you want. It's exactly what I would do if I were in your position."

I glance down to avoid his gaze, but all I see is his erection, still tented in his pants.

"I should be angry with you, but I'm not," he says. "I'm impressed by your mind games."

Regret floods over me.

"You'd be a master at court politics as my queen." His voice is steady despite the bloodlust still gripping his body. "I'll make you a counteroffer."

He nuzzles my ear with his nose, and I don't know how it's possible to feel so disgusted with myself and what he wants to do to me—but also to crave him and crave *it* at the same time.

The Crimson Vale is a total mindfuck.

Caspian continues. "My light one can come to the ball, just like any other guest. All three of us will be disguised, but none of us will have any knowledge about what the other two are wearing. I'm sure he will be seeking you out at the ball, but so will I. Whichever one of us finds you first gets to spend the night with you until morning... *however* we please. But if I find you first, he goes back to the dungeons immediately. Do we have a deal?"

I consider his words for a moment, trying to find any downsides to his proposal. Caz gets a night of freedom if he wins, and I get to spend the night in the arms of one of them. Either way, I win, right?

I lift my head to meet his gaze. "Fine. Deal."

Within seconds, my leggings and underwear are bunched at my ankles—along with the bloodied cloth I'm using as a panty liner.

I cover my face with my hands.

Caspian knees at my feet, and I press my thighs together on instinct.

"Spread your knees, Bri."

Wincing, I pull my hands away from my face to look down at him. He's wearing a dark look on his face that says, *I may be on my knees for you, but I'm in charge.*

I slide my feet apart until he has a clear view of my pussy, and I want to die of embarrassment.

As he stares between my legs, his eyes glow an even brighter shade of red, giving his face an eerie, yet captivating quality.

The lascivious way he licks his lips is utterly obscene. "I've been waiting a long time to taste your blood, Bri." His voice is hoarse. Parched.

And with that, he dives forward. He wraps his arms around me, pulling my against his face. His fingers digging into my ass as he sucks my folds into his mouth, lapping up my blood.

His tongue punches inside me, and I scrabble for purchase against the wall to no avail. "Oh, God. Oh, *God.*"

Caspian lets out a low moan against me, sending a delicious reverberation up from my core. My head rolls back as his mouth moves against my mound, and I run my fingers through his thick, dark hair. My hips buck against his face as he sends shockwaves of pleasure through my body.

I shouldn't be enjoying this. Everything about this is wrong and forbidden and taboo, so... dirty. But finding pleasure in the humiliation, sharing something so personal with a man, proves there are no barriers left between us. There's nothing more intimate than that.

He glides his tongue along my clitoris, and I nearly fall over. One of my hands is wrapped in his hair while the other grips his shoulder for support.

Caspian grabs my legs and hoists them over his shoulders. He stands up, keeping his face flush between my legs the entire time. On instinct, I gasp and clench my thighs around his head, engaging my core for support.

But he doesn't let me fall. He keeps a firm grip on my waist as he walks me over to the bed, and when we reach it, he pushes me back on the bed with him pressing over me. The mattress groans beneath our weight.

His lips only leave my sex for a moment when we land, and then he's back to work. The adrenaline has my heart racing a million miles a minute, hurdling me toward climax. Moments later, I'm screaming his name with reckless abandon.

Holy. Fucking. Shit.

When I finally come down off my high, my eyes refocus and land on Caspian, who is sitting up between my legs. His face has blood—*my blood!*—smeared across his chin, nose, and cheeks.

He looks crazed and raw and untamed, his eyes glowing bright in the dim room. "I'm not finished yet. Turn onto all fours and bend over."

I do as he says, but my arms are boneless and struggle to hold me up. Within seconds, he's behind me, stripped down to nothing as he presses his hard erection against my ass.

He covers his body over mine, bringing his lips to my ear. "I want to taste everything your body has to offer. To explore every inch and claim it as my own." Caspian leans back, pressing his finger at the entrance to my *other* orifice, and I gasp in surprise at the unfamiliar sensation.

"Is your asshole untouched?" he asks.

I give him a hesitant nod in response. I was always too chicken to try anal, but I didn't trust drunk frat guys in college to do it right.

"Do you trust me, Bri?"

But Caspian isn't a drunk frat guy. His experience far surpasses them. "Yes."

He pushes his finger inside my ass, and my body reacts on instinct at the foreign sensation.

"Breathe," he soothes. Slowly, he withdraws his finger and pushes it in again, working slowly. My face is scrunched in discomfort, but as soon as I take a deep breath and unclench, I adjust to the sensation.

"Very good," he praises, leaning over to give me a kiss on my back. His other hand grabs my butt cheek with a firm grip, and as his fingers dig into the soft flesh, it sends shockwaves of renewed desire through my veins.

"You have the most perfect ass, Bri," he says. "Remember when you asked me to spank you?"

I gasp for air. "Yes."

"I'm going to grant your wish." His hard erection positions itself at the barrier of my womanhood. He slowly pushes himself in until he is fully submerged in my sheath, and I let out a deep moan.

Between the feeling of him and his finger in both holes, it gives me a feeling of fullness I never thought possible. Every sensation is enhanced, every touch electric against my skin.

SMACK!

His palm slaps me across the backside, making me cry out in surprise. It wasn't too hard, but it certainly caught me off guard.

"Again," I whisper, closing my eyes. I give my body over to him completely, suppressing my other senses and focusing only on his touch.

SMACK!

I gasp. *Yes.*

He begins to move in and out of my pussy, keeping the same slow, gentle tempo as his finger. I'm not sure if I could take much speed or aggression with everything else going on, and I'm panting and shaking with need as it builds and builds.

SMACK!

I clamp down on my lower lip to stifle a deep, primal moan.

Caspian continues to pump behind me, bringing me closer to the edge. "How does that feel, Bri?" His voice is ragged.

I shudder. "Amazing."

SMACK!

"I'm so close..."

"Good."

That's the only warning he gives before burying his bloodstained face into my neck. As soon as his fangs pierce my flesh, I cry out at the sharp pain. On instinct, I buck backward to throw him off me, but I only take his finger and his cock deeper.

However, when he begins to suck, the pain melts away into a pleasurable warmth, which spreads from the site of his puncture through my entire body, including my pussy.

Especially my pussy.

I careen over the cliff's edge and find my release. His bite sends an orgasm straight to my core, ripping through my body with so much force I see stars dancing in my vision.

I grab the pillow for something to hold on to as I writhe beneath him, turning into a wild, feral mess for this man. "YES, CASPIAN! YES!"

Caspian groans when I cry out his name, and he spills his seed within me with a roar.

I'm soaring, and yet, I know this ecstasy is only a taste of what's possible. If this is ecstasy, then having Caz and Caspian take me at once would be fucking nirvana. One in my pussy, the other in my ass.

And now, more than ever, I want that forbidden fantasy to come true. A fantasy that's been locked inside my dreams, except now my body knows what it's missing out on.

Caspian delivers a few more short thrusts to finish off before withdrawing his manhood and his finger, leaving a feeling of emptiness in my body as I collapse onto the bed.

He rolls off and lies next to me, grazing my back with his fingertips as I lie there catching my breath.

"That was, without a doubt, the most delicious blood I've ever tasted in my entire life."

I peer at him through my eyelashes. Caspian is leaning against the pillows with my blood smeared across his rich, sepia skin—his mouth, his neck, and his groin.

He gives me a wicked grin, revealing blood on his fangs.

It gives him a wild, violent appearance. This is Caspian's rawest self as a vampire, and he is so sublime and breathtaking.

How can such profound pleasure can be wrought from so much brutality?

It is, without a doubt, the most beautiful sight I've ever seen.

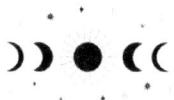

The next morning, I wake up in my bed beside Caspian. He must have taken a shower at some point in the night—there isn't a trace of blood on his face, and his hair is sticking out in different directions like he laid down with it still wet.

When he's awake, he's vigilant. Alert. Ready to tackle any threat to his reign. Even when he lets himself be vulnerable with me.

But this rare sight of him asleep offers a glimpse at what he could have been without the weight of the crown or the curse on his shoulders. It's disarming how at peace he looks.

Caspian opens his eyes and catches me staring at him. The corner of his mouth pulls into a sleepy smile. "Good morning."

"Good morning."

He wraps his arm around my waist to pull me against his chest. "I like having you at my side when I wake up in the morning. I could get used to this."

My chest tightens.

Tonight will mark my sixteenth night here in the Crimson Vale. My time here is more than halfway over, and I'm no closer to making a decision about whether to stay or go.

When Caspian first made his proposal, my mind was made up. My intention was to return to Earth with Caz, the boy I've known my whole life who I fell head over heels in love with this summer.

But after these intimate nights with Caspian, my attraction to him is growing into something else, something deeper I can't explain. I'm starting to imagine building a life for myself here by his side, as his queen. I don't know what my future on Earth looks like after messing it up so much, but here? The path ahead is so clear, even if it's fraught with danger.

Perhaps that's why I'm drawn to Caspian and his world. The lure of danger and excitement and adventure. Things I thought I'd never experience after getting sick.

"What are your plans for today?" Caspian asks.

His question is a welcome distraction, and I plaster a smile on my face. "I want to get a head start on planning the masquerade ball. But only if the council is on board with our plan."

I sit up to get a better look at him. He stretches his arms behind his head, sprawling out on the pillow. His taut muscles flex with the movement, and I trace my gaze over every hard line of his body, all the way down to the sheet sitting low on his waist.

Damn, he really is exquisite to look at.

Caspian stares at the ceiling, deep in thought. "The council won't care about the theme. As long as there's a ball on Saturday and we're in attendance, that's all they care about." He glances at me. "But are you sure you want to do this? After everything that happened—"

"I'm sure. I need something to focus my attention on. Malrick's locked away where he can't hurt anyone, right? I'll be fine."

"Then I'll consider the matter settled." He reaches toward me and twirls a lock of my hair around his finger.

Last night we had great sex. Not just great sex, but mind-blowing, life-changing sex that took me to forbidden places I never thought possible.

But I took advantage of Caspian's bloodlust to achieve my own agenda and get him to agree to let Caz out of the dungeons. And while I could pretend I have the moral high ground and justify it for Caz's benefit, it was selfish. I wanted Caz to be let out for my own protection and my desire to see him, to be with him, and be loved by him. And I used Caspian to achieve it.

I bite my lip. "We should talk about last night."

Caspian throws me a wicked grin. "Already needy for another round?"

"No." *Yes.* "I'm talking about the deal we made. Letting Caz out of the dungeons."

He releases the hair from around his finger and drops his arm to his side, avoiding my gaze. "Ah."

I take a deep breath. "Are you mad at me?"

He lets out a low sigh. "No. I know how you feel for my light one. If the roles were reversed I would have done the same."

"But?"

"But I am having... second thoughts. About our deal." He sits up, and I can't help but watch the sheet fall lower on his waist. "I wasn't in my right mind when I made that deal with you. Bloodlust makes a vampire act irrationally. But I'm a man of my word, and I won't back out now. However, I have some concerns that I overlooked last night in my... altered state of mind."

"Look, I know you're jealous of Caz—"

The words die in my throat when he climbs out of the bed. The sheet slides all the way off, revealing his chiseled naked form, and all I want to do is drag him back into bed and forget this disagreement.

He crosses over to a chair in the corner where his clothes are laid out, and he begins to tug them on. "My only concern is your safety, and if neither he or I can identify you in a crowd, then we can't protect you. I am not the simpering, jealous fool you believe me to be."

Caspian is throwing his walls up again, and it's my fault; he was vulnerable with me, and I betrayed his trust.

"I don't think you're a fool," I say.

He shakes his head. "I failed to protect you from Malrick, and now you don't feel safe in my care. I'm not enough. You need my light one, too." He peers over his shoulder at me, offering a glimpse of the sorrow etched on his face. "At the very least, make sure Elowen knows what you're wearing so she can keep an eye on you." Throwing his jacket over his shoulder, he takes a step toward the door.

"Caspian, wait—"

But he's gone before I can get the rest of the words out.

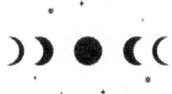

"I want the event to be themed with the colors of House Nezara," I say. "Black and red like on their house flag, and let's do gold accents to give it a luxurious vibe. I want long, black ceiling drapery to hang from the ceiling." I gesture above my head.

The castle staff tails me through the ballroom as I go over my ideas for the masquerade ball. After Caspian left this morning, I wanted to throw myself into event planning, and I wasted no time calling the staff together for a meeting.

There's nothing in my life I have control over. I'm sick, I'm stuck in the Crimson Vale until the full moon, I have Caspian' enemies out to get me, and the Royal Council is using me as a pawn in their political maneuvers. On top of all that, things are tense with Caspian. This masquerade ball is the only thing I have control over right now, so I might as well direct all my energy and attention on it.

"Elowen, do you know of any elves that can manipulate light?" I ask.

"I do, Lady Briar." Her violet eyes sparkle with excitement.

"I want hundreds of floating orbs of light to be suspended in the air with magic," I explain. "With the black backdrop above, it will look like stars in the night sky."

The entire staff *oohs* and nods their heads.

"Oh, that is marvelous," Elowen agrees. "I will send a message to my friend who can help."

I gesture for everyone to follow me to the opposite end of the room. "For the buffet tables, let's do red tablecloths with gold serving dishes."

However, when I turn around, I halt at the sight of Caspian's grandmother, Queen Sybil, striding in through the ballroom doors. When her cane raps sharply against the floor, the staff grow quiet and bow their heads.

She pins me with a murderous stare. "Lady Briar. A word."

My stomach lurches. "Excuse me, everyone. We'll reconvene here tomorrow. Same time."

The staff shuffle out of the ballroom, leaving me alone with the dowager queen. As I approach her, she peers down over the bridge of her nose at me. I've only spoken to her once before, and it was unpleasant enough that I didn't want to encounter her again.

She looks so much like Caz's grandmother, who I've always known to be a compassionate, kind woman. But that is where the resemblance ends—their mannerisms, dress, and even their presence couldn't be more different. Queen Sybil is cold and snobbish, caring only for securing the power of the monarchy over her family's happiness.

"I see you're making yourself right at home here in the castle." Her voice is dripping with contempt as she begins to circle me, like a vulture homing in on their dead prey. "Using the royal treasury to plan parties as though you've already secured your position as my grandson's queen."

"I'm doing it as a favor to King Caspian, at his request," I reply, keeping my voice steady. "I know how important these events are to remind the realm of the royal family's wealth and power."

"Indeed." She comes to a stop in front of me. "Which is why we cannot have any more embarrassing incidents."

I quirk an eyebrow. "Embarrassing incidents?"

She scoffs. "Our alliance with the Ravenrock Clan is critical to the stability of the monarchy, and yet, my grandson threw that all away to lock up their alpha because of *you*. You haven't even been here a month and you're already stirring up trouble. Your presence here makes him act recklessly, and I will not allow it."

I grit my teeth. "Malrick was inappropriate toward me, not the other way around. I didn't ask for this to happen."

"And yet, you turned it into a scandal," she hisses, her eyes flashing a dangerous shade of red. "Rather than be discreet, you made sure to get my grandson and the guards involved, and now the entire kingdom knows what happened."

Anger ripples at the edge of my voice. "Are you saying I should have let Malrick do what he wanted to me?"

"I'm saying that a human girl has no business trying to bewitch my grandson nor any man here in the Crimson Vale." Her lip curls in disgust. "And after Saturday's incident, your reputation is in question and unbefitting of a future queen."

My blood is boiling with white-hot fury, and I bite my teeth down on my tongue so hard it hurts.

"I know how you spend your time," she continues, her voice low. "You lounge around in luxury all day while fornicating with my grandson at night. You're lazy. You lust for a powerful man who will take care of you for the rest of your life, just so you don't have to lift a finger. You have no idea of the hard work and cunning it takes to be a queen of the Crimson Vale. Do you think it's about planning parties? It takes much more than that to keep a Nezara on the throne."

My hands are shaking so much that I ball them into fists and dig my fingernails into my skin. I can't let her see that she's getting to me.

She narrows her gaze. "My grandson thinks he's going to marry you after the full moon, but I won't allow it. Your presence here is an abomination against the laws of nature—against the ancient curse. Grimwalkers do not belong in the human world. You were never meant to cross paths with Caspian, so I suggest you stop misleading my grandson about your intentions and leave as soon as the portal reopens. Do I make myself clear?"

I let out a hollow laugh. "You know what? I actually feel sorry for you."

Surprise flashes across Queen Sybil's face. I catch her off-guard just long enough to continue without interruption.

"You were born knowing that you'd never meet your fated mate. You grew up reading fairy tales about true love and knew you'd never experience it for yourself. But now that your grandson has a chance at true happiness, you want to rip it away from him." I meet her ruby gaze straight on. "Are you so miserable that you want to make everyone else around you just as unhap—?"

Before I can finish my sentence, the wind is knocked out of me. With a gasp, I collapse onto my knees, clutching my stomach at the sharp pain exploding there.

When I look up, Queen Sybil is standing over me with her cane in her hands like a baseball bat.

She hit me.

She fucking *hit me*.

As I wheeze, she brings her cane down to the floor with a sharp rap. "I am not a woman to be pitied. I am a woman to be feared." Her lip curls. "Do not forget that."

I blink, and she's gone.

It takes a few moments to process what happened, but when I'm certain she's not coming back, I let out a shaky sob. Hot tears prick my vision as violent shivers wrack my body, and when I inhale a breath, it hurts.

Once I'm able to, I stand up, but I double over from the pain. Wincing, I clutch my stomach and hobble slowly out of the ballroom.

It's an arduous journey up the stairs to the top floor of the castle, but I want to escape to my room, which has become my sanctuary in this dangerous, cruel realm. When I reach it, I lock the door behind me and press my back to the wood, sinking to the floor as my chest heaves with ragged breaths.

I lift the hem of my dress to inspect my stomach, and sure enough, a bruising welt stretches across my flesh from Queen Sybil's cane.

CHAPTER 16

"**B**ri?" I hear a voice say. "Bri, it's time to wake up."

When I open my eyes, Elowen is standing at the foot of my bed, holding a breakfast tray.

I pull the covers over my head. "I'm not hungry."

She shifts the tray in her hands. "You can't keep sending your meals back to the kitchen. You need to eat."

After getting caned by Queen Sybil, I've managed to avoid dinner two nights in a row with Caspian. I sent Elowen in my place to relay a message each night: I am too ill to leave my room, and I'm too ill for visitors. Which isn't exactly a lie; my stomach is killing me.

But the truth is Queen Sybil got into my head, and as much as I hate to admit it, she has a point. My intention was always to return to Earth with Caz during the next full moon. Caspian distracted me from that mission with his good looks and devilish charms, and as I spent more time with him, I began to entertain the idea of staying here as his queen.

But Queen Sybil was right. I'm not cut out for it, and I was stupid to believe otherwise.

To my surprise, Caspian didn't come barging into my room like the Beast demanding the Beauty to dine with him. Although, given the way we left things after our last conversation, he must think I prefer Caz to him.

Is he giving up on me? On us?

He should. It will make it easier for us to part ways. And yet, the idea of losing him sends me into a pit of despair.

My chronic symptoms are on full blast this morning. I can't remember a day I felt this bad since my initial infection. My body feels heavy, and I'm not sure I have enough energy to walk to the bathroom if I need to. The room wavers in and out of focus as a wave of nausea washes over me, so I curl up into the fetal position and wait for it to pass.

My head hurts. My stomach hurts. And my heart hurts.

Breathe in through your nose, breathe out through your mouth...

"I don't feel well," I murmur to Elowen.

There's nothing for me to do anyway. The staff knows what to do for the masquerade, and the invitations were sent out yesterday. No one needs me for anything, so I might as well sleep.

"Of course," Elowen says. "I'm sorry to disturb you."

A pang of guilt hits me when I hear her close the door.

That's Briar Casey for you—always disappointing those closest to her.

Familiar faces stand around me in a circle. My parents, my doctors, the mage, and even Queen Sybil are closing in on me, whispering vicious words.

Pathetic.

Selfish.

Lazy.

"Stop!" I clap my hands over my ears and fall to my knees.

Caz and Caspian step forward into the circle and stand in front of me.

"I thought you loved me, Bri," Caz says. "How could you sleep with him?"

"I can't take this anymore," Caspian says. "So, choose right now. Me? Or my light one?"

"Please, I'm not ready!" My shoulders quake with sobs. "Please, don't make me choose..."

"Bri? Bri, wake up."

Ripped from my nightmares, I gasp, sitting straight up in bed with a cold sweat on my brow.

"Shh, it's okay, my love. I'm here."

I turn to find concerned, burgundy eyes staring back at me. "Caspian?"

"You were having a nightmare." He helps me lie back on the pillows but doesn't let go of my hand. "This is the third night you didn't come down for dinner."

"I've been sick," I say flatly, turning my head against the pillow to avoid his gaze.

"Elowen says you've sent back almost every meal untouched since I saw you last."

"I'm not hungry."

"I don't care. Eat." His commanding voice leaves no room for negotiation.

"If I eat, will you leave me alone?" I can't bear to look at him as the words leave my mouth, so I pull the bedcovers over my head.

He doesn't respond. My heart pounds harder the longer the silence lasts, and the seconds stretch into infinite tension. I squeeze my eyes shut, wishing I could wake up in my bed in Los Angeles and forget about the Crimson Vale and grimwalkers.

Caspian sighs. "Bri, what happened?" He pulls the covers off my face and takes my chin in his fingers, tilting my head up to look at him. "Tell me what's wrong."

"Nothing."

"Don't lie to me." His tone is more desperate than angry, like he's begging me for the truth. "You've been avoiding me for nearly three days. Are you... disgusted with me? By my bloodlust?"

"What? No, not at all."

He rubs his thumb over my chin. "Then why won't you see me? Whatever has happened, I will fix it. If someone has hurt you, I will have their head. I will keep you safe, Bri, but you have to let me."

His face is twisted in pain, and the worst part is knowing I'm the cause of his suffering. As he holds my gaze, tears well up in my eyes.

"I-I can't stay here," I tell him, my voice trembling with emotion. A tear slips down my cheek as my chest heaves with a ragged sob. "I don't belong here."

"Of course you do. You belong with me."

"No, I don't." I wipe a tear away with my fingertip. "A human doesn't belong in the Crimson Vale, especially not as its queen. I'm not up for all the responsibilities. I'm just too tired. I'm so tired I can't even think straight. I just... want to go home."

He starts speaking in fast, whispered words. "Please, don't say that. You're wrong; you're perfect as my queen. If you feel too overwhelmed with all the responsibilities, I'll hire enough staff to do it for you. You'll never have to lift a finger because I'll take care of you."

That statement makes me cry even more. "No. You have to let me go home, Caspian."

"No, I can't let you leave," Caspian says. "Not after everything we've shared. Please don't give up on us. Just give me until the full moon, and you'll see. I know you'll fall in love with me."

I break from his grasp and stand up, trying to put some distance between us. "That's the problem. The longer I stay, the more I hurt you." A wave of lightheadedness overcomes me, and I grip the railing of the bed to keep from falling.

He comes around the bed to stand in front of me and grips my shoulders. "You're not hurting me. What we've come to share is so special. I've found my fated mate, and now that I have, I'll never let you go. You'll stay here, with me, and we'll be happy. I just need more time to prove it to you."

"Caspian, please don't make this any harder than it already is."

He drops to his knees, gripping onto my hands for dear life. "I'm begging you, don't leave. I'll do whatever you want, but please don't leave me."

My resolve is crumbling. I fall to my knees in front of him so we're eye level with one another, the rug digging into my skin. "Then come with me. Come back to Earth with me."

He shakes his head. "I can't. I'm physically bound to this realm by the ancient curse."

"If I stay, could Caz stay, too?" I whisper.

His face twists. "Share you? With *him?*"

My heart is beating so fast it feels like a hummingbird is trapped in my ribcage. It's wrong to have this conversation without Caz here, but if I don't get this out, I might explode.

"Do you remember the Manor of Salacious Appetites?" I ask.

He scoffs. "Of course I do, but what does that have to do with—?" As he stares at me, his eyes grow wide with realization, and he drops my hands. "The threesome."

I give him a single nod and avert my gaze to the floor.

"When we were at the Manor of Salacious Appetites," he continues, "that's what you were imagining: having both me and my light one at once."

It's not a question; it's a statement. A fact as clear as a cloudless day.

"Yeah." A fresh wave of tears streams down my face as shame and guilt consume me. "Is it so wrong to want you both? I'm your fated mate, but I'm also Caz's. Why would destiny bring us together only to make me choose between you two?"

The weight of my admission hangs heavy between us.

He lets out a long breath. I'm desperate to hear his thoughts, to tell me it's okay to feel this way, and that he wants to fulfill my deepest sexual desires and fantasies to get me to stay.

But that's not what I get.

"I... I need time to consider." He stands up and turns for the door.

"Caspian, wait!"

He stops in the doorway and rests his hand on the frame, but he doesn't turn to face me. "I will never be enough, will I?" Somber resignation laces his tone. "I'm only one half of a broken soul. An incomplete man."

And with that, he's gone.

Queen Sybil was right about me. She knew my greed would only bring pain and suffering to Caspian.

After the Manor of Salacious Appetites, I thought I would have difficulty living up to his expectations of sex, not the other way around. I never thought I'd be the one to push him too far, but it seems as though everyone has a breaking point. Even Caspian.

I wanted too much and asked for too much. I thought I could have both my men at once, but I ended up pushing Caspian away. And if Caspian's reaction to my selfish, twisted desire was so jarring, I can't imagine how Caz would react.

I cried most of the night, falling in and out of a fitful sleep. When Elowen brings in my breakfast tray, I turn away from her, pulling the bedcovers up to my chin.

"Good morning." Elowen is tentative, tip-toeing around me and hoping not to set me off. "I set up a meeting with Valerius before lunch, and I was hoping you'd come."

"Who's Valerius?" I ask flatly.

"He's the elf with light magic. He's here to help with the ball at your request."

A pang of guilt spears through my chest, making my heart clench. Elowen is asking for my help, and I can't turn down my only friend. She's been nothing but patient with me as I've wallowed in my own problems for the past few days.

It takes every ounce of strength—both physically and emotionally—to get up and start getting ready. If it weren't for Elowen, I would opt for leggings, no makeup, and a messy bun, but she would never allow me to roam the castle in such disarray.

After my bath, Elowen combs my hair in front of the mirror. "You can talk to me, you know. About anything."

I can't exactly talk about wanting a threesome with the king, not that I'd want to if I could. This is a secret I need to keep to myself, one that I should push from my mind and forget. Caz can never find out about my erotic fantasy, and I need to find a way to salvage my relationship with Caspian. If I leave the Crimson Vale on bad terms with him, I'll never forgive myself.

I give Elowen a weak smile. "Thanks. I just have a lot on my mind."

Once I'm ready, Elowen and I make our way downstairs, though my pace is rather sluggish. Her friend, Valerius, is waiting for us in the empty ballroom.

The elf is rather handsome—his long, platinum-blond hair is pulled back into a low ponytail, and his golden eyes sparkle in the sunlight streaming in through the windows. One could guess he possesses light magic just by looking at him.

"Hello, Valerius," Elowen says, and a deep red blush blooms across her cheeks when he smiles at her.

"Elowen, it's truly wonderful to see you again." His voice is steady and warm. "And this must be Lady Briar, yes?"

"Nice to meet you." I glance between him and Elowen. "I appreciate your help on such short notice."

He gives me a deep bow. "It's a pleasure to serve House Nezara."

Elowen watches Valerius with a yearning expression, her violet eyes wistful.

Holy shit. She likes him.

"The king appreciates your loyalty," I tell Valerius. "As a token of our appreciation, why don't you attend the ball as our guest? Elowen can accompany you as your date."

Her eyes grow wide, and the flush on her cheeks deepens.

Valerius looks surprised, but his expression brightens when he glances at Elowen. "I would be honored, Lady Briar." He gives me another deep bow. "I look forward to it."

I clap my hands together. "Great! Then it's settled. Elowen, if you wouldn't mind explaining to Valerius what we need for Saturday, I have a few other matters to attend to."

"Of course," she squeaks. She steals a glance at Valerius before averting her gaze to the floor.

I turn and head straight for the doors, leaving the two of them alone in the ballroom. I burst through the exit and round the corner as quickly as I can, eager to put some distance between me and them.

I'm happy for Elowen, and I want her to pursue her interest in Valerius, but my heart physically hurts at the sight of other people's happiness. Her relationship is just beginning to blossom while mine crumbles to ash.

When I turn the next corner, a couple of servants are making their way toward me, so I slip into the first set of doors I find, which open up into the royal library. I'll hide in here for a while, at least until I can pull myself together. No one needs to see me fall apart.

In this world, you get eaten alive at the first sign of weakness. That's what Caspian said.

The tears begin to fall as I press my back to the door, but when another opens on the opposite end of the room, I startle and clutch my hand to my chest.

Caspian steps through from his attached office, but he freezes when he spots me in the library. "I heard a noise and came to inspect it." A few tense moments of silence pass between us as we stare at one another, and he clears his throat. "Excuse me. I'll give you the room."

"Caspian, wait. Please." I blow out a breath. "I hate this."

He roves his gaze over my face. "I told you, I need time."

"But we don't have time." Afraid of startling him, I cross the library cautiously. He gives me a wary look as I close the distance between us. "There's only twelve more nights before the next full moon."

"You know, you don't have to leave during the next full moon." He shrugs, his gaze distant and guarded. "You can stay for two moon cycles. Three. Five. You can stay as long as you want while you decide if I'm enough to make you stay."

"I can't leave Caz in the dungeons for that long." I shake my head. "If you could let him out for longer than just the night of the masquerade—"

"It would appear we're at an impasse," Caspian cuts me off. It's clear from his tone the conversation is over, and he turns his back on me, slamming the door in my face.

Elowen brings a dinner tray to my room, along with the news that the king is otherwise engaged and won't be dining with me this evening.

I toss and turn all night long, and when morning arrives, I'm too exhausted to get out of bed. Elowen invites me to attend another meeting with Valerius, but the thought of watching them stealing flirtatious glances at one another the whole time makes my stomach churn.

Tomorrow night is the masquerade ball, and I wonder if my deal with Caspian is still on. Will he let Caz be the first to find me? Or will his jealous, possessive side take over and steal me away to his bed for the night?

The easy thing to do would be to forget about Caspian. Find a way to get through until the full moon arrives and return with Caz, just like I always planned, and he and I could live out our days together on the ranch. I know we'd be happy together.

But deep down, I know something would be missing from my life. A crucial piece of my heart I'd have to leave behind in the Crimson Vale.

When night falls, I head down to the dining room, even though Elowen said he wouldn't be dining with me tonight. I hold on to a small glimmer of hope that he will be there anyway, and if he's forced to sit down for a meal with me, then we can figure things out. I can't navigate this mess on my own; I need Caspian.

But the dining room is empty. The only sounds that fill the room are the seconds of the grandfather clock ticking by at an excruciatingly slow pace.

Tick tock, tick tock...

The door opens, and my heart jumps, but when I see the servant hastening toward me, I deflate. "He's not coming, is he?"

"No, he is not, Lady Briar," he replies. "But I'll serve your meal in here tonight if you'd prefer?"

I shake my head. "No, it's fine. I don't have much of an appetite."

He gives me a quick bow before retreating through the door to the kitchens.

I heave a heavy sigh, closing my eyes. Pressure builds in my chest as disappointment, sadness, even anger swirl within.

How dare he?

Why should I apologize? What right does he have to be mad at me for vocalizing what I want when he's known all along that I love Caz?

Despite the ancient curse, fate quite literally hurled me into the Crimson Vale and into the arms of Caspian. He's the one who told me I'd come to care for him as much as I care for Caz because they are two halves of the same man. I didn't ask for any of this, but now that Caspian has gotten his way, he's upset at me for it?

Caspian took me to the Manor of Salacious Appetites. Caspian told me he wanted to fulfill my every whim and desire. And yet, when I tell him what I want deep down, he shames me for it? Ices me out?

How dare he? How *fucking dare he?*

With much more force than I intend, I shove my chair back from the table, which sends it tipping backward onto the floor with a clatter. I storm out of the dining room, past two guards at the door who step away to give me a wide berth.

That's right. They should fear me. Hell hath no fury like a woman who's fucking had enough.

I make my way through the castle corridors along the familiar path to his private bedroom. Without bothering to knock on his door, I barge inside, earning me a startled look from the guard stationed down the hall.

Caspian is seated in front of the fireplace on his sofa, staring into the fire with a glass of red liquid in his hand. His eyes dart toward me as I storm into the room and slam the door shut.

"What's your problem?" I storm across the room to pace back and forth in front of the fireplace, glaring daggers at him.

"Bri, what—"

"No! You don't get to speak right now," I interrupt. "You promised me you would do everything in your power to convince me to stay before the next full moon. You knew going into this how I feel about Caz, but you set out to make me feel the same for you. So, how dare you push me away after making me fall in love with you, too? This is all *your* fault!"

A heavy silence falls over the room, and Caspian stares at me with a startled expression. His mouth parts as he sucks in a sharp breath. "What did you just say?"

"I said, 'How dare you push me away after making me fall in love with you'." My frustration and fury are about to boil over, and I might start throwing things any minute now. Especially if he continues to look at me like I've just grown two heads.

"You... you said you loved me," he says.

"Yes, you idiot, I love you!" I take a breath before laying into him even further, but I stop myself.

I've just confessed those three little words to Caspian: *I love you.* They came out so naturally I didn't realize the weight they carry.

It's true—I love Caspian. I love Caspian just as much as I love Caz. I love the two halves of the same whole, the light one and the dark one equally. I need one just as much as I need the other because they're my fated mates.

I can't fight fate any longer, nor do I want to.

Caspian jumps to his feet, closing the distance between us as his hands grab me and pull me into the most passion-fueled kiss I've ever experienced. If he weren't gripping me so tightly, I'd lose my balance from the lightheaded feeling he gives me, which takes my breath away as his mouth consumes mine.

He wraps one of his arms around my waist while snaking his fingers through my hair with the other, pulling my face against his. His wild tongue explores the chasm of my mouth as his hips move against me, and even though our bodies melt into each other, we still yearn to be closer.

He breaks apart from our kiss for a moment, and the expression of pure devotion on his face stuns me. He's grinning with unadulterated happiness as his burgundy eyes start brimming with tears of joy. "Say it again," he whispers.

"I love you, Caspian." I can't help but grin from his infectious euphoria.

He lifts me up into a joyful embrace and swings me around, laughing with pure bliss. "I love you too, Bri. I love you so, so much."

He stops spinning me, setting me down to plant another deep, passionate kiss against my lips. Our legs become butter, and we sink to the floor in front of the fireplace. The thick fur of the bearskin rug grazes my legs as we kneel facing each other, and the warmth from the fire heats my skin as Caspian slips my dress off over my head, exposing my bare breasts and panties.

Caspian yanks off his shirt, revealing that broad, muscular chest that drives me wild. No man should be this beautiful, but there are two of them that exist in this world, and they're both mine.

He shimmies out of his pants and underwear, his growing erection coming to full mast.

I lean back onto the floor, slipping off my panties to expose myself completely to him. He lunges forward, kissing me urgently and lying me back on the rug, which is thick and soft against my bare back.

The tip of his shaft teases my entrance as he settles his weight on top of me.

Finally, he thrusts inside, drawing his face away just enough to watch my reaction. I let out a gasp at the contact, but I hold my gaze steady with his.

Caspian begins to rock back and forth, our eyes drinking the other in the entire time. I watch every muscle in his face react to my body, just as he's watching me, and I've never felt an intimacy on this level before. Our sexual experience tonight transcends pure lust... this is something that runs much deeper.

We are completely in sync as we move in tandem. His length continues to spear into my core as though our bodies were custom made to fit together in perfect harmony. We undulate faster without a word, our lovemaking heated and needy as we hurdle toward the brink. Our breathing is labored as we gasp for breath, sweat clinging to our naked bodies as we give each other our all.

As one, we both career over the edge, crying out each other's names as we find our release. His seed fills my lower belly with warmth as I convulse beneath him, losing myself in the depths of my love for this man.

I want him to stay buried within me forever, just like this, and never let me go. I don't care what Queen Sybil says... I want to stay by his side, even if I'm unworthy. As long as he'll have me, I'll stay.

Whatever the future may hold, I don't care. As long as we love each other, we'll figure it out.

All three of us.

CHAPTER 17

The following morning, I wake up exhausted in Caspian's bed, his hard, naked body pressing against mine. If I could, I would stay in his arms all day.

We didn't do much sleeping last night. After we made love on the floor, we continued on the sofa, then the bath, then the bed. Heat creeps to my cheeks when I replay those moments in my mind.

Caspian stirs beside me, and when his burgundy eyes meet mine, he smiles. "Good morning."

"Good morning. How are you feeling?"

"I'm great." He sits up and leans his back against the headboard. "The question is, how are you?"

I grin. "Exhausted, but for good reason."

"Breakfast should be here shortly." Caspian glances at the clock on his bedside table. "Or, should I say, lunch?"

"Good. I'm starved." I stretch my arms over my head and yawn, and the sheet slips down to my waist.

His eyes darken as he licks his lips. "Instead of lunch, why don't I eat you instead?"

I wrap my arms around his neck and give him a kiss, which he meets with fervor. "Are you referring to my pussy or my blood?"

He growls against my lips. "I'm greedy, so both."

I laugh and slip out of bed, giving my bare ass a little shake as I cross over to his wardrobe. "I'd take you up on your offer, but I've got to get a start on the day. Especially since I woke up late." I throw a playful glance over my shoulder.

All of Caspian's clothes are black, so I grab the one hanging closest to me and put it on. It hangs just low enough to cover my sensitive areas.

He smirks. "Looks better on you than it does on me." He crosses the bedroom, takes me in his arms, and plants a deep kiss on my lips. Like a drug I can't get enough of, I lean into his mouth, pressing my hips against his.

Instantly, he starts to grow hard.

We're interrupted by a knock on the door, and he breaks away to put on his robe. Moments later, a servant wheels in the meal cart. His eyes widen when he sees me, but he quickly averts his gaze and sets up our meal quickly before bowing and leaving us.

I grab my plate and take a seat on the sofa while Caspian pours a glass of blood from the pitcher. "Any hints on what you'll be wearing?"

"That would give you an unfair advantage." Although, I honestly don't know yet. Aurelius hasn't told me what he's designed.

"That's the point." A dark expression crosses his face as a tense silence falls between us.

Caz will be at the ball tonight, and I'm both nervous and excited to see him. So much has happened since I saw him last—like falling in love with his dark one.

Who will find me first before midnight? Caz or Caspian?

We don't speak for the rest of the meal. I worry he's going to fall back into not speaking to me again, but before I leave for my room, he takes me in his arms.

"I'm going to win tonight," he whispers in my ear. His nose grazes my cheekbone, sending a shudder through my body.

"I love you, Caspian. No matter what happens tonight, remember that."

He nods, his expression somber, then steps out of my embrace. "I love you more."

When I walk into my room, Elowen is already waiting for me. She draws a fresh bath, but I don't have any time to linger in it because Aurelius arrives for my dress fitting. His assistants are setting up my dress on the mannequin when I emerge from the bathroom in my robe.

"Lady Briar!" he exclaims, giving me a quick kiss on each cheek. "You're going to make a marvelous peacock!"

I blink. "A peacock?"

"Yes, come take a look."

He leads me over to the dress, which looks like something Marie Antoinette would have worn in the French court, except that the colors are a mixture of teal, navy, emerald green, and purple. Black lace ruffle details adorn the sleeves, collar, and hem of the skirt, and the colors shimmer in an ombre pattern under the light. In the back is a high collar made entirely of peacock feathers.

"Wait until you see the mask." He waves over one of his assistants, who steps forward with a black lace mask in her outstretched hands. A few large peacock feathers are attached to the side at a jaunty angle, and two black ribbons hang off the ends to tie it around my head.

"Is it to your satisfaction?" Aurelius asks, trying to gauge my reaction.

I nod as I sweep the edge of the mask with my fingertip. "It's incredible. Really."

"Oh, Lady Briar, you honor me." He gives me a deep bow, and the assistants begin to applaud.

I wonder if he pays them extra to do that.

Aurelius straightens up and claps his hands. "Let's do a quick fitting before Elowen steals you away for hair and makeup."

Once we finish the fitting, the assistants put the dress back on the mannequin to make the last-minute adjustments, and I return to the bathroom with Elowen.

As she dries my hair, I glance at her in the mirror. "What will you be wearing tonight?"

She smiles. "I'm going as a butterfly."

"And what will Valerius be dressed as?"

Her cheeks turn beet red, and I lift my hand to my mouth to cover a laugh.

"He says his mask will look like the sun," she says, glancing at the floor.

"You two will make a cute couple." I waggle my eyebrows.

"Oh, Bri!" Her hands fly up to cover her cheeks. "Thank you for inviting us."

"Of course. We'll have lots of fun tonight."

With Malrick locked away in the dungeons and increased security, I'm not nervous about tonight like I was a few days ago. In fact, I'm looking forward to the ball, and I'm looking forward to seeing Caz—if we can find each other in the crowd.

On the one hand, I hope he finds me first, because we have a lot we need to talk about. But, if Caspian finds me first, I'll be able to put off a hard conversation for a little while longer.

Either way, I win tonight, one way or another. But one of them loses, and that guilt gnaws my stomach.

Once Elowen finishes my hair and makeup and Aurelius's assistants help me into my dress, I send Elowen downstairs. Caspian will expect me to head down early to make sure the ballroom is ready for the guests, so sending Elowen in my place will throw him off the scent.

He's made it clear that he doesn't play fair, but I'm not going to make it easy for him.

By the time I arrive downstairs, a large crowd has already gathered in the ballroom, allowing me to blend in with the sea of people. The guests are wearing ostentatious outfits like mine in an array of colors and textures, and the party feels more like a Venetian carnival. The energy is electric.

"Lady Briar has done it again," someone says in front of me. "This party is marvelous."

I grin, enjoying the anonymity my mask provides, and scan the room for any man that matches Caz and Caspian's height and weight. But everyone is masked in elaborate costumes, and I can't make out any distinguishing features of the guests.

A cocktail server with a gold Venetian mask walks by with a tray of champagne, so I pick one up and begin to sip, continuing my survey of the crowd.

Someone in a pink, purple, and white butterfly mask stands next to someone in a sun mask—I assume Elowen and Valerius. They seem comfortable with each other as they talk and laugh, and I'm glad to see her enjoying her night off. She deserves it.

I scan the black silks hanging across the ceiling, along with Valerius's magic orbs of light dancing delicately above like fireflies. The room is bathed in luxury, and the royal family crest is displayed on the flags covering the walls. Caspian will be pleased.

If I'm lucky, Queen Sybil will see this party as the power move it is and leave me alone for a little while, though I'm not holding my breath. This masquerade is so much more than a party—it's a display of the might of House Nezara. That the king is strong and unafraid of his enemies.

It's an idea that Caspian and I came up with together, and if I became his queen, he and I would be unstoppable. I just have to figure out how Caz fits into that dynamic.

The small chamber orchestra ends their lively song and begins a slow, sultry waltz. Someone taps my shoulder and my heart rate skyrockets.

Did Caz or Caspian find me already?

When I turn, I come face-to-face with a man extending his hand out to me in an invitation to dance. He's wearing a black cloak over his head, and his mask is a full-faced,

Venetian-style gold mask. Black mesh covers the holes around his eyes, so I'm unable to tell what color they are.

Without a word, I set my empty glass of champagne on a nearby table. When I place my hand into his leather-gloved palm, he leads me through the crowd to the dancefloor. His hand rests on the small of my back, while the other holds my arm extended from our bodies, and at the top of the melody, he begins to spin me in time with the music.

It's hard to make out his build beneath the cloak, but his height is about right for Caz and Caspian. The way he guides my dance steps makes me think it could very well be Caspian. I can't be absolutely certain, although I wouldn't put it past him to engage a servant to tip him off about my costume. If that's the case, I'll be really fucking pissed, because it means he never intended to give Caz a chance in the first place.

The song comes to an end, and all the couples on the dancefloor stop and bow to their partners. My masked man takes my hand and begins to pull me toward the balcony outside.

Yep, it's definitely Caspian. No one else would act so familiar with a stranger like this. I won't call out the king in front of everyone, but as soon as we're away from the crowd, I'm going to go off on him. I'm so furious I'm shaking.

We head through the glass doors outside to the balcony, and as he leads me down the steps into the garden, the sound of the party grows more distant.

"Caspian, you better not be dragging me out here to have sex." I yank my hand out of his and stop along the path. "You cheated, which means you forfeit your night with me." I untie my mask so he can get the full effect of my rage.

He stops and turns to face me, but he doesn't lower his hood or remove his mask. In fact, he doesn't say a word; he just stares at me and tilts his head to the side.

I scoff. "Don't act innocent. You broke our deal by getting tipped off about my costume, didn't you? Did you really think I wouldn't figure it out?"

He takes a step toward me, but I hold my ground. "Don't you have anything to say for yourself?"

Hard footsteps catch my attention, and I turn around to see who followed us into the garden. But before I have a chance to find out, someone grabs my arms as a hood is shoved over my head. I start to scream, but a hand clamps over my mouth to stifle it.

Another pair of hands lift my legs while someone else pulls my arms. Adrenaline pumps through my veins and I fight back. I manage to get one of my legs free and start kicking at my unseen kidnapper, but before I can deliver a hard blow, something heavy crashes against my skull, and the world around me plunges into darkness.

The throbbing pain in my head wakes me up. My vision is blurred, so I can't tell where I am. I reach up to touch my head gingerly, and dried blood is stuck in my hair.

The floor I'm lying on is cold and rough. I blink a few times to bring my surroundings into focus, and I find myself in a small room made out of stone bricks. There are no windows, so I have no idea if it's day or night, and the only exit is a wooden door. Hanging by the door is a pillar candle, illuminating the room in an eerie, flickering glow.

I glance down at my ballgown and find it stained with dirt and the lace detail ripped in a few places.

I try to stand up, but I'm too dizzy to find my balance. Instead, I crawl over to the door and lift the handle, only to find it locked.

Where the hell am I?

My chest heaves with ragged breaths as panic sets in. I keep telling myself to stay calm, but it's no use. I crawl backwards into the corner and hug my knees to my chest, rocking back and forth as a sob sticks in my throat.

This room is completely empty, devoid of a bench or a bed to lie on. There's not even a bucket to use for a toilet.

Unless someone brings me food and water, I'm going to die in here.

I burrow my face into my knees as tears well in my eyes.

Time passes at an excruciating pace. I'm too on edge to drift back to sleep, but I'm going insane without anything to keep my mind occupied. Instead of panicking, I count the stitches on the hem of my skirt. When I finish, I count the stitches on the hem of each sleeve.

And then I do it all over again.

The lock clicks on the door, and I freeze. Terror grips me as the door creaks open, and I press my back against the wall, trying to put as much distance as I can between me and the intruder.

When Malrick steps into the room, I stiffen. His long, greasy hair is slicked back, and his pointed, yellowed teeth stretch into a leering grin. Our eyes meet, but he's only looking at me with one golden eye. An eyepatch covers the other where Caspian plunged his dagger.

He closes the door behind him and crosses the small room. He stops in front of where I sit, looming over me. "Good. You're awake."

I swallow the lump in my throat. "Where am I?"

His grin widens. "Somewhere your bloodsucker will never find."

My heart sinks. I don't know how long I've been out, but surely Caz and Caspian have noticed my absence by now.

"What do you want?" I ask quietly.

Malrick crouches in front of me until our gazes are level and points at his eyepatch. "Caspian took my eye, so I took his mate. But don't fret. You'll be free soon enough."

I sit up straighter. "I will?"

"I'm going to make him an offer: your life in exchange for his throne. I'm certain he will accept, and then a true werewolf will be crowned the King of Alphas. You're just a means to an end." He reaches out to caress my knee over my dress. "But in the meantime, you and I can have some fun. I'll show you what a real alpha cock can do."

I shrink back further against the wall, trying to make myself as small as possible. "How did you even get out of the dungeons?" I have to keep him talking, keep him distracted. Buy myself some time.

"While everyone was preoccupied with the ball, my pack overpowered the guards to the dungeons. They brought me a costume to enter the party and find you, and an informant told me which costume to look for." He sneers. "And you made it so easy to get you alone."

"You? You were the one I danced with?" A chill washes over my body.

He slips his hand beneath the hem of my skirt. "You enjoyed our dance, didn't you?"

It takes me back to that night of the garden party when he tried to come onto me in the hedge maze before Caspian arrived.

Except Caspian isn't here to rescue me this time.

Malrick's stale breath fans my face as his rough hand touches my skin. "When that bloodsucker trades you for his throne, my scent will be all over you, and he'll have to live with the knowledge that I took everything from him." He slides his hand further up my leg.

Something awakens within me. I don't know if it's my survival instinct or if I've finally come to my senses, but I kick my leg out with as much force as I can muster. My heeled shoe lands squarely on his chest, and he topples backward to the floor.

While he's stunned, I waste no time scrambling to my feet and rush toward the unlocked door. However, when I fling it open, another man is standing in the doorway, blocking my path.

He's shorter and a bit burlier than the alpha; his face is covered in uneven scruff, and he's rather plain without any distinguishing features. He's not ugly, but he's not attractive either, although he could certainly use a bath.

He grabs my arms and pushes me back into the room. "I don't think so."

"You bitch!" Malrick roars. His body begins to tremble and shake, and the sound of his bones breaking cracks through the air. As he shifts, his clothes tear apart and fall to the floor, and within moments, his wolf form fills the entire room.

He lets out a vicious snarl, baring his teeth as saliva drips from his maw. Enraged, the wolf lashes a paw out at me, and his claws rip into my skin. I cry out and scramble backward, trying to avoid another attack.

"Alpha Malrick!" the other man shouts from the doorway. He waves his hands to get the wolf's attention. "We need her alive to make the trade for the throne!"

The wolf whips his head to snarl at him, but he doesn't attack. After a tense standoff, the wolf transforms back into the naked form of Malrick, and I avert my gaze.

"We need proof of life," Malrick says, unbothered by his state of undress.

"Perhaps a finger?" his pack mate suggests.

I shove my hands behind my back, burying them in the skirts. My chest and arm sting where Malrick slashed me, but I ignore the sensation and press my back against the wall.

"I have a better idea." Malrick glances over his shoulder at me. "Collect a vial of her blood, now that she has fresh wounds. Once that vampire takes a single whiff of it, he'll give up anything to get her back."

Malrick turns, giving me a view of his chest where I kicked him and the round indent matching the heel of my shoe. I didn't draw blood, but that'll definitely leave a bruise. Serves him right.

He gives me a long look, but the desire in his eye is long gone. Instead, loathing fills his gaze. Better loathing than lust.

Without another word, Malrick walks out the door, followed by his pack mate. The lock clicks after they leave, only to unlock a half hour later, and Malrick's pack mate walks in holding a tray of food. He sets it on the floor and plucks a glass vial off it.

He's dirty, like he hasn't showered in days, and I detest the idea of him getting near my open wound with grungy hands.

He crosses the small space and grabs my arm in his rough grip, making me whimper in pain. Three large gashes go across my entire chest and right arm, and the front of my dress is ripped from Malrick's claws. Blood stains my dress around the wounds, and when he squeezes my arm, more blood drips down my skin. He holds the vial up to it, pressing my arm in different places to squeeze out as much blood as possible.

When he's satisfied, he corks the vial and walks out of the room, slamming the door shut behind him. A moment later, the lock clicks.

I sink to the floor, shaking violently from the sharp pain. I need to clean the wounds, so I crawl over to the tray of food he left behind. My stomach growls at the sight of a loaf of stale bread and a goblet of water, which is all he provided.

I devour the bread and drink some of the water, but I leave enough to clean my wounds. With a loud rip, I tear off a few strips of fabric from the bottom of my dress and soak them in the remaining water before applying them to my gashes.

It stings as I lay each strip of cloth across my chest, but I grind my teeth and endure it. After a few minutes, the stinging feeling goes away and is replaced with a dull throbbing.

How the hell am I going to get out of here? There isn't any route for escape besides the door, which is locked at all times. The only time it's unlocked is when someone comes in.

Running from Malrick didn't work because he had backup. However, I doubt his pack mate had backup when he came to collect my blood.

A plan begins to form in my head.

It's crazy, and there is so much that can go wrong, but I have to try.

Chapter 18

They haven't brought me another plate of food since the stale bread and glass of water, even though it feels like a full day has passed since then. Without windows or something to occupy myself, it's difficult to gauge exactly how much time has passed.

My body is too stressed to sleep for long, so between fitful bursts of rest, I contemplate my escape plan in my head. It's flawed—*very* flawed—but I can't see any other way out. Even though I'm starving, I appreciate Malrick and his henchmen leaving me alone. A part of me worries that I'll lose my nerve the next time I see them, and I can't. Not if I'm going to pull this off.

But it's hard to think in here. Aside from the overpowering stench of urine in the opposite corner, my body is heavy with fatigue, and every thought feels like wading through sludge. My joints and muscles are sore, and the nausea comes and goes the longer I sit here on the cold stone floor.

When my symptoms become too overwhelming, my mind disassociates from my body, and I'm going to need that to get through what comes next.

The lock clicks in the door, and terror renders my body frozen, with the exception of my racing heart. Moments later, a figure enters the room—Malrick's pack mate who brought my meal and collected my blood yesterday.

It doesn't look like he's showered since, either.

With a grunt, he strides in with another stale loaf of bread and a cup of water and sets it down beside me on the floor.

"Thank you." My voice is weak and hoarse. "What's your name?"

He stops and gives me a guarded look. "Why do you need to know my name?"

"I-I just wanted to thank you." I avert my gaze in submission. "Would it be possible to get some more food?"

"No." He gives his head a firm shake before turning toward the door.

"Wait! Maybe we could... work something out?"

He peers over his shoulder, brow furrowing. "What are you talking about?"

"I mean, I could give you something in exchange for more food." I inject as much allure into my voice as I can muster.

At first, he doesn't say anything, so I bat my eyelashes up at him a couple of times, trying to entice him. When I shift to sit on my knees, his eyes widen, and after a few moments, he breaks the silence of the room.

"I'm Vane," he says gruffly, taking a step toward me. "I'm the beta of the Ravenrock Clan."

"Vane." I give him my best come-hither look. "That's a strong, sexy name."

"You think so?" He smirks and takes a step closer, and then another until he comes to a stop in front of me, my head eye-level with his belt.

"Yeah." I reach out to run my hands up his thighs. "I wonder what else about you is strong and sexy."

His laugh rumbles low in his chest, but he doesn't stop my hands from fiddling with his belt.

"If you'll do this for a piece of bread, I wonder what you do for the king for dresses and jewels." Vane watches me with a hooded gaze. "I can't wait to see what all the fuss is about over the king's whore."

I resist the urge to glare at him and focus on unbuckling his belt. With an aggressive yank, I pull his pants down to his knees, and his hardening erection is directly in front of my face.

It takes every ounce of willpower not to gag. With a deep breath, I remind myself that escape is within reach.

"Take it." He fists my hair and thrusts forward into my mouth before I can chicken out.

I gag as his shaft hits the back of my throat. Vane begins to rock his hips back and forth while holding my head firmly in place. Tears begin to stream down my face as I choke on his length.

On his next thrust into my mouth, I bite down as hard as I can with my teeth.

Vane's scream rings out around the small room as he stumbles backward. With his pants bunched below his knees, he loses his footing and falls onto his backside, cradling his exposed manhood in his hands and writhing on the floor. Judging from the taste of blood in my mouth, I got him good.

I snatch the loaf of bread and scramble to my feet. Before reaching the door, I deliver one last kick in the balls to Vane. A fresh round of screams echoes around the small room as I search his pockets for the key, and when I find it, I run.

Outside, I shut the door behind me and lock him inside.

Much like my holding room, the floor and walls of the corridor are constructed from stone bricks. The ceiling hangs low, and only a single wax pillar candle illuminates the narrow passageway. There are no windows, and the temperature is unusually cold, which makes me wonder if I'm underground.

I follow the dim corridor around the corner, and then another until I finally reach a set of stairs leading up to a closed hatch overhead. With caution, I climb the stairs and push the door upward just a crack.

Fresh, cool air hits my face as I peer through the gap. A clearing of grass surrounded by trees glows red beneath the moon in the night sky. There's no sign of Malrick or his other henchmen, so I open the door wider and climb outside.

Upon closer inspection, the clearing is full of crops. With a 360-degree view of the field, I turn in a circle and find a barn nearby, along with a thatched farmhouse. Light shines through one of the windows of the farmhouse, revealing a group of men sitting in a circle playing cards and drinking—including Malrick.

I need to get out of here before they realize Vane is missing and come looking for him. My plan didn't account for what I'd do after escaping my cell.

So, I hike up my dress and run as fast as I can in my heels, seeking cover beyond the forest edge surrounding the farm. The wind whips through my hair as my skirts billow behind me. My breathing comes in ragged breaths, and my legs start to burn the more I push, threatening to give out from beneath me. But I ignore the sensation and press forward until I'm tucked away in the dark forest.

Pressing my back against a tree, I peer around the trunk to check if I've been followed. The field is empty.

But there's no time to breathe a sigh of relief. I have to keep moving, but journeying deeper into the forest is difficult with only the red crescent moon illuminating my path. The thick branches of the trees block much of the light, so I take careful steps forward, my hands outstretched to prevent me from running into a tree trunk.

The heel of my shoe catches on a tree root, and I tumble forward to the ground. When my chest hits the forest floor, rocks dig into the wounds from Malrick's claws, and a sharp cry of pain rips from my throat.

But there's not enough light to inspect my injuries. I use a nearby tree to steady myself and stand up, and with much more care, I press on, taking tentative steps to avoid any more exposed tree roots.

I continue moving until my legs begin to shake and lightheadedness takes over. Sinking to the ground, I pull my bread out and begin to eat. If I ever see Aurelius again, I'll have to thank him for the dress pockets.

My mouth is parched, but until I come across a creek of water, I'll have to suffer through. At this rate, I won't be getting very far in the dark, and I need to conserve my energy to move during the day. I fumble around in the darkness for an appropriate shelter, and if I'm lucky, Malrick's pack will get so drunk they won't notice mine or Vane's absence.

It doesn't take long to find a tree with thick, exposed roots, which form a small shelter to hide me from view. I slip off one of the petticoats of my dress and ball it up to make a pillow before lying down, though the twigs and rocks dig into my back.

As my breathing slows, the forest buzzes with life. An owl hoots and crickets chirp rhythmically as leaves rustle in the breeze. It should calm me, but my senses are on high alert for any sign of danger.

All I want is to be back with Caspian and Caz, but I have no idea how far away they are. I'm sure Caspian has his armies searching the entire kingdom for me, but will it be enough? How long do I have before Malrick and his men realize I'm gone?

Who will find me first?

After tossing and turning on the rough ground all night long, dawn arrives. I can forge ahead at a much quicker pace and scavenge for food along the way. My stomach twists with hunger and growls as a reminder that I've been living on stale bread for the past two days.

Blisters line my feet from wandering the forest in heels, and for a moment, I consider taking them off. But rocks and twigs litter the ground, so I keep them on when I stand, dusting the dirt off my dress.

Birds chirp in the trees and insects buzz around me, and for a moment I forget I'm in the Crimson Vale. This forest is so similar to the ones back on Earth.

An hour or two passes on my journey before the sound of a gentle creek reaches my ears. My heart leaps with excitement, and I follow the noise until I find it. When I reach the bank, I drop to my knees and scoop the water into my mouth with a voracious thirst.

It's cool, but not so cold that I couldn't take a bath. Cleaning my wounds would be beneficial, so I strip naked and fold my dress up to place it on the bank. My makeshift bandages have started to stick to my dried wounds, so with a sharp intake of breath, I peel the fabric away from my skin like I'd rip off a Band-Aid. I lay them on top of my dress and step into the water.

The first few steps are cold as I slowly submerge myself. It's shallow enough that I can kneel with my head above the water, so when my shoulders are beneath the surface, I lean back to rinse my hair.

After last night's encounter with Vane, it feels cathartic to wash myself, as if I'm purifying my body after being tainted by his touch. Just thinking about him in my mouth makes me gag.

I take a moment to enjoy the cold water while I plan my next move. To cover my tracks, I should get out on the opposite bank of the river downstream. I have no idea if this is the same river that flows under the bridge below the castle, but if I follow it, I should eventually hit a village along the way where I can ask for directions.

A distant howl echoes around the trees. The birds stop chirping and the insects stop buzzing as the forest comes to a complete standstill. I freeze, recognizing the distinct call of a werewolf.

As quietly as I can, I grab my dress and my bandages off the nearby rock and wade downstream, holding them high above my head to prevent the fabrics from getting wet. When I emerge, I slip my dress back on quickly and shove the bandages into my pocket. I don't have time to clean them and redress my wounds.

Another howl makes my blood run cold. This time it's closer, and it's joined in by more werewolves. They've probably locked onto my scent, and I can't outrun a pack of them.

I spot a tree nearby with branches low enough to climb. It's going to be tough with my dress, but it'll provide cover in the forest canopy. They're gaining on me by the second, and it's the only option I can think of. I take my heels off and shove them into my empty dress pockets.

My arm muscles are weak, but I manage to crawl up onto the lowest branch. I'm breathing hard, and my arms begin to shake, but it should be a tad easier from here.

Adrenaline fuels my ascent as I shimmy up the tree, hanging on to the branches for dear life. The howling continues to grow louder, and the trees reverberate with the sheer power of their voices. I scramble toward the top, but the more energy I expend, the clumsier I get.

My foot slips on one of the branches, and I throw my arms around the tree trunk to steady myself as a small yelp escapes my lips. "Ah!"

The howling stops.

Oh, God, did I just give my location away?

I stop breathing or moving and listen for any sign of my pursuers. But the forest is completely silent... *too* silent.

Minutes later, voices float through the forest, and my heart hammers hard against my ribcage.

"...and her scent just stops at the river."

"We need to check the other side of the bank. You two go that way. The rest of you, follow me."

They're closing in on my location, and there's nothing I can do except wait and pray I won't be discovered.

Minutes later, a voice I recognize as Malrick's speaks. "Larold, have you got a scent?"

In response, a beast snorts, and my stomach sinks when I realize the werewolves are acting as sniffing dogs. I never stood a chance at getting away.

"Close by, you say? Good. Lead the way."

The massive paws of the werewolf shake the ground with each step. After a couple of minutes, dark fur appears through the branches below, and I hold my breath once again, praying silently for them to move on.

The werewolf, Larold, leads the way, while Malrick and Vane follow behind in their human forms. Panic rises higher in my chest, constricting my throat and paralyzing me in terror.

"Come out, Lady Briar, wherever you are!" Malrick calls in a sing-song voice. "I promise I won't bite too hard." He lets out a low, dangerous laugh.

Malrick holds my balled-up petticoat in his grasp, which I left behind under the tree where I slept last night. He presses it to his face and takes a deep inhale, closing his eyes.

I led them straight to me.

Fuck. Fuck, fuck, *fuck.*

When the werewolf gets to the base of my tree, he sniffs the trunk and pauses before sitting down.

"The scent goes cold?" Vane asks. "How is that possible?"

"No!" Malrick bangs his fist against the tree. "You idiots! I'll sniff her out myself."

Malrick begins to transform into his wolf, and the sound of his bones breaking cracks through the air. It sends a shudder down my spine, which sends my whole body trembling, and my muscles ache from clinging to the branches.

He stands on his hind legs before stomping down on his front paws, forcing the trees to quiver in response to the sheer power of his weight hitting the forest floor. My tree shakes, and I grip the trunk tighter into my chest, which presses bark against my wounds.

I bite down on my tongue to keep from crying out from the pain.

In his wolf form, Malrick begins to throw a tantrum, and he paces below, swiping his massive paw at a nearby tree and leaving claw marks along the base. My eyes widen with horror as Malrick slams his paw into my tree, causing the leaves to rustle and fall as the trunk reverberates.

The branch beneath me starts to crack, and I clutch desperately to the trunk. When Malrick's wolf slams his body against the tree, the branch snaps.

I fall and emit a loud scream as I crash through the lower branches on my way down. And when my body slams to the ground, my world goes black.

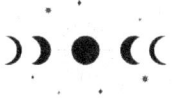

When I wake up, I let out a soft moan at the throbbing pain all over my body. I try to reach up to touch my head, but my wrists are bound behind my back.

I open my eyes to find myself in the same holding room at Malrick's farm, and my stomach churns.

It was all for nothing. Sucking off Vane, the blisters on my feet, all of it. My escape attempt failed.

"Welcome back," a sinister voice says. *Malrick's voice.*

I turn my head in his direction, where he's leaning against the closed door, blocking the exit.

"Don't even think about trying anything," he says. "My pack is stationed just outside the door, and they'll barge in if I give them the signal."

Tears of frustration well in my eyes, and I choke down a sob. "Have you made a deal with Caspian yet?"

"We'll have his answer tomorrow night. We've instructed him to send a messenger to meet ours at a remote location. You better hope you're worth an entire kingdom to him." Malrick takes a menacing step toward me. "But before I send you back, I'll cover you with my scent so Caspian knows I laid claim to his mate."

My throat constricts.

I try to back away from him as he steps even closer, but with my hands tied behind my back, it makes movement difficult. When I try rolling away from him, he grabs my ankle and pulls me closer, my chest scraping across the floor. A sharp pain hits my wounds as I cry out.

"Don't expect to fall for that little stunt you pulled with Vane." He pulls his belt off with one hand while tightening his grip on my ankle with the other. "Your mouth won't be anywhere near my cock."

Fresh tears stream down my face as he sits on my back, pressing my injured chest to the cold, damp floor. I'm unable to escape or struggle as he ties his belt around my face, and my teeth bite down into the leather strap.

I try to plead with him to let me go, but my words come out muffled and incoherent. He shifts off my back before pulling my hips upward so my ass is in the air. My face is pressed against the cold stone floor, and I'm unable to move with my hands tied behind my back.

There is no getting out of this.

I'm completely at his mercy.

All I can do is squeeze my eyes shut and hope it'll be over soon.

I try to focus on my breathing instead of my situation, but his roaming hands keep me grounded in this horrific reality. Malrick lifts my skirt over my back, and he groans when he sees my panties.

Just breathe, I tell myself repeatedly, waiting for the inevitable. His rough, calloused hands rip my panties apart, exposing my bare ass for his view. He squeezes my butt so hard I whimper.

Malrick removes his hands to shove his pants down. I feel violated already, and he hasn't even penetrated me yet. My heartbeat is thumping in my ears, and I want to curl up into a ball and cry.

Just when the tip of his cock brushes against my flesh, a loud commotion on the other side of the door erupts. Something heavy thuds against the door as shouting and screams of agony ensue.

Malrick pauses. "What the hell?"

The snarl of a werewolf shakes the small room as the door bursts open on us. I turn my head to the side, my cheek pressed into the floor, and when I do, my heart soars. Relief washes over me at the sight of Caspian standing in the doorway, smeared in the blood of Malrick's pack.

CHAPTER 19

CASPIAN

"Lady Briar has done it again." My hearing locks in on Bri's name from across the room. "This party is marvelous."

Grinning behind my mask, I glance toward the ceiling to admire her handiwork, including the red and black color scheme she chose as a nod to honor House Nezara. She truly has a queen's instinct for subtle political power moves; even my mother's parties never measured up in comparison.

Bri will be the perfect consort to rule by my side.

I stalk around the masquerade ball in search of a woman whose features look like Bri's: blonde hair, blue eyes, and a body to kill for. But the room is quite crowded—more crowded than usual. Perhaps last Saturday's incident with Malrick has drawn in people's morbid curiosities.

I try to sniff out Bri's scent, but it's disguised by the heavy perfumes and colognes of the hundreds of guests, and the sensory onslaught gives me a pounding headache.

Frustrated, I snatch a glass of champagne from a passing butler tray and down its contents in one gulp. I cannot let my light one get to Bri before I do. She cannot be reminded of her reasons for leaving.

The moment she said she loved me, it was all over for me. I'll be damned if I let her go.

I cannot help that Bri is mated to both me and my light one. Parting the two of them would bring her immense pain, but when she suggested a threesome, I was stunned.

Bri deserves every whim and desire fulfilled. But I've never had an interest in sharing a woman with another man... even if that other man is, technically speaking, me.

After seeing the two of them together in the dungeons, I thought I might go insane with jealousy, so how could I control myself while actively participating in her indiscretions?

The champagne flute shatters in my fist, earning me a couple of strange gazes from the guests. If they knew I was their king, they wouldn't dare look upon me with such judgment. But no one knows who I am with this black mask on, although it's taking every ounce of strength to not reveal myself and call out for Bri.

I cannot let my light one win. He's a thorn in my side that I cannot get rid of without hurting the woman I love. Only she could convince me to agree to this ridiculous arrangement.

When it comes to Bri, I truly am a simpering fool.

I spend the next hour searching the party, but I have no leads on either her costume or my rival's. Resisting the temptation to find out in advance proved difficult, but for Bri's sake, I refrained.

Someone taps on my shoulder. "It's me, Your Majesty. Marcellius."

My valet, Marcellius, is the only person in this castle who knows my true identity tonight. His tone is urgent.

"What is it?"

"Malrick has escaped," he says. "The guards were overtaken—"

Before Marcellius can finish, one of the guards stumbles into the ballroom with a cry of pain, which reverberates against the vaulted ceilings. The guests' chatter quiets into whispers as they turn toward the commotion, and the crowd parts to make a path for him. A few shocked gasps ring out as the full figure of the guard comes into view. Blood covers his uniform, and his gait is uneven as he limps into the party, clutching his stomach.

"Malrick's escaped!" he cries out, wincing in pain. "His pack has ambushed the guards!" He falls to his knees in the middle of the ballroom.

If Malrick has escaped, Bri is in danger. If he lays a hand on her...

My stomach lurches, but I push down the feeling and let my instincts as king take over. I push through the crowd to the nearest table and leap on top, taking off my mask to reveal my face to the entire room. "Everyone, remove your masks at once! If Malrick is among us, we will find him."

My discerning eyes scan the room for anyone not complying with my command and for Bri. Our deal is off—I'm going to keep her by my side all night, my light one be damned.

Speak of the devil.

My eyes fall onto my light one, who is looking back at me with a confused and worried expression on his face.

Ugh, he makes me sick. His innocent demeanor makes me look weak. As soon as I find

Bri and take care of Malrick, he needs to be thrown back into the dungeons, away from view. If Malrick finds out about him, that would be disastrous for me.

Marcellius approaches the table through the crowd. "Your Majesty, I cannot find any sign of Malrick."

My stomach twists. "What about Lady Briar?"

A somber expression crosses his face as he shakes his head, and an unfamiliar feeling rises in my chest: fear.

If Malrick is responsible for her absence, I will rip him and his entire pack limb from limb and burn what's left of their bodies.

"Marcellius, sequester all the guests for questioning." I stand back up to address the crowd. "No one leaves until everyone has been interrogated. Elowen, check Lady Briar's room, the library, and anywhere else she may have gone. Guards, follow me!"

I leap off the table and push through the crowd toward the doors, leading the guards from the party and into the corridor. Malrick did not escape on his own—he must have had assistance from his pack. If we're fortunate, they left behind clues to their whereabouts.

When we enter the courtyard, at least a dozen bodies are strewn across the ground in front of the entrance to the dungeons, each of them wearing a uniform of the royal guard. The iron gate is swinging open in the wind, unlocked and unguarded.

A croaked voice whispers nearby. "Y-Your M-Majesty…" One of the guards stirs on the ground, reaching a shaky hand toward me.

I rush to his side and kneel, where I support his head with my hands. The scent of his blood is enticing, but I resist the urge to drink. "What happened here?"

"The R-Ravenrock Clan… it was an ambush. They… overpowered us and released their alpha. They g-gave him a mask and cloak, and I overheard them say… they were going to kidnap Lady Briar…"

His words are a punch to the gut, sucking all the air from my lungs. The courtyard tilts in my field of vision, and I lay the guard back down to steady myself.

Slowly, I stand up, my chest heaving with labored breaths. "Search the kingdom! I want all soldiers on the search for the Ravenrock Clan and Lady Briar!"

The guards scatter to give the command; however, I remain frozen in place, reaching out for a nearby column to steady myself. I'm in free fall, plunging into a black pit of immobilizing terror, an emotion I've never encountered before.

I should have killed Malrick after he touched Bri in the garden.

I should have canceled the ball tonight.

I should have never agreed to allow her to hide from me behind a mask.

There are so many things I should have done differently, and now she is paying the price for my inaction.

"Bri's been kidnapped?"

I spin around at the sound of my own voice, except it wasn't me who said it. My light one stands behind me, eavesdropping.

It unnerves me to gaze upon my doppelgänger. It's unnatural.

I grit my teeth and push past him. "I'm handling it."

I dart inside the castle. Perhaps Bri felt unwell and returned to her room early, and Malrick gave up and left without her. That's the only hope I have right now, and as a desperate man, I cling to it.

My light one's footsteps echo behind me. "Let me help with the search."

"Absolutely not. I've already had one man slip through my clutches tonight."

"Why would I escape without Bri?" he asks. "I'm just as desperate to find her as you are. Let me use my heightened senses as a werewolf to track her down."

I scoff. "I have armies of werewolves who can do that for me."

"But no one knows her scent better than I do."

"I know her scent as well as you!" I bellow, rounding on him. I bring my face inches from his, staring into those strange, brown eyes with a challenging gaze.

His face is contorted into a grim expression. "You're not the only one in love with her. I've always loved her."

Does my face mirror his right now? Do I look that weak and broken?

"Fine." I turn my back on him. "We leave in ten minutes."

With my vampiric speed, I rush up the stairs to Bri's room and escape my light one.

The door to Bri's room is open, and Elowen is turning over every sofa cushion and piece of furniture in her search.

"Have you found her?" My question is clearly futile, but the desperation in my voice is thick.

"Your Majesty, the only trace of her we've found was a peacock feather in the garden," she explains. "I helped dress her tonight, so I know what her costume was. She was the only one with peacock feathers on her dress."

Without another word, I sprint downstairs, pushing my way through the ballroom until I burst through the doors toward the balcony. Her sweet scent lingers in the night air without the interference of the guests' perfumes.

I follow my nose down the steps, but when I turn the corner into the garden, my light one is already there.

I pause. Closing my eyes, I take a deep breath before I fly into a rage. I need to remain focused if I'm going to find Bri.

"Why are you on the loose without supervision?" I ask through gritted teeth.

His eyes remain on the ground as he takes cautious steps forward. "I tracked her scent on the balcony and followed it down here, but with all the flowers, I'm having trouble locking onto it."

Without warning, his knee snaps backward with a loud crack, and he hinges forward with a groan. His other leg inverts in a similar, grotesque manner, and he falls to the ground on all fours, shifting and changing as his clothing rips off his back. Muscles tear open and rebuild themselves as he transforms into a werewolf, and when he's done, I take a step back at his sheer size, which dwarfs Malrick's wolf in comparison.

His eyes glow a bright shade of gold, and his fur is the same dark shade of brown as his eyes. It isn't often I'm rendered speechless, but a small part of me can't help but admire this impressive specimen.

If we were joined as one into the body of a grimwalker, this would be the form I would take on.

I shake my head. No use in dwelling on what isn't meant to be.

The werewolf sniffs the ground before taking off deeper into the garden, keeping his nose to the path. I follow him until the light from the ballroom windows disappears behind us, though neither of us have trouble seeing into the darkness.

He's a good tracking dog; I'll give him that.

He continues around the exterior of the castle and follows the path toward the stables. Eventually, he reaches the side entrance of the castle, and he comes to a stop at the cobblestone path leading down the hill.

"What is it?" I ask.

His wolf form shrinks until he returns to his unclothed human form. When he turns to face me, my gaze inadvertently slips toward his manhood, and I'm disappointed to find it the same size as mine.

Damn. We're physically identical in every way except for our eyes.

My light one huffs. "Her scent just... disappears. It leads up to this cobblestone path before going cold. If I had to guess, they threw her onto a horse or into a carriage and rode off to keep us from tracking her scent. And because of the cobblestone, there aren't any tracks." He clenches his fists. "They could have gone in any direction."

"No!" I slam my fist into the side of the castle wall. Chunks of stone break apart and fly in all directions, and dust lingers in the air.

"So, what's next?" my light one asks, looking to me for guidance.

My expression darkens. "First, put some clothes on."

It takes time to gather my army of ten thousand men and march toward Malrick's estate in the western region of the realm. Armies move slowly, so we won't reach our destination until nightfall. I send my fastest scouts to ride ahead and check out the estate before we arrive, just in case they are mounting a defensive attack.

I ride at the helm of my army on a horse of my own, with my brother, Sebastian, and my light one riding a few paces behind me. So far, we have traveled in an awkward silence, but as the day wears on, I grow weary of it.

"Would you stop staring at me?" Sebastian barks, at last breaking the tension.

"Geez, sorry," my light one answers. "It's just weird that you're my brother, but you're not my brother—"

"I'm not your brother," Sebastian says. "No brother of mine would speak like such a simpleton."

My light one huffs. "We didn't all grow up as spoiled princes with private tutors. Some of us had more important things to do."

"How dare you—?"

"Enough!" I snap. "Brother, join the back of the line."

Sebastian scoffs. "I am your second-in-command. I ride at the front."

"You serve at the pleasure of the king," I say, "and it would please me for you to join the back of the line."

"But—"

"Without complaint," I add, cutting him off. "Go."

Sebastian veers his horse out of formation and rides back toward the end of the formation, but not without murmuring a few choice words under his breath.

My light one chuckles, though the sound grates on my ears. "Your brother is more of a grump than you are."

"And you," I hiss, throwing him a scowl over my shoulder. "Be quiet. You're already drawing too much attention as my doppelgänger."

My dark, malicious, jealous side is eager to establish my dominance over him, and to remind him that Bri belongs to me. I am the dark one, after all, and when it comes to my mate, I have no honor when it comes to others vying for her affection.

I tug on the reins to slow my horse and ride side-by-side with my light one. "Bri confessed her love for me, you know." With a smirk, I watch him closely for a reaction.

His eyes widen with surprise, but he refuses to meet my gaze. A somber expression crosses his face as he mulls over my jab. "Maybe that's true, but she loves me too."

This fool.

"From what I understand," I say, "you come from a world where you have no means. You're a meager ranch hand; what do you possibly have to give her? I am a king. I can make all her dreams come true and spoil her with everything her heart desires. If you truly love her, you'll agree that she deserves only the best."

"At least she's safe in our world," he says quietly. "She hasn't even been here a month, and she's already been kidnapped by one of *your* enemies."

My fists tighten on the reins of my horse. All I want to do is dismount and punch my light one's cherubic face. Just looking at him makes me angry. His innocent demeanor is sickening, and his mere presence weakens my position as king.

But... he makes a fair point. From what Bri has told me of her world, safety is not a concern except for pestilence and disease. If she were to remain here as my queen, her life would be constantly under threat.

"If Bri loves you, that's fine," my light one says. "I decided a long time ago that I would forgive her for anything—even if she fell in love with someone else."

My own jealousy and pain are reflected in his face like a mirror image, caused by the same woman we're both mated to. In a strange twist of fate, Bri was brought into both of our lives, but where we go from here is uncharted territory.

There is no precedence for this scenario. I am the first dark one to meet my fated mate since our ancestors cast the curse centuries ago.

I don't know why Bri or my light one are here in the Crimson Vale, but things feel… unstable. Breaking the curse is within my grasp, but despite all my library research in recent weeks, I'm no closer to finding the answer.

If I can get Bri to stay longer, I'd have more time to figure it out. But I need to find her first.

"Why haven't you marked her?" I ask. Werewolves are able to mark their mates, a visible indication to the world that they have laid claim to them. From what I understand, it strengthens the mate bond.

My light one scratches the back of his neck. "It's, uh, rather personal."

I snort. "Good thing we're the same person."

He glances sideways at me. "Bri only recently found out I was a werewolf. It probably would have freaked her out if I'd marked her."

"But you had the opportunity the first night you arrived in the Crimson Vale." I cast my gaze over the open field, surveying the path ahead. "My men reported that they found you both in a barn the morning after you arrived. You are me, after all, and I know what I would do if I were stuck in a barn with Bri, alone, all night long."

He gulps. "So, you two have…?"

"Of course." My lips stretch into a wide grin. "All night, every night."

He shakes his head, as though trying to erase the image of Bri and me from his mind. "Okay, I get the picture."

I feel rather smug, if I do say so myself. "So, why didn't you mark her?"

My light one stares straight ahead, though his gaze isn't focused on anything in particular. He takes a deep breath as he considers my question. "I guess it's because I didn't feel like she fully belonged to me. She said she loved me, but something about it felt… incomplete."

"Because she also loves your dark side, which you do not currently possess." Just as I know her heart does not fully belong to me, either.

As much as I hate to admit it.

I can never fully claim Bri's heart as my own, even if my light one was in a different dimension. He will always have a piece of her heart.

It's too bad I can't kill him without meeting my death also. I'd love nothing more than to get him out of my way and have Bri all to myself.

A movement in the distance catches my attention, and I hold my hand up to bring my army to a halt. Upon closer inspection, I make out the face of one of my scouts galloping across the landscape toward us.

"Take these!" I toss my reins to my light one and leap from the horse. Using my vampiric speed, I race across the clearing to meet him, much faster than if I were on horseback.

My scout brings his horse to a stop when I reach him.

"What did you find?" I demand.

He bows his head toward me. "Your Majesty, the estate is completely abandoned. There is no sign of Malrick or anyone from his pack."

"And of Lady Briar?" I ask, my voice tight.

"Our werewolf scout did not pick up on her scent at all," he answers. "However, we did find a messenger waiting for us at the gate. He knew we were coming and gave us this." He reaches into his satchel and pulls out a small package, which he passes to me.

I rip the wrappings open to find a small box inside. When I lift the lid, a scroll of parchment sits inside the box, and I unfurl it to find handwritten text scrawled across the page:

I have your precious mate in my custody. I will return her alive under one condition: you relinquish all claims to the throne and acknowledge me as the one true alpha king of the realm.

These terms are non-negotiable. My messenger awaits your reply. Do not attempt to follow him to our location. If you do, I will not hesitate to kill Lady Briar. The sample inside is just a small taste of what we're willing to do to her.

I look forward to unburdening your heavy crown from your head.

—Alpha Malrick

Fear grips me as I dig through the rest of the package. What does he mean by *the sample inside?* What have they done to her? Has he cut off her finger?

Bile rises in my throat.

A glint of something red catches my attention at the bottom of the package. I pull out a glass vial of what is unmistakably blood, and I immediately uncork it. I'd recognize that scent anywhere—Bri's blood.

I salivate and quickly cork it before I lose control to my bloodlust.

Hooves gallop closer behind me, but I ignore them as I read through Malrick's letter once more. Relinquish the kingdom to Malrick? How can I throw away everything my family has built over centuries? The entire realm would descend into chaos under the rule of the Ravenrock Clan.

But if I'm to save Bri, do I have a choice? Now that her life hangs in the balance, I find myself prepared to throw it all away to save her.

There is nothing to consider. I've already made my choice.

My light one comes to a stop beside us and spots the package. "Can I see that?"

I pass him the note and the vial of blood. "It's Bri's blood."

As my light one reads through the letter, his eyes grow wide. When he's finished, he looks at me. "Are you going to give up your throne?"

"I don't have a choice," I answer quietly. "If it means saving Bri, I'll do it."

My light one uncorks the vial to sniff the contents. "There are witches and mages in this world, right? Can one of them enchant this to lead us to her?"

I stare at him for a moment, considering his words.

"Lucius the Wise!" I bellow across the field. "Come!"

The elderly mage breaks rank and gallops toward us on his horse. As he approaches, I narrow my eyes at him, remembering how he upset Bri when he attempted to treat her illness in such a pathetic way.

"You better prove your worth to me this time, old man." My voice dips with a threatening tone. "Tell me, is there a way to enchant this vial of blood to lead us to Lady Briar?"

"I aim to please Your Majesty," he squeaks. "Allow me to consult my spellbook." He bows his head in submission before searching through his saddlebag with shaking hands. After a moment, he pulls out a tattered old book and begins flipping hastily through the pages.

Several minutes go by while we wait. All ten thousand of my men are silent as the seconds tick by. The only sound is the occasional horse snorting with impatience, but otherwise the only sound is the mage's fingers flipping from page to page.

Relief passes across the mage's face. "Ah, yes, here is something! 'A werewolf may drink the blood of their fated mate, and it will allow him or her to find their true love, no matter how distant they may be.'"

I could strangle this useless old man. "I am not a werewolf, you idiot."

"No," my light one says quietly. "But I am."

Lucius and I turn toward my light one, who wears an expression set with resolve.

"Let me drink it," he says, holding out his hand. "Once I do, I'll be able to lead us all to her."

After a moment of stunned silence, I let out a hollow laugh, earning me some concerned looks from Lucius and my scout.

In a cruel twist of fate, my light one is the only one who can reunite me with Bri. To find her, I must put my faith in my competitor to lead me to the woman we both love.

The moon goddess has a wicked sense of humor.

Reluctantly, I hand the vial to him. "Don't screw this up."

He takes the vial and uncorks it, sniffing it with a look of disgust.

I scoff. "Such a waste. You can't even appreciate the divine taste of her blood."

My light one sighs. "Bottoms up." He throws back the contents of the vial, swallowing every last drop as he squeezes his eyes shut.

Chapter 20

Briar

C aspian is here—actually here—and he's come to rescue me. He's standing in the doorway, smeared in the blood of his enemies, like a dark angel of vengeance. The sight steals the breath from my lungs.

I call out his name, but with the leather belt in my mouth, it comes out muffled as fresh tears roll down my face to the cold, stone floor my cheek is pressed against.

Malrick shifts behind me, and Caspian's eyes burn bright red as he tracks the movement.

"She's in here!" Caspian bellows right before he lunges toward us.

Caspian knocks him flat onto his back and pins him to the floor. Malrick's legs are tangled in his pants bunched around his knees, making it impossible to escape the series of brutal punches Caspian lands on his face.

With my wrists bound, I try to scramble away from the skirmish, but my foot catches on the hem of my dress, and I fall to the side.

The snarl of a werewolf in the doorway pulls my attention away from the fight, and I see a pair of familiar golden eyes peering out from dark brown fur and blood dripping from its maw.

I'd recognize my werewolf anywhere.

When I call out to him, it's a muffled scream, but I implore him to come closer with my gaze. The wolf shifts back into his human form in a matter of seconds, revealing the stark naked figure of Caz. As a wolf, he wouldn't have been able to fit through the doorway, but in his human body he rushes into the cell toward me.

"Bri!" He closes the distance between us in two long strides. Caz crouches beside me and pulls my skirt down over my exposed backside, then unties the ropes keeping my wrists bound behind my back.

I rip the belt off my head. "Oh, Caz…" My voice catches, and I fling my arms around his neck, clinging to him for dear life. I let out a raw cry and burrow my face into his chest.

"It's okay, Bri. You're safe now. I've got you." He wraps his strong arms around me, shielding me from the aggression of Caspian as he continues to beat Malrick into a bloodied mess.

"How. Dare. You. Touch. Her!" Caspian thunders, enunciating each syllable with a blow to the face.

"Let's get you out of here." Without waiting for a response, Caz lifts me off the ground and carries me effortlessly out the door.

I glance back once more at Caspian and Malrick, who doesn't appear to be moving. "W-What if he transforms into a werewolf?"

"He can't transform," Caz explains, carrying me through the narrow passageway toward the basement doors. "He's unconscious."

The corridor leading to my cell is strewn with the bodies of Malrick's pack mates on the floor. Members of the king's guard are placing shackles on the ones who are still alive and dragging them up the stairs into the open air.

"How did you fit in here in your wolf form?" I ask.

"It was a snug fit, but I managed." Caz follows the soldiers up the stairs and steps onto the soft earth. He walks a few yards further toward a set of clothes strewn on the ground. "Can you stand?"

I give him a shaky nod, and he helps me down onto my feet, holding me steady. Shock starts to set in as my body erupts into violent trembling, and I reach out to touch his chest, making sure he's real. "How did you find me?"

"Your blood." Caz tugs his shirt over his head, then tugs on his pants. "A werewolf can drink their mate's blood to find them. It led me straight to you."

I shake my head. "I can't believe you're really here. If you hadn't come in time..." My voice trails off.

"I'm just sorry we didn't get here sooner." His voice catches before he wraps his strong arms around me, pulling me against his broad chest.

We stand there in silence, holding onto one another tightly, as Caspian's army rounds up the entire Ravenrock Clan. The field is full of soldiers milling about.

Malrick's pack never stood a chance. Caz and Caspian took them completely by surprise and outnumbered them.

After a few minutes, Malrick's bloodied and bruised body flies out the basement doors, landing on the ground with a dull thud—like a ragdoll being tossed in the air. Caspian steps out behind him and dusts off his clothes.

Everyone turns to watch the scene unfold. Caspian approaches Malrick's unconscious body and lands a strong kick to his side. "Wake up."

Malrick groans as he writhes in the grass and reveals his face, which has been beaten beyond recognition. His unpatched eye is bruised and swollen shut, and blood streaks down his face from cuts on his forehead and nose.

Caspian gestures to Malrick and faces the crowd of soldiers. "Let this serve as an example of what happens when you defy me. This traitor, along with his entire pack, will be erased from existence. I will wipe their legacy from the history books of this kingdom, and they will be completely forgotten."

His threat sends a shiver down my spine. I know Caspian means every word.

Caspian digs the heel of his boot into Malrick's ribcage, forcing a choked cry from him. "Someone get him out of my sight."

A few guards step forward to shackle Malrick and drag him off to where the other prisoners are rounded up. Each of them has rope tied around their wrists, and I'm not sure if it's a trick of the sunlight, but I swear the ropes glow.

Caz catches the direction of my gaze. "Enchanted rope. Apparently, it prevents werewolves from shifting. You're safe, Bri. They can't hurt you."

Once Caspian tears his eyes away from Malrick, he seeks me out in the crowd of soldiers. When his gaze lands on me, he materializes at my side, using his vampiric speed to reach me in under a second.

I step out of Caz's embrace to wrap my arms around Caspian, inhaling his scent.

"Bri, I'm so sorry," he whispers against my hair. His arms hold me tight as he rocks me from side to side. "I'm sorry we didn't get here sooner."

"I'm okay." I burrow my face into his shoulder. "You got here just in time."

"But you shouldn't have had to go through this to begin with." He takes a step back to look me in the eye, keeping a firm grip on my shoulders. "He used you as a pawn in his vendetta against me. You should never have been involved."

I step back and take each of their hands, clasping onto both of my men. "I just want to go home."

Caspian nods. "Yes, let's get you back to the castle. We have a long ride ahead."

"Our home is back on Earth," Caz says, narrowing his gaze at Caspian. "Not here in the Crimson Vale."

"Home is where the both of you are," I reply, squeezing his hand.

Caz lets go of my hand and steps away, clearing his throat. "Let me find you a horse. I'll walk beside you in my wolf form."

"Caz, wait." I reach for him, but he walks away until he has enough space to transform. The sound of breaking bones cracks through the air, making me wince and turn away, but when I look again, his majestic wolf huffs.

It's an excuse not to talk to me.

"He knows about us," Caspian murmurs. After a pause, he adds, "Give him time to come to terms with it."

Caz refuses to look at me, and I don't blame him. He turns around and pads off toward the horses, his tail hanging low behind him.

The ride back to the castle takes us the entire day, and by the time we arrive, the red sun is already setting beyond the horizon. Elowen runs out into the courtyard to greet us, and I jump off my horse to run into her waiting arms.

"Oh, Bri, I was so worried about you!"

I'm too exhausted to respond. All I can do is clutch her even tighter.

"Can you walk to your room?" she asks. "Or do you need assistance?"

"I can walk," I say weakly. "All I want is a hot bath and some food."

"Of course." She nods and gives me one last squeeze before taking my hand.

Before she leads me into the castle, I glance over my shoulder at Caz and Caspian. I wave to them both to let them know I'm heading upstairs, and Caspian nods in understanding. Caz's wolf snorts at me, which I take as his acknowledgment.

Thank goodness I have Elowen to lean on as I climb up the stairs. My bones are stiff and achy as I hobble to my room, and once we're there, I sink onto the couch, staring straight ahead at the wall in a daze.

"I'll draw the bath," Elowen says. "I have the kitchen sending up some finger foods that you can eat while you soak in the water."

She leaves the room, and I realize this is the first moment I've been alone since Malrick tried to...

When I close my eyes, images of him standing over me flash through my mind, as if those memories are branded into the inside of my eyelids. The way he spoke to me, the way he bound my wrists, the feeling of his hands and his tip touching my skin...

"Bri? Bri, are you okay?"

I open my eyes to find Elowen kneeling in front of me, staring at me with a concerned expression on her face. My chest is rising and falling with my ragged breaths, and I'm gripping the armrest so hard my knuckles have turned white.

"Bri?"

I shake my head, unable to put my thoughts into words. If I speak, I'm afraid I'll break.

She guides me to the bathroom before disappearing into the living room, giving me a moment of privacy while I undress and step into the warm bubbles. As I submerge myself up to my chin in the steaming water, Elowen reappears with a tray of bread, cheese, and dried meats.

"Will you stay?" As difficult as it is for me to admit, I'm afraid to be left alone again.

Elowen nods and takes a seat on the side of the tub. "Of course."

Washing off the dirt and grime of the past few days is a healing experience. I slowly scrub my body with a sponge, taking my time to wash off every inch that Malrick and Vane touched.

When I emerge, Elowen has a comfortable set of long-sleeved, flannel pajamas waiting for me. Where they came from, I have no idea, because they certainly weren't in my closet full of satin negligees. They feel protective and soft against my skin as I slip them on, and when I'm finished, Elowen helps me to bed. My legs have turned to gelatin after the long day of travel, and I can hardly walk without assistance.

As I settle under the bedcovers, a knock raps at the bedroom door. Elowen opens it to reveal Caspian, who's wearing an unrecognizable expression. He looks... broken. Dark circles sit beneath his eyes, and his posture is slouched and defeated.

"I'll just excuse myself," Elowen whispers, curtsying to Caspian before closing the door behind her.

"What's wrong?" I ask, sitting up straighter.

Without a word, he approaches the bed and sits down beside me, taking my hands into his.

My brows knit together. "Caspian, talk to me."

"Bri…" He lets go of one of my hands and runs his palm down his haggard face. "I've been thinking all day about how to say this." His struggle is etched onto every inch of his face as he finds the words he's hesitant to tell me. "You should return to your world when the full moon arrives. With my light one. Leave this place behind and forget me."

"What?" I yank my hand out of his grasp. "Where is this coming from?"

His expression twists with sorrow. "The Crimson Vale is dangerous. When I walked into that cell and saw you, and I saw what Malrick almost did to you… my world crumbled. I thought I could protect you, but I was wrong, and if you hadn't met me, this never would have happened…" His voice trails off as he shakes his head.

"Listen to me." I press my hand against his cheek and force him to meet my gaze. "The danger has passed. Everything bad that's happened is because of Malrick and the Ravenrock Clan, and you're going to make sure that they can't hurt anyone else again."

He leans into my touch as though memorizing it. Savoring it. "They're not my only enemies. We're going to execute their entire pack, but who's next? Who else will come after my throne? Who else would use my love for you as a weapon?"

"Caspian—"

"Please, let me finish before I lose my nerve." He holds a finger to my lips. "Letting you go is the single most difficult thing I will ever experience in my life. But the thought of you in danger, or worse, killed… that's a thought I can't even bear. At least I know you'll be much safer in your world. My light one has proven he can protect you."

Why does this feel like goodbye? I'm not ready for this, and I refuse to accept that this is our fate. Why would destiny bring Caspian and me together, allow us a chance to fall in love, only to rip us apart?

"There has to be a way to break the curse," I reply with shaky breath.

"Believe me, that's all I've wanted since I met you." Caspian clenches his fist. "I've spent countless hours in the library searching for a way to break this blasted curse. If I could give this all up for you, I would."

I sniff. "You would?"

"Of course, I would." He brings my hand to his lips to plant a long kiss on my knuckles. "But it's because I love you so much that I must let you go." Without warning, Caspian leaps to his feet and turns away from me. This conversation is causing him immeasurable pain, and he doesn't want me to see it. "Rest now, my love."

A moment later, he disappears through the door and closes it behind him.

It sounds so final, like he's closing the door on us for good.

I fall back against my pillows and curl up into a ball, tears freely streaming down my face.

The weight of everything that's happened over the past few days suffocates me. A lump in my throat constricts my airways as I struggle to come to terms with losing Caspian, and my heart shatters into a million pieces, making each breath feel like I'm inhaling glass shards into my lungs.

I have no idea how long I've been crying when the door opens again. When I glance up, Caz is standing in the doorway, eying me with a worried expression.

"Caz..." I devolve once again into a fit of sobs.

Caz crosses the room and crawls into bed with me. Without a word, he pulls me into his chest, wrapping his muscular, warm arms around me. I burrow my face into the crook of his elbow and let my emotions pour out onto him.

With Caz, I've always felt safe. His strong, gentle presence is a familiar comfort that I desperately need right now.

At least I have Caz. At least half of my heart is still intact.

It just won't ever be whole again.

CHAPTER 21

I awaken with a start, sucking in a sharp breath as sweat drips down my forehead.

"Bri? Shh, it's okay. I'm here," Caz whispers into my ear as he strokes my arm. When I realize it's him, my pulse slows, and I take a moment to catch my breath.

"Bad dream?" he asks.

"Yeah." I nod. "What time is it?"

"It's almost dinnertime," he says. "You've been asleep since last night."

"Holy shit." My entire body aches from being still for so long, and I sit up gingerly in bed. "You haven't been here that whole time, have you?"

He smiles and sits up beside me. "I haven't left your side."

I arch an eyebrow at him. "Even to go to the bathroom?"

His head lolls back against the headboard as he laughs. "Except for that."

The lighthearted moment is a welcome distraction from my nightmares, and I curl up against his chest. My ear rests over his heart, allowing me to hear the steady rhythm of his pulse.

"Have you eaten?" I ask.

"Yeah, your maid's really nice," Caz says. "She's brought meals throughout the day. She said she'd bring dinner up as well."

My stomach sinks. "We're not eating with Caspian?"

Caz's smile falters. "No, we're not."

I immediately regret opening my big mouth. "I'm sorry, Caz. That was careless. So much has happened since we got here…"

"Yeah, I know." He lets out a heavy sigh. "He told me you're in love with him."

I sit up and grab his hands. "But I'm in love with you too." I gaze into his eyes, imploring him to believe me.

He gives me a weary look before entwining his fingers with mine. His thumb rubs the back of my hand in gentle strokes. "I know you are. And your feelings for him don't change how I feel about you. You're my mate, and you have no idea how much I love you. I know I shouldn't be jealous of him, but...."

"You don't have to be jealous." A lump forms in my throat, and I struggle to say my next words. "He's not coming back with us to Earth. It's just you and me now." I bite my lip. "I owe you an apology."

He furrows his brows. "Why's that?"

"Because while you were locked away in the dungeons, I've been up here living a life of luxury... with him." I take a deep breath to steady my shaky voice. "And I felt so guilty about it, especially because I betrayed you."

His throat bobs as he swallows. "I know. He told me. But I don't want you to feel bad about it, okay?"

Only someone good like Caz could forgive me for cheating on him. I hurt him, and he's telling me not to feel bad about it.

It's proof that he's too good for me.

"Don't say that." I shake my head and swipe at the tears in my eyes. "I deserve to feel guilty."

He laces his fingers with mine. "No, you don't. You're attracted to both me and my dark one, which is proof you truly are my fated mate. You love both sides of me, the good and the bad." Caz shrugs. "Not even you can resist fate, Bri."

"Oh, Caz." Tears well anew in my eyes. "I've missed you so much. You have no idea."

"Me too." He leans in to give me a long, sweet kiss, his lips familiar and gentle.

I lean back. "He's not going to send you back down there, is he?"

He chuckles. "No. In fact, he ordered me not to leave your side until the full moon arrives."

"Oh, so you're taking commands from King Caspian now?" I poke his side, eager to lighten the mood.

"This command I'll obey." He gives me a goofy grin before wrapping his arms around my waist. He pulls me against him and begins to lay a trail of kisses along my face, making me giggle.

We're interrupted by a knock at the door, and Elowen comes in, wheeling an elaborate dinner cart for us.

"Oh, Bri, you're awake!" she exclaims. "I'm sure you're hungry."

"I'm famished." I don't know why I'm embarrassed to get caught with Caz, but I quickly untangle myself from his embrace.

If she's judging me for sleeping with two men, she doesn't show it. "Good, because there is a lot of food on this tray for the two of you."

When she lifts the covers off the plates, the savory aroma of beef Wellington and bread wafts to my nose, and my stomach growls.

But the best part is that Caz and I get to eat it all while in bed, chatting away like old times. I've missed this, how comfortable we are with each other.

Caz is the only person in the Crimson Vale who knows my past, who understands where I come from and what our world is like. He tells me about his encounter with Prince Sebastian when they marched to rescue me, and we compare the dark Nezaras to his family on Earth, even imitating their stuck-up, obnoxious attitudes.

I remind myself that this was my plan all along—to return home with Caz at the end of my thirty nights with the alpha king. Caz and I will make a life together on my grandparents' ranch, and I need to accept that and move on from Caspian. He'll always have a piece of my heart, but we weren't meant to be together. Fate is cruel like that.

Caz and I stay up for hours past sundown talking about our future until we fall asleep in each other's arms.

The next morning, I wake up feeling more refreshed than I have in a while. As I yawn and stretch my limbs, Caz stirs awake beside me.

"You seem to have slept better," he mumbles, appraising me with a sleepy gaze.

"I did." I snuggle against him beneath the sheets, pressing my lips to his bare chest. "Can we just stay in bed all day again?"

"There's nothing I'd love more," he says, but his voice sounds constricted.

I sit up, staring down at him with a curious gaze. "What's wrong?"

With a heavy sigh, he sits up and takes my hands in his. "I wasn't sure how to bring this up to you. Caspian didn't want me to tell you, but I think you have a right to know."

I raise my eyebrows at him. "Now I'm *really* curious."

He swallows. "Today is Malrick's execution, along with the rest of the Ravenrock Clan."

I sit with that news for a moment. Either Caspian wants to protect me from the violent display of his strength, or he wants to keep me hidden from the realm now that I won't become his queen. Perhaps it's a bit of both.

But deep down, I know I need closure on this chapter with Malrick, and I'll always be watching my back unless I see his death for myself.

Malrick tried to steal Caspian's kingdom, but he also tried to assault me on multiple occasions. This is my vengeance too.

I crawl out of bed. "Let's get dressed."

"I thought we were staying in bed?"

"I want to go to the execution."

Caz scrambles off the bed and follows me into the bathroom. "Are you sure that's a good idea?"

I pause in front of the sink and turn to face him. "Caz, I need this. I need closure, and I need to make sure Malrick is truly, finally gone. If I can't stay in the Crimson Vale, I want to leave knowing Caspian is safe from the Ravenrock Clan."

He studies me with a wary gaze. "Okay, but I'm coming with you."

I nod. "Okay. Go get Elowen. I'm sure she'll find something suitable for you to wear."

Caz blinks. "What's the proper attire for an execution?"

I shrug. "Honestly? I have no idea."

While I wash my face, Caz goes to find Elowen. Unlike yesterday, I'm grateful for a moment to myself to steel my resolve for what I'm about to witness.

When I exit the bathroom, Elowen is waiting for me with a breakfast tray. Caz takes a bath while I munch on a couple of berries, but I don't have much of an appetite.

A heaviness sits in the air between Caz, Elowen, and myself as we get ready. Elowen has laid out two outfits, one for me and one for Caz, and they are both black and red.

"The colors of House Nezara," Elowen explains. "To show a united front."

I examine the dress she's picked out for me. It's a full-length, long-sleeved gown in a deep shade of burgundy.

Just like Caspian's eyes. A pang squeezes my heart.

I slip into the dress, which Elowen finishes off with a black cloak and the beaded crystal necklace Caspian gifted to me. She adds a tiara made completely of dark silver and onyx stones.

Caz comes up beside me, fastening the cuff of his swallowtail jacket, and if I didn't know any better, I would have thought it was Caspian coming to stand beside me. His velvet jacket is a deep shade of burgundy, which sits atop his high-necked black shirt underneath. He tugs at his collar. "These clothes are so itchy."

I laugh. "You get used to it."

Caz comes over to stand beside me in front of the mirror, and we stare at our reflections. The heaviness in the air returns, and he reaches for my hand.

"You look powerful, Bri. You look like—"

"A queen," I finish. "A queen of the Crimson Vale."

And hell, I feel powerful. I'm ready to go downstairs and make Malrick regret ever fucking with me in the first place.

"I'm ready." I turn to face Caz and Elowen. "Let's go."

When we reach the courtyard, I step into the red sunlight with Caz and Elowen flanking me on either side. Despite the crowd gathered, the atmosphere is silent, so silent that my footsteps echo against the cobblestones. Everyone is gathered beneath the breezeways, and their eyes turn toward us as we begin to cross the open space of the courtyard toward Caspian.

The tension in the air is palpable. Ignoring my pounding heart, I keep my chin held high and my eyes forward as I walk.

Caspian stands on a platform in the middle of the courtyard, watching me as his lips form a thin line. His silver crown adorned with onyx stones sits atop his head of wavy, dark hair, and he wears an all-black, Victorian-style suit, very similar to the day we first met. Except he has a red velvet cloak draped around his shoulders with a fur trim.

He truly looks like a king in all his regal glory.

This is the first time I've seen him since he told me we couldn't be together. My heart breaks all over again as I keep my gaze trained on his, but I keep a strong façade beneath the crowd's scrutinizing gaze.

Caspian's grandmother and his brother, Sebastian, stand beside him on the platform, watching me with haughty expressions as I approach.

When I reach the platform, Caspian reaches his hand out to help me up the steps. "Bri, what are you doing here?" he mutters under his breath.

"I need to see this for myself."

Keeping my hand clasped in his, he guides me toward the center of the platform while Caz and Elowen remain at the bottom of the stairs. I keep my gaze trained ahead with a serious expression on my face, but I feel Caspian's intense gaze on me.

"You are truly amazing," he whispers.

Surprised, I turn to face him, and for a moment, it feels like just the two of us.

"I didn't know it was possible to love you even more than I already do. You continue to surprise me with your bravery." He gives me a sad smile. "You would have made a magnificent queen."

His words affect me, and I fight back a fresh wave of tears as my throat constricts with emotion. But there's nothing I can do or say to change our circumstances.

Unable to look at him any longer, I turn back to face the courtyard, steeling my resolve for what's next.

"Bring out the prisoners!" Caspian's commanding voice echoes around the silent courtyard.

Within moments, the guards march out a long line of prisoners, each with their hands and feet shackled to a long chain. There must be over fifty members of the Ravenrock Clan, though I'm surprised to see women included in that count. A few of the members even appear to be young teenagers.

They come to a stop in front of the platform, forming four rows, each with a guard standing behind them.

I glance sideways at Caspian, but his hardened gaze continues to examine the prisoners. He waits as the guards force them all down to their knees before issuing his next command.

"Bring out their disgraced alpha!"

A pair of guards bring out Malrick in chains, filthy and disheveled. He's wearing the same outfit that he was taken prisoner in, and bruises cover his face and arms. The guards bring him out in front of the platform and shove him to his knees, just like his pack behind him.

"Malrick," Caspian says, loud enough for the entire courtyard to hang on to every word. "You are a traitor to your king. You have disgraced your entire pack, and you are the reason they will die here and now. As conspirators to the traitorous plot against the throne, I hereby sentence the entire Ravenrock Clan to death by beheading. Their heads will be placed on pikes in the village, to serve as reminders of what happens when you betray House Nezara."

"Not the women and the children," Malrick begs, keeping his head bowed. "Some of the boys are barely older than pups."

Caspian narrows his gaze at Malrick. "I am a man of my word. I promised you the legacy of your entire pack would be wiped from this kingdom. You should have considered their lives before you went after my throne and my mate. Their blood is solely on your hands, Malrick, and you will witness the consequences of your actions."

Caspian nods to his guards, who are standing behind each prisoner. They begin to shove them to the ground so that they are lying flat on their stomachs. My gaze lands on Vane, and our eyes briefly meet before he's shoved to the ground as well. Some of the pack members begin to plead for their lives, while others cry silent tears, readying themselves for the inevitable.

The guards raise their axes above their heads and swing them down. Metal grinds against cobblestone and bone with a sharp squeal, echoing through the courtyard the moment before severed heads roll across the ground. Blood spurts everywhere and pools beneath the bodies of the victim, and many of the onlookers bring scarves up to their noses in shock and disgust.

A pathetic sob escapes from Malrick, his shoulders trembling as he hangs his head.

"Weep for your pack, Malrick," Caspian says, his face schooled into an unreadable expression. "Bring out the pigs."

A stable hand comes out with two massive black pigs, each with glowing red eyes. Their appearance is startling, and they remind me of the pegasuses in the barn the first night Caz and I arrived in the Crimson Vale. The pigs snort and huff as they are led across the courtyard on leashes. As they pass the bodies, the pigs grow restless and tug on their ropes, eager for the taste of flesh.

When the pigs come to a stop in front of the platform, two guards flanking Malrick yank him to his feet and turn him toward the crowd. A third guard approaches with a dagger and pulls Malrick's pants down, exposing his bare ass to those of us behind him.

I think I know what's coming, and if I'm right, I'm thankful he's facing away from us.

The guard brings his knife down, and Malrick's screams of pain fill the air as blood pools on the ground beneath him. The guard tosses what appears to be Malrick's severed penis toward the pigs, who shove and push to get to it first.

I've never seen anything so cruel and disgusting in my life, and yet, I'm unable to tear my eyes away.

Vindication. That's what I feel right now.

I'm certain I'm not the first woman Malrick has assaulted, and if he were allowed to live, I wouldn't be the last. Knowing that stops here, today, brings a strange sense of peace I didn't know was possible.

Feeling Caspian's eyes on me, I turn to meet his gaze. We say nothing to one another, but we don't have to.

He did this for me. He exacted his revenge on my behalf. Yes, it was cruel, but it was necessary.

Caspian gives me a subtle nod before turning back to the grisly scene. "You have a choice to make, Malrick."

The guards pull Malrick around to face Caspian, but his eyes are scrunched together as he squirms with pain. On reflex, I glance down between Malrick's legs, but all I see is blood spurting from the place where his manhood used to be.

"Malrick, you have the option to die a quick death right now," Caspian says to him.

"P-Please," he chokes out between pained sobs.

"All you have to do is recognize me as the one true alpha king and rightful ruler of the Crimson Vale. Simple enough, yes?"

Malrick says nothing. His face is twisted in pain as tears stream down his dirty face.

"If you do not, my men will continue to torture you by cutting off other pieces of your body," Caspian says. "Your fingers and toes will be first, and then they will cut you limb from limb, piece by piece, until there is nothing left of you. Would you prefer that to a quick death?"

"N-No..."

"Then say it!" Caspian bellows. "Say it for the entire kingdom to hear."

"Y-You are His Majesty, King Caspian of House Nezara, Ruler of the Crimson Vale and... K-King of Alphas."

Caspian nods, and the guard standing behind Malrick raises his ax, holding it in the air for a moment as it glints in the afternoon sun. He brings the ax down on his head, delivering a swift blow that ends Malrick's life.

"Justice has been served," Caspian announces to the crowd.

Applause erupts.

"Long live the alpha king!" the onlookers shout.

My eyes land on one of the youngest members of the Ravenrock Clan, whose severed head lies near his body in a pool of blood.

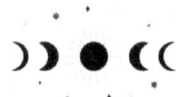

Caz's heavy sigh cuts through the thick silence of the dark bedroom. I roll onto my side to get a better look at him, and in the light of the red moon through the window, I can make out Caz's haggard face.

"Can't sleep, either?" I ask.

He shakes his head as his gaze drifts toward the window, looking out over the night sky.

"Hey." I touch his chin and force him to look at me. "What's going on in that head of yours?"

His Adam's apple dips as he swallows thickly. Caz opens his mouth to speak, but then shuts it and shakes his head again.

I caress his cheek with my thumb. "Today was a total mindfuck, wasn't it?"

Caz rolls onto his back and shifts his arm behind his head, staring up at the ceiling with his brows knitted together with worry. "Can I ask you something?"

"Of course."

He takes a deep breath, as though struggling with the weight of his thoughts. "I'm supposed to be the light one, right? I'm supposed to embody the true north of my soul's morality."

I lie still. So still, my muscles begin to protest.

"But if that's true, then..." Caz's voice breaks. "Then... why did I enjoy what they did to Malrick? After what he did to you, I wanted to kill him. I wanted to take my hands, wring them around his neck, and squeeze while I watched the light leave his eyes." He lifts his hands above his head and chokes the air. "But if that's true, I'm no better than Caspian." Caz lets out a ragged breath and sits up, swinging his legs over the side of the bed. With his elbows on his knees, he buries his head into his hands and shakes his head. "The longer I stay here, the darker my thoughts become. It's like there's something at war inside me, but the darkness is winning, and I don't know what that means for us, Bri."

His shoulders tremble with unshed tears.

"Hey, this changes nothing between us." I sit up in bed and crawl to him, pressing my chest against his back. I wrap my arms around his neck from behind and embrace him as tight as I can to ground him. "Wanting Malrick to pay for his crimes doesn't make you a bad person, Caz. It means you love me. It means you're human, and no human is truly good or evil. We're complex with conflicting emotions, and that's what makes us beautiful."

He leans into my touch, resting his head on my arms. "But if I'm becoming darker, what do you need me for? You have Caspian for that. I'm supposed to be the light one—I'm not supposed to have these dark thoughts."

"Of course, I need you, Caz." I burrow my face into his neck and press a long kiss against his warm skin. "You're my best friend, and you know me in a way no one else does. Not even Caspian." Another kiss. "You have no idea how badly I need you."

He cranes his neck, his hooded gaze coming to rest on my mouth. "I need you too, Bri. So, so much..."

His lips crash into mine, desperate and needy, seeking comfort to quell the raging storm within him. He twists his body to face me, to lean deeper into our kiss, and I pull him closer, entreating him to rejoin me in the bed.

When he pulls back, I'm left breathless and bereft and longing for his touch.

"I shouldn't." He stands up from the bed, rather abruptly, and runs his fingers through his hair. "I should give you space after what Malrick did. I'm sorry."

My eyes rake over his hard chest, the lines of muscles etched over years of manual labor. The only clothing on his body is a pair of cotton sleep pants, which ride low on his sculpted hips and are tented above his groin.

When he catches me staring, he pauses. "You need time before we..." His voice is tight.

I tear my eyes away from his dick and meet his gaze. "I need *you*." I slip my negligee off over my head, the silk sliding over my bare body. I lie back against the pillows and spread my legs, offering myself to him. "Please, Caz."

Caz's hesitation is proof that he's good. He's considerate of my feelings after my ordeal with Malrick, but I don't need to be handled with kid gloves right now. I need him to remind me how good it feels to be with him, to push away the memory of Malrick's cock brushing against my bare ass on that cold, hard floor in his basement.

The same cock that became pig food hours ago.

Caz licks his lips. "Are you sure, Bri?"

"I'm sure."

His hands hook into the waist of his pants. "If at any point you need me to stop, just tell me."

I nod, even though I won't need to.

Caz takes off his pants, revealing his thick erection, before climbing back onto the bed, hovering above me on all fours. He lines himself up at my entrance and gazes down at me, and the love I find there makes my heart swell.

"Are you ready?" he asks, brushing a strand of hair off my face.

"Yes."

When he slides in, he moves slowly. Deeply.

We've only been intimate on a couple of occasions, and when we have, there's been a sense of urgency, like the clock is ticking before the fantasy shatters. But tonight, there's no rush, and he takes his time to worship my body, keeping a steady tempo as he pushes himself inside, then slides out to the tip.

His touch is safe. Tender. He sweeps his thumb across my cheek, an action so small but weighted with love, pure and good.

Like him.

His eyes shine with adoration as he exalts my body. "You're so beautiful, Bri. I love you so much..."

And they aren't empty words. I feel the truth in them deep in my core.

When we come, it's like a rising tide, lifting me to a place of clarity and rapture. I cling to him, calling out his name and his name only, unwilling to let him go.

He's all I have left, the only intact piece that remains of my broken heart.

CHAPTER 22

T he next morning, Caz and I are eating breakfast on the sofa in my sitting room
    when the door bursts open. Aurelius strides into the room in a flurry of excitement,
followed by a parade of assistants and fabrics and mannequins.

I forgot. It's Saturday, which means the Crimson Vale is hosting another ball. Not even
a mass execution could put a damper on the festivities.

"Ah, so it is true what they say!" Aurelius approaches Caz and gives him a deep bow.
"You truly are the spitting image of His Majesty."

Caz, who has an entire boiled egg in his mouth, swallows too quickly and ends up
coughing.

"Lady Briar, a pleasure." Aurelius stands in front of me and takes my hand, placing a
gentle kiss on my knuckles when he bows.

I share a glance with Caz. "Hey, Aurelius. What have you got for us today?"

Aurelius pauses, his flamboyant smile faltering.

I quirk my eyebrow at him. "Is everything alright?"

"Yes, Lady Briar, not to worry. I have a demure pink gown for you to wear." He waves
his assistants over, who scramble to bring forward a mannequin with a blush pink dress.
It's an A-line ballgown with multiple layers of horsehair tulle curling softly around the
skirt. The top consists of long lace sleeves and a high, frilly neckline. As if that wasn't
enough, a white, furry cowl sits on top of the shoulders.

"Uh, wow." My voice is flat. "It looks so…"

Modest. Like the entire point is to cover me up.

"Ah, yes, well…" Aurelius lets out a shrill laugh. "I mean, given those awful rumors, the
queen dowager insisted upon something that exuded—how should I say this?—*purity*."

The room falls completely silent, and everyone refuses to meet my eye, including
Aurelius.

"Hold on," I say. "What rumors?"

Aurelius lets out another nervous laugh. "Oh, it's nothing, really—"

"Aurelius." My patience is wearing thin.

"Ah, you see..." Aurelius takes a cautionary step back. "There is, shall I say, a question as to what occurred between you and that dreadful Malrick fellow during your, ah..."

"My kidnapping?" I supply.

"Yes, that." He bows his head.

I'm speechless.

So, the entire kingdom is gossiping about what a whore I was while in Malrick's captivity. And of course, Queen Sybil, the reigning bitch of the Crimson Vale, had to stick her big nose where it didn't belong.

A low growl erupts from Caz beside me. "That's bullshit."

Hearing a cussword fall from Caz's squeaky-clean mouth takes me by surprise, but when he moves to stand up, I tug him back down onto the sofa. "It's fine. It's not Aurelius's fault."

"I did coordinate your suit, sir," Aurelius says, his voice jumping an octave. "A gray suit with a blush tie and pocket square."

"We don't have to go," Caz says in a low voice. "You don't owe these people anything."

No, but I do want to see Caspian at least one more time. Ever since he told me he was sending me back through the portal, he's been avoiding me. It's probably too painful for him to be close. The more time we spend together, the harder it will be to let go.

I tug at the lace around my neck. "Aurelius couldn't have made this less itchy?"

Caz and I stand at the end of the corridor, watching the crowd enter the ballroom from a safe distance.

He loosens the knot of his tie. "You think Aurelius is trying to suffocate us to death?"

I snort. "That would be pathetic if that's how the Crimson Vale finally gets us: death by fabric." I place my hand on Caz's chest, admiring the way his muscles are taut beneath his shirt. "But I'd be lying if I said this suit didn't do things to me."

He gives me a bashful grin. "You look beautiful tonight, Bri. Really."

"Me?" I glance down at my dress. "I look like a cupcake."

He shrugs. "I like cupcakes."

I give his arm a playful slap, which makes him laugh.

"By the way, I almost forgot." He reaches into his suit jacket and pulls out a small velvet box.

My eyes practically pop out of my sockets. That isn't...?

But when he opens the lid, a small flower bud sits on top, and as if by magic, it unfurls and blooms into a pink peony.

"Caz, this is incredible," I say on a breath.

"I never got a chance to go to prom." He takes the flower out of the box, revealing the ribbon attached to it underneath, and he begins to tie it around my wrist. "With a little help from Elowen, I made you the perfect corsage."

I run my fingertips over the velvety petals. "Caz, this is so thoughtful."

He ties off the ribbon and admires his handiwork. "Ready?"

I nod and snake my arm around his, and together, we walk toward the ballroom. Uniformed guards are stationed all along the perimeter, and I can feel their eyes on me as we pass.

Woe to anyone who tries to kidnap me tonight.

"Did you ever go to prom?" Caz asks.

"I did. I actually lost my virginity at my junior prom." I laugh out loud at the memory. "It was *so* bad."

Caz stiffens beside me. "He didn't force himself on you, did he?"

"Oh, no, nothing like that." I wave my hand. "More like neither of us had any experience, and it was awkward. We did it in the bathroom, and he ended up leaving with another girl."

"Well, he's an idiot," Caz says, leaning in to whisper in my ear. "And for what it's worth, I'm glad my first time was with you." He plants a soft kiss on my cheek. "My first and my last."

A small chamber orchestra begins to play a waltz, and Caz offers his hand to me. "Shall we dance?"

"Do you know how to waltz?" I ask, giving him a dubious look.

"No, do you?"

"Not really."

We both burst into laughter.

"Maybe we should just stand by the punch bowl, then," Caz suggests.

"I didn't bring any alcohol to spike it, though." I grab his hands and lead him toward the dance floor. "Besides, I'm not a wallflower, and neither are you."

With a grin, Caz follows me to the dancefloor and wraps his arms around my waist. I respond by wrapping my arms around his neck, and we sway slowly from side to side as other couples dance and twirl around us.

"You definitely have the prom-style slow dance down," I tease.

"Oh, good. That's what I was going for."

As we turn in a circle, my eyes land on Caspian across the room. A couple of people are talking to him and his brother, but he's not speaking. His gaze keeps wandering toward the dancefloor, and when our eyes meet, my heart stops.

His burning red irises widen as he drinks me in. The heat there strikes me in my core, and I suck in a sharp breath at the effect he has on me. With just one look, I melt for him into a mewling puddle of need and longing.

There are only two more nights left before Caz and I return to Earth. How am I supposed to stay away from him when he's looking at me like he wants to devour me whole?

"Caz?"

Caz looks down at me as we continue to sway to the music. "Yeah?"

"I have a favor to ask."

"Anything."

Caz's warm smile makes my stomach lurch. This man would do anything for me, and yet, what I'm about to ask him is going to break his heart.

I came here tonight with Caz as his date, but I have no plans to leave with him. It's like my junior prom all over again, except this time I'm the villain of the story.

"I want to spend the night with Caspian."

His smile falters.

"We have the rest of our lives to be together," I explain. "Once we step through that portal, I'm one hundred percent yours. But I only have two nights left with Caspian, and I want the chance to say goodbye."

We've stopped dancing. Caz studies me with a conflicted look on his face, and he glances across the room at Caspian.

"I know I have no right to ask you this," I whisper. "And I'm going to spend the rest of my life making it up to you. Just, please. Let me have this before I say goodbye to him forever."

"Bri." Caz grabs my shoulders and looks at me. "Of course you have a right to ask. He's your fated mate, too. I understand." He swallows. "It's hard, but I understand."

I step forward and give him a long hug, which he returns. "Thank you," I whisper against his chest.

The music changes to a slower, sultrier tune, and moments later, I sense a familiar presence beside me.

"May I cut in?"

When I glance up, Caspian is there.

"I take it you overheard?" Caz asks, his tone holding a hint of annoyance.

Caspian nods, his hands folded behind his back, looking every bit like a regal king. "I did."

Caz looks down at where our hands are joined, lingering there for a long moment before reluctantly letting go. Without a word, he steps away to allow space for Caspian to step in.

As Caspian wraps his arm around my waist, I watch Caz head off into the crowd. He turns around with a sad smile on his face and gives me a nod.

He's giving me his permission to be with Caspian.

Thank you, I mouth at him. *I love you.*

Caz gives me a tight nod before disappearing into the crowd.

"Don't feel bad," Caspian whispers to me. "You're a woman who knows what she wants. That's nothing to be ashamed of."

"But I hate hurting him. He's too good for me."

Caspian spins and dips me in time to the music, his eyes boring into mine. "You have nothing to apologize for. You are mated to both of us, and he knows that as well as I do."

He lifts me into a standing position until my bosom presses against his chest, and we stand here for a moment, staring into each other's gaze.

Caspian begins to spin and sway me in an elegant waltz to the music. Our feet glide across the ballroom floor as he leads me in our final dance together, and I cling to him, wishing this moment could last forever.

I want to savor every second I have with him before we part ways for good, to make memories with him that I can take with me. To remember the way he makes me feel like I'm flying when we dance, and how his touch sends an electric thrill weaving through my body.

The music stops, and he leans down to whisper in my ear. "Shall we get out of here?"

I'm breathless. "Won't your grandmother have something to say about that?"

He quirks an eyebrow at me. "All I want to do is fuck you senseless, and you bring up my grandmother at a time like this?"

I shake my head and laugh. "You're right. What was I thinking?"

With a devilish smirk, he grabs my hand and leads me off the dancefloor as fast as my legs will allow me to keep up. The crowd parts for us and bows to the king as we pass. Queen Sybil is glaring at me from the corner of the room, but I ignore her as I follow Caspian out of the party and up the stairs.

"So much for convincing everyone I'm 'pure,'" I mutter under my breath.

Caspian snorts. "Trust me, I plan to defile you every which way tonight."

His words send explosive anticipation between my thighs as we wander further and further from the ballroom.

"Caspian!" I gasp. "You're going too fast... I can't keep up!"

He turns and picks me up, and I squeal as he heaves my body over his shoulder like a sack of flour. His hand rests on my ass, holding me steady while he wraps his other hand around my legs.

I giggle as he takes off up the stairs at a breakneck speed. "What are you doing?"

"I don't want to waste another minute," he answers, giving my ass a smart slap.

When we reach his room, Caspian opens the door, carries me inside, and kicks it shut behind him. Without setting me down, he shifts my body until my back is pressed against the door, and my legs wrap around his waist for support.

He pushes up the gown of my skirt to expose my underwear. I'm already slick with arousal as the back of his hand brushes against my panties while he fiddles with the button of his pants. With one hand, he slides his pants down just enough to expose his erection. He hooks his finger in the bottom of my panties and moves them aside to give himself access to my entrance.

With desperate urgency, he pushes himself inside, and we both moan at the familiar, delicious contact. I hold on to his shoulders, my fingernails digging into his jacket as he moves in and out of me.

The idea that he couldn't wait to have me before we even reached his bed makes me explode with desire. As he thrusts in, pressing me against the door, we both quickly approach the brink of climax.

"I love you, Bri," he gasps as sweat rolls down his face.

"I love you too." I press my mouth against his.

I snake my fingers into his hair, knocking his crown to the floor. Our tongues dance wildly in each other's mouths, stifling my screams of pleasure as I reach my orgasm, and Caspian groans as he finishes and releases inside me.

Our faces pull apart, chests heaving as we both gasp for air, and we gaze at each other as we come down off our high.

Slowly, Caspian withdraws himself from my sheath, and I unwrap my legs from around his waist and slide to the floor on my feet.

"Come here." Caspian takes me by the hand and leads me to the bed.

I lie down on the mattress, my breathing ragged as I watch him strip down to nothing but his underwear. My gaze snags on the sharp lines of muscle, and his beauty takes my breath away.

He lies down beside me. "I've thought long and hard about this, Bri."

I turn over in the bed so that our faces are almost touching as we lie side by side.

He lets out a long sigh. "I want to give you everything you want before you leave me for good. So, I'll do it. I'll do the threesome with you and my light one."

I stare at him, dumbstruck and speechless.

Surely, I heard that wrong. Or maybe I'm dreaming.

"I'm sorry if I ever made you feel ashamed of wanting this," Caspian continues, stroking my cheek. "I promised I would fulfill your wildest dreams, and this is me fulfilling that promise."

I'm stunned. My deepest, darkest fantasy is within my grasp, so close to becoming my reality. But Caspian is only one part of this equation, and until all parties agree, I can't allow myself to even dare to hope.

"I appreciate this so much," I say. "But I'm not sure Caz would agree to it."

"That matter I will leave to you, but know that I'm on board. We can do it tomorrow night, if he's amenable."

He says it so casually, like he's scheduling a dentist appointment or a business meeting.

I weave my fingers with his. "That's our last full night before we leave."

"I know." He pulls our hands up and places a kiss on my fingers.

I close my eyes and relish his touch. "I'll worry about talking to Caz tomorrow. Tonight, I just want to focus on spending every moment I can with you." I lay my head on his chest, listening to his steady heartbeat and committing it to memory.

Caspian and I stay up all night long until the red sun peeks through the windows into his bedroom. He takes his time with me, and it allows me to memorize every line of his hard body, every curve of his sculpted face, and the way his burgundy eyes brighten when he looks at me.

I think that's what I'll miss the most about him—the intensity of his love. How he devours me with his gaze, drinking me in from head to toe with a ravenous thirst he can never seem to quench.

How he sees right through me and my flaws and accepts me not in spite of them, but *because* of them. The good and the bad as equal sums of my parts.

The stamina of this man is truly astounding, although the frequent blood draws from various parts of my body certainly aid in his swift recovery. Every time he drinks from me, it's euphoric, and I know he's leaving bruises on purpose to mark me as his.

I hope they scar so he'll be branded on my body forever. A physical piece of him I can carry with me as proof of our love. That Caspian and I found our way to each other, overcoming ancient curses and fate and dark ones.

Because after he's gone, I'll have nothing else to prove he was more than a beautiful, dark dream. Nothing except my memory of him.

CHAPTER 23

I'm standing outside the door to my room with my hand on the knob. Caz is on the other side, waiting for me to return to him after spending the night (and day) with his dark one, and I'm about to hit him with a proposition for a threesome.

What could possibly go wrong?

Bracing myself, I take a deep breath and open the door.

Caz sits in the living room, staring into the fireplace with his chin resting on his hands. The sun is setting outside the window behind him, rimming him in golden light.

He startles when I enter the room. "Oh, you're back?"

"Yeah." I shut the door and come over to sit beside him on the sofa.

Caz swallows. "I didn't expect you back until tomorrow night."

"Well, I wanted to have dinner with you."

The corner of his mouth tugs as he fights a grin. "Already sick of him?"

I doubt I could get sick of fucking Caspian, but I decide to keep that tidbit of information to myself.

Caspian and I stayed in his bed all day, exhausted after staying up all night long. My circadian rhythm is off, and it's making everything feel a bit surreal.

That's the only reason I'm bold enough to bring up my forbidden fantasy.

"Actually, I wanted to talk to you about that," I say. "You see—"

The door opens, and I practically leap off the sofa in fright. Elowen comes in wheeling a dinner cart and begins to set up our meal in front of the fireplace. It takes a moment for me to collect myself, and when I bring my hand to my chest, my heart is thumping beneath it.

"His Majesty said you would be taking dinner in your room with Sir Caz tonight." Elowen begins listing off the menu for the evening, but I don't hear a word. Oblivious, she carries on while Caz and I sit in silence.

I look at her—really look at her. Not only am I leaving Caspian behind, but I'm leaving behind my dear friend, too. She has proven herself loyal and kind, and the idea of not seeing her again brings a fresh wave of melancholy.

She turns her violet gaze onto me with a serene smile. "Enjoy your meal."

I want to say something to her, but the words don't come. Nothing seems adequate for everything she's done for me, but I only have another day left to think of something profound.

"Thanks, Elowen. It looks delicious."

She curtsies to the both of us before exiting the room and closing the door behind her.

Caz digs into his meal, but I leave mine untouched. How the hell am I supposed to ask him for a threesome when he only lost his virginity a few weeks ago? I can count on one hand the number of times he's had sex, and I'm not sure a hand job in the dungeons counts.

So, I stall. I talk about every other subject I can possibly think of to distract myself, to put off this difficult conversation for a little while longer. The evening passes with polite conversation.

Caz leans back in his seat. "You're acting weird, Bri."

"Weird? I'm not weird."

"Yes you are." He levels me with an amused look. "You haven't touched your food all evening."

"Actually, I... I have something I want to run by you," I stammer. "But I'm afraid of how you're going to react."

"Geez, this sounds serious." Caz shifts in his seat and sets down his wine glass.

"Caspian made us an offer," I begin.

Caz groans and leans back against the sofa pillows. "Oh, great. What does he want?"

Am I really about to ask this aloud? I guess it's now or never.

"He, um, offered to have a threesome tonight. With us." I chew my lip and wait.

Caz's brows knit together as he tilts his head to the side, and I can see the gears churning in his mind.

However, what I don't expect is for him to start laughing.

It's a thunderous laugh erupting from his belly, and his entire body shakes with mirth. He throws his head back and clutches his stomach as he tries to regain control of himself. "A threesome?" he repeats, wiping a tear from his eye. "That's the last thing I expected out of him. How did you react?"

I want to burrow my face into the sofa pillows and hide. In fact, the sofa should just swallow me whole at this point. "Well, the only reason he suggested it is because... well, I wanted it."

Caz's laughing fit ends as abruptly as it began. "Wait, are you being serious right now?"

I nod.

He glances around the room, as if he'll be able to glean answers from the drapes or the furniture. "But... where's this coming from?"

I take a deep breath and launch into my explanation—how Caspian took me to the Manor of Salacious Appetites, what I witnessed there, and how I haven't stopped thinking about it since.

I stop rambling and wait for Caz to react.

He picks up his silverware and cuts off a bite of cake, which he pops into his mouth. It takes him forever to chew, all the while staring absently into the fire. He sets the silverware back down and swallows.

The wait is so excruciating I think I might pass out. "Please, say something."

"I'm not really sure what to say." He runs his fingers through his hair. "I don't know the first thing about having a threesome."

"Neither do I, honestly, except for what I saw at the Manor. I figured we could explore it together."

He's looking rather pale, like he might be sick all over the coffee table.

"I know this is a bit of a shock." I wring my hands together. "But I really want to do this. We can go at a pace we're all comfortable with. If you just want to watch for a while, that's fine. Even if you don't want to go all the way, I'd understand. I just want to share something with the two of you before"—I take a deep breath—"I have to leave him behind forever. One last memory to hold on to, and then we'll never mention it again."

Caz opens his mouth to respond, but before he can say anything, a knock comes at the door.

"Oh, shit," I whisper.

Caz glances between me and the door. "Is... is that him?"

"Yeah," I reply. "He's early. I'll tell him we need more time to talk."

I stand up, but then he wraps his warm hand around mine, keeping me still. "It's fine," he says. "Bring him in."

"What?" I pause and stare down at him. "Are you sure?"

He gulps, then nods. "Yeah. He should be included in the conversation, don't you think?" Caz lets out a hollow laugh.

"Yeah, I guess that's a fair point."

Caz gives me a reassuring nod, though I swear there's a hint of green in his complexion. I give his hand one last squeeze before letting go and crossing over to the door.

When I open the door, Caspian stands on the threshold looking dapper as always in his suit.

"Hi," I whisper.

"Hello," Caspian murmurs. "And I'm not early, by the way. This is the time we agreed on."

"You heard that, didn't you?" I frown and fold my arms. When I glance behind me at the window of the sitting room, it's already dark outside. I spent more time rambling than I realized. "Fine, come in." I wave him into the sitting room and close the door behind him.

The three of us sit in an uncomfortable silence until Caspian clucks his tongue. "So, are we doing this?"

I wince at his bluntness, but I glance over at Caz for a response. He is sitting on the sofa, wide-eyed and still, and guilt stabs me in the gut.

I rub my temples and begin to pace the room, eager to release some of this tension. For a girl who was thoroughly fucked over the past twenty-four hours, you'd think I'd be more relaxed, but instead, I'm wound up tighter than one of my grandma's canning jar lids.

This is not how I wanted things to go. Everything tonight is going wrong, and I'm handling this all wrong.

"Fucking Christ," I mutter, pacing back and forth.

"So..." Caz says, "how does this even work?"

I pause mid-step, and my head shoots up to look at Caz. He's wearing a wary expression, but at least he's opening himself up to the experience.

He's opening himself up to the experience.

This is happening. This is really happening.

Oh my God.

I've imagined this moment so many times, experienced this secret fantasy in my dreams, but I never believed it would become a reality. My breathing speeds up as a small thrill knots in my lower belly.

I will admit, though, that my fantasies never included this much awkwardness. Caz's question still hangs in the air, and I glance at Caspian for direction.

He shrugs. "I've only ever been with two women in one bed. Never two men and one woman."

I put my hands on my hips. "Okay, so... this is new for all of us."

"Bri, you mentioned that I could, uh, watch?" Caz shifts on the sofa. "Maybe we start there, I guess? I'm still wrapping my mind around this."

"Yeah, okay." I give him an eager nod. "That sounds like a good place to start."

"Perhaps we move this into the bedroom?" Caspian gestures toward the open door leading into my room.

"If you don't mind, I'd like to get changed first," I chime in. "I'll go get ready in the bathroom while Caz finishes his dessert."

"Don't worry about me; I don't have an appetite." Caz pushes his plate away from him on the coffee table.

I give him an apologetic smile. "I'll just be a minute. Don't kill each other while I'm gone." With a pointed look at Caspian, I head toward the bedroom and make a beeline for my wardrobe.

Sexy lingerie. That's what this moment needs, and perhaps it will help us all get in the mood.

Caspian made sure to stock my wardrobe with plenty of skimpy pieces, and the options are overwhelming. Flustered, I grab the nearest set and tuck it under my arm before darting into the bathroom.

Before changing out of my dress, I brush my teeth and run a comb through my hair. My makeup from last night is smudged, but I don't have time to fix it. My fear is that if I keep them waiting, they'll change their mind and back out.

Again, this is not how I wanted things to go. I thought I'd have more time to prepare.

I quickly slide out of my dress and slip into the lingerie I picked out—a sheer black chemise with a floral lace pattern. It comes with a matching thong in the set, but I decide to leave it off, exposing my pussy through the sheer fabric. I don't want to throw any additional obstacles into the mix. Getting the guys to agree to this was enough of an obstacle in itself.

When I emerge from the bathroom, every inch of me is shaking with nerves. Caspian is pacing by the bed, and Caz is settled into a chair in the corner, wiping his sweaty palms on his pants.

But when their eyes land on me, they both grow still.

"Bri, wow, you look..." Caz's voice trails off as he admires me with wide eyes.

Caspian licks his lips as I approach the bed, closing the gap between us. "I think he means to say that you look absolutely divine."

Beneath their twin gazes, heat rises to my cheeks. Heat is spreading to other areas of my body, too, as I stand between them, exposed and accessible. I press my thighs together to keep the arousal from coating my legs.

Their desire for me is eroding the awkward tension, turning the air thick and heady.

Caspian slowly undresses, taking his time to take off his jacket, followed by his shirt and then his pants. With a quick glance over at Caz, the first glimpse of uncertainty crosses his face. He turns his gaze back onto me, and with a deep breath, he slides his underwear down and removes them, adding them to the pile of clothes on the floor.

I bite my lip as my eyes stare at his manhood. He's not yet fully erect, so I step closer and place my hand around his length. With gentle strokes, I begin pumping on him and glance over to check on Caz.

Caz is one to wear his emotions on his sleeve, but as he watches us with wide eyes, his expression is unreadable. I can't even begin to imagine what's going through his mind as I stroke his doppelgänger right in front of him.

Caspian's broad hands snake around my waist and lift my chemise to reveal my ass. He palms my cheeks, spreading them apart as he kneads them with his fingers. "Does that turn you on?" he growls. "Seeing our mate's bare ass exposed to you?"

The bold way he addresses Caz startles me, but not as much as the hard slap he lands across my backside.

Smack!

Closing my eyes, I take a sharp intake of breath at the contact.

"See how she's turned on when I spank her?" Caspian asks in a low voice.

I don't know why, but the filthy way Caspian talks about me to Caz—like I'm not even here—might be the sexiest thing he's done in the time I've known him. And Caspian has done a lot of filthy things to me.

But it's more than that. He's taking control of the situation the way I'd expect from the alpha king, and it's setting off dynamite between my legs.

I need Caspian to captain us through this. Caz and I both do.

"Caspian, please," I beg, tightening my grip on his erection. He's fully hard now.

"Please what, Bri?" He lays another loud *smack!* across my ass that echoes around the dark bedroom.

My breath comes in ragged gasps. "Fuck me."

Caspian glances at Caz in the corner. "Do you want to watch me fuck our mate?"

Caz runs his hand along his jawline, his eyes glued to the scene unfolding before him. His chest is rising and falling with rapid breaths, and his tongue darts out to wet his bottom lip. After a moment, he gulps, then gives us a single nod.

I shudder. That small signal of agreement nearly sends me to climax.

Caspian shoves me down onto the mattress in a seated position, my feet planted on the floor as I face Caz's chair.

"Spread your legs," Caspian commands. "Show us that wet little cunt of yours."

I do as he instructs, spreading my knees apart as the chemise rides up. Both Caz and Caspian's eyes drift south, making the heat burn hotter in my cheeks. I feel so exposed, so raw, and yet I'm basking in their lust-fueled gazes, the singular object of their desires.

"Touch yourself," Caspian says.

I do as he says, lifting the hem of my chemise to give myself better access. Slowly, I begin rubbing circles at my entrance with my three fingers, glancing between Caz and Caspian and finding curiosity and desire in their expressions. Their reactions feed my lust, and I bring my other hand up to massage my breast over my lingerie.

My breathing is growing quicker, shallower, as I work faster against my pussy. Caspian fists his cock in his hand, and Caz's pants start to bulge at the junction of his thighs.

"Don't come just yet, Bri," Caspian warns, taking a step closer to me. He grabs my waist and shoves me further back on the bed until I'm lying back against the pillows.

Caspian climbs onto the bed, prowling like a jaguar. He shifts closer so that he's positioned between my legs, which he spreads apart.

His fingers find my entrance, and when he makes contact, I gasp and buck my hips.

He smirks. "She's wet for us. Wet and ready for our cocks." Caspian slams his erection into me, which makes my back arch off the mattress. "You like how that feels?" Caspian grips my knees, forcing my legs wider apart. "Let's put on a show for my light one, shall we?"

He begins to pump inside of me, starting slow until he finds his rhythm. With each thrust, my body is pushed further back into the pillows, but then Caspian pulls me back against his hips, forcing me to take every brutal inch of him. With increasing intensity, he continues to thrust and withdraw, bringing my body closer to the brink of climax.

He keeps my legs spread wide, staring down at our joining with fascination. "Do you like watching our mate get fucked?" he asks Caz. "Is it like watching yourself fuck in the mirror?"

My head lolls to the side to look at Caz, and what I see makes my mouth fall open with a gasp. Caz's pants are undone to reveal his long, hard erection, and he's stroking it while watching Caspian and me in bed.

My sweet, innocent Caz is touching himself while watching me, and it is a sight to behold. Mesmerized, my gaze locks with Caz as Caspian continues to thrust inside, over and over again, until a searing, white light blinds my vision. Ecstasy grips me as my body erupts with involuntary convulsions, and I cry out at the height of my pleasure.

My heart is racing as sweat beads along my brow, enraptured by this perfect moment shared by all three of us.

It is everything.

I'm boneless as I blink the white spots from my vision, and I become aware that Caspian is still inside me, thrusting harder and faster, using my body to get off.

"Are you going to join us?" he asks Caz. "If you aren't, I'm going to release my seed inside of her right now."

Caz is silent.

"Tell me now," Caspian growls.

Caz becomes deathly still at the precipice of his indecision as he fists his cock in one hand while digging his nails into the armrest in the other. After a moment, he pushes out of his chair and crosses the room. "I'm coming." His voice is gruff as he tugs at his shirt.

Caspian pulls out, his throbbing length glistening with my essence. "Get up, Bri. He'll lay beneath you while I take your virgin asshole."

I shudder with delicious anticipation at his words, and butterflies erupt in my stomach. Even though I just came, my body is craving another round, knowing that I'm about to fulfill my deepest, darkest fantasy.

What's about to happen between the three of us is going to change me forever. I can feel it, and God, I'm ready for it.

When Caz approaches the bed, I shift to the side and allow him to lie back on the pillows.

"Bri, get on top and ride his cock." Caspian helps me crawl on top of Caz before resting his hands on my hips, guiding me into place. When he pushes me down, I sink along Caz's length until he's fully seated inside me, and Caz lets out a low groan, his eyes rolling back in his head. With a moan, I lift myself off of him until I reach the tip, then slide back down his shaft, lubricated with my own arousal.

Caz reaches up to knead at my breasts through the lingerie, and I lean forward into his touch. I spread my palms flat on his chest, pushing against him to keep me upright.

"Good girl," Caspian encourages. "Now, bend over and kiss him."

I do as he says, leaning down to meet Caz's mouth as I suck on his lower lip. He meets my kiss by slipping his tongue into mine, and his arms wrap around my back in a tight embrace.

"Yes, exactly that." Caspian moves away and picks up his coat from the floor to rummage in his pockets. He pulls out a small jar and twists the lid off before setting both down on the dresser.

Gripping his stiff erection at the base, he uses his other hand to dip into the jar, emerging with a gelatinous substance coating his fingers. He smears it over his entire length before climbing onto the bed behind me. "Bri, remember to relax. We'll start with my thumb."

His finger presses against my rear hole, testing me as Caz's hips grind against me from below. Caspian pushes, but my body resists.

"Relax, Bri," Caspian croons. "Let me in."

It takes a moment, but once I manage to relax, his thumb slips in.

"I feel so full," I whimper, my senses overloaded with the feeling of Caz's thick cock and Caspian's thumb buried inside me.

"Just wait. I'm about to bury my cock inside of your ass." Caspian withdraws his thumb, leaving me with an empty feeling. But it doesn't last long as Caspian lines the tip of his manhood at my rear entrance. "Ready?"

I nod, and Caz stops his thrusts for a moment. I gaze down at him as Caspian pushes inside my rear entrance, and I let out a sharp hiss at the unfamiliar sensation. Caz watches me from below, his brows furrowed in concern, keeping me still with his arms wrapped around me.

Caspian pauses, allowing my body to adjust around him. "Relax, my love."

Both of my men are buried inside me at once, and my lower half feels so full I might burst. How the fuck is there room for both of them at the same time? We must be defying the laws of physics. That's the only explanation.

"She's ready," Caspian says. "Begin to pump inside her again, but move slowly."

Caz withdraws himself as Caspian burrows deeper. As Caz begins to push back up, Caspian pulls out, and they begin to alternate inside of me in slow, careful strokes.

"It's... so much." I let out a moan, holding still as they both slide in and out of my body.

Caz gasps and shudders beneath me. "I'm going to come!" His fingers dig into my shoulders as his control loosens.

Caspian groans. "Me too. She's so tight."

I'm shaking and trembling as my body barrels toward release. My arms and legs wobble beneath me as Caz and Caspian take turns inside of me, unhurried and deep.

So fucking deep.

Caz is the first one to reach the pinnacle, and he lets out a gasp beneath me. Warmth spreads in both openings as Caspian echoes him, releasing his seed into my ass.

I've never felt anything like this before. It's indescribable and perfect, having both these men unravel around me as we blur the lines between light and dark.

I did this to them. Two strong, striking men who shatter at my touch, revealing the rawest versions of themselves only to me.

The power that gives me is the final push I need to career over the edge, screaming both their names in quick succession. "Yes! Caz! Caspian! Oh, *God*..."

My men grow still as they empty themselves inside of me, and wave after wave of infinite euphoria crashes over me, consuming me and pulling me out to an endless sea of ecstasy.

If it's possible to drown in one's own pleasure, this is it.

It feels so good I can't breathe. My screaming fades into a soundless whisper as my lips hang open in an O-shape. My eyes are scrunched together as white light dances behind my eyelids.

Just as I'm starting to come down, Caspian wraps his hand around my throat and pulls me upright. Both of them are still buried inside me as my back presses against Caspian's broad chest. He burrows his face into the crook of my neck before biting down.

Hard.

A sharp pain comes down on my shoulder, followed by another orgasm ripping through me, sudden and unexpected.

"Oh, God, it's too much!" I cry. "It feels too good…"

It's overwhelming how much pleasure they have to offer, and yet, my body, weakened with illness, continues to take and take and take from them.

Through my lidded gaze, I see Caz beneath me, staring up at us with a wide-eyed expression, equal parts fascination and horror.

But when his mouth falls open, his canine teeth are revealed, and they're growing sharper and longer.

"C-Caz?" My shaky voice is spent.

When Caspian has had his fill, he licks my puncture wounds and sits back, his hips still angled forward against me.

Caz reaches up, wrapping his hand around my neck to pull me down. Rather than kiss me, he burrows his face into the crook of my neck, the same place where Caspian just drank.

And then he, too, sinks his teeth into my flesh.

I gasp as another wave of pleasure washes over me. "W-What's happening? Oh, my fucking God…"

I can't take it anymore. My body can't handle any more pleasure, and I don't have a safe word to find relief.

I collapse on top of Caz's glistening chest, my consciousness slipping.

When I wake up, I'm pressed between two warm bodies—my breasts are pressed against Caz, and my camisole is pushed up above my backside, which is settled against Caspian's hip. Caz's fingers are entwined with mine, while Caspian' arm is resting across my waist in a possessive hold.

My body is sore all over. But I would take this ache tenfold if it meant I could experience another night of pleasure with Caz and Caspian.

I've never felt more complete. I could die right now with zero regrets.

My eyes take in the bedroom, at the clothes scattered across the floor, at the chair Caz sat in last night. Everything has a hazy quality to it, like I'm still stuck in a fever dream I never want to wake up from.

Caz stirs beside me, rubbing his sleepy eyes before his brown gaze settles on me. He grins. "Good morning, beautiful."

My cheeks grow hot. "Good morning."

"I was going to ask how you're feeling, but I already know."

My brows knit together. "What do you mean?"

His fingertips graze the place where he bit me last night. "Your mate mark. We're connected now." He leans over to place a gentle kiss there.

"My what?"

"Your mate mark," he repeats. "Now that I've marked you, we share the mate bond. I can feel all of your emotions. If you close your eyes, you should be able to feel mine, too."

I let out a soft laugh. "It's called a hickey, Caz. There's nothing special about it."

His grin grows wider. "Trust me. Close your eyes."

After giving him a skeptical look, I close my eyes and play along. "Okay, now what?"

"Just focus on me, not on your own emotions." He presses his palm over my chest. "Feel my hand on your heart."

There's something about his touch that soothes the ache in my muscles. I take a few deep, steady breaths, and my body relaxes against him.

And that's when I feel it—a warm fuzziness in my chest. Overwhelming emotions of intimacy and love that don't belong to me, yet I experience more deeply than my own.

A tear slips down my cheek. "Oh, wow."

I'm a broken, chronically ill college dropout, and yet I feel the way Caz feels when he looks at me. He doesn't see me as any of those things; he sees perfection, beauty, and kindness.

Despite everything I've put him through, his love for me is unwavering.

He's too good for me. I don't deserve his love.

"Bri." He sweeps his thumb across my cheek, wiping my tears away. "How could I not love you? You're incredible. I'm the one who doesn't deserve *you*."

His statement makes my heart stutter. "Wait, what? How…? Can you read my mind?"

"No, but I can feel your emotions, and they're really strong right now. Whatever is going through your mind, just know that you are the most incredible woman I've ever met, and if I have to remind you every day for the rest of our lives, I will."

"I concur," a voice says behind me. "You are the most incredible woman in all the realms."

I look over my shoulder to find Caspian staring back at me with his ruby gaze. He's awake with his head propped on his elbow, listening to our conversation.

I lean over to give him a lingering kiss. "Thank you for last night." I take their hands into mine. "Both of you. I'm going to treasure it forever."

Everything is so perfect, and yet, I'm hit by a debilitating feeling of grief. Grief so deep, my heart hurts, and I bring my hand to my chest to quell the ache. When I glance at Caspian, his face is twisted with sorrow.

"I can feel your emotions, too," I whisper, reaching to touch his face. "Oh, Caspian..."

It hurts so much. Not only can I feel his emotions, but they're amplified through the mate bond. A bond created by Caz's mark.

If I can feel Caspian now, will I be able to feel him on Earth?

Caz sits up in bed. "I can feel both of you, but I only marked Bri. How is this possible?"

Caspian settles back against the pillows with his arm behind his head. "You seem to forget we are the same person. If I had to venture a guess, marking her bound her to both of us, and Bri is now a conduit between you and me."

Caz lets out a long sigh. "Great."

I dig my fingers into my chest, trying to distract myself from the pain, while my other hand covers my mouth to stifle a sob. "It feels like my heart is breaking all over again."

Caspian gazes up at me with a longing expression. "I'm sorry, my love. I'm causing you pain."

"No, I wouldn't trade this for anything." I caress his jawline, feeling the prickle of his morning stubble beneath my fingertips.

Tonight is the full moon, which means Caz and I leave tonight. These are our final hours together, and I refuse to let him out of my sight until the last possible minute.

"If the portal reappears, we could visit from time to time—"

"Absolutely not," Caspian cuts me off. "You're in danger every moment you spend here in the Crimson Vale. And I... I will be expected to find a queen. Produce heirs." A dark expression crosses his face. "It's best if your paths do not cross. For your own safety."

This is the first time he's discussed what his future looks like without me in it. Caspian has his duty as a king to continue the Nezara line, as painful as it is to think about.

Caspian must sense my jealousy because he grabs my hand. "I'll never love her. I'll never love another woman. That is a promise."

My lip quivers. "If Caz can go through the portal, why can't you come back? I mean, have you ever tried?"

Caspian shakes his head. "The curse is designed to keep the dark ones out of your realm." He runs his hand along my arm. "My light one will keep you safe. He will make you happy." His voice catches. "Move on without me."

"I... I need a minute." I untangle myself from between Caz and Caspian and crawl out of bed. The lump in my throat is so thick I can't even breathe, and my eyesight is watery as I stumble toward the bathroom.

Once inside, I sink to the cold, marble floor, naked and sobbing. I hug my knees against my chest in the fetal position and let out a raw, tormented cry that echoes off the title.

How am I supposed to carry on when I'm carrying the burden of emotions for three people? It's all too much. I can't do this without Caspian. I need him as much as I need Caz.

I thought that maybe, just maybe, I was brought here to the Crimson Vale to break the curse. To end centuries of pain. But I'm just a broken girl who thought herself special enough to take on an ancient curse. It's delusional.

Footsteps pad across the tile, and a pair of strong arms lifts me off the floor. Caspian carries me over to my chair in front of the mirror and sets me down, with Caz following from behind.

"I want our final hours together to be happy," Caspian says. "Cast thoughts of the future from your mind. Can you do that for me, my love?"

I meet his gaze in the mirror. He gives me an encouraging smile, but I still feel his heartache through our bond.

I can do this. For Caspian.

I give a resolute nod.

Caz and Caspian stand behind me like twin gods and meet my gaze through the mirror. I can't help but admire them side-by-side in their naked splendor, my eyes tracing the lines of their muscular physiques down to their...

"Show Bri her mark." Caspian runs his fingers along my neck. "My light one did good work, if I do say so myself."

Caz stands a little straighter, and quiet pride ripples through the mate bond. With a gentle sweep of his hand, he moves the remaining strands of hair off my neck. "Take a look."

I angle myself in front of the mirror to get a better view of the spot Caz and Caspian seem so obsessed with—the juncture of my neck and shoulder. When the mark comes into view, I gasp.

This is so much better than a hickey.

It doesn't look like a bite mark at all. A jet-black tattoo appeared on my body overnight—a detailed symbol of the sun with a smaller crescent moon embedded inside of it.

The sun and the moon. The light and the dark as one, branded onto my skin.

I trace my fingertips over the top of it. "Did you pick this design?"

"No." Caz rakes his eyes over the mark. "No one knows why mate marks look the way they do, but some say it's a gift from the Moon Goddess. It's unique to every individual."

A small smile crosses my lips. "It's perfect. I love it."

All dreams must come to an end when we wake up.

The carriage ride to the village square is quiet. Outside the window, the full moon sits in the night sky, its eerie shade illuminating the path in a red, foreboding glow. Caspian's hand grasps mine while Caz sits across from us.

I'm teetering on the edge of a breakdown, and if I utter a single word, I'm afraid I'll devolve into uncontrollable sobs. I have to stay strong for Caspian, even though our mate bond betrays my true feelings.

Caz is wearing dark pants and a loose, cotton shirt from Caspian's closet. I'll never wash that shirt for as long as I live, and I pray that Caspian's scent will linger on the fabric for many years to come.

Elowen saw us off in the castle courtyard, and after our lengthy, teary goodbye, I'm already missing my friend. She took care to wash the clothes I arrived in, which I'm wearing for my return home.

I'll never see her again. I have no way of knowing if she'll be alright or if Valerius will take care of her, so I made Caspian promise me to keep an eye on her.

Elowen slipped something into my hands before we left. I look down at the small care package in my lap—a wrapped cloth full of cheese, nuts, and cold meat. She always made sure I ate and kept my strength up.

The carriage rolls to a stop, and my hands begin to shake.

No, no, no. Not yet. I'm not ready.

We step out of the carriage at the end of the village square, which is lined by a dark forest of trees. Caspian grabs my hand and guides me forward. "The portal is just through here."

His heart is breaking through our bond, making me clutch at my chest from the pain it's causing me, too.

We descend deeper into the forest, with twigs and leaves crunching beneath our shoes. Soon, a soft, scarlet glow becomes visible ahead, which beckons us forward, lighting our path. As we approach, the light grows stronger until the familiar, rectangular outline of the portal emerges into view.

A portal home. *We're finally going home.*

From the moment Caz and I fell through this portal, all I wanted was to return home with him. But then Caspian happened, and I fell in love all over again. Is Earth really my home if Caspian isn't there with me?

Caz clears his throat. "I'll give you two a minute." He moves closer to the portal and turns his back to us, allowing us a moment of privacy.

I turn to face Caspian, craning my neck to meet his glassy eyes. Through our bond, I feel him using every ounce of his strength to not break down.

If I speak, I risk losing my composure, and I don't want that to be his final memory of me.

I fling my arms around his neck, jumping into his embrace. He burrows his face against my mate mark and inhales my scent. His arms hold me so tight I can hardly breathe, but I don't want him to loosen his grip on me.

"I love you, Bri."

"I know. I can feel it." Leaning back, I bring his hand to rest over my heart. "At least you'll always feel me with you. I'm so glad we found each other, even if it kills me to let you go."

Caspian lets out a stuttering breath and turns away. He runs his hand along his face as his resolve crumbles.

This is why the dark ones never meet their mates. It's infinitely worse to know true love and have it ripped away than to never know what it feels like at all. For centuries, the dark ones have lived in ignorance, and in this case, ignorance is bliss. Caspian is condemned to a life of misery, knowing he'll never experience true love again.

I put my hand on his shoulder. "I'm so sorry, Caspian."

In the distance, the clock tower in the square strikes midnight. Each ring reverberates through the forest, counting down to the moment when we have to leave.

The portal glows brighter, pulsing with energy.

Caz approaches me from behind. "It's time, Bri."

Panic has me in its wicked grip, stilting my breathing in quick, shallow gasps. I bite down on my trembling lip as that familiar lump in my throat grows bigger.

"Kiss me goodbye," I beg.

Caspian whirls around and plunges his mouth upon mine, his passion stealing the breath from my lungs. My body melts against his as he devours me with wild desperation, knowing these are our final moments together.

He grabs my shoulders and pushes me back. His chest heaves up and down, his face twisted with raw pain. "Go."

I'm frozen in place, unable to move. My limbs are trembling.

Caspian glances behind me at Caz. "Take her. Go now, before it closes."

Caz slips his hand into mine and pulls me toward the portal.

With a sob, I rip my gaze away from Caspian. Before me is the dark abyss in the middle of the glowing crimson outline, eager to swallow me whole.

"We'll jump on the count of three," Caz says.

I nod and close my eyes.

"One."

A strange emotion takes hold in my gut. One I'm unfamiliar with, but a powerful one. I've never felt sadness this deep in my bones.

Everything feels... hopeless.

And that's when I'm hit with a jarring realization—I don't want to live anymore.

"Two."

These thoughts aren't mine; they belong to Caspian. Through our bond, an explosion of fear and desperation overwhelms me, suffocating me like a noose.

Caspian is about to do something reckless.

"Wait—"

"Three!"

I'm too late. Caz jumps into the portal, pulling me with him, and I scream.

A hand wraps around my wrist, and I turn to find Caspian falling into the portal after us.

"CASPIAN, NO!"

But the portal swallows us into its pitch-black oblivion, and I'm falling, falling until nothingness consumes me.

CHAPTER 24

Tall grass tickles my face. My eyes flutter open and find the full moon overhead, shining white and bright in the sky.

A *white* moon.

I scramble into a seated position, though the swift movement makes me lightheaded. It takes a moment to recover, but when I do, my surroundings become visible beneath the light of the moon.

This place is familiar.

We're back on the mesa ridge on my grandparents' ranch, and the portal is gone.

"Caz?" I call out into the darkness.

The last thing I remember is jumping into the portal with Caz. And Caspian...

The dark Nezaras are cursed to remain in the Crimson Vale. He never told me what would happen if they tried to cross into the human world, and now I know why.

I felt what he felt in those final moments through our bond. Caspian would have rather died than live without me, and when he jumped in after us, he was planning to end it all.

"Oh, God..." My voice catches. "C-Caspian. No..."

It can't end like this. Not after everything we've been through.

"Damn it!" I pound my fist into the grass. Tears well in my eyes as my chest grows so tight I can't breathe. "Caz? Where are you?"

Someone groans behind me, and a rush of relief floods my veins. I whip my head around to find a figure stirring in the grass behind me.

"Caz?" I crawl over to him and help him sit up. "Caz, talk to me. Are you okay?"

He rubs the back of his head, but when he opens his eyes, I gasp.

Eyes glinting like rubies in the moonlight.

"Caspian?" I run my hand across his face, unable to trust my eyes. "Caspian, how...? Wait, why are you wearing Caz's clothes? Where's Caz?"

The overwhelming joy at seeing Caspian alive is replaced with blazing panic. My mind is a jumbled mess, racing so fast I can't seem to latch onto a single thought. Nothing makes sense right now.

Caspian is here, but Caz is not. Something went wrong with the portal.

"Caz? CAZ!" A sob is wrenched from my gut, and I climb unsteadily to my feet. "Get up. We have to find him!"

Caspian grabs my wrist. "Calm down, my love. He's here."

"Where?" I whip my head back and forth, scanning the mesa and the ranch below. "There's nobody here except us!"

Caspian rises to his feet, though he clutches his head and stumbles. I catch him, supporting his arm to hold him upright.

"You're in no state to look for him," I say. "Wait here while I—"

"My light one is here... inside my mind."

Fuck. He hit his head and now he's lost his mind.

"We need to get you to a hospital," I say. "Come on, we need to hike down the mesa and get a car—"

"Bri, stop."

The warning in Caspian's voice makes me shudder.

He runs a hand along his jaw and closes his eyes. "Would you be quiet?" he mutters under his breath. "I'm trying to calm her down, but I can't think with your incessant talking."

"Who are you talking to?" I ask.

Oh, God. He's hearing voices. He must have really hit his head hard.

"My light one." He lets out an annoyed huff. "It would seem we share one body now, and I must say, it feels rather crowded in here." Caspian taps his head.

I take a step away from him. "I don't understand. So Caz's body is gone, but he's here?"

Caspian glances down at his outfit and makes a sour face. "Actually, I believe I am in *his* body, and my body is gone. But I assure you, we are both here."

I grab both sides of Caspian's face and stare into his eyes. "Caz? Are you in there? Can you hear me?"

"He says he can hear you," Caspian says. "If you calm down, you might be able to feel him through the bond—"

"That doesn't make any sense." I step back, shaking my head. "This isn't fair. It wasn't supposed to happen this way."

"It's okay, my love." He brushes a lock of hair from my face. "He will take over when the sun rises, and I will retreat within our mind until sundown."

"What does that even mean?" I ask, my voice shrill. "How do you know that?"

"I don't know. I... we... we just know. Deep down somehow. We feel it." Caspian lets out a long exhale. "Bri, I think we broke the curse."

Silence falls over us as the weight of his words sink in.

The ancient curse is broken. Two halves of the same soul are back together again.

"I have... so many questions," I whisper.

"As do I." Caspian pauses. "My light one says we must see his grandmother immediately. She will know what to do."

"Okay." I give him a determined nod. "I'll take us to the Nezara's homestead."

When Caz and I first fell through the portal a month ago, we left behind my grandfather's truck. However, it isn't where we left it.

Our families must have found it after we disappeared.

Explaining our absence is going to be a difficult task. So much has happened in a month.

"Before we do that, come here." Caspian pulls me against his chest, burrowing his face into my neck. With a deep breath, he inhales my scent. "Let me hold you."

His broad chest moves with his breathing, and soon my own falls into rhythm with his. It has a calming effect on me, and as we stand here, embraced beneath the moon, it hits me.

We're home. All three of us. It might not be the way we expected, but it's better than not having him at all.

Caspian's relief radiates through our mate bond, along with joy and love. It sends a warmth through my chest, which spreads through my body even on a cool summer night like tonight.

I feel relief, but I also feel another emotion. Confusion, and a hint of bitterness.

I tighten my grip around his waist. "Caz doesn't like sharing his body with you, does he?"

Caspian chuckles, the sound rumbling in my ear. "No, he doesn't. But he'll get used to it. We'll be fine."

The rumble of an engine in the distance catches our attention. Caspian breaks our embrace and shoves me behind him, shielding me with his body. Every muscle in his stance is tense, and the urge to protect me from danger is evident through our mate bond.

The engine noise grows closer, and soon the headlights of a vehicle appear over the ridge of the mesa. Caspian and I both bring our hands up to shield our eyes, until the vehicle turns off and the headlights go dark.

I blink furiously, trying to get my eyes to adjust to the sudden darkness.

The doors of the vehicle open and slam closed.

"Sebastian?" Caspian says. "Seraphine?"

"CAZ!" Seraphine races forward and flings her arms around Caspian's neck.

Seb hurries toward us. "Thank God you're both here. Do you know how worried we all were about you? We were afraid we'd never see you again."

"It's a long story," I reply.

Seeing the light Nezaras is such a relief. This is the Seb and Seraphine I know, and the familiarity in their eyes is a welcome relief after interacting with their dark ones for the last month. Seeing their joy at our return makes me realize how much I missed them.

But for Caspian, this is his first time meeting them. He doesn't hug Seraphine back but rather stands still like a statue, and it doesn't take the mate bond to sense how this is catching him off-guard.

There was not much affection between the dark Nezara siblings, and this is completely new to him.

Seraphine pulls back from Caspian wearing a relieved grin. However, when she catches a glimpse of Caspian's face, her smile falters. "What's wrong with your eyes?"

"Like I said, it's a long story," I interject. "Do you think you could give us a ride back to the homestead? We need to speak to your grandma."

Seb nods. "Yeah, she'll be glad to see you. We have a lot to catch up on." He waves for us to follow him toward the truck, and I grab Caspian's hand to pull him forward.

Seraphine gives him a skeptical look but says nothing. It's probably best to wait until she's sitting down to explain that this is her brother's dark one, and that the brother she knows is trapped inside for the time being.

"What are you two doing up here in the middle of the night?" I ask.

"We stayed up to keep an eye on the mesa." Seb gives Caspian a sideways glance. "I'm assuming Bri knows everything now?"

"Yeah, I know all about the grimwalkers and the ancient curse," I answer with a wave of my hand.

"Okay, then you'll know we're always on alert during the full moon for any signs of unwanted visitors from the other side," Seb explains. "As soon as we saw the lights, we jumped in the truck and drove up here."

We reach the truck, and Seb and Seraphine start climbing in.

Caspian comes to a stop in front of the Chevy and gives it a dubious look. "What in the nine hells is this?"

"It's okay," I whisper in his ear. "It's like a carriage but without the horses."

Seraphine and I climb into the back while Seb gets behind the wheel. Caspian hesitates for a moment before getting into the front passenger's seat.

Seraphine gives him another strange look. "Why are you acting so weird?"

Seb turns the keys in the ignition, and the lights on the dashboard come alive. The clock indicates we still have a few hours until sunrise.

A few hours until Caz appears—hopefully. Because if Caspian is wrong about Caz "taking over" at sunrise, we're going to have problems.

I haven't even had a chance to wrap my head around it. And until I lay eyes on Caz, I won't be able to rest easy.

Neither Caspian or I answer Seraphine as Seb turns the key in the ignition. When the engine roars to live, Caspian flattens his back against the seat and grips the door handle.

I place my hand on his shoulder. "It's safe, I promise."

The truck takes off down the rocky path toward the bottom of the mesa, but Seb and Seraphine keep me busy with questions about the Crimson Vale. I answer everything as best I can while avoiding any mention of their dark ones, which is next to impossible.

The Nezara's homestead comes into view. It's a modest, rectangular dwelling made of stucco, and I have no idea how they fit all seven children and their grandmother inside.

Caz's grandmother, Sybil, is visible through the window, sitting at the kitchen table with a cup of coffee in her hands. As soon as the truck pulls up to the front, she glances up at the front door.

As we climb out of the truck, the front door flings open, and Grandma Sybil rushes outside with surprising agility for an old woman. She gathers Caspian into her bony arms and squeezes him tight. "My grandson! Oh, I've been so worried about you."

Again, Caspian is unsettled by the encounter, but he pats her gingerly on the back.

She draws away from him, holding him by his arms as she inspects him from head to toe. Like Seraphine, when her gaze falls on Caspian's eyes, she pauses.

"Everything is okay. Caz is okay," I interject. "But we have a lot to catch up on."

Grandma Sybil gives a sage nod. "Yes. It appears we do." She turns to me and wraps me in her embrace. "Bri, I am so thankful you've returned safely."

As she holds me, I realize how much I've missed my world. How much I've missed familiarity and family, and this sense of safety. I dreaded returning here because of what it meant—losing Caspian—but now that the curse is broken, relief washes over me.

I'm home. But my home is wherever Caz and Caspian both are.

Slipping her arm through mine, she leads me toward their house and into their small, cozy kitchen. She gestures for us to sit down at the table while she starts to busy herself at the stove. "How about some coffee? The three of us haven't slept a wink all night. I was hoping you'd return on the full moon." She begins muttering a short prayer.

Caspian stands back in the corner, peering around the tiny home with a guarded expression.

"I'm assuming your grandparents don't know you're back yet?" Grandma Sybil asks, directing her question to me.

"No, we came straight here." I glance at Caspian and pat the wooden chair next to me. "A lot happened in the Crimson Vale, and Caz said you might be able to help us make sense of it."

Caspian takes the chair beside me, but the rigid way he sits in it is regal, like he's sitting on his throne.

It's not at all the slouched, casual way Caz sits in a chair, and the Nezara siblings take notice.

"Okay, what's going on with him?" Seb hikes his thumb at Caspian. "Seraphine's right; his eyes look funny."

Grandma Sybil brings over a few cups of coffee and sets them on the table for us. I take a long sip, savoring the warmth it brings me after being outside in the cool Utah night.

Sybil takes a seat and turns her focus to Caspian. Her scrutinizing gaze rakes over him. "Where is my grandson?"

Caspian meets her gaze head-on, studying her with equal measure. "He is safe. He will emerge at sunrise."

Seb glances between Caspian and me. "What's he talking about?"

Sybil seems unphased by this news and instead gives a slow nod. "In that case, Bri, tell me what's happened since you went through the portal. Help me understand."

I speak in quiet tones so as not to wake the younger Nezara siblings. Grandma Sybil, Seb, and Seraphine hang on to my every word as I launch into full detail of the night we fell through the portal—although I leave out the part where I took Caz's virginity. I describe our first encounter with Caspian, how he sent Caz to the dungeons, and how I fell in love with both of them as their fated mate. All the balls and the encounters with the dark Nezaras.

I lean on Caspian to fill in the gap about how they rescued me from Malrick's clutches, but I pick back up after our return to the castle, all the way up until our return through the portal tonight—again, leaving out the sordid details of my sex life.

By the time I finish, the lack of sleep and the emotions of the past few days begin catching up to me. My brain fog and fatigue flare near the end of my tale, and I sink lower into my seat.

"I think we broke the curse," I finish breathlessly. "Caz and Caspian reside within the same body now."

"And you are Caspian," Grandma Sybil says, examining her grandson.

"I am. But not for much longer." He nods toward the window.

All of us turn to follow his gaze, where the first signs of light appear below the horizon, turning the sky from black to early morning navy.

Caspian squeezes my hand, and I glance at him. His exhaustion is painted all over his face, except for his eyes. His ruby eyes are staring at me with the depth of his affection and love for me, and I feel it through our mate bond.

I love you, he mouths.

He squeezes his eyes shut. When he opens them, they've returned to a deep shade of brown.

"Caz!" I fling my arms around his neck. "Oh, thank God you were right!"

Everyone turns back to look at him, and when they see his relaxed, lopsided grin, they know their brother has returned.

As soon as I release Caz, Seraphine and Grandma Sybil rise from their seats to embrace him, and Seb claps him on the back.

"Geez, give me a little space," Caz says with a laugh. He stands up from his chair and starts stretching his limbs. "It feels weird not being in control of my body."

"But Caspian is still in there, right?" I ask.

Caz taps his head. "Yep, he's already complaining and demanding more space."

Well, that certainly sounds like Caspian. I let out a sigh of relief.

"I'm just glad we're home in one piece, even if it's a little crowded," Caz says. "It'll take some getting used to."

Grandma Sybil taps her finger to her chin. *"Until the dark becomes light once again, you will remain cursed."*

"What was that, Grandma?" Seraphine asks.

"It's the words of the ancient curse," Sybil murmurs. "They've been passed down through stories over generations, though I never quite understood what they meant until now."

"I remember the words, but I'm not sure I follow," Seb says.

"Caz's dark one was absorbed into his body," she explains. "The dark one became the light one. By the way, have any of you tried to shift into wolves since they returned?"

A silence falls over the group as the siblings glance between each other with wide eyes.

Seb pushes his chair back from the table with a loud scrape, stands up, and walks outside. The rest of us watch him through the window as he stands there, closing his eyes and clenching his fists.

But nothing happens.

He comes back in with a pale expression. "I can't shift."

Grandma Sybil lets out a rattled gasp and brings her hands to her mouth. "The Curse of the Werewolf has broken."

"But how will we protect the ranch?" Seb asks. "We're defenseless without the ability to shift into wolves."

"I imagine that if the curse is broken, that also means the portal is sealed," she answers. "The threat is over."

"Aren't we descended from grimwalkers?" Seraphine asks. "Shouldn't we be able to change into any animal we want and have a thirst for blood?"

Grandma Sybil lets out a chuckle. "Do you feel the need to drink blood?"

Seraphine thinks about it for a moment. "No."

"Caspian still does," Caz mutters. "But he'll have to wait until night falls."

"Then you sound quite human to me." Grandma Sybil taps Seraphine's nose, making her giggle. "The stories passed through the generations depict grimwalkers as evil beings who drank blood to fuel their wicked magic. The knowledge of their blood magic has been lost to history, and that is for the best. Without it, we are simply human."

"I have a question," I interject. "If Caz and Caspian are now merged into one, why haven't the rest of you merged with your dark ones?"

Grandma Sybil ponders my question for a long moment, then hums. "Caspian threw himself into the portal after Bri. He would've rather sacrificed himself than live a life without love." She takes my hand in hers. "But you and Caspian are connected through Bri, through the mate bond. It allows you to understand and accept the opposite half of your soul. And when Caspian made his sacrifice, I believe that was the moment the curse broke."

Caz nods in understanding. "So now my soul is whole again."

"For the rest of us, the connection with our Dark Ones is severed." Grandma Sybil smiles. "Future generations of Nezaras will not be burdened by the curse. They will be born into this world whole."

The weight of this revelation sinks in, and all of us sit in a moment of silence. Things feel lighter, like a heavy weight has been lifted from our shoulders.

Seraphine wipes a tear from her eye. "Does this mean we can leave the ranch?"

"I believe so," Grandma Sybil says. "If the curse is broken, so is our connection to this land."

For the first time in a long time, I find myself looking forward to what the future has in store for me. If the curse is broken, Caz isn't bound to the ranch. I can go anywhere with Caz and show him and Caspian this vast world. In an instant, his future has opened up like an oyster, full of possibility and hope beyond what fate dictated for him at birth.

And Caz won't have to worry about passing his curse down to his children anymore.

Grandma Sybil turns to me and pats my hand. "Bri, our family owes you a great debt of gratitude."

"Me?" I ask. "But I didn't do anything. Like you said, Caz and Caspian accepted one another."

She gives me a subtle wink. "But you brought them together."

Oh, I sure brought them together, alright. Just not in the way she might be thinking. Although, the knowing twinkle in her eye is making me wonder...

The heat creeps up my neck to my cheeks, and I glance away.

Instead, I turn to Caz, who stares back at me with a warm, gentle expression. For a split second, I swear there's a flicker of ruby red behind his gaze, but it's gone in an instant.

Caz and I walk up the steps of my grandparents' front porch. With a deep breath, I lift my fist and knock on the door. And then we wait.

We've been gone for a whole month without so much as a note to my grandparents. Grandma Sybil knew my grandparents would go to the police, and if they started poking around, it would open up the Nezaras to unwanted questioning about what really happened on the mesa.

So, Seb told everyone he dropped Caz and me off at a bus station so we could run away together. But according to him, it hurt my grandparents, especially my grandma.

When I fell through the portal, I left behind a family that cared about me. It's going to take a long time to repair the damage my absence left behind.

That's why I'm nervous.

Caz squeezes my hand. "It's going to be okay. Whatever we face, we face it together."

The door opens to reveal my grandmother on the threshold, and when she sees me, her jaw falls open. The coffee mug in her hand falls to the floor, shattering against the hardwood planks as hot liquid goes everywhere.

"Oh, Bri…" she whispers, tears welling up in her eyes. "Is it really you?"

"Grandma, I'm so sorry…"

She flings her arms around me, pulling me into her tight embrace. "None of that matters now. I'm just glad you're home safe."

EPILOGUE

S **ix Months Later**

After dropping my bags at the foot of the bed, I collapse on the mattress in our hotel room.

Caz sets the rest of our bags against the wall. "You feeling okay?"

I throw my arm over my eyes to block the light, which is making my migraine worse. "Just tired from the travel."

"Here, drink this." He pulls out a sports drink from my backpack. "You need your electrolytes."

"Okay, *Dad*," I tease, taking the bottle from him and unscrewing the cap.

Caz ignores my comment and shuffles through my bag. "I'm setting your meds on the nightstand. You forgot to take them this morning."

"Well, it was a little crazy between getting packed and making sure we left for the airport on time." I take a sip of my drink. "But thanks for taking care of me."

After we returned from the Crimson Vale six months ago, Caz and I moved back to Los Angeles and rented a tiny studio apartment in a more affordable neighborhood north of the city. One of the perks of living in a major city is the access to top doctors, and at last I found a specialist who understood my condition. I'll live with chronic illness for the rest of my life, but at least I'm able to manage it better now.

After I re-enrolled in university, my parents decided to reward my "good behavior" with a trip to Hawaii for Caz and me. They think that Caz is a good influence, and they credit him for getting my life back on track in their eyes. Still, I avoid them as much as possible.

Caz found a job working as a security guard for a high-end resort in Beverly Hills, and he's saving up to go to college. I wasn't able to get my original internship back, but I'm applying for other positions while I finish up my degree.

I swallow the sports drink in my mouth. "Oh, I almost forgot to tell you, I spoke with my grandma yesterday."

He takes a seat on the edge of the bed beside me. "Oh, yeah? How are they doing?"

"They're good. She mentioned how there hasn't been any new cattle mutilations or crop circles in a while."

Caz grins. "Hmm, imagine that."

"Yeah, they think that Findley kept to his word after the sheriff got involved. Poor guy never did a thing." I stand up and cross over to the dresser to pick up the hotel directory. "Are you hungry? This resort has a lot of great restaurants we can go to for dinner."

"I'm starving," Caz growls.

I turn around to find Caz standing right behind me. He pushes me against the dresser, his hips grinding against mine. His face is only inches away, except his brown irises are now a deep shade of burgundy.

I peer out the window over his shoulder. Sure enough, the sun has dipped below the ocean horizon.

With a swift movement, Caspian picks me up and tosses me over his shoulder. I let out a squeal as he lays a playful smack across my backside.

He carries me out onto the balcony, where a private hot tub awaits us, and only then does he set me on my feet. Taking a step back, he begins to tug off his T-shirt over his head.

I'll never get used to seeing him in human clothes.

"Take your clothes off," he commands.

"Yes, sir." I smirk at him. "You certainly don't waste any time."

"I only get a couple of hours with you before you fall asleep, and I plan to spend every minute ravishing your body until you do."

My breath quickens, and I begin to peel my shirt over my head. I leave my bra and underwear on as I kick off my shoes and shimmy out of my jeans.

He steps out of his briefs, revealing his growing erection. "*All* of your clothes."

I bite my lip to suppress a grin. "Make me."

Caspian takes a prowling step forward, and then another, closing the distance between us. He grabs my shoulders and spins me so that his chest is at my back. "Are you testing me, my love?"

"Always."

His fingers unfasten my bra before making quick work of my panties, which he slides over my hips until they fall at my feet. He pushes on my back to bend me over the hot tub, and I grip the edge as his hand palms my backside.

When his finger slips inside my pussy, I push my hips back to meet him. "Oh, fuck, that feels good."

He slips a finger out. "Only good girls get to come."

I let out a pathetic little whine of frustration as he moves away. He leans over to inspect the dials on the hot tub, and after a brief pause, he sets to work turning on the jets. Caz must have walked him through the steps in their shared mind, because Caspian is oblivious when it comes to human technology.

I slip into the warm water with Caspian close behind. He takes a seat and guides me to sit on top of him, positioning my hips so that the tip of his erection presses against my eager entrance. When he eases me down on top of him, I let out a low moan as he sheathes himself inside me inch by delicious inch.

"Oh, fuck, Bri," he groans in my ear. "You feel so good."

Caz and Caspian feel what the other feels, but I imagine it's better when you're in control of your movements rather than taking a backseat to the action.

"Don't stop." My fingers run through his thick, raven hair as I pull his face closer. My kiss is needy and passionate as I begin to ride his cock, the warm water around us enhancing my arousal.

I love it when Caspian takes me like this, desperate and urgent and fast and rough. Like I turn him on so much that he can't take it anymore and needs release *now*.

I feel the same way. I need him so bad it hurts, and the only relief is for him to make me come.

Caspian digs his fingers into my hips and bounces me faster on top of him. Our breath comes in ragged gasps as we move in tandem with one another. His mouth moves down my jawline to my neck, sucking hard at my mate mark.

Fangs pierce my flesh, drawing the blood from my veins as I grind against him. It's this final action that sends me reeling over the edge, making me cry out at the top of my lungs into the quiet night.

Who cares if the entire resort can hear us? I'm too far gone to care about that, lost in my own whirlwind of euphoric pleasure.

Caspian slows his thrusts as he empties his seed inside of me. He licks my wound clean to seal the puncture marks before sitting back to gaze into my eyes. I remain on his lap, savoring the sensation of my sheath relaxing around his cock, which is still buried inside me.

I rest my forehead against his and close my eyes, relishing his touch. "I love you."

He tightens his grip on my hips. "Marry me."

I open my eyes and lean back, staring at him. Did I hear that right?

His ruby gaze peers into mine. "Marry me, Bri."

It's not a question. It's an order, and I wouldn't expect anything else out of Caspian.

Still, I'm stunned by the abruptness of it all.

Caspian sighs and rolls his eyes. "My light one is unhappy. We had planned a more romantic marriage offer."

"A marriage offer?" I repeat. "It sounded more like an order from the king."

He smirks. "He agreed to let me do the proposal since he'll be the one to stand on the altar with you on our wedding day. So I'm doing it my way, and I don't want to wait another second."

He reaches over the edge of the tub to pick up his jeans, which are lying on the deck of the balcony in a crumpled heap. After rummaging through the pockets, he pulls out a ring box and opens it. "Marry me," he repeats. "Agree to be mine—ours—forever."

Inside the box is a silver band, and in the center, a circular diamond ensconced in a crescent-shaped ruby.

I run my fingers over the gemstones. "The sun and the moon."

"We felt it was appropriate." Caspian gives me a conspiratorial grin. "So, is that a yes?"

I tear my eyes away from the ring and stare into Caspian's gaze. Both his and Caz's love for me radiates through our mate bond, and their feelings are so powerful, so overwhelming, that it brings tears to my eyes.

I'm not sure I'll ever get used to this feeling, of basking in their love for me. But I want to hold on to it forever.

"Yes." I plant a soft kiss against Caspian's lips. "Yes, I'll marry you. I'll marry both of you."

Triumph brings a golden glow to his face as he pulls the ring out of the box. He slides it with care onto my ring finger before pulling me into his embrace. "Words cannot describe how much I love you."

I nestle my face into his neck. "You don't have to. I can feel it through our bond."

With Caspian still inside of me, I begin to grind against him once again. This time, our pleasure is not for carnal reasons, but to show each other the depth of our love and intimacy.

An intimacy that all three of us share.

My mates. My loves. Together for the rest of our lives.

The story continues in the second and final installment of the Moons of Fate Duology...

A Kingdom of Ice and Sorrow: Coming Fall 2026

A new king sits on the throne of the Crimson Vale—and he's determined to destroy the last remaining threat to his crown: Caspian.

He'll start by claiming me as his queen... and erasing the bond that ties me to my fated mates.

ALSO BY K.R. MCRAE

ROMANTASY

THE MOONS OF FATE DUOLOGY
A Kingdom of Blood and Fate
A Kingdom of Ice and Sorrow *(Coming Fall 2026)*

Also by Kati McRae

Contemporary & Urban Fantasy Romance

THE DARK LOVE SERIES

Alek & Willow's Story:

Love to Fear You: A Dark Bully Romance

Love to Defy You: A Dark College Romance

Love to Find You: A Dark Stalker Romance *(Coming Soon)*

Prisha's Story:

Love to Praise You: An Age Gap Novella *(Free to newsletter subscribers)*

Mikhail & Anastasia's Story:

Love to Save You: A Dark Mafia Romance *(Coming Soon)*

CALIFORNIA ROMANCE NOVELS

All Tied Up: A Spicy Friends to Lovers Romance

All Tied Up Again

THE OUTBREAK ZONE DUET

Outbreak Zone: A Dystopian Werewolf Romance

Danger Zone

STANDALONE NOVELS

17 Sexy Short Stories

LET'S CONNECT

Visit K.R. McRae on the web at:

www.katimcrae.com

Facebook: @kati.mcrae.author

TikTok: @katimcrae

Instagram: @kati.mcrae.author

Want more behind-the-scenes info about this book? Join other readers in the **Books & Mimosas with Kati McRae** group on Facebook!

Sign up for K.R. McRae's newsletter for exclusive access to bonus content:

www.katimcrae.com

ABOUT THE AUTHOR

K.R. McRae writes lush romantasy and paranormal romance infused with unapologetic spice. Drawn to stories where desire collides with destiny, she crafts emotionally charged worlds led by morally gray male leads and beautifully imperfect heroines. What began as a love for romance that never faded to black has evolved into immersive tales that linger long after the final page.

When she's not writing, the author can be found exploring the wild beauty and culinary delights of Arizona with her family.